Reckless Association

Books by D. C. Shaftoe

Forged in the Jungles of Burma
(Finalist in the 2011 Canadian Christian Writing Awards)

Assassin's Trap
(Winner in the 2013 Word Awards; Editor's Choice)

Enemy by Association

Lethal Intentions: The Battle for Gideon
Book 1 in the *Second Chance* Series
(Finalist in the 2014 Word Awards)
Republished as **Imperfect** in December 2014

Praise for D. C. Shaftoe

"… Shaftoe's gift for suspense and willingness to put her characters in real danger ups the stakes, resulting in a vividly realized adventure that one can easily imagine seeing on the big screen. A highly enjoyable thriller with lots of intelligence and heart."

- Kirkus Reviews on **Assassin's Trap**

"D.C. Shaftoe has written a well-researched fiction that tells of the struggle of a young man who is trying to turn his life around…**HIGHLY RECOMMENDED.**"

- Allbooks Review International
on **Reckless Association**

"The story is riveting, exciting, full of suspense…it's hard to put the book down…there is excitement from beginning to end…truly a book that all students learning about autism should read."

- Customer Review
on **Lethal Intentions: The Battle for Gideon**

Reckless Association

D. C. Shaftoe

Cornerstone Research & Publishing
2014

Reckless Association

www.dcshaftoe.com

Dedication

"I have come that they may have life, and that they may have it more abundantly."
John 10:10

To all those courageous men and women who've chosen recovery, and the many who have helped them.

To my wonderful husband and my amazing children.

Acknowledgements

As always, I want to thank my husband and children who listen to my ideas, provide insight, and who are my most rabid fans. I couldn't do it without you! I also want to thank Drew Toth and Norm Arnold who gave up their time to help me understand the life of Ayden Breckinridge and the struggles of recovery. I want to thank Linda Beard for connecting me with them. I also want to thank Betty, Tanya, Carolyn, Joan, Mary, and Helen for their support. I want to thank my mother and father who first taught me about unconditional love. I'll add a "thanks" to my mom as well, for reading the original, unfinished manuscript for this book and encouraging me to complete it. In conclusion, I want to thank everyone who buys my books and reads them. Thank you, all.

Dear Reader,

I was well into the plot of Book 2 of the *Second Chance* series when my second novel, *Assassin's Trap*, won at the 2013 Word Awards. I went home and started a new book, the story of Ayden Breckinridge, an ex-con raised on the gang-ravaged streets of inner-city Cincinnati. As I researched the themes in the story, prison, the psychological effects of imprisonment, street crime, et cetera, I reached out to one of my children's teachers from the past, Linda Beard, whom I had heard was involved in a Canadian prison fellowship organization. Linda connected me with Drew Toth, a Shelter Resident Services Coach at the Southridge Shelter. Drew told me his story and connected me with Norm Arnold. Norm was able to grant me a new insight into the character of Ayden Breckinridge, his life and recovery. Drew and Norm, above all, gave me a new insight into the power of God to transform a life. Thank you.

Prologue

The chimes over the door sounded as Ayden "Reck" Breckinridge, stepped through into the Book Wyrm fantasy bookstore. Empty of customers, every available surface in the store was laden with a mismatched assortment of new and used books. The dark mahogany shelves and arched ceiling lent the dimly lit space an aura of earthen deep, like a dragon's lair minus the treasure hoard.

But now the dragon had entered the shop. Though this dragon wasn't especially tall or brawny, his compact frame was toned and trained from years of violence. His occupation was written on his skin in ink and scars, and in his eyes with a look of steel.

"Hey-ho. Be wit' ya in a sec." Sid Zucker's disembodied voice rang out from beneath the sales counter. A former merchant sailor, he was the current proprietor of the Book Wyrm.

Flipping the **OPEN** sign to **CLOSED**, Reck engaged the deadbolt. At the sound, Sid's head appeared above the counter, their gazes connecting for an instant. The bald fear in his eyes belied his earlier friendly greeting. "I, uh, don' need yer he'p." His eyes darted about as he searched for escape or rescue, neither of which he would find today.

"Yeah," Reck said in a lazy drawl, sauntering over with his hands in his back pockets. "Ya do."

"We'se, uh, doin' jus' fine…" Tugging nervously at the collar of his florid shirt with his left hand, Sid reached beneath the counter with his right.

"No, ya ain't." What a fool to think he could get the drop on The Wrecker. Vaulting the counter, Reck pinned Sid to the wall, the V of his hand fitting perfectly beneath his jaw.

"Reck. Please! I gots no problem wit' you, man."

Reck tightened his grip, leveraging Sid half an inch higher up the wall until only the tips of Sid's navy blue deck shoes touched the pale green linoleum. Sid's weather-beaten hands clawed at Reck's sure grip to no avail. "I step out that door empty-handed, yer gonna have a problem, 'cept it won't be with me." Reck knew that if he reported Sid's reluctance to pay, members of the Grex, one of Cincinnati's most violent street gangs, would arrive soon after and then Sid would quickly remember his agreement with Roarke, their sergeant-at-arms. Likely from the dubious comfort of a hospital bed. Sid knew it, too.

"You want protection?" Reck emphasized the word, fully aware of the irony. "You do as I say and give me what I want." He squeezed, cutting off Sid's air supply for just a moment, not long enough to do any permanent damage, just enough to anaesthetize a few brain cells. Not that Sid could afford to lose many.

"Okay, man. I agree." Sid's voice rasped over the words as he inched his palms up the wall trying to gain enough height to escape Reck's grip. "Was on'y foolin'."

When Reck loosened his hold a fraction, Sid rasped in a breath, his eyes watering. "The till."

Releasing Sid to huddle on the ground at his feet, he warned him, "Don't doubt my cred, man," aiming a kick at Sid's hip.

"Never." Sid shook his head so vigorously that Reck thought it might spin off into space. He kicked him again, harder this time, to get him moving. Hands trembling, Sid punched the button to open the cash register. Lifting the drawer, coins rattling in time with his fear, he removed a wad of neatly stacked bills captured in a blue elastic band, and handed it over.

Pocketing the cash, Reck scanned the piles of bestsellers beside the counter and snatched one up, zipping it into his black leather jacket. Offering Sid a one-fingered salute, he said, "See ya next month," and then let himself out, flipping the sign to **OPEN** on the way through.

Job completed, Reck mounted his top-of-the-line marble-yellow Suzuki Hayabusa motorcycle, spinning his rear tire to send a spray of slimy grey water onto the Book Wyrm's front window, decorating it in Cincinnati grime. Stopping at the Grex's clubhouse, he passed over the eighteen hundred he'd been ordered to collect, keeping the two hundred he'd skimmed off the top in his pocket, and then drove home.

Riding straight in the rear door of his apartment building, he parked, leaving his bike blocking the bottom of the stairs. He didn't take the time to secure it. No one in this neighborhood would dare to steal from The Wrecker. As an independent street-level enforcer for the Grex, his security was ensured. Unless he ever crossed them. Or they decided to dispense with his services. Or he failed to deliver. In which case, his dismembered corpse would likely be found on the shores of the Ohio River.

Mounting the stairs to the second floor, Reck stepped through the door of his dingy apartment. He didn't bother to remove his boots before walking down the hall to the kitchen because whatever he'd tracked through this afternoon in the denizens of Over-the-Rhine was certainly cleaner than the filthy carpet.

"Wipe yer boots."

"Hey, Gram." Planting a kiss on her weathered cheek, he tried not to inhale the unpleasant odor emanating from the stove, something that didn't truly smell like food. Though he appreciated her presence in his sister's life, he rarely dared to eat anything his grandmother cooked. "Cassie home? I got her somethin'." Reck's prize, the newest volume of the supernatural cat books his sister loved, lay nestled in his jacket. Why anyone would want to read a story about cats who were people was beyond him. But then, he wasn't a fourteen-year-old girl.

Turning, Gram laid a cold, thin hand on his cheek, patting it not quite gently. "Wit' yer ill-gotten gains, Ayden?"

Stilling at the rebuke, his eyelids dropped to half-staff, his gaze intense. "If you want to know, just come out and ask me."

Shaking her head, she gave the pot another stir. "Somet'in' wrong wit' yer sister."

Alarm penetrated Reck's chest somewhere near his shrivelled heart. If the Grinch's heart had shrunk two sizes, Reck's was smaller still, shrivelled and puny, holding only love for Cassie and gratitude to Gram for rescuing his little sister from their mom. "Where is she?"

"Chesterfield."

Gram followed him down the hall. "She shakin' a fair bit. Can't get 'er warm. Why 'm makin' soup."

"What happened?" he asked her, gazing at the pale oval of his sister's face.

"Don't know. Won't say." Gram patted his arm and then returned to her chicken noodle soup.

At twenty-two, Reck had experienced rage, fear, despair, but between him and Gram, they'd tried to protect Cassie from the harsh realities of life. Settling beside her on the sofa, Reck tucked a lock of her straw-blonde hair behind her ear, tickling her neck in a familiar gesture. Cassie flinched, the first sign she'd shown of his presence, but her eyes continued to stare blankly into the middle-distance.

"What happened, honey?" When she didn't respond, he pulled the book out of his pocket, the same book she'd begged him to buy for her since its release four days ago. He could have bought it for her, he had the money. But it was so much more fun to obtain it the way he had. Who said violence didn't solve anything? He felt a brief thrill at the memory of Sid's fear. "I got you a present." He set it on her knee where her fingers gripped the fabric of her jeans. "That werecat book." Her hand reached out to take it but the book dropped from nerveless fingers and lay forgotten on the filthy carpet.

All thoughts of cats fled as Cassie turned to him, her eyes dark with an ancient pain. "Who?" he said harshly.

Out of the voluminous depths of the quilt Gram had wrapped around her, Cassie raised her other hand, opening it to reveal the crushed petals of a daisy. That piece of filth was always giving the girls daisies.

"I'll kill him."

Chapter One: Second Chance

<u>Eight years later</u>

Sophie Anne Paetan stood, linking her hands behind her head
and stretching out her back. For the past twenty minutes, she'd
been stooped over the refreshment table beneath the shade of a
seventy-five-year-old Locust Tree at the side door of the Hope
Wesleyan Methodist Church in Ancora, Ohio. Three plates of
chocolate chip cookies sat next to thirty vanilla cupcakes
decorated in *Jonah's Whale* blue. When the Sunday school picnic
commenced an hour from now and the mini-hordes descended,
not a crumb would remain.

As Sophie covered the cupcakes with a plastic lid, she
scanned the area around the church. The lawns were freshly
mown, sloping gently toward the river to the north and Riverside
Park to the west. Kiran Rao, Tristan Paetan, and another man, a
stranger, emerged from the parsonage, a single-storey fifties-era
brick house with sagging eaves, carrying the church's ancient
sound system. Ancora was a quaint little town about twenty
minutes or so from Cincinnati. It didn't see many strangers,
particularly not one like this. His hair was long, springing out
over his ears and brushing the collar of his white cotton T-shirt,
looking as though he'd had it trimmed with a weed whacker and
then let it grow out. But it was nice hair, thick and chestnut
brown with auburn highlights glinting in the sun. His jeans were
faded a pale blue except where stress had bleached the knees and
seat nearly white. The hard planes of his features were rugged,
but striking. He appeared strong and wholly confident in that
fact.

Sophie started across the lawn, not knowing if she was more interested in going over the day's agenda with Kiran or discovering the identity of the scruffy newcomer. Actually, she did know.

"Higher, Reck, we don't want it to drag across the grass," Kiran said to the new guy.

Sophie didn't hear his response but she did see the microphone wobble on top of the massive pile of speakers, receivers and transmitters. Rushing over, she grabbed for it and, in the process, bumped into Reck and sent the entire leaning tower precariously close to tumbling to the ground.

"Sorry," she cried at the same time he said, "Hey!"

Reck performed a quick-step and got under the pile once again. Within two more steps the three men were able to rest the items on the portable plastic table which Sophie and her best friend Gaelen Somerset had set up for that purpose.

"If you can't be helpful, Sophie, then stay out of the way," Tristan said sharply.

"Sorry," she said again, a little more angry than contrite. "I was trying to help."

"Try helping someone else next time," Tristan said contemptuously.

Sophie watched her big brother walk away, her fists clenching involuntarily at her side. People would think they were still ten and sixteen rather than twenty-four and thirty. Sometimes she missed the days of childhood when she could have hauled off and punched him in the arm.

"Thanks for your help, Sophie," Kiran said, drawing her attention away from her dork of a brother. Kiran adjusted his black-rimmed glasses, winking when she met his gaze, his obsidian eyes conveying his amusement with the blatant display of sibling rivalry. Raised with his older brother and younger sister by his traditional grandparents, Kiran well understood the trials of family. "I hope I remember how to set this thing up. Old Pastor Cooper was here last year to do it. Do you suppose the retirement home would let him out on good behavior?"

Sophie chuckled politely at the joke while sneaking a peek at the rugged man beside Kiran. Now that she was closer, she could see that he was clean-shaven, bearing a scar on his chin and another that ran in a slant from the corner of his right eyebrow to his hairline. There was a colorful image of a ridgeback dragon, its open maw devouring a village, on his right forearm. This man definitely stood out amongst the small town crowd.

Kiran must have noticed her studying the man—ministers were good at picking up on the subtleties of human behavior— because he said, "This is a friend of mine, Ayden Breckinridge. He's just moved to the area."

"It's nice to meet you," Sophie said in greeting, extending her fingers toward Ayden. His sun-kissed hand was rough, calloused, but warm. Four letters, CASS, were tattooed in blue ink across his knuckles. "I thought I heard Kiran call you Reck."

"Nickname," Ayden said, stuffing his hands in his back pockets and rocking back on the heels of his black leather boots. "You know, short for Breckinridge," he rolled the 'R's dramatically.

"Oh," she said because she wasn't sure how to respond to the tone in his voice. It wasn't charming, that was for sure. Seductive, maybe? Aggressive? His eyes wandered over her body, but then he seemed to catch himself, shuttering his expression and averting his gaze.

Tristan sauntered back over with a can of iced tea. She capitalized on his typical self-centered behavior to cover her uncertainty over how to react to Reck. Or Ayden. She certainly didn't think she could call him Mr. Breckinridge. "Did you bring one for everyone?"

Tristan shrugged and gestured with his head toward the refreshment table near the back door of the church. "They're over there."

Sophie could feel Ayden's gaze on her again, the intensity of his attention drawing a blush to stain her cheeks. When Kiran cleared his throat softly, just a quiet "ah-hem", Ayden glanced at him then dropped his gaze, raking his fingers through his hair. The movement raised the sleeve of his T-shirt revealing a previously hidden tattoo, the image of a sun on the horizon with birds flying overhead.

Tristan pointed at Ayden with the middle finger of the hand holding his iced tea. "That's a prison tattoo." Tristan nudged her with his elbow. "Let's go." When she didn't immediately comply, he gestured with his head toward the church. She suspected the point was to get her away from Ayden-Reck not to get her a beverage. Sophie ignored him.

"What makes it a prison tattoo?" Sophie met Ayden's eyes as she asked. They were a pale blue like the sky on a hot summer's day, but rather than warmth, they conveyed hardness, ice.

"Because it is." Tristan interrupted before Ayden could reply. "Come on, Sophie."

She turned on him. "Tristan, that's rude. Go away if you want to go."

"Yeah, Tristan," Ayden murmured quietly, but loudly enough for Tristan to hear the sneer in his voice matching the expression on his face.

Eyes narrowed, Tristan stepped toward Ayden. Kiran intervened, placing his five-foot-seven body courageously between the two taller, more muscular men. "Could you please get my CD player from the parsonage, Reck?"

Ignoring him, Ayden held Tristan's gaze over Kiran's shoulder. Sophie could feel the sizzle in the air between them. And she didn't want her brother to win.

"Come on, Tris, let's go find Rhona and her pies," Sophie said, tugging on her brother's sleeve. "There she is, looking for you."

Rhona was Tristan's fiancée and the only useful thing she seemed to be able to do was attend committee meetings and make cherry pies. Not apple or blueberry or peach, just cherry.

Tristan released Ayden's gaze and looked over toward the church where—glory be—Rhona Miller was indeed standing outside, her raven hair impossibly stiff in the morning breeze, her fifteen-hundred-dollar *Donna Karan* sleeveless black sarong hugging her narrow waist, hips and thighs. Her dark eyes scanned the crowd, coming to rest on Tristan. And then her ring-laden hands moved from her hips to cross her chest, transmitting her annoyance with unerring skill across the space.

With one last baleful glare in Ayden's direction, Tristan left.

"Sorry about that," Sophie said to Ayden. "He can be a real toad."

Kiran chuckled breathily as he flicked a nervous glance at Ayden's fervid expression before saying, "Tristan's the same as I remember him from high school."

Ayden shifted his gaze to her face and then flicked Kiran a peripheral glance. "You went to school with that guy?"

Slowly, Kiran replied, "No."

"Tristan went to a private school in Pennsylvania and my older sister Vivian went to a private girl's school in Virginia," Sophie said.

"And you?" Ayden asked.

"I went to the local high school with Kiran's sister, Pia."

"Pia, Gael and Sophie were the Three Sisters, the terrors of Ancora High," Kiran said, grinning.

Ayden narrowed his gaze. "Shakespearean bad? She don't look too terrifying to me."

"You'd be surprised," Kiran muttered.

Sophie chuckled as she remembered the night she and her friends had tormented Kiran and his girlfriend, Melinda or Melody or whatever her name was. The relationship had been doomed from the get-go with or without Pia and Sophie's assistance. One look from Kiran's traditional grandfather had made it more than clear that the fair Melinda would never be joining the Rao family.

"There's a story there, I can tell," Ayden said. His face relaxed a little.

"Yeah, maybe, but one she's *not* going to tell." Kiran's voice was light and humorous but his feelings were betrayed by the blush that darkened his dusky complexion right to the roots of his straight, black hair.

Still laughing lightly, Sophie wiggled her fingers gaily. "I need to go check on the kids setting up the fishing pond so, on that note, I'll say, toodle-oo." As she walked away, she could feel Ayden's eyes following her.

"That would be complicated," Kiran said, adjusting his glasses.

"Don't know what you mean," Ayden said.

"Don't be a twerp," Kiran said, punching Ayden companionably on the shoulder.

"A twerp?" Ayden snorted in derision. "Were you always such a…" Ayden searched for a socially acceptable, non-profane word to use, "nerd?" He was trying hard to clean up his language as a part of his new life. Profanity identified him in a way that he no longer desired.

"Yep. You just didn't notice because ministers are supposed to be the nice guys."

Ayden snorted again. "What's her story, anyway?"

Kiran turned to meet his gaze directly, all humor gone. "If you want to know, you'll have to ask her."

Ayden nodded solemnly, agreeing. But still…his eyes sought Sophie's form across the lawn. She was lovely, feminine but full of spirit. She moved with lithe grace and a vigorous energy that made her look ready to dance and climb a tree with equal enthusiasm. Her deep brown eyes revealed her every thought; they conveyed humor and pique and curiosity. As he watched, the breeze riffled her thick tawny hair. She brushed it away and tucked it behind her ears. She was utterly charming.

He could tell that she was curious about him. And he had enough experience to tell when a woman was attracted to him. But how would that spark of attraction fizzle when she discovered how he'd spent the first twenty-five years of his life? If Ayden was wise, he'd turn away and never give Sophie Paetan another thought.

But he wasn't wise. "Nope."

"No what?" Kiran said, pausing in the process of assembling the stereo equipment.

"Nothing," Ayden muttered. "I'm thirsty."

Kiran called after him, "I'll take a root beer."

"Hmm." Ayden made his way to the refreshments table.

"Well, howdy, handsome."

Ayden turned to see a striking brunette, all lean and willowy. "I'll take a couple of colas." He gestured at the table.

"Honey, I'm not handin' out soda pop. Although I may reconsider, gorgeous," her eyes scanned him from his toes to his ears, "if you tell me your name."

"Reck," Ayden replied, using his camouflage of choice, the nickname he'd borne since childhood. It was comfortable. Safe.

"Oo. Reck for reckless, I'll just bet." She held out her hand in that odd limp manner that some women seemed to feel was sophisticated. Ayden took it and pumped it just a little more enthusiastically than was polite.

The glamorous grin faltered but quickly returned. "I'm Vivienne Paetan, that's with two E's and two N's."

"Like Anne with an E?" Ayden asked.

So this was Sophie's sister. He could see the similarity now, but where Sophie was blonde and freckled, Vivienne's hair was the color of black coffee and he couldn't imagine a freckle having the audacity to light on her perfect patrician nose. Where Vivienne might be considered slender and alluring, she didn't elicit a single mote of attraction in him. He much preferred Sophie's softness and the sparkle of joy in her deep brown eyes, a sparkle that hadn't diminished even when she'd seen his tattoos and was given a hint to the origins.

Vivienne was watching him with an expression of confusion. "I do declare I don't know what you mean."

"I'm sure," Ayden replied, reaching across Vivienne to retrieve the first two beverages he could reach. He saluted her with the cans, saying in his best southern drawl, "Ya'll take care now, y'here?"

Putting a few paces between him and the now miffed Vivienne, Ayden paused and turned a circuit, locating the inimitable Sophie exiting the side door of the church that came directly up from the basement. Three under-tens walked with her, two girls and a boy. Sophie's head was thrown back in laughter, her hair loose and spilling over her shoulders.

Ayden jogged to catch up with them. "Hi," he said.

While the kids continued on their way past the old shed, casting him only a brief, vaguely curious glance, Sophie stopped on the grassy knoll that overlooked the riverbank. She turned at his approach, greeting him with a smile. "Hello, Ayden. How's the stereo system coming?"

Ayden glanced over to where Kiran looked about ready to pop a blood vessel in frustration. "Kir's got it well in hand."

Sophie followed his gaze and then laughed knowingly. "Uh huh."

Ayden held up a can of iced tea. "Thought you might like a drink."

She hesitated and then accepted it. "Thank you. I hope you got one for yourself as well."

"Yeah." He opened the other can, a can of cola, and took a sip.

Sophie held her can in both hands, her thumbnail lightly flicking the tab.

"You know who Anne with an E is, don't you?" he asked.

"Of course," she replied, continuing to gaze across the lawn toward the children. "Anne of Green Gables. Lucy Maud Montgomery."

Of course she does. He only knew it because Kiran had read the story to him while he was in the hospital. With his jaw wired shut, he'd been unable to protest the choice. Thus he'd also been forced to listen to Shakespeare as well. He gestured at the can in her hand. "Go ahead."

Glancing first at the can in her hands, she then met his gaze sheepishly.

"What's wrong?" he said.

"I don't want to be rude, but I don't like iced tea. I mean, really don't like it. Or I'd drink it to be polite," she said. "Sorry."

"Don't be," he replied. "Moron." The shocked expression on her face had him backpedalling. "Not you. Me." He berated himself internally. Did she think he was calling her a moron? How did he fix that? He'd obviously gone a little too far in learning to express his inner thoughts.

She looked away so he could no longer read her expression. "It's okay," she said softly.

Profanity scrolled through his brain but at least he managed to keep from expressing it, though he could feel his fists clenching as his blood pressure rose. "I should have asked what you'd like." Trying to salvage the situation, to pull it back from the awkward state it was morphing into, he held his can out toward her. "We could trade?"

Meeting his gaze, she hesitated.

Immediately he retreated and turned to go, muttering, "Never mind." *What an idiot.* An innocent like Sophie Paetan was not going to share spit with an ex-con. Especially not one she thought had just called her a moron. He scanned the swear words in his vocabulary, trying to choose just the perfect one to call himself. He sighed out his regret. Even though his relationship with the Ohio State penal system had concluded over three years ago, and he'd left the mean streets of Over-the-Rhine behind him, he would carry the stain much longer, maybe forever.

Sophie grabbed his sleeve. Not only did she halt his egress but she moved until she was face to face with him. "I'm not sure what you interpreted from that moment, but I don't want to share your pop because I just finished scolding Todd and Philippa for sharing a piece of gum."

Ayden felt an inexplicable relief. She wasn't repulsed by him. She was only trying to be a good example to the kids. Shuddering in mock horror, he said, "That's grim."

"Philippa! Beatrice! Todd!" A voice called across the lawns. The two girls and the boy ran off toward the speaker, a grandmotherly type in a blue striped cotton house dress.

"Okay. Now I can trade," Sophie said, holding her iced tea out to him.

"You sure?" Ayden said, watching her closely.

"Is there any reason I shouldn't be sure?"

He could tell that, though she used a light and easy tone, her question was serious. Matching her tone rather than her message, he replied, "Nope. I don't have any horrible diseases." That was the first thing he'd checked after his release from the Ohio State Penitentiary. And continued checking.

"Neither do I," she said and he could sense that she relaxed a little.

"Truly?" he asked. "You didn't share gum with Todd?"

She laughed. "That's gross."

He found himself smiling back at her, an inexplicable giddiness bubbling in his chest. When was the last time he'd felt giddy?

Her smile faded as her gaze drifted over his shoulder. "Uh oh," she said. "Big brother patrolling."

Ayden glanced back to see Tristan stomping across the grass in their direction. What did he want? "He's a bit overprotective."

"He's a self-important twit. My father's little watchdog." She added in an undertone, "It's certainly not because he cares."

Tristan brushed past Ayden to stand between him and Sophie. "I warned you that this guy was no good." Sophie's face clouded. Tristan's hand darted out to grasp her elbow. "Come on."

It wasn't the first time that Ayden had been judged by his past. It certainly wouldn't be the last.

Sophie pulled back but couldn't dislodge her brother's grip. "Stop it, Tristan. You're being really rude."

Tristan was virtually vibrating with anger and he must have tightened his grip because Sophie flinched. Ire rose up within Ayden and he reacted without thought, fisting Tristan's shirt and jerking him around. He couldn't tolerate aggression against women. When Tristan released Sophie's arm, Ayden hesitated a moment, struggling internally until he could finally bring himself to relax his grip and thus release the man. *Gotta let go. Can't let this escalate.*

Tristan's expression went from menacing to afraid for a split second before a mask of superiority fell into place. "You." Stepping in, Tristan poked Ayden in the shoulder. Ayden stiffened, combating his instinctive desire to remove the guy violently from his personal space. *Lord, give me patience.* "If this wasn't the church picnic…" He jabbed Ayden once again, raising his blood pressure incrementally. He hated being poked. "Don't test me. One more word and I'll have you arrested so fast you'll think you'd never left the big house." He flicked a gesture toward Ayden's arm, presumably indicating his prison tattoo.

Ayden refused to back down even as he heard the ring of truth in Tristan's words. If the man followed through on his threat, Ayden could very well land back in prison. He'd certainly spend the night in jail before anyone would bother to stop and ask whether a man known to have a violent past had actually broken any law.

"Back off," Sophie said acerbically, shoving her brother back a step and insinuating herself between him and Ayden. Ayden felt his eyes widen in surprise. "And stop pretending you care."

"Father was right about you," Tristan said spitefully, striding away.

As soon as he turned the corner around the church, Sophie's shoulders slumped and she hugged her elbows tightly to her body.

"Hey," Ayden said. His fingers extended toward her then flexed into his palm. He didn't like the defeat in her posture but he wasn't sure if he should touch her. "You okay?"

After a shuddering breath, she nodded once. "Yeah." Her voice was hoarse. "Sorry."

Her sadness softened his resolve. Reaching out, he touched her shoulder gently, just a glide of his fingertips on the silky sleeve of her vibrant yellow blouse. "You have nothing to be sorry about."

She took another deep shuddering breath. "My family's been divided for a while. After my parents divorced, I stayed with my mom but my sister and Tristan went to live with my father, hence the private school education."

"So he thinks he's better than you."

Finally, she turned to look at him. "He certainly thinks he's better than you."

"But you don't?" *Could it be true?*

She shook her head. "What did you go to prison for?"

"What makes you so sure that I did?" he asked, using the voice that usually persuaded the gullible that he was above reproach.

"Tristan may be a waste of good air but he knows about criminals. He's the sheriff of Clermont County."

Of course he is. "Does it matter? Aren't all ex-cons cut from the same cloth? Shackles and chains? Black and white stripes? A grungy orange jumpsuit?" He could feel the edge of bitterness creeping into his voice. Five years ago, just after he'd gotten parole, he'd given his heart to Christ. But he was still new to salvation and, no matter how hard he tried, his past haunted his present, old reactions governed new.

Unmoved by his question, she waited, tilting her head quizzically, expectation in her gaze. She wasn't going to be pulled into debate or pity or anything but the truth.

So he gave it. "Aggravated assault."

"Who did you assault?"

Most people didn't ask. As a matter of fact, most people didn't ask what he'd gone to prison for. Once they knew he'd spent time inside, they assessed, weighed and found him wanting. "The man who raped my sister."

"Oh, my." She gasped. "How long…were you…"

"Inside?" he said, filling in the blanks. "Three years. Parole for two. Been free and clear for three years now."

"And you're a friend of Kiran's?"

He nodded, his eyes dropping to her mouth and he wondered for a moment what she would taste like. Cola, probably.

"Eyes," she said.

Frowning, he looked up to meet her gaze. *What?*

"That's better," she said, tilting her head to watch him more carefully. "How did you and Kiran meet?"

"Through his brother. You know him?" he said.

"Yes. Well, not really. Pia and her grandparents don't seem to have any contact with him. I didn't know that Kiran did either," she said. "Ram Rao is famous, though. Well, infamous is probably a better word. The story I heard is that Ram came under threat from a Mumbai Mafia don for losing a shipment of laundered money. So Ram, Kiran and Pia were sent here to the 'States to get them out of danger in India. I don't think the change took for Ram, though, for several more years. He's a lot older than me and Pia but every teenager at Ancora High knows of his reputation. Last I heard he was a nurse or something at one of the hospitals in Cincinnati."

"Mercy Hospital. Where I landed about five years ago. Ram was one of my nurses. I guess you could say he took an interest in me." *Because he recognized my prison tats. Because he'd spent time inside. For drugs.* After which time, his family had disavowed any relationship with him. But eventually Ram had found Christ, repaired his relationship with the part of his family that was willing, and gone to college for nursing. "He sent Kiran to visit me when he was off-shift. Thought I needed a pastor, I guess." So Ram, with his common experience of crime and punishment, had become his mentor, ushering him into recovery. But Kiran was his friend. Because of Jesus and the Rao brothers' tenacious good will, Ayden was starting a new life.

"Did you?"

"Did I what?" He'd pretty much done everything after all.

"Need a pastor?"

He felt his features soften at her kind voice. "Yeah."

"Kiran's a good guy," she said.

"Yeah." They lapsed into silence for a moment, the laughter of children filtering across the grounds, joining the calls of the ice cream vendor from across the road in Riverside Park.

"What do you do for a living, Ayden?"

"Carpentry. I work at Hagerty's Handmade Furniture in Eden Park, but I got my carpentry papers while I was on parole. One day I hope to make my own furniture." *Why had he told her that?* He knew that the chance of him ever being able to do that was slimmer than a calorie-wise candy bar.

Sophie's eyes brightened at his words. "I know that area of Cincinnati. I work at East 9th and Vine," she said. "Have you made anything yet?"

"A few things. I have a project on the go," he said suddenly feeling shy. How stupid was that?

"I'd love to see it sometime."

"Sure," he replied, knowing full well that this woman would never spend enough time around him to have the opportunity to see the teak wood dining table he was fashioning with his own hands.

A tan and black SUV and a yellow Classic VW Beetle pulled into the church parking lot, children debarking almost before the vehicles had stopped. Sophie cast a glance their way, greeting the newcomers with an enthusiastic wave. Turning back to him, she said, "Well, welcome to Ancora, Ayden Breckinridge." Then she smiled at him, her deep brown eyes soft and warm.

"Thanks."

"I'll see you around."

"Sure."

But he knew it wasn't true. Even as she turned back to give him a little wave, he was confident of one thing, women like that, wholesome, sweet, church-bred women didn't go out of their way to spend time with violent criminals. But, oh, he wished it were true.

Chapter Two: Family Matters

Parking along the curb in front of the first home he'd truly known, Jaxen Foxx debarked from his Jeep Liberty, gathering two paper grocery sacks from the trunk before engaging the locks. His uncle, Arlo Kimutai, lived in a row house, reminiscent of New York City's Brownstones, the characteristic brownish-red sandstone domiciles of *Sesame Street*. The sun's burnished rays dipped behind the roofline, the last glimpse of daytime before nightfall, as a gentle breeze wafted along the tree-lined street. Just a block in from Main Street and abutting the Greenland Forest to the southwest, the air carried the mingled scents of exhaust and pine. The muted sounds of traffic masked the gentle sweep of the nearby Little Miami River.

Mounting the front steps, Jaxen knocked several times before the door opened a crack. "It's me, Uncle Arlo."

"You bring them twitter-pated girls?" Arlo asked grouchily. It seemed that most things made him surly, except those that made him sullen.

"Nope. I left Angie and Saffi at home." In fact, Jaxen's teenaged daughters, Angeline at fifteen and Sapphire at fourteen, had staged a protest this morning, refusing to spend anymore Friday evenings with the cantankerous man. It was difficult to tell if Arlo was pleased or annoyed by the girls' absence. "How are you keeping, old man?"

Arlo muttered something derisive about "youth" before he replied. "New neighbor. Quiet gal. You bring me some beer?" He accepted one of the bags Jaxen was carrying and shuffled to the kitchen, unloading it piece by piece onto the kitchen counter.

"You know the doctor said you can't have alcohol with your medication. I did bring you some of the ginger beer you like."

Arlo scowled, muttering darkly something unintelligible. Jaxen didn't bother to ask for clarification.

"I brought the fixings for cabbage and corned beef. Would you like it if I made that for your supper?"

"Suppose so," Arlo mumbled, straightening a photograph of Angie and Saffi as toddlers that hung on the wall over the moss-green Arborite table, before lowering himself gingerly into one of the four matching upholstered brass bucket swivel-chairs. A wooden highchair still sat in the corner, testament to the kind heart beneath Arlo's gruff exterior.

As Jaxen prepared the meal, chopping the cabbage and setting it to boil in the frying pan before adding the spiced corned beef, he studied Arlo. An African-American man, prematurely aged by the grief of life, he moved through life glowering at everyone and the world. His close-cropped afro was completely grey. His features were wrinkled and gaunt, thinner than the last time Jaxen had visited.

"You still teachin' them kids?" he asked.

Jaxen smiled. His change of career was still a bone of contention between them. "Yes."

"Can't believe you gave up bein' a cop to wipe snot."

Jaxen had been a police officer with the City of Cincinnati Police Department for one year, partnered with a crooked cop, Orion Vanderzalm, a veteran who survived on the streets of the inner-city through a combination of graft and extortion.

Jaxen remembered his last day on the job...

"You hear what happened to Keshia?" Jaxen Foxx had asked his partner.

"Course," Vanderzalm replied while passing the bag of maple bacon donuts he'd just purchased at Hopkins Donut Shop across the street. "She didn't have no choice. Kid pulls a gun on you, you take him down." He bit into the doughy pastry, humming in pleasure.

"The kid was twelve years old."

Vanderzalm turned in the driver's seat of the cruiser, pushing his white hat to the back of his prematurely grey head while stuffing the rest of his donut into his mouth, licking the sticky icing off his fingers before speaking. He was a short powerhouse of a man who disdained chasing down suspects as much as shaving and so he carried a perpetual half-grown beard. "What are you getting at, Rookie?"

"Don't you ever get the feeling that, by the time we're dealing with the youth on the streets, it's too late?" Within an hours' drive from Hopkins which was nestled in the relatively affluent neighborhood of Mount Auburn, some of the countries' poorest citizens lived in some of the most violent and gang-ravaged neighborhoods.

"You're not from around here so I'll cut you some slack." Vanderzalm cut off Jaxen's protest. "You never spent one single hour in Camp Washington or Over-the-Rhine. You h'ain't seen the filth of humanity runnin' those streets. These kids are born bad and most of them die that way. Don't matter when you know 'em. Catch 'em all and put 'em away."

"There is always—" Jaxen didn't get to finish his thought because the dispatcher's voice interrupted. *Hope,* Jaxen had meant to say. But without Uncle Arlo, would there have been a path out of the gangs for Jaxen? God was speaking to all the youth of Cincinnati, he didn't question that, but with no experience of love and forgiveness, it was hard for them to hear, just as it had been for him in inner-city Seattle.

"William 66 respond. 10-27 in progress at Mount Auburn High School. Assailant known to the department."

"10-4." Jaxen responded to dispatch as Vanderzalm activated the sirens and put the cruiser in gear, peeling away from the curb, down Dorchester past Hopkins Park, and south onto Sycamore. They passed supermarkets, high-end retailers, and newly developed condominium complexes constructed to match the historic buildings around them.

...that night they'd arrested a man who should have gone free and released a man who went on to re-offend. The case that should have been prosecuted never was. And Jaxen had walked away. Three weeks later his wife had died of a heart attack and he was alone with his two little girls, in desperate need of a stable income and a career that didn't break his heart.

CR80

Why am I here? Sophie wondered. Ever since her parents' divorce when Sophie was ten, she had been expected to attend her father upon command for Friday supper. So, once again, she'd made the journey through the forested backcountry roads of Greenbriar and Elklick to the stately homes of some of Ohio's most moderately wealthy. She'd parked her Cypress Pearl Toyota Avalon between the tennis court and the four-car garage which generally sheltered Stuart's conservative black BMW Gran Coupé, Tristan's canary yellow Porsche Cayenne, and Viv's silver H3, not to mention the tan Chevy Cavalier sedan kept for the servants' use.

Her mother greeted her at the front door of the 3800-square-foot colonial-style red brick mansion. Rita, clad in her grey maid's uniform, ushered them inside. As usual, there was not a mote of dust on the veneered hardwood floors or the curving mahogany staircase. The flush-mount crystal chandelier sparkled and Sophie wondered whether it was the petite Rita's job or the gardener's—Tad she thought his name was—to scale the twenty-foot ladder to the vaulted ceilings to polish it.

"Sophie Anne. Lucille." Stuart greeted them. "Dinner is ready."

As Sophie followed her mother into the dining room where Tristan and Viv were already waiting, she wondered why her mother also still attended these so-called family dinners. She wasn't privy to the reasons for the break-up of her parents' marriage although there were plenty of rumors about her father's infidelity; rumours, which for some reason had never impacted his position of trust as mayor of Ancora. But if her father had betrayed his marriage, then why did her mother continue to respond to his every beck-and-call the way she did?

According to the original custody agreement, Tristan and Vivian had been required to visit their mother on a weekly basis but they'd simply refused to come. Tristan had found his time better spent pursuing his career, better interpreted as any activity which Stuart was seen to value. Already fourteen at the time, Vivian had always been too busy dating the *right* kind of men, those chosen by their father.

Wait, her sister now had the new spelling of her name with two V's, two E's and two N's, which she felt was so much more sophisticated. Sophie had an abrupt and vivid vision of the goose from *Charlotte's Web* by E. B. White and her exaggerated spelling of terrific. T double E double R, et cetera. A quick glance aside at Vivienne made Sophie chuckle. With her long neck and haughty expression, the similarity was reinforced.

"Sophie Anne!"

Her father's reprimand carried down the lace-and-linen-covered mahogany table. He would never do anything as crass as slapping the table, setting the fine bone china and silver rattling. However, as usual, his displeasure was enough to silence his family.

"I really don't think world hunger is a laughing issue," Stuart Paetan said. His face was stern and forbidding but Sophie no longer found it intimidating. She simply knew too much about the man. Like the fact that, rather than running her grandfather's pharmaceutical business, he'd chosen to cash in on his father's hard work and sacrifice to sell-up. The fortune he'd collected was ostensibly used to prop up the local economy but actually went a long way to garner influence and power.

"I wasn't laughing about world hunger," she said wearily. "I simply had a private inner thought that was humorous. I am allowed to have private musings, am I not?" She worked to keep the challenge from her voice though by the narrowing of her father's stony gaze, she guessed that she hadn't quite managed.

"There's no need for impertinence," he said. He brushed his right palm down the left side of his face, tracing his neatly coiffed beard to its point and then skimmed the backs of his fingers up the right side. It was his one tell, a sure sign that he was annoyed.

Sophie didn't bother to respond, she simply began eating again. The vichyssoise was quite delicious.

"I checked out that Brokeback guy for you," Tristan said, lifting his glass of sparkling mineral water. "Ran him through the database."

Who? "Ayden Breckinridge?" Sophie asked.

"Yes. Sophie, what were you thinking, cavorting with a violent criminal?" Stuart said.

Sophie huffed in surprise. "I wasn't *cavorting*," she emphasized the ridiculous anachronistic choice of vocabulary, "with anyone. He's a nice man."

"A man," Stuart said, "who assaulted a fifty-four-year-old high school teacher, beat him nearly to death. If the police hadn't been nearby, he would have killed the man in front of the entire teaching staff."

"He said he beat up the guy who raped his sister," Sophie said.

"Allegedly," Tristan said haughtily. "The teacher was never charged."

"Not every guilty person is charged," Sophie said narrowly.

"He was hot," Vivienne added. She looked like she wanted to eat Ayden for dessert. "But really, darling, one has to have standards." Vivienne flipped her long coffee-black hair over her shoulder.

Stuart frowned at his older daughter. "Viv." That was all he needed to say and she wore contrition like a mask. "That teacher guided the girls' volleyball team to victory six years in a row. How many other coaches have the dedication and skill to accomplish such a thing? He called them his daisies."

"Volleyball? That's his excuse?" Sophie said, taken aback.

"That is what speaks of his character," Stuart said tightly.

"Did the police investigate the allegations against him?" Sophie insisted on knowing.

Wearing the same haughty expression that Viv had adopted earlier, Tristan said, "Of course not. A man like that deserves the benefit of the doubt, particularly when it concerns a fourteen-year-old slut well known to have circled the block with many a man."

Wait a minute. "Fourteen? The girl was only fourteen?" *How could that be?*

"And a known liar and drug user. She was picked up for prostitution the very next week. She was asking for it," Tristan said. Stuart looked on his eldest child, his only son, with approval.

"I wonder what cook has made for dessert." Lucy Paetan was trying to bring peace to her family, a futile attempt.

"Lucille, really," Stuart said sternly. "The ruination of a man's reputation is somewhat more important than lemon meringue pie."

All she managed to do was bring the contempt of her ex-husband down on her head. Flushing, Lucy ducked her head. "Of course you're right."

"I'm not a big fan of lemon meringue," Sophie said. Step one in diverting her father's attention. "Where's Rhona today?" Step two and...

"Where is Rhona?" Stuart asked—bingo—turning his attention to Tristan.

"She's meeting with her Arts and Opera committee, planning some fundraiser or other," Tristan said cautiously.

"She will make a suitable wife for a career-minded man, son. You've done well," Stuart said.

The conversation moved on from there while Sophie counted the bites to finish her Boeuf Wellington and the minutes until she could depart. She always made plans for Friday evenings so that she could escape "family time" as soon as possible. "*Oh, sorry, I need to leave. I have a commitment.*" Tonight she was going out for coffee and dessert and then bowling with her friends, Pia, Gael, Sam, and Reggie. Perhaps next Friday Sophie would decline her father's standing orders altogether. She simply couldn't face another dinner with a group of people who thought it was okay to vilify a fourteen-year-old girl.

Chapter Three: Reckless and Irresponsible

Ayden twisted the millionth bolt on the hundred thousandth end table so that Archibald Hagerty could claim that his furniture was handmade. As he worked, he recited his mantra, "I am grateful for my job." It wasn't easy for an ex-con to find employment, much less to find a job somewhere in the vicinity of his interests. No one wanted to employ a man with a record. It didn't matter that his crimes had nothing to do with theft or drug violations; it was as though by committing one crime, he'd committed them all. Why did employers assume that he'd fail a drug test, steal from them or attack them in the alley behind their store? Okay, so maybe he understood why they might be afraid of violence, but he wasn't that man anymore. At least he didn't want to be.

Keeping his morose sigh internal, Ayden forced himself to repeat his mantra, gritting his teeth and twisting the next bolt. His eyes scanned the cavernous space. Gus and Little Pete assembled plywood drawers while young Brandi assembled boxes which Stewie taped closed. Arvin ran the Ripmaster, cutting foam bales for cushions, and the arms and backs of sofas. Yannie and Douglas drove the forklifts, delivering bales of foam to Arvin, cardboard crates to Brandi, and stacks of plywood to Rod who had the awesome luck to operate the CNC panel saw.

Unfortunately, due to his lack of math and computer skills, Ayden had been ineligible for a job running the Computer Numerical Control machines. There were occasions, many occasions if he was honest with himself, when he regretted his *laissez-faire* attitude toward education in his youth. As if an ex-con didn't have enough strikes against him when seeking employment, it was doubly difficult to get a good job when you had organized your high school schedule around your illegal activities.

At times like this, it was tempting to see history through a revisionist haze, to remember the way money had flowed through his fingertips in the old days collecting for the Grex. For someone who was skilled at instilling terror, at making his victims believe in their own imminent demise, money was easy. But hard, he reminded himself. Violence led to fear of reprisal and, inevitably, to prison. Aggravated violence led to hard time in federal prison, no matter that his actions had seemed justified at the time. Prison was an experience that Ayden had no desire to repeat.

If not for the Rao brothers entering his life at that lowest moment, he wasn't certain what would have become of him. Two weeks out of prison, lonely and alone, with Gram dead of a massive stroke just six months after Cassie overdosed, ending her young life, Ayden had allowed himself to be provoked by the wrong men.

The next morning he'd awakened in Mercy Hospital, groggy, pain vibrating through his head and chest…

Something was squeezing his arm. Reaching over, Ayden tried to shove it away. A warm hand restrained him and the tightening increased.

"Relax, pal. I'm just taking your blood pressure."

Too disoriented to understand, Ayden tried to rise, to escape, but he was trapped. Aluminum bars guarded his sides, an intravenous tube tethering him to the convex mattress on the narrow bed. White light reflected off the equally white walls sending a spike of pain through his forehead, forcing him to close his eyes against the glare.

"Hey, buddy. I'll give you something to help you sleep."

Opening his mouth—his mouth wouldn't open! He couldn't speak. Ayden panicked, groaning.

"You're okay, man. Calm down."

A figure loomed over him and large hands pressed his shoulders into the bed. A warm tingling spread through his body. His arms and legs felt heavy, unresponsive, and the panic resolved into a mysterious sensation that tugged him toward sleep.

"You're safe, man."

Ayden stopped struggling, drifting away. The next time he surfaced, there was a robust Indian man in blue surgical scrubs adjusting his IV. "Hey. Good afternoon. That was some fight you had."

Memories returned in a series of snapshots. Nausea roiled in Ayden's belly as he remembered the sensation as his ribs cracked and the explosion in his head when his jaw broke.

"Where'd you do your time?" The man, a nurse, he supposed, pointed at Ayden's right biceps. "I was born free and should be free." Only someone who'd spent time in prison would know the meaning of that, or someone who spent time in the company of violent men.

Sleep tugged him back under and Ayden's eyes drifted closed.

"We'll talk later. Get some sleep. You're safe now."

Ayden had drifted off, waking later to find another Indian man at his side, this one clad in a white dress shirt, beige tie, and brown slacks. He resembled the Indian nurse but was leaner, softer, and shorter by a good four inches. He wore black-rimmed glasses.

"Hello."

Shutting his eyes, Ayden dismissed the man. Had he somehow been transported to a hospital in Mumbai?

"I could read to you, if you like. Help you pass the time."

Ayden ignored him. He'd rather speak to the nurse who'd spent time in prison than this delicate man who'd clearly never been near that life.

"I've got Tom Clancy, C. S. Lewis, *Fanny Hill*…"

Ayden's eyes sprang open.

D. C. Shaftoe

The man chuckled. "I thought that would get your attention. I don't in fact have *Fanny Hill* but I do have *The Hobbit* and *The Hunt for Red October* with me today. Shall I just pick one?"

Ayden closed his eyes again. The man took it as permission. "I'm Kiran, by the way." Ayden glanced at him and then closed his eyes again. "Nice to meet you," Kiran said wryly and then he began to read. At least it wasn't a story about cats.

In spite of Ayden's feigned disinterest, Kiran kept showing up, moving through *The Lion, The Witch and The Wardrobe* and, for some inexplicable reason, *Anne of Green Gables*. He learned that the nurse and the preacher were brothers.

"I've brought an extra book today," Kiran had said one afternoon. "Do you remember the story by C. S. Lewis about Aslan and the children?"

Ayden grunted his affirmation. There wasn't much else he could say with his jaw wired shut.

"I have another book by that author but it's not a story." Kiran handed over *Mere Christianity* by C. S. Lewis. "Would you be interested?"

Ayden gave him a hard stare. Was he interested? He hadn't the faintest curiosity about Christians and God but he did know that he needed a new start in life. If he didn't learn to control his temper, he was going to die. In fear and violence. And Kiran *had* given up his time to make Ayden's life a bit more bearable. He liked the guy. If it mattered to Kiran then maybe he could quell his skepticism and read the book.

Ayden had shrugged and agreed. And now here he was, five years later, twisting another bolt.

Ayden *was* grateful for his job, and even more grateful that God gave second chances. After the life he'd led, the mistakes he'd made, to believe…to know, that the God of all creation wanted a relationship with reckless and irresponsible, angry and bitter, Ayden Breckinridge, was an astonishing joy. And maybe, just possibly, Sophie Paetan could be a part of that new life.

Ayden found his mind drifting to her every day, several times. It wasn't just her smile or the way her eyes sparkled with humor. It was the way she looked at him. Like he was a real man, a normal person who deserved the same respect as people who hadn't spent half their adolescence in juvenile detention or who hadn't taken a baseball bat to a well-respected man of the community. She treated him as though he didn't carry the shame and fear and violence of prison with him at all times.

"Reck." Ayden turned to see his shift supervisor approaching. "Hagerty says you'll have to take the whole evening. Says he's not splitting a shift. Your pay'll be deducted." Barney Tomlinson wasn't a bad guy. He was just delivering bad news. Losing those wages was no small thing for Ayden. But he was trying to find a place to live in Ancora and the landlord, Hamish Oskar, had demanded that their meeting take place today, Friday evening at six, even though Ayden had told the man that he was scheduled to work.

"No problem," Ayden muttered. Hagerty wasn't the sort of man you argued with. If he told you to stay after hours, or insisted on paying you in cash, denied your health benefits, or in any other way betrayed your civil rights, you put up and shut up. Without him, there would be dozens more unemployed ex-cons.

"See you Monday," Barney said as he moved down the line to speak to Ford Carver, the guy who stuck the little felt pads on the legs of the end tables and chairs.

"Wait," Ayden said, reaching out to stop Barney. "I thought I was scheduled for Saturday."

"Not this week. They're cleaning the spindle carvers." Barney continued on his way.

Great. So now he'd lost not only his Friday evening shift but all of Saturday as well. Ayden sighed. *Lord, why does it have to be so hard?*

At his locker, Ayden removed his work gloves and then shoved his coveralls down and off his body. One sniff of his armpits told him he stank. But why bother rushing home to shower. If Oskar thought the meeting had to be at six, the least the man could do was put up with a little stink.

Removing his work boots, Ayden pulled on his black leather riding boots and then grabbed his leather jacket, sunglasses, and helmet from his locker. Pocketing his keys, he headed out.

The meeting with Oskar—which had been more like an interrogation—was over in fifteen minutes and Ayden had the rest of Friday night ahead of him. Stopping at the Red Barn Market, he picked up milk, coffee, eggs, and apples, his staple diet, as well as a few other things he needed. Arms laden with paper grocery sacks, he walked down Beckwith Street toward Main, heading past Stohl's Jewellers toward Paxton's Pharmacy to pick up some antibacterial ointment and bandages. Kiran had found some ancient chisels in the parsonage shed and lent them to Ayden who had nearly sliced the skin off the heel of his hand using them. This weekend he wanted to be prepared.

Dodging a group of slow-walkers who felt the need to stop and discuss every shop they passed, including the pet store and a used book store that looked like a library had exploded in its front room, Ayden started across Main Street, taking advantage of the conversation ongoing between a white-haired man leaning out the window of his battered pickup and a much younger woman, neither of whom seemed to have an issue blocking traffic as they conversed.

"Ayden."

When he heard his name, he just kept on walking, past the abandoned theater whose last showing had obviously been *Star Trek: The Wrath of Kahn*, the original version with Shatner and Montalbán. It was most likely a greeting for someone else. Only his grandmother had called him Ayden. He'd been Reck since he was ten years old and had thrown a brick through his school principal's window.

He missed his grandmother. She'd loved him in spite of his lifestyle, even warning him repeatedly that he'd wind up in prison if he didn't change. Little old grey-haired prophet she was. The old broad had laid a wooden spoon across his flanks in his younger years but she'd also been quick to laugh and always ready with a hug and forgiveness. If it wasn't for Gram, Ayden wasn't certain he would have even understood Kiran when he'd first told him of God's forgiveness.

"Ayden."

This time he stopped and scanned the sidewalk. Of course, the other person who called him by his given name was Sophie. And there she was standing in a crowd, waving him over.

She smiled at him when he started toward her and he smiled back. He couldn't help it. However, the smile faded once he saw the hostile expressions on the faces surrounding her. There were two men and two women, aside from Sophie. One of the women he immediately recognized as Kiran and Ram's sister, Pia, because he'd seen her picture. She had her long, silky black hair pulled into a ponytail. Her ebony eyes reflected apprehension. The other, a buxom woman with hair dyed a brilliant blue he'd seen at Kiran's church but had never spoken to. They both frowned at him.

The two men in the group moved closer to flank Sophie, whether by instinct or by design, perhaps in some misguided attempt to protect her from Reck the ex-con. Both men were shorter than Ayden's five-eleven and while one had the artificial muscles of a health club member, the other was lean and pale.

"I don't know if you've met." Sophie indicated her friends. "This is Pia Rao. But you probably know her since you know Ram and Kiran." Sophie gestured to the blue-head. "This is Gaelan Somerset." Health club guy was... "Sam Jeong." And skinny guy was... "Reggie Dundas."

They all, each one of them, scowled at Ayden.

Sophie continued, "Guys, this is—"

Ayden interrupted her. "Reck." He extended his hand first toward the health club dude who, given his stance and manner, clearly considered himself the alpha dog in the group of friends. Ayden held on just a little too tightly and just a little too long. Sophie frowned, probably at his arrogant manner, but maybe not. He knew he was overcompensating because he was embarrassed; he knew he stank and was covered in sawdust from the factory. But he refused to broadcast the vulnerability he felt because he worked with his hands.

"You're new in town." Sam tugged his hand free, massaging it a few times before shoving it into his front trouser pocket.

"Yeah."

Sophie was watching him closely. "Picking up a few groceries?"

Ayden looked pointedly at the bag and then back at her. No need to answer that.

While tugging urgently on Sophie's sleeve, Pia glanced at Ayden with an expression of mild panic in her eyes. "Come on, Sophie, we'll lose our table if we don't leave soon."

"Get the car, Reggie. I'll be right there." Sophie was still watching Ayden quizzically.

"Are you sure?" Sam narrowed his gaze at Ayden.

As if. Sam didn't have a clue how to look truly mean. He just came off as constipated. He wouldn't last a day in Over-the-Rhine, the capital of violent crime, where Ayden had grown up. And prison? Ayden had thought he was tough when he went inside. He'd been proven wrong. Sam wouldn't last an hour.

Ayden shifted back on the heels of his boots. It was hard to keep up the façade of disinterest when what he really wanted to do was to reach out and take Sophie's hand. And then kiss her mouth, to taste her and see if she was as sweet and spicy as he suspected.

"Well, go on. You're the ones who're worried about being late." Sophie nudged Sam's shoulder, waving them away.

The others muttered among themselves, casting dark looks in Ayden's direction. Finally, they departed.

"How are you?" Sophie asked, her voice suddenly unsure, her eyes holding doubt.

"Fine." Ayden stepped closer. It was a good thing his arms were full of groceries or he might be tempted to touch that soft-looking lock of tawny hair that fell across her cheek. "You?"

"Good." His eyes followed the movement as she spoke. "We're, uh, going bowling later. Would you like to come?"

Wait. What? "Bowling?" His eyes flickered up to meet her gaze.

"You know, it's that sport where you take a big black ball and roll it down a wooden floor," she said with a glint in her eye.

He furrowed his brow in mock disgust when he realized she was teasing him. "Not hardly a sport."

She smiled and her eyes sparkled. "Would you like to come with us?"

No. The answer he should give was "no" because her friends clearly didn't like him. And though she didn't seem to mind his status as *persona non grata*, she would soon enough. The allure of the criminal element always faded once the reality became known. He could soften his dialect, eliminate profanity, even remove his tattoos, but he couldn't erase the years of violence he'd both inflicted and received. He didn't fit with her friends and never would.

"Okay," he said, much to his own surprise.

"Great." And she looked like she truly believed it. "We'll be at Hondo's on First Avenue about nine. See you then." She gave him a little wave and then jogged off to join her friends around the corner.

Bowling? Had he really agreed to spend the evening with people who looked at him like he was sidewalk gum? People who acted like they wanted to find a stick and scrape him off?

Ayden forced himself into motion finishing his shopping and heading home to his dingy basement apartment on his metallic red 1998 Suzuki Marauder motorcycle. He'd found it abandoned behind Hagerty's factory at the end of his first week of work and had been scavenging parts to keep it running. It wasn't as fast or as fancy as his Hayabusa which had been the last of his possessions sold to pay Cassie's and then Gram's medical bills, but it cost little to run and released him from dependency on public transit, allowing him a sense of freedom.

For the next few hours he lost himself in woodworking, sanding the surface of his current project, a teak dining table. Growing up, he'd never had anything permanent like a dining room table. He'd never had a dining room. The many apartments he'd lived in, first with his mother and then with Gram, had never had much furniture and certainly nothing as beautiful as the table he was fashioning with his own hands.

Eight-thirty rolled around and Ayden was forced to stop. He needed to buy finer-grade sandpaper but his budget was spent on groceries and bandages. No more carpentry supplies for two weeks. Ram had been working with him, helping him set up a budget and stick to it, allotted portions of his salary for food, tithe, incidentals, and carpentry supplies.

Speaking of incidentals, he'd need money to go bowling with Sophie and her friends. He sniffed his pits. *Phew.* And a shower and fresh clothes. But did he really want to go? The answer to, "did he want to see Sophie again", was "yes". He was attracted to her, but it was more than that. She sincerely seemed to like him. But he wasn't good for her. So, the answer to, "*should* he see Sophie again", was a deep, resounding "no". His friendship was only going to bring her pain. And for what? He wasn't worth losing her friends, irritating her brother…who was the sheriff…or any other inevitable social consequences.

So maybe the answer was to go, see Sophie, and give her a sample of what life as his friend would really be like. And then, when he saw the revulsion in her eyes, he'd find it easy to stop thinking about her. Plan confirmed.

He dressed like they expected him to dress, in old blue jeans that were faded and torn, and an old used-to-be white T-shirt which had a faded blood stain across the bottom. He'd gotten the stain staunching a bloody nose after inhaling too much varnish early on in his apprenticeship. But they wouldn't know that. They'd assume something more sinister.

Pulling on his leather motorcycle boots and jacket, he donned his black helmet, slipped on his sunglasses, and drove his Suzuki to Hondo's on First Avenue. Considered a dicey neighborhood, First and Foundry was substantially upscale as compared to Clough-Pike where Ayden now rented. As compared to the Cincinnati neighborhood he'd grown up in, it was positively affluent.

Situated between a vacant lot and an ancient Dairy Queen, Hondo's had that saggy, rundown appearance of a building that hadn't seen repair or upgrade since the seventies. A white mini-bus, two sedans and three motorcycles populated the parking lot which offered an unobstructed view of the local toughs smoking pot in the adjacent alley.

The bowling alley wasn't very full given that it was a Friday night. There was one under-tens birthday party in the far left lane, a couple clearly more interested in gazing into each other's eyes than bowling, and what looked like a church youth group given the "bowl for Jesus" T-shirts they wore, the girls pointing and giggling at the embracing couple, the leaders frowning in disdain. They clearly had no understanding of passion.

A few lanes to the right of the teens were Sophie and her friends. Pausing a moment, Ayden wondered if maybe he'd made a mistake leaving the city, uprooting himself from the familiar to this little town. In the city, he knew the rules, knew how things worked, unlike in Ancora where everything about him made it clear that he didn't fit in. Taking a bracing breath, he reminded himself that what he was about to do was for Sophie's own good.

Sauntering over, he stepped directly into the center of the group and flopped into the corner of the U-shaped bench, slouching, spreading his knees and resting his arms on the back. In every way taking up as much room as possible. Opening his jacket to reveal the blood-stained T-shirt beneath, he reached into his shirt pocket to retrieve a matchstick which he slipped between his teeth. He knew that in that pose he looked sexy and dangerous. "Hey, girl," he said, tugging on the hem of Sophie's blouse.

"Hi…Ayden." Sophie's eyes flickered with doubt as she greeted him.

"You can't wear those in here," Reggie said, pointing at Ayden's leather boots. His voice actually shook nervously as he spoke. "You need to get a pair of bowling shoes."

Ayden dropped his gaze to Reggie's feet, examining the scuffed leather shoes, and then speared him with an expression of disdain. "You have *got* to be kidding."

Reggie flushed scarlet from his ugly tan-and-green bowling shoes to his carrot-top. Backing away, he took a seat as far away as possible from Ayden. Ayden felt a moment of remorse. The skinny guy really didn't seem to carry himself with much confidence. He didn't need Ayden's spite adding to his already low self-esteem.

"Fine. So he doesn't bowl," Sam said, smoothing a hand over his cropped black hair. "Gael, you're up."

Gael spared Ayden a sneer before stepping into the lane to take her turn. Ayden tilted his head as the woman bent to retrieve her bowling ball.

"You're disgusting," Pia said. "If you want to ogle women, go somewhere else." Turning her back to him, she crossed her arms and sat angrily across the space beside Reggie.

"Hey, babe, I was invited," Ayden said. Removing his jacket, he flung it over the back of the bench, creating even more distance between himself and the others. The tight T-shirt rode up his arms, displaying his tattoos.

Sophie was watching him as she awaited her turn to bowl. Her posture spoke of her tension but her eyes looked confused. "What's wrong?" he asked her insolently. She didn't answer him but instead turned to watch Gael bowl.

When Sam got up from the scoring table to take his turn, Ayden used his foot to swivel the chair around and then plonked his booted feet on it.

"Get your filthy boots off there," Gael said, coming to loom over his legs. He grinned nastily up at her. "You're a real jerk, you know. Tristan told me you're a criminal."

Ayden maintained his expression but he knew his eyes grew harder, colder, because he felt it in his chest.

Arrested by Gael's words, Sam paused in the upswing and then walked over carrying the ball cradled against his chest. "What?"

Gael looked over at Sam. "He attacked a teacher at his sister's high school; beat him with a baseball bat."

"That's awful," Pia said. Her eyes widened in dismay while her hand clapped to her mouth.

Ayden clasped his hands together in a mock-swing and made a pop sound with his mouth. "Home run."

No one moved. Ayden could hear the giggles of the teenage girls in the next lane along with the laughter at the children's birthday party, but around him there was silence.

"Ayden," Sophie said softly. He looked over to see a deep sadness on her pale face. "Please put your feet down. Sam, please take your turn."

Deep regret burned in Ayden's chest but he couldn't ignore the disdain in Gael's voice. Then again, he couldn't ignore Sophie's soft-spoken plea. Keeping his eyes on hers so no one could mistake whose words motivated him, he slowly removed his feet. Sam followed the movement with his eyes.

"Sam," Sophie said. Her voice was stronger now. "It's your turn."

Sam glanced at her and then at Gael who nodded once. He returned to the lane while the others returned to their seats across the way from Ayden, all except Sophie.

"I'm going to get some food," Sophie said.

"I'll help," Reggie said eagerly, following her but making a wide berth around Ayden.

Sam returned to the scoring table after his turn, brushing it off first with a tissue Gael handed him. Pia stepped up and bowled a spare. Ayden simply stared off into the distance while he replayed the look of hurt and disappointment in Sophie's eyes.

"You know, you are odious. You don't need to watch her bend over."

Ayden looked up into Gael's flinty eyes. He hadn't been looking at any part of Pia, in fact. But if that's what they expected of him...

"Hey, doll, I'll watch you, too," he said in the street-charm drawl he'd perfected years ago. It drove the upper class girls wild with anger and lust. He could see it had the same effect on Gael. She was disgusted by him at the same time as she wanted to be noticed by him. "Your turn next, babe," he said and swung his arms wide. "There's plenty of me to go around."

His hand connected with something and he heard a gasp of surprise and pain. Turning abruptly, half rising, he saw what he'd done. Nacho cheese and corn chips littered the front of Sophie's top, giving the impression of a jumble of fossils trapped for all time in the ooze. The cheese was hot as tar, still steaming where it clung to her clothes.

"Ow, it's burning," she said, pulling the fabric away from her skin. Turning away, she took off toward the bathroom.

Ayden rose to follow her but Gael shoved him back. "You've done enough, don't you think? Doll?" Her words had no impact in spite of her scathing tone. Because he already felt like a jerk.

"Yeah," he muttered because, though Gael's disdain made little impact on him, the pain in Sophie's eyes had made a significant impact.

As Gael followed Sophie to the ladies' room, Ayden started after her but halted when Reggie shoved something at his chest. His jacket. "Don't come back," he said. The guy had grown some chest hair in the past few minutes.

Ayden took the jacket, ignoring Reggie, and followed Gael. He couldn't go into the ladies' room so he sat in the metal folding chair beside the pay phone across from the toilets, his head in his hands. He could hear Gael and Sophie arguing inside.

"What did you think would happen? The guy's a convict. He's violent. Did you think just because he went to church now, he'd somehow become something else?" Gael said.

"You're not helping, Gael. Just leave me alone."

Gael gasped. "He's burned you. Look, your skin is all red."

"It's the cheese. It stuck."

"Stay away from him Sophie. He's no good."

"Just go, Gael, before I lose my temper," Sophie said.

Ayden heard the paper towel dispenser and, before long, Gael stormed out of the washroom. She didn't even notice Ayden sitting in the shadows.

Burned. He'd hurt her, something of which he didn't think he was capable. Why did he do it? She had asked him to spend time with her and, instead of enjoying her company, instead of making her want to see him again—because, he sure as shootin' wanted to see her—he'd humiliated her in front of her closest friends and then covered her in burning hot cheese.

Rising, he went to the canteen. After practically begging, when what he really wanted to do was wipe the smug smile off the soda jerk's face with his boot, and then paying for a drink he didn't want, he was able to get a cup full of ice.

Ayden knocked on the Ladies' Room door. "Sophie?" He swallowed hard. She was crying. "I brought you some ice."

He heard the towel dispenser again and then some running water. "Come in," she said finally.

Cautiously, he opened the door, peering inside. "Is there anyone else in here?"

She sniffed. "No. I'm alone." She was standing in a pale pink tank top, rinsing her blouse in the sink. The skin across the top of her chest was an angry red.

Holding the cup out toward her, he said, "I brought ice."

She accepted the cup, placing it on the edge of the sink.

"It's not blistering," he said. "That's good."

Squeezing the water from her dark pink blouse, she said, "Yeah," not meeting his gaze.

When she moved to pull the wet blouse on, he stopped her. "Here." Taking it from her, he spread it across the basin. Then he dumped the ice into the shirt, rolling it up and stepping close to her. When she backed away, he forced himself to stop and explain. "We can use it like an ice pack. You can wear my jacket over it and no one will see."

Nodding, she lifted her arms so he could fasten it around her upper chest like a large bandage. Then he shrugged out of his jacket and put it on her, zipping it closed. He gestured at the mirror. "See," he said, keeping his voice gentle and soothing. "You look like a hot biker chick."

Her eyes widened a moment and then she snorted in disbelief. "Hot?"

He got his unintended pun and grinned cautiously. It faded quickly. "I'm really sorry, Sophie. I never meant to hurt you."

Her humor vanished. "You were just acting like a punk and got carried away?"

"Not a punk, Sophie. A thug maybe." He met her gaze squarely. "I'm sorry for that, too."

"Why did you do it?" she said earnestly.

He lost eye contact for a moment and then glanced back at her face. "I just wanted you to see what you were getting into being friends with me."

"It was stupid, Ayden. And cruel."

"I'm not a nice guy, Sophie," he said and met her gaze, holding it.

"But you're not this guy either," she said, gesturing at him with both hands.

"I have been," he admitted.

"So? Who are you now?"

A knock sounded on the door. "Sophie? Gael thought you might need my help. Don't worry, that Reck guy is gone." There was a short pause. "Can I come in?"

"Yeah. Come in." Sophie watched the door open, flicking a glance at Ayden just before Pia entered. "I need to know," she whispered at him.

"Oh." Pia gasped and then frowned at Ayden. "You shouldn't be in here." Her frown deepened when she noticed the jacket that Sophie was wearing, using her expression to clearly convey her opinion that anything he possessed was tainted and unworthy.

"He got me some ice," Sophie said, defending him. Now how about that!

Pia skirted around Ayden, giving him lots of space, on her way to Sophie's side. "Are you okay?"

"I'm fine. I'm going home, though." Sophie embraced Pia briefly. Ayden saw a flash of pain across Sophie's features when Pia gripped her harder. He wanted to pull Pia back, to stop Sophie's pain, but he didn't dare touch either of the women, not when Pia looked ready to call the cops any second.

"I can drive you home. If you want," Pia said but she didn't sound completely sincere.

Sophie smiled sadly. "No, Pia, you stay. Can you please let the others know, though? And get my purse for me?"

"Sure," she said, throwing Ayden another filthy look before leaving.

"I'd like to take you home," Ayden said, prepared to beg if his soft words weren't enough to earn him the opportunity.

"I don't know who you are," she said, meeting his gaze.

His throat tightened. Who was he? "I guess I'm the jerk who's trying to figure out how to be a good guy," he finally said and then held his breath. How could he ever be good enough for this sweet and wonderful woman?

She scrutinized his expression for a long moment before she finally said, "Okay."

Pia met them at the door to the toilets, giving Sophie a peck on the cheek before returning to the alley. Ayden didn't speak as he walked beside Sophie to the door of the bowling alley and then led her to his Suzuki.

"I only have one helmet," he said, removing it from his saddlebag. "You wear it. I'll, uh, buy another one. For next time." Hoping there would be a next time. But he didn't have that kind of cash, and wouldn't for another two weeks at least. And he'd have to forego any carpentry supplies, and coffee, in order to pay for it. But he would do that for her. "As soon as I can."

"I'll buy my own," she said, surprising him, and then added with a mock-scowl, "You might buy a pink one or something. If I buy my own, I can have one of those cool ones with a dragon." A smile appeared at the corner of her mouth.

Was that some sort of acceptance of his tattoo? Probably not. But still…Ayden's face relaxed into a grin. "I like you, Sophie Paetan. You're my kind of girl." His expression blanked as he realized what he'd said.

He opened his mouth to clarify but she interrupted him. "We'll see."

His mouth snapped shut and then he nodded once, slipping his sunglasses on. "I need to get on first and then you can climb on behind me," he said, taking hold of the handlebars and straddling the seat.

She put the helmet on, buckled it after a few attempts and then swung her leg over the motorcycle behind him. He held the bike steady, watching her over his shoulder.

"You can hold my belt loops if you want or just put your arms around my waist." *There's a strap at the back as well you can hold on to.* He thought those words but never said them. He wanted her up against his back.

Sliding her hands around his waist, she failed to find a handhold. When she looked down to find a belt loop to hold onto, she knocked him on the head with the helmet. He blinked away the stars without comment.

Finally, she settled and he started up the motor. As he put the bike into gear, she tapped him on the shoulder.

"You don't know where I live," she said, yelling over the sound of the engine.

"Kiran told me."

"Kay," she replied and then took a hold on his waist again.

It was mostly true. After meeting Sophie at the Sunday school picnic, Ayden had mined any unsuspecting soul for information about her, as well as some, like Kiran, who suspected a great deal. Her address he'd found in the church directory. He'd even taken to coming home from work past her Brownstone-style row house even though it meant crossing Foundry Avenue and the Little Miami River to Main Street, detouring around the tree-lined block and then driving back to Foundry. It gave him a feeling of proximity and promise.

Sophie was silent on the way home. Ayden held himself back from using all the little tricks to get a girl to hold on tight on the back of a motorcycle. He was going to have to cultivate his best *gentleman* if he was going to have a hope with Sophie.

Parking at the curb in front of her Brownstone walk-up, he waited for her to step off, offering her a hand to keep her balance.

She pulled off the helmet, handing it to him. "Thanks for the ride."

"Do you have anything for that burn?" Ayden asked her.

"I probably have something," she replied, removing the leather jacket and handing it to him. "Good night."

He grabbed her hand. "Do you have any lidocaine spray?"

"No, what's that?" To his relief, she didn't yank her hand away.

"It's an external analgesic. For burns. I'm going to run home and get mine for you." Releasing her hand, he started the bike again. "Can I come up when I get back?"

She nodded. "I guess I'll see you soon."

"Keep ice on the burn. I'll be back in about half an hour or so."

"Okay."

Ayden was lucky. Kind of. Paxton's Pharmacy was still open so he got back to her home in fifteen minutes, with further depleted funds. Dating Sophie was going to be hard on his wallet.

Taking the steps two at a time, he rapped on her front door. She didn't answer and he wondered if she'd changed her mind. He knocked again.

"Hey. You."

Ayden turned to see an aged African-American man glowering at him out of what seemed to be the man's kitchen window which, incidentally, also overlooked Sophie's front stoop. All of his hair was completely grey, even his eyebrows which were furrowed angrily.

"Whatchyou want with our Sophie?" the man asked gruffly.

Ayden held up the paper bag from the pharmacy. "She's expecting me."

Sophie's door opened and Ayden turned his back on the grumpy neighbor to see her clad in a mint green ankle-length bathrobe. Her hair was wet and a towel hung around her shoulders. She'd had a shower.

"Hello, Mr. Kimutai. I see you've met my new friend, Ayden," she said brightly to the neighbor.

The man humphed, retreated and slammed the window down.

Sophie chuckled. "He's like having a watchdog." Ayden gazed at her, seeing that hint of a twinkle back in her eyes, and continued watching even as the twinkle gradually dimmed. "Ayden?" she said, a question in her voice, as if to say, "did you come here for a reason?"

He jerked to awareness. "Uh. Yeah." He held the bag out to her. "Here."

She accepted it from him. "Thanks."

Yeah, thanks. He so didn't deserve her gratitude for anything. "Sophie. Again. I'm really sorry."

Her eyes grew serious. "I know. I think. Will you be in church on Sunday?"

"Yes."

"Good," she said. "Maybe I'll see you then."

"Yes. Thanks. See you." He stumbled verbally and physically down the stairs. Hope burned in his chest. "Sunday." A better day.

"Sunday."

It had to be a better day than today.

Chapter Four: History of Violence

Sophie was running late for church. She'd forgotten to print out the picture of Daniel in the lion's den for her kindergarten Sunday school class and, of course, when she remembered this morning, her printer was out of ink. With the extra time it took to find her spare black ink cartridge, remember how to remove the empty one and replace it, she would have had to jog to church to get there on foot. So she hopped into her Toyota Avalon. And when the gas gauge pinged a warning, she pulled in at the familiar orangey-red triangle—or was it reddish-orange—of a Citgo on the corner of North and S 3rd streets. Sliding her credit card through the reader, she filled her tank and then set off once more, taking Wood Street to Kilgore Avenue and the Hope Wesleyan Church. Parking, she hefted her bag-of-stuff out of the trunk and started across the lawns.

"Sophie, wait up." Slowing at Gael's voice, she watched her friend lean in just a little too close to Kiran before sauntering over, swaying her hips suggestively, presumably for his benefit. "You are hopeless, girl," Gael said as she reached out to fluff Sophie's hair. "Are you even wearing makeup?"

"Um." Sophie thought about it. Wake up. Read. Shower, dress, blow-dry hair, change ink cartridge... "Nope. Forgot."

Gael whipped out her compact and started brushing powder over Sophie's cheeks and beneath her eyes.

"You know, you would have made a good chimpanzee," Sophie said.

Gael paused, nonplussed. "What?"

"All your community grooming skills." Sophie grinned as she said it.

Gael's fists landed on her hips. "You are lucky I'm such a good friend or I might be tempted to leave that gargantuan zit completely unconcealed." Sophie gasped as she covered her cheek with her hand. Gael's grin was superior. "Gotcha."

"You truly do have a cruel streak," Sophie said sincerely.

"What do you care about looking good anyway? I haven't seen you encourage any male interest since freshman year in college," Gael said. "I can understand from a certain point of view." Gael returned to her dabbing. "There hasn't been a new face in town for the past two years."

"There's a new guy in town." Sophie felt her cheeks heat.

Gael straightened, her hands dropping to her side. "Do *not* tell me you mean that hoodlum friend of Kiran's."

"He's a nice man, Gael," she said and then added softly, "He's had a rough life."

"Of course he's had a rough life. He's a criminal. It's bad enough that Kiran's brother is a convict. But you? You have a perfectly good family, and a trust fund. If you would just date one of the guys your father likes, your life would be set."

Sophie stiffened. She didn't often see this side of Gael but it would be wrong to think she didn't know it existed. It had simply never been an issue between them in the past.

"I'm going in to church now," Sophie said tacitly. She ascended the front steps into the plain white pioneer church, Gael following behind with her makeup still in hand. They pushed through the heavy oak double-doors into the foyer.

"Wait up," Pia called, doing a little jog up the stairs from the basement on her three-inch heels to join them. Even with the added height her shoes provided, she barely topped Sophie's eyebrows.

Immediately, Pia launched into a replay of the current conflicts in the community, the debate over whether to install a bell in the steeple, whether the Carter's would approve of Plexiglas to replace the cracking glass in the three-part Gothic arch windows along either side of the Carpenter Gothic style building. She seemed particularly interested in the heated discussion which evidently took place the night before between her grandparents and Kiran with respect to replacing the heavily varnished oaken pews with padded chairs.

Making noncommittal murmurs of interest, Sophie led the way through the swinging doors separating the foyer from the sanctuary. The interior of the church was white, painted plaster with little ornamentation or decoration apart from the quilt produced by the Missions Society which hung on the west wall. Wainscoting, stained to match the original hardwood floor, extended from the vestibule throughout the sanctuary and the front foyer. An unadorned wooden cross hung in the center on the wall at the front.

Pausing at the rear of the sanctuary, Gael said, "Let's sit down front. Then I get a good view."

"Of what? My brother?" Pia said, scrunching up her nose in distaste. She pointed to the middle row of pews to the right of the central aisle. "There's Rhona and Viv. Let's sit with them."

"No thanks," Sophie said wryly. "You two go ahead. I'll sit in the back. It makes it easier to get out for Sunday school anyway."

"Okay," Pia said brightly, not even looking back as she waved an enthusiastic greeting to Vivienne.

Sophie wondered sometimes if it made sense to keep the same friends she'd had from childhood. It was comfortable but at times it seemed they had nothing at all in common anymore. Pia still sought acceptance with the popular crowd and Gael seemed bound and determined to marry a man of influence. What Sophie couldn't understand was why she'd currently set her sights on Kiran. He was a good man, but hardly a man of influence in the traditional sense.

"I'll sit in the back with you..." Gael's words tapered off and Sophie followed her line of sight to see what had caught her interest.

Ayden was leaning against the back wall of the sanctuary watching them. He was wearing jeans again though they were definitely nicer than the ones he'd worn Friday night, and an ill-fitting, plain white button-down shirt. His hair was still damp and slicked back from his face. A pair of sunglasses was hanging from the pocket of his shirt.

Pushing off the wall, he approached them. "Hey, Sophie. Gael."

"How dare you? After what you did?" Gael hissed at him, glancing sideways, probably to make sure no one saw her talking to him.

Sophie nudged Gael with her elbow, narrowing her brows in warning. "Why don't you sit with Pia? I want to say hello to Ayden."

"Don't make this mistake, Sophie," Gael warning, flouncing away in a huff.

Why were her friends behaving this way? What had happened to the notions of Christian charity and giving the benefit of the doubt? Gael clearly wasn't giving Ayden the benefit of the doubt. Tristan certainly would never apply charity to Ayden. Would he to a rapist? Would her father decide it was less of a sin to take advantage of a poor girl from the wrong side of the city than to beat up a pillar of the right community?

"Go ahead and sit with your friends. I can catch you after the service," Ayden said, pulling her attention back out of her head and into the moment. His expression was studiously blank.

"That's okay. How are you?" she said.

"Fine. You?" Even though he looked relaxed with his hands shoved into his back pockets, rocking back on his heels, she suspected the posture was meant to conceal his nerves. "Did you, uh, have a good weekend?"

"It was okay. There's a new collection at the library so I spent Saturday organizing it and coming up with some displays."

"You work at a library?"

"I'm the children's librarian at the Public Library of Cincinnati and Hamilton County," she said.

"That's great," he replied, his gaze softening minutely.

"Um, did you want to sit down?" she asked, gesturing toward the back pew.

"Yeah. No, wait," he said and drew something from his shirt pocket, handing it to her.

"What's this?" she asked and then her eyes widened in pleased astonishment. It was a flower fashioned from a deep honey-gold wood, finely grained and exotic. It was only about a quarter of an inch thick but intricately carved. He'd even glued some fine pink sand over the petals and a pale yellow in the center. It was a Gerber daisy. "It's beautiful. Ayden, did you make this?"

He shrugged. "Yeah. I had a little extra time yesterday."

"Whoever you give this to, is going to be so thrilled," she said, holding it out to him.

He looked confused for a moment. "I made it for you, Sophie."

Pleasure suffused her. "It's the most beautiful thing that anyone's ever given me." She whispered because her throat had gone tight with emotion. Holding the four-inch piece of wood tenderly in her hands, she traced the carved lines and curves with her thumb. "Thank you," she said, looking into his eyes. No one had ever made her a gift before unless you counted the paste-and-crayon renderings she received regularly from her Sunday school students.

"You're welcome."

Reaching out, she took his hand and tugged him toward the back pew. His palm was calloused and warm. "I, uh, like to sit at the back so I can slip out after the singing for Sunday school."

He stepped aside to let her sit first. "You teach Sunday school?"

"The kindergarten class. I love the way five-year-olds see the world," she said, smiling.

"I've never spent much time with kids."

Just then the service started with a video and Sophie and Ayden turned their attention to the front.

After the service, once all the parents had finally made their way downstairs to pick up their children, Sophie packed up. She found Ayden waiting outside, leaning his shoulder against the corner of the church building, straightening as soon as he saw her.

"How was Sunday school?" he asked, plucking the bag off her shoulder and carrying it.

"Good. Tommy Tripper—he's the little fellow with the bright orange hair that sticks up in all directions—well, when I asked the kids why the lions didn't eat Daniel—we read Daniel and the lion's den today—he looked up at me with those bright green eyes of his, so serious, and says, 'stinky feet?'." Ayden chuckled as Sophie laughed over the incident again. "Kids are great," she said. "How was the sermon?"

"Good. Kiran's a good speaker. He talked about, uh, grace. Um, how grace saves us because...you know..." His voice drifted off.

"'For by grace you have been saved through faith and that not of yourselves; it is the gift of God, not of works, lest anyone should boast.' What did Kiran have to say about it?"

His cheeks pinked but he kept his expression flat. "Mostly that, no matter how hard we try to be good enough for God, we can't. Our idea of goodness is nowhere near God's goodness. But we can accept salvation as God's gift." He shrugged. "It makes me feel a bit better."

"Me, too," she said softly.

"Reck."

They both stopped and turned toward Kiran as he jogged over. "I wanted to see if you were still up for supper Thursday."

Ayden nodded. "Sounds good."

Kiran narrowed his eyes at Ayden and then softened his expression as he met Sophie's gaze. What was that about? "How are you? I heard you had a little misfortune on Friday."

Ayden groaned and muttered something that sounded like, "Thanks, buddy".

"Just an accident with some nachos," she said. Ayden's neck was flushing red and she wondered if he was embarrassed or angry, or maybe just getting sick. As a matter of fact, if she had to guess, she'd surmise that he was more uncomfortable by the blushing than the comment.

"I'm looking forward to seeing your new display at the library. Is the reception Wednesday?" Kiran asked. "Do you still want me to come and read?"

"Thursday." Sophie added in an aside to Ayden, "I often ask him to read at events because I figure he should use his speaking skills for more than just nagging at the rest of us." She grinned broadly as she said it. This was an ongoing joke between her and Kiran.

"Oh, daughter," Kiran said gravely. "The wicked shall receive their due."

"By the way, you're off the hook," Sophie said to Kiran, chortling. "They have some adult literacy specialist coming in to read."

A voice called across the churchyard and Kiran turned to look. "Mrs. Carter needs to bend my ear, I see. You two have a good day. See you later, Reck." After narrowing his gaze at Ayden, he jogged over to Imogene Carter where she stood frowning down at the flower beds alongside the church steps.

"He's been the best thing for this church and this community," Sophie said, watching her friend fondly. It was true. Somewhere along the way, Kiran had gone from being the annoying older brother of one of her best friends to being a friend himself, and a fine man of God.

"Would you…do you have to be anywhere right away…would you like to take a walk?" Ayden said with his hands shoved in his pockets again.

"I usually have Sunday dinner with my mother but she's visiting her sister in Cleveland for the week," she said. "Where did you want to walk?"

He gestured at the paths in Riverside Park across the road. "I was thinking just there."

"Okay. Let me put my bag in the car and I'll join you," she said. The beige pumps she had on weren't the best for walking but they'd be okay for a short journey.

Ayden walked with her to her Toyota Avalon and even took the keys from her hand to stow her bag in the trunk before handing them back to her. She slung her purse across her chest and fell into step beside him.

"How's your…burn?" he asked.

"It's fine. That spray you gave me is great. I don't have any discomfort at all. I had sunburn last summer that was far worse."

"Sorry," he muttered.

"You can stop apologizing now." She wanted to get him onto a better topic. He looked awkward and half miserable and totally wrong in that shirt, like he was trying to be someone else. He should be wearing bold colors and styles that complemented his ruggedness. "What did you do yesterday?"

He slipped his sunglasses on and that improved things somewhat. "I was supposed to have a shift at work but they were cleaning one of the machines so I did a little woodworking at home."

"Like the flower." She put her hand in her pocket so she could trace the whorls. "What kind of wood is it?"

"Teak. From India."

They walked in silence for a few more minutes.

"Are you okay, Ayden? You seem bothered or something."

He laughed in surprise. "I guess I'm not used to being forgiven so quickly. I'd prepared a series of grovels but you don't seem to want to hear them."

Sophie smiled. "Nope. But I would like to hear other things. Tell me about your family."

"Hey, look, ice cream. Would you like a cone?"

"Is that a distractor?" she said mischievously.

He shrugged. "Do you want one?"

"Sure. Chocolate, please. What are you going to have?" she asked, walking over to the vendor with him.

"I'm good." Ayden pulled out his wallet, glanced inside and then took out a five.

"One chocolate cone." He turned to Sophie. "Do you want one scoop or two?"

"Oh, two, absolutely. What are you going to have?"

"Two scoops," Ayden said to the vendor, a jolly man with bushy grey eyebrows that flapped like bird's wings when he nodded.

"Ayden, you have one, too, okay. I don't want to eat by myself," she said but he just ignored her, paying for the cone, getting his fifty cents in change and pocketing it. He passed the cone to her and turned to walk away.

"Where's yours?"

He kept walking.

"I can buy you one if you don't have enough."

His whole body stiffened while his hands clenched into fists at his sides. After a moment, he jerked into motion again stalking away from her at a rapid pace. She jogged to catch up with him while rescuing a melting chocolate drip with her tongue.

"Hey," she said, grabbing his arm. "I'll buy you one if you can't afford it."

He spun, knocking her hand off his arm. "I don't want a frigging ice cream cone!"

Shocked, Sophie stepped back a pace from the raw anger blazing in his eyes. Looking down at the cone, she gulped. The chocolate ice cream no longer looked appealing. Spotting Jenkins, the homeless man who called the park his bedroom, she handed him the cone. He graced her with a toothless grin and a, "Shanks".

Without even a glance at Ayden, she stormed away, back toward the church. He caught up to her before she'd taken four steps.

"Sorry," he said but it was an apology given through gritted teeth.

"Whatever," she said, waving him away.

"Why did you have to push it?" he muttered, removing his sunglasses to pinch the bridge of his nose.

Stopping, she spun on him, suddenly furious. "I don't know what your problem is but I was just being friendly."

"No you weren't. You were being pushy and condescending. If I want to buy a girl an ice cream cone and not have one myself the least she can do is refrain from impugning my manhood while I do it."

"What are you talking about? I didn't impugn anything. I simply said I'd pay for it. I know you don't have much..." She stopped because he'd gone completely still. His face flushed crimson and there was plain misery having a no-holds-barred war with fury in his eyes. "I embarrassed you."

"Ya think?" he said and then brushed his hands over his face. The movement seemed to bring some calm with it. "Look, I've got some hot button issues, okay? I'm not a good guy and I don't know why I even try. But I really do want to spend time with you." He flung his arms out. "So here I am again making things impossible between us."

"What are they?" she asked.

"What?" he said clearly confused.

"Your hot button issues."

Drawing in a deep breath, he then expelled it on a long sigh. "There are too many to list."

"I understand you've had a tough life and that you're trying to change it, but that doesn't give you the right to go off on me like that. If we are going to spend time together then you either have to control yourself or tell me what I need to know."

He met her gaze, just watching her for the longest time. "Does that mean I still have a chance with you?" he asked softly.

"I don't think we've really started anything yet," she said. "But if you want to, then you have to..." She sighed in vexation. "Look, I've got my own issues. My father's controlling and cold.

And my brother wants desperately to be his clone. My sister's vicious and vapid and my mom couldn't grow a backbone if you injected her with adamantium."

A grin pulled at his mouth. "Nice comic book reference," he said and she felt herself soften. "I am trying." She stiffened and he reacted quickly, moving closer and raising his hands in that universal *calm-down* gesture. "I will try harder."

"Will try or will control yourself or will tell me when something I've said or done bothers you or steps on your hot buttons," she said, her voice rising in passion.

A grin pulled at his mouth and then he roared with laughter. He laughed so hard that she expected tears to fall from his eyes. She watched him wide-eyed. Had he gone crazy?

"You have no idea what you just said, do you?" he asked, still laughing but in a more constrained fashion. "Never mind. It was…complimentary. Sort of."

She scowled at him. "Whatever," she said, again in that Valley-girl way. "How are we going to deal with this problem we have?"

"I'll just have to do better," he said, his smile gone.

"What if I try to take your first answer and not push?" she said. He began to respond but she stopped him with a gesture. "But you would have to promise…and I mean *promise*, to tell me what the deal is as soon as I want."

"In private." His gaze was riveted on her face.

"Fair enough. But I have one question I would like to have answered right now."

"Five dollars."

"Oh." Did he mean he had five dollars left in his wallet? "Really? How long does that have to last you?"

"Is that your question?"

"Um." She thought about that a moment. Was that the most important question she had for him right now? Because she was pretty sure he was not going to allow another. "No." She took a deep breath and then released it in a rush, checking left and right to be sure that no one could overhear. "My brother told me that you beat a high school teacher with a baseball bat."

"That's not a question."

"You told me that you beat the man who raped your sister." She paused but he didn't say anything so she continued, "What happened?"

His gaze scanned the vicinity. "That's a big question."

"It's my price to trust you enough to see where this thing between us leads."

She read trepidation in his eyes then resignation. Then blankness. "Let's go back to the church. I think Kiran leaves it opened on Sunday afternoons. We can talk there."

"Okay."

When they reached the church, Kiran was coming out of the side door with Gael walking very closely behind him. "Hey, Reck. Sophie."

Sophie watched Gael's eyes darken then spark with anger. Then she seemed to catch herself and pasted a smile on her face. "Hello, Sophie. Aren't you due at your mother's?"

Sophie narrowed her eyes, suspicious of the question. "Mom's at Aunt Cecile's for the week."

"Kir, can we borrow your office for a few minutes," Ayden said.

"Sure." Kiran dug in his jacket pocket for his keys and tossed them to Ayden.

"Are you sure that's a good idea?" Gael said as though she couldn't not say it.

"You're not planning to do anything that shouldn't be done in a minister's office?" Kiran said with a knowing expression on his face.

Ayden didn't smile as Kiran had obviously intended. "We just need to talk."

An awkward silence ensued and Kiran and Ayden did that odd silent communication thing they had going. Kiran sobered. "Sure. Lock up when you leave."

"Kiran, I'm not sure—" Gael began, continuing even when Kiran took her arm and led her away. Sophie was pretty sure she heard murmured comments as they turned the corner including words like "criminal" and "trust" though she was pretty sure it was part of a longer word like "untrustworthy".

Without a word, Ayden led the way inside. He pulled Kiran's desk chair around to sit opposite one of the padded leather armchairs kept for visitors.

Once Sophie sat in the desk chair, Ayden began pacing the small space, clenching and unclenching his fists. After a while, he flopped into one of the leather chairs, spread his knees and dropped his head into his hands. "I don't know where to start."

"You have a sister," Sophie said.

"Yeah, but that's not a good place to start." He blew out a breath. "My mother was an alcoholic, a drug addict, sometime dealer and sometime prostitute to pay for her habit. We lived in Over-the-Rhine. I don't know if you've heard of it." He glanced at her face.

She nodded. "Cincinnati is something like the third poorest city in the 'States and Over-the-Rhine is one of the most violent neighborhoods."

His mouth tipped in a feral grin. "Home." There was no humor in his eyes. "When I was about seven or so, my mother was...assaulted."

"How do you know that?" Sophie asked. Her voice was barely above a whisper, her throat tight with emotion.

"I saw them."

"Them?" she mouthed.

"Yeah. I heard her screaming. Went to check then went for help. She wasn't much of a caregiver but she was my mother. I ran down to the landlord's apartment. He was a regular with my mom so I thought he might help. I was wrong."

Sophie felt sick to her stomach that a young boy had witnessed such horrific violence. "What did he do?"

Ayden stood and faced the window, rocking back on his heels, his hands shoved in his back pockets. "He beat the, uh, snot," clearly not the word he'd first intended to use, "out of me and locked me in a closet until morning."

"Oh, Ayden. Why?"

"The…assault…was her punishment. She'd stolen money from her dealer."

"Why did that man hurt you, though? Even if he didn't want to help her?"

"He was her dealer." Ayden brushed his hands over his face. "Anyway. Nine months later, my sister was born. Cassandra Marie." His voice softened and she noticed that he was running his thumb over his knuckles, caressing the name written there. "She was a pretty baby and so good. She hardly cried." His shoulders drooped. "My mother hated Cassie, but how can you blame a baby for being born?" She saw anger flash across his eyes. "I protected her when I could. She was such a sweet little thing. But I had to go to school sometimes." He drew in a breath and released it. "One day, when Cassie was a little over a year old, I came home to find my mother boxing up the baby stuff. Cassie was nowhere in the apartment. I was scared, uh…stupid but my mom just laughed in my face. Someone had reported her to the Children's Aid Society and they'd come and taken Cassie."

Head down, he was silent for a long time and Sophie realized that tears were streaming down her cheeks. She swiped at them before Ayden noticed, instinctively knowing that he wouldn't like her sympathy.

"My grandmother fought for her. She eventually got Cassie out of foster care and then she came for me. By that time I was thirteen and already a well-accomplished thief and part-time drug dealer." His shoulders drooped in what she could have sworn was a parody of shame. "My mother refused to let me go with Gram, largely because she could steal drugs from me. So I ran away to Gram's house. What could my mother do? Call the police? Hardly. So Cassie and I lived with Gram after that."

"Was that a better time?"

Ayden turned to her and then strode over to crouch beside her. "Don't cry for me."

She sniffed, trying to hold back a full-blown sob. "Sorry."

He held her face gently between his hands, caressing her cheeks with his thumbs. "Don't cry."

"How did you survive?" she said and then she just couldn't resist offering him comfort. Leaning forward, she kissed him on the forehead and hugged him around the shoulders. He went very still, moving his hands to the arms of her chair so that he wasn't touching her anywhere except where she touched him. When she realized he was holding himself tightly in check, she pulled back, murmuring, "Sorry."

He rose from a crouch and backed up to lean against the window ledge, clearly putting some distance between them. She wasn't sure if that was an escape strategy or him maintaining self-control. "What happened next?" she said, remaining seated, letting him choose the proximity he needed.

Sighing, he resumed the story, "Things were better with Gram but Cassie was a very shy and withdrawn child. Then one day, suddenly, it seemed, overnight, Cassie became this bright and enthusiastic student. She kind of…floated through the apartment every night, spent hours working on her homework in her room. She started staying after school two or three times a week. She'd never been involved in extracurricular activities before. I was happy for her." He shook his head with an expression of wonder at his own stupidity. "I thought she was coming into herself."

Sophie guessed what was coming. "It was that teacher."

"He did this regularly, picked out a needy young girl to lavish attention on, 'tutoring' them after hours, giving them daisies. I don't know why he gave them daisies. But she trusted him, enough to go into his office alone, enough to take the pills he gave her and drink the wine." His body tightened into an aggressive pose. "When I got home from, uh, work…that evening, Cassie was huddled in a pile of blankets, pale-faced and…" he searched for the right word, "vacant on the sofa." When Ayden looked up, Sophie could see fury in his eyes. "He…assaulted her. He gave her alcohol, told her she was special, and then he took her. She was fourteen, Sophie, just a girl." He straightened away from the window ledge and, Sophie knew, if he'd looked half this fierce when he went after that teacher, the man must have been terrified.

"So, yeah, I took a baseball bat to him." Ayden snorted in disgust. "He deserved it."

"Oh, Ayden."

He tipped her chin up with his knuckle, touching her softly, gently. "Don't do that, Sophie. Don't feel sorry for me. I'm a bad man. I would be ashamed to tell you the things I've done. I deserved to go to prison, not only for smacking that guy."

"Did anyone investigate the teacher?"

"Nah. With my record, no one listened."

"But you became a Christian in prison?"

"After. When I was on parole." He smiled sadly. "I was desperate never to go back, knew I needed to change my life. I'm, uh, very grateful that God doesn't look at rap sheets."

"Me, too." She drew in a deep breath, blew it out and brushed the tears from her eyes.

He shrugged. "That's my story."

She smiled encouragingly. "Not all of it, I would guess. But what I asked for. Thank you for telling me."

"Go out with me tomorrow night." He blurted the words, belatedly realizing they sounded more like an order than an invitation.

But she didn't seem to mind. "Okay. What do you want to do?"

Ayden was brought up short. In the old days, he'd have dropped a hundred dollars on weed and wine just to warm up for a date. But today, he had five measly dollars in his pocket. What could they do with that?

Sophie was watching him, clearly calculating something from his expression, hopefully not his exact thoughts. "There's a park a couple of blocks from my place. They have rowboats and a basketball court and…well, we could hang out."

A grin grew on Ayden's face. "I'll see you about seven."

"Great!"

When she said it like that, he almost believed it.

Chapter Five: Testimony

Monday afternoon, Sophie arrived home from work to find Pia, Sam, Reggie, and Gael gathered on the front stoop of her Brownstone walk-up. "Hey, guys. What's up?" she said, jogging up the steps with her packages and workbag.

Pia, still in her pencil-thin skirt and three-inch heels, clearly fresh from a day's accounting, shifted uncomfortably, saying, "Can't your best friends show up just to see you?"

In fact, they had each obviously come straight from work; Sam in his gym shorts and purple tank top, straight from Riker's Fitness Center; Reggie in his deputy's uniform; and Gael dressed in bubble-gum pink scrubs from a shift at the Clermont County Retirement Home.

"I suppose," Sophie said hesitantly, her brows dipping in a frown. There was something guilty about Pia's expression. Sam and Gael looked censorious. And Reggie? Reggie just looked remorseful with a heavy blush on his cheeks. They were clearly not just "showing up to see" her.

"Do you mind if we come in?" Reggie asked querulously.

"Okay." Sophie unlocked the door and led them in. "Coffee anyone?"

A chorus of "sure"s followed. "What's this?" Sam asked, honing right in on the wooden flower on her bookshelf and picking it up.

"It's a Gerber daisy."

Suspiciously, he asked, "Where did you get it?"

"Ayden made it for me. He's a carpenter," she said, her fond smile slipping when all four of her friends turned to gape at her.

Sam cleared his throat. "Forget coffee. Let's sit." He dropped onto the sofa. Obeying without question, Pia sat beside

Sam while Reggie pulled over a kitchen chair. Gael sat on Sam's other side. Sophie felt a spurt of irritation at the way he took over the situation even though this was her home.

"We wanted to talk to you, Sophie. We're...concerned." Sam said the word as though searching for the right descriptor.

Sophie sat in the overstuffed easy-chair across from the sofa. "What exactly are you concerned about?"

Gael leaned forward, clasping her hands and tapping her lips thoughtfully with her steepled fingertips. "Sophie. You've always had an independent spirit." She paused meaningfully. But what exactly was her meaning? "We are your closest friends and have been since kindergarten, well, Reggie moved here in grade one." She waved vaguely in his direction. "You're one of us. We feel responsible to look after you."

"Gael, this is sounding really weird. What's going on?"

Sam leaned forward to push himself right into the conversation. "That criminal you insist on hanging with is trouble, trouble we don't want you exposed to. I mean, how dare he come into our midst and think he can mingle with the good people of our community. He is filthy, tainted with the violence of his upbringing." Sam brushed off his pant legs as though he wished he could wipe away the unclean fragments of Ayden Breckinridge.

"He is not tainted. He's accepted Christ as his savior. He's clean," Sophie said.

"Of course he's clean in God's eyes," Gael continued Sam's diatribe, "but you can't expect us to trust him." She shuddered.

"We got together after Gael told us she saw you spending time with the guy after church yesterday at Riverside Park and agreed that this was for your own good." Sam drew a circle on the coffee table. "We care about you," Sam added. Gael nodded in agreement.

"I'm afraid he'll do something to hurt you," Reggie added, his voice quiet, tense. "Have you any idea of the recidivism rates amongst ex-cons?"

"He already has hurt you," Pia muttered.

Sophie's mouth tightened involuntarily. "Is this how you feel?"

"We do," Sam said, speaking for them all.

"And if I choose to continue to see him, to see him as a man like any other, who's been saved by grace, set free from sin? What then?" Sophie asked.

Deliberately, Sam rose. "I won't stand by and watch this happen."

"Then you'd better leave," Sophie said. She met Sam's gaze directly, fiercely.

"If that's what you want. Come on, Gael. Pia. Reggie." Sam strode to the door. "When you come to your senses, call me."

Anger rose up within her and suddenly, their absence wasn't enough. "How can you behave like this? We're Christians. Sam, you went forward at the same camp meeting that I did. You said the same words, 'Jesus, come into my heart'. Why do you assume that Ayden wasn't afforded the same grace we were?"

Sam paused at the door, turning back with his hand on the knob. "One day he may earn a place among us." He said the words but he clearly didn't believe it possible.

"Salvation is not something that can be earned." Ayden's words from Sunday came back to her. "'For by grace are you saved through faith...' Nobody is good enough to earn it."

"Yeah, but some are a lot further away." Gael rose to join Sam.

"You honestly think you're closer to God than anyone else?" Vexed, Sophie gestured around the room.

"Not everyone," Sam said.

"You need to leave now because he's going to be here in a couple of hours and I don't want him to have to see you, any of you." Reggie blanched at her words. Sophie rose and, nudging Sam aside, opened the door, gesturing them out.

"Fine. Come, Gael." Sam and Gael departed hand in hand.

Pia hesitated at the door. "Why, Sophie?"

"If I decide to stop seeing Ayden then it will be because of who he is now not because of his past."

"I don't understand," Pia said, her eyes damp with unshed tears.

"You of all people should, Pia," Sophie said dismissively. "Now, you better go."

"Reggie?" Pia said.

His earth-brown Stetson in his hands, Reggie stood. "I don't think he's good for you, Sophie. I only hope you know what you're doing." He hugged her abruptly, too quickly for her to push him away. "I'll call tomorrow to make sure you're okay."

"I'll call you, too," Pia said. "I don't want to lose you as a friend."

"You don't have to, unless you force me to choose between you and Ayden Breckinridge."

Visibly distressed, Pia walked out but Reggie paused a moment. "Be careful," he said, squeezing her hand.

Alone, Sophie curled up on the sofa and wrapped her grandmother's afghan around her shoulders hoping the bright colors and happy memories would bring comfort. She regretted her return to Ancora, never more than at this moment. If her mother hadn't begged, she wouldn't be here. If Sophie hadn't clung to the vain hope that perhaps her return would enable her to know her father better, she would have taken the job she'd been offered at the Cleveland Public Library and stayed away.

However, if she hadn't returned, she wouldn't have met Ayden. She sensed something in him that reminded her of integrity and strength. And maybe even a little sweetness, though he probably wouldn't appreciate that thought. Angry as he was at times, he truly believed that God loved him. The truth of that was indisputable in Sophie's mind; of course God loved Ayden just as he loved her and everyone. The more difficult question was whether the circumstances of his birth dictated the path of his life; could someone from the mean streets of Over-the-Rhine really change?

Her birth, into a family where no one seemed to see who she really was or understand her, did not dictate her life. She had left home, gone to college, and been happy. She had returned with a purpose, to reconnect with her family. Perhaps her error had been in thinking that life had stalled while she'd been away, that old relationships had remained static. If she had moved to Cleveland, she would have had to make new friends and forge a new life. Perhaps that's what she needed to do here in Ancora.

Oh, Father, I love you and I want to do Your will.

Casting aside the scarlet, indigo and daffodil afghan, Sophie stood, determined to cast off the pall of her so-called friends' visit as easily as she displaced the wool. She showered and changed for an evening at Pike Park. Loading her backpack with a container of homemade oatmeal cookies and two bottles of water, she changed into jeans and a candy red T-shirt. If she dressed like him, maybe he'd feel more relaxed around her. At the last minute, she shoved her raincoat into her pack. They could sit on it if nothing else.

A knock sounded on the door. Sophie could hear Mr. Kimutai's voice as she approached and then opened the door.

"You got comp'ny," he said.

"Good evening, Mr. Kimutai," she said.

He huffed and then turned away, muttering something unintelligible.

Waiting until Mr. Kimutai's window was shut, Ayden greeted her with a "Hey" and an appreciative expression in his eyes as they slid down her body. And then he seemed to catch himself, locking his eyes on her face. Her heart gave a little leap, but she wasn't sure if it was in response to his open regard or his acknowledgement that ogling was not appropriate behaviour.

"Hi. How was your day?" she said, inviting him in.

He shrugged, shoving his hands in the front pockets of his jeans. "How far is it to this park? Do you want to walk? Or we can use my bike."

"Oh, yeah." She retreated to the bedroom without explanation and returned waving her brand new glow-black motorcycle helmet. It had a red fire-breathing dragon painted on the outer shell. "Let's ride over."

Clearly pleased, he grinned at her and she felt lighter, the remnants of her argument with Sam and the others retreating. Whatever happened between them, she refused to see Ayden as merely a product of his past. She wouldn't want to be judged for all the stupid things she'd done and said as a teenager.

Relieving her of her backpack, Ayden loaded it in his pannier as she locked the door on the Brownstone. He really was a gentleman at heart. She fastened her helmet and climbed on behind him like an expert. At least this time she didn't bump him on the head.

"Where to?" Ayden asked. He felt nervous, but more excited than he could remember feeling in a long time.

She gave him directions and then he fired up the ignition, shoulder-checked and pulled into the lane. The park wasn't busy. There was a group of teens playing basketball on one court and a few younger kids engaged in a game of something that looked like soccer-basketball. A few small children romped on the equipment with parents hovering nearby. No crack-heads. No knife fights. No couples making out. None of the equipment had been removed to use as weapons or shelter for the homeless. It was a far cry from any park that Ayden had frequented as a child.

"I guess the basketball courts are in use. Do you want to go out in one of the rowboats?" Sophie asked.

"Sure." *How hard can it be?*

Making their way down to the booth by the river, they found a couple of life jackets and two oars, launching the boat which looked least likely to sink. None of it was locked up, yet it hadn't been stolen. New life. New rules.

Ayden had always been a quick study. With only a few tips from Sophie, he quickly picked up the method, rowing them easily into the middle of the Little Miami River and then upstream, away from the mini-waterfall that hissed and burbled near a bend in the river. Sophie settled in the stern, using her backpack as a cushion. He was pleased to have her face-to-face.

They rowed in silence for a time, following the sweeping, verdant riverbanks with their eyes. The water was calm, a murky greenish-brown in the evening light. A pair of ducks paddled along the shore, occasionally dipping below the surface in their perpetual search for food. It was peaceful. Nice. And Sophie was there. There weren't many people that Ayden truly relaxed around.

"Ayden?"

"Hmm." He shifted his gaze from the sentinel trees lining the far riverbank to her, appreciating the hint of mystery created by the play of shadows across her face.

"What was prison like?"

Startled by the question, he tried to fob her off, not wanting her touched by his past. "Rough."

"Like a dog?" she asked, her eyes twinkling. "Ruff ruff."

He raised a brow. "Ha. Ha."

Her smile slipped. "Is it too hard to talk about?"

He frowned, considering what to tell her. Then decided. *Nothing.* "It's just…it's bad, Sophie. I don't think you really need to hear about it."

"But I'd like to. I want to know more about you."

Why? His defenses immediately rose to protect and defend his inner self. Sighing, he battled to make a path through them for Sophie's question. "I, uh…hmm…" He leaned on the oars for a moment. "In prison, you have to choose sides."

"You mean like good guys and guards versus the bad guys, the violent criminals?"

He snorted, subconsciously slipping into the street vernacular of his youth. "Inside, doll, ain't no good guys, no doubt. They's all—"

"Are you talking that way on purpose?"

"What way?" He wondered what he'd said and if he'd sworn at her. She didn't seem upset, just a little confused, so probably not. He determined to monitor his speech more closely.

"Never mind," she said, gesturing for him to continue. "So the scary people run the place, in prison."

"If you want to survive, you need to join a gang. I chose...poorly, and don't ask because I'm not going to tell you about it. It's enough to tell you that I never want to go back. And I refuse to be defined by my time there."

"Ayden." There was a clear reprimand in her voice.

What was she upset about? He'd said he didn't want to go back to prison. Wasn't that what she wanted?

"You think you can just refrain from answering the question?" she said.

Ah, she was upset about that. "Soph, I don't want you to know about it. That life is in my past. It's over. Done."

"But it still affects you."

He shrugged, beginning to row again. The ducks, disturbed by the sudden movement, took off in flight.

"Okay," she said and he thought she'd given up. "How about your testimony?"

"My what?" he asked, pausing, oars raised a moment before dipping back into the murky water.

"Your story. The story of how you met Jesus."

"Oh. Well." He pulled one of the oars into the boat, buying himself a little time to formulate a response by unwinding a stem of seaweed that had entangled with the oar.

When he didn't respond, Sophie adopted a lilt, as though she was telling a fairy tale. "You were a model citizen. You always did what you were told and never caused any trouble because everybody liked you and..."

Her naiveté amused him. "Yeh. No." Lights he hadn't noticed along the riverbank flickered on.

"Are you sure? Cause you never cause any conflict here." Her grin broke through.

"Do you want to hear this story or not?" he asked wryly, frowning at her.

"Uh huh, but I think I can probably guess it all with my vast experience in life."

He sobered quickly. "There are a lot of things that are better not experienced." *Like being on the receiving end of violence. Like the sick feeling you get after hitting a grown man so hard that he actually starts to weep like a baby. Like hunger and privation. Poverty. Like prison.*

"Yeah, but..."

"If you want the story then you have to shut up and stop interrupting."

Narrowing her eyes at him, Sophie mimed zipping her lips.

"Amusing," he replied, wryly. "Where was I?"

She lifted a brow.

"Sophie?"

She remained silent.

He was not tempted even for a moment to let her remain silent, to be without the happy lilt of her voice, even though she constantly demanded that he respond in new ways, ways that were so different from his past behaviors. She forced him to admit his mistakes, like telling her to shut up—*uh oh, that was probably a bad idea*—and reveal his inner self to her. He stifled a groan. "Sorry. Please talk to me."

"Talk? Really? Can I ask questions?" Her tone was acerbic. "Cause, you know, I might have a question or something that I'd like to ask to clarify..."

"Okay. You win. I shouldn't have told you to shut...anything. Sorry."

She looked very satisfied. "Tell me how you and Kiran met."

"Those first few months after you get out of prison are rough." He glanced at her and he just knew from the smile dancing around her lips that she wanted to bark again so he frowned at her. Remaining silent, she gestured for him to continue. "The rules on the outside are different. I suppose it's a kind of culture shock. Rou—difficult to deal with. That morning, the girl I'd been staying with told me she was leaving town. So I lost my place to live. I'd had an argument with my parole officer about the stupid job he'd gotten me. As if I had any interest in cleaning public toilets." He sighed. "Let's just say it was a bad day. So when I saw that guy smackin' his kid, I lost it. I can't stand it when people hit kids. Unfortunately, it wasn't his kid, it was his lookout. And he wasn't alone. I woke in Mercy Hospital with my jaw wired shut and a coupla broken ribs, a bruised kidney, other stuff. Ram Rao ended up bein' my nurse. He, uh, recognized my tat." Ayden lifted his sleeve to reveal the tattoo he'd gotten in the Ohio State Pen from Guido, artist extraordinaire and convicted forger. "Took an interest in me. Common heritage, that sort of thing. Got Kiran to visit me too." Ayden's chest warmed at the memory. "He came every day that I was in the hospital to read to me. Didn't preach at me, which was good. I knew at that point that I wanted a new life, wanted to leave the violence behind. But I wasn't interested in really putting much effort into changing myself. I sure wasn't interested in church things. God had never done anything to make my life any better so I just discounted him.

"Ram invited me to move into his spare room when I was released from the hospital. It was a lot nicer than where I'd been staying so..." He shrugged. "Ram was attending these Narcotics Anonymous meetings. He kept inviting me to come along but I'd never been an addict," he flicked a glance at her, "not after watching what it'd done to my mom. I was bored, though, so eventually I went with him. All during the meeting they kept talking about recovery. And lots of those guys had the same issues with..." he broke off searching for the right word, "self-control. I wanted what these guys had, some level of peace. Ram and I talked for a long time that night. Kiran showed up the next day with a Bible. He was my friend, someone who seemed to like me for who I was. So when he gave me a Bible, I read it because he asked me to." Ayden met her gaze directly. "The, uh, idea that someone loved me was pretty foreign. The notion that someone would go to the cross for my benefit, well, that blew me away." His mind drifted back to that moment when he'd given in and accepted that God really wanted him, loved him, and the warmth and peace that'd flooded him when he'd surrendered. Amazing!

He returned his attention to Sophie. "You're lucky, you know?" he said. "To be raised in the church."

"With the family I have, I never really thought of myself as lucky, but, I guess I am," she said dubiously. "My testimony isn't very exciting. When I was nine, I went forward at a camp meeting and gave my heart to Jesus. As I matured through high school, partly, but mostly in college, I realized that though I believed in Jesus as my Savior in a practical sense, I didn't really engage with him emotionally; I didn't trust my life to Him. It's one thing, a good thing, to understand that John 3:16 is true, that God gave His only Son as a sacrifice for our sins, and by faith in Him, we have eternal life, but it is quite another to trust Him with the decisions of our lives." Sophie met Ayden's gaze directly and he was mesmerized. "That's what I want, to be Jesus' own, so that one day He'll say to me, 'Well done, thou good and faithful servant'." Her face tightened with emotion.

"That's remarkable, Soph. You're lucky. Wonderful," Ayden said. "I think your testimony is amazing. You get to walk through life without a load of regrets as heavy as the links of Marley's chains."

"Thanks," she replied quietly.

Silently, thoughtfully, they returned to shore beneath the flickering lights casting the tree-lined shore into silhouette.

Spreading her jacket out on the grass beneath the branches of an Ohio Buckeye tree like a picnic blanket with sleeves, they ate cookies and watched the activity around them. Ayden found himself preoccupied with the crumbs around her mouth. He wanted to nibble them off, to press his mouth to hers and stay there, breathing her in. The more he knew about her, the more time he spent with her, the more his attraction grew.

"Eyes," she whispered.

He lifted his gaze from her mouth and, reaching out, brushed the crumbs away carefully with his thumb. She drew in a sharp breath. She felt the attraction, too. He could see it in her eyes. *Relationship* was a foreign concept in his world. Love, fidelity, intimacy, he just didn't know how it all worked.

"That boy is a lot bigger," Sophie said, nodding toward a ruckus at one of the basketball courts.

Huh? Following her line-of-sight, Ayden noticed one boy, about twelve or thirteen, clearly bullying a younger, smaller boy by bouncing a basketball off his head and chest. The younger tow-headed boy was on the verge of tears.

Rising abruptly, Sophie started toward them. Ayden reached out, stopping her. "Soph." He nodded toward the group of teens on the other court who were clearly watching the interaction with interest. No way was Ayden letting Sophie become an object of interest to them.

"We have to help him," she protested.

"Let me deal with it. Stay here," he said sternly, pointing back toward the jacket on the ground.

As he approached, Ayden reached out, scooping the basketball out of the air. "Knock it off." In response, the older boy swore quite profusely. Ayden pinned him with a glare. He didn't want Sophie to have to listen to that filth. "You think you're a tough guy?"

The boy puffed out his chest. "I know I'm tough."

"Because you can intimidate someone smaller than you?"

"You gotta get respect in this 'hood."

"Nuh uh. You act the fool. You scared." The boy bristled but Ayden kept speaking, slipping into the street vernacular of his youth. "You 'bout t' lose yer water, dawg, you so scared. You about t' do anythin' for a glance, a peek, even when you do what be wrong. You thinkin', if no one see me, I gonna disappear." He snapped his fingers.

The boy glanced over his shoulder at the teens. Their grins had faded but they were clearly interested in the conclusion to this scene. "Gotta have respect," the boy said but it seemed to be more of a question this time.

"Strength ain't beatin' shrimps. Strength be fightin' 'gainst the odds." Ayden let the boy think about that a moment. "Whose dis?"

"Um. It's my ball," the younger boy said, wiping his tears from his eyes.

Ayden handed it to him. "Go." Once the littlest boy had scampered away, Ayden turned to the older boy who glanced nervously over his shoulder toward the teens.

"They'se at it again," Ayden said. "Not seein' us. Whatsa name, dawg?"

"Sasha."

He jerked his chin toward the boy. "You want a oatmeal cookie?"

Sasha's eyes brightened. "Yeah." Then he shoved his hands in his jacket pockets and shrugged. "Whatever."

"Soph." Ayden turned. He realized that she was closer than he'd thought, close enough to hear. He fought the blush that wanted to creep up his neck, keeping his reactions under control. "You got a coupla cookies for my man, Sasha?"

She handed the container over to him. There were still five or six cookies inside. He gave them all to Sasha.

"Thanks, man," Sasha said, bumping Ayden's fist with his own and then jogging away, as though he needed to escape quickly before Ayden could change his mind and retake the cookies.

Ayden felt Sophie's hand twine around his. "That was kind of you to help," she said, looking up at him with admiration in her eyes, an admiration he didn't deserve.

"That used to be me."

"You were bullied?"

"Nah, I was the other guy." Ayden released her hand and walked away, gathering their things and then shoving them into his pannier. He felt her eyes on his back as she followed him. Shoving his helmet on his head, he straddled the bike. Sophie stood beside him, staring. She tilted her head, shrugged and then pulled on her helmet and sat behind him. He drove to her house.

Once he'd cut the ignition, she knocked on his helmet. He pulled it off.

"You're a nice man, Ayden." Leaning forward, she kissed the side of his neck, the sensation shooting through his belly to his toes.

"I used to think that a real man takes what he wants. But I have learned that a real man has no need to take. He earns. He earns respect."

Sophie wrapped her arms around his shoulders, resting her cheek on the back of his neck. Warmth filled him at her affectionate gesture. "The library is holding a reception to unveil the new children's exhibit on Thursday. I had an artist in to paint an extensive mural on the wall of the reading room and we'll be showing it off. Would you like to come? There'll be fruit punch and snacks," she added in her most persuasive tone.

"What time?" He still didn't know what to make of her reaction to what had happened at the park so he was grateful that she wasn't expecting a debriefing session.

"I'll be there setting up all day but the ceremony will take place at seven."

"You need help setting up?"

"Sure. When do you get off work?" she said, shifting off the bike to stand beside him.

"I only have a morning shift on Thursdays but I'll need to drop home and then come back into the city."

"Okay. I'll pick you up at your house at two."

"I'll pick you up," he said.

She shook her head. "Won't work. I have things to bring from home, *and* I'll be wearing a skirt."

"I'll meet you at the library then," he said.

"Why can't I—"

"Soph," he said in reprimand.

"Right. I don't push and you..." She left the sentence unfinished, gesturing for him to do his part and explain his reluctance.

"My neighborhood is not safe."

"Okay. I'll meet you at the library at two-thirty," she said, accepting his reasoning.

"Agreed."

Chapter Six: Big Brother is Watching

As Jaxen cleaned up the last of the markers and play clay, a warm satisfaction filled him. Little Tammy Watkins had finally spoken up in class today. The shy girl was gaining confidence.

Jaxen had had to do some pretty fast talking five years ago to convince Ms. Byers, the no-nonsense veteran principal of Ancora Elementary School, to hire a male teacher for the primary division, especially one who was six-foot-two and built like a Cornerback. Aside from his sheer size, he'd had to convince her that a black man raised in the Rainier Vista Projects in Seattle, a man who'd run with a gang from the age of twelve, could be trusted to nurture young children in the largely Caucasian middle-class community. Aside from Mrs. Ouchi, whose name the children thought was wonderfully hilarious, he was the only non-pale-faced staff member at the school.

Locking the classroom door, Jaxen continued out of the school, settling in his Jeep Liberty. His cell phone rang.

"You still comin' over? Or you gotta box up them crayons?" Uncle Arlo began without a greeting.

"I'm coming as planned. Angie is going to the movies with friends and Saffi has drama practice."

"Didn't ask for no biography. Get chicken." Arlo disconnected.

Jaxen shook his head, wondering wryly at the bitterness which his uncle just could not seem to release. Still, Jaxen would not forget the kindness that Arlo had shown to him as a young man, arriving on his doorstep with his pregnant girlfriend, a violent past and nothing else.

Stopping for chicken as requested, Jaxen added in a salad and a chocolate milkshake, Arlo's secret delight. Mounting the steps, he greeted Arlo's pretty, young neighbor on her way out.

Arlo's door opened before Jaxen could knock.

"Bout time," he said gruffly, snatching the bag from Jaxen and peering inside.

"I got a family Caesar salad. I thought we could share it."

"Suppose so." Arlo grumbled something about hippy-food, shuffling into the kitchen where two place settings were waiting. "Want some coffee?"

"Sure. I brought you a milkshake."

Arlo's grumpy demeanor lightened a moment. "Ye don't say." Accepting the cup, he put the straw to his lips, sucked in and then sighed, happy for a moment. "Good. Thanks."

"You're welcome. Remember the day I showed up on your doorstep with Sherise? You fed us hamburgers and chocolate milkshakes. That was the best meal I'd ever tasted."

Arlo quickly turned away to pour a cup of coffee but not before Jaxen saw the softness in his gaze. "Dora, that sister o' mine was no good. Runnin' off to Seattle with a drug addict. Don't even know if he was yer father. Leavin' you to be raised by that gang and whatever foster parents had the misfortune to get ye. Hoodlum yourself for…how long?" He met Jaxen's gaze as he sat.

"I left the gang when I was seventeen, joined when I was twelve and still puny for my age. Running drugs through enemy territory. I was good at it."

"Course ye were." Arlo looked proud for a moment before scowling. "Not much call for that skill with decent folks."

"Very true. I'd like to ask the blessing." Jaxen continued without waiting for permission, thanking God for the food and for Arlo.

"God and me ain't on speakin' terms. You don't gotta remember me."

"I remember you, Uncle Arlo. God does too. And I'm grateful to you."

Once a year, every year on his birthday, Arlo had sent Jaxen, his only living relative after Dora had died when Jaxen was ten, a card with twenty dollars and a plea to come home. Jaxen had happily accepted the money, when he could retrieve it before his mother spent it on drugs. But he'd never considered leaving the bosom of his gang family until the day everything changed.

Among a variety of other crimes, he'd shuttled drugs, running the streets and alleys across enemy territory to deliver smack, weed, E, whatever, where he was ordered. He'd had an uncanny talent for escaping notice until one culminating event that had changed his life forever. Captured by a rival gang, he'd been held in solitude in a dank basement without food or water for three days, fearing every moment for his life. Wracked by trepidation and loneliness, he'd missed even his foster mom's tearful prayers.

When his isolation had finally ended, life got worse. The lieutenant of the Hispanic gang, a violent psychopath named Jean Baptiste, smoked and watched as his men beat Jaxen within an inch of his life, giving advice from time to time. "Ribs. Use the pipe. Don't let him up."

"You got a choice, *ladrón*," Baptiste had said. Jaxen had instinctively reacted to the accusation but Baptiste had neither noticed nor cared. "You work for us or you die. Bloody and hard. We be back *mañana. Elegir sabiamente.*"

"Water." Jaxen moaned out the word.

When Baptiste spat on him, the others followed suit.

Jaxen thought he'd die from thirst. He got so desperate for water, he drank from a puddle in the corner, the oily liquid making him vomit, fire bursting through his broken ribs. He'd hit bottom. His skills on the street, his gang, his girlfriend, Sherise, nor the baby he'd put in her belly, nothing could help him now. Except maybe his foster mother's God. After all the prayers she'd prayed and the tears she'd shed for him, God just might listen.

So Jaxen made a promise. "Please, God, if you get me out of this, I'll change my life."

When he was released the next day, he never knew why or how, only that he was suddenly free. He picked up Sherise and they left, hitching their way to Cincinnati, to Uncle Arlo. Five months later, Angeline was born and a year after that, Sapphire burst onto the scene.

Jaxen got a job as a janitor for a building maintenance company while Sherise looked after the babies. At least that was the plan. Sherise, however, had other ideas. She chafed at Arlo's rules and the mundane tasks of child-rearing. She missed the parties and the drugs. They struggled to keep their family together. But more and more she disappeared for hours or days at a time, returning with red-rimmed eyes and shaking hands. More and more often, Jaxen returned from a night's work to find Arlo alone with the babies.

"You can't make her change, boy. She is what she allas was. Yer priority's gotta be these tiny babes. Ye gotta give 'em a better chance. Ye need t' go t' school, ye need a education to get by in this world."

In spite of the impact on his own life, Arlo encouraged Jaxen to attend college and make a better life for his children than he'd had. Arlo paid for daycare and let them stay in his home, helping out as much as he was able, becoming the grumpiest, reluctant caregiver ever. Even once Jaxen was accepted onto the police force, Arlo kept them close because Sherise was spending half their budget on drugs.

One day Sherise simply didn't come back. She'd overdosed, inducing a fatal heart attack.

"She's gone, boy. Stop yer grievin' and move on."

Through it all, God had walked beside Jaxen, urging him step by step to keep his word.

∞

D. C. Shaftoe

Ayden arrived home from work to find Sheriff Tristan Paetan leaning against the front corner of the ramshackle house where he rented a basement room. The two-storey Saltbox with its flat front and steeply slanted rear roofline was situated on Huylick, an L junction just off Clough-Pike, past Foundry Road. There were only four houses on the gravel road, Oskar's piece-of-crap rental unit, a bungalow which Ayden was pretty sure belonged to the grow-op hidden in the forest across the road, an abandoned hunting shack, and, at the end, a faded orange A-frame which he was convinced contained a meth lab given the frequent noxious odors emanating from it. This was the first he'd seen law enforcement in the vicinity and, of course, it had to be this man.

"Ayden Breckinridge also known as The Wrecker," Tristan said, swaggering toward him with his thumbs hooked in his gun belt. "Fancies himself a marauding dragon."

Tempted to stay on his motorcycle and simply ride away, Ayden instead planted his feet on the ground, straddling his bike and removing his helmet. In his experience, cop equalled trouble. Brother of girlfriend definitely compounded that. But he forced himself to ignore his bleating instincts which told him to run or fight.

"Two arrests, assault, possession with intent to distribute, for which you spent eleven months total in juvenile detention."

Ayden carefully blanked his expression. How had the sheriff obtained that information? Ayden's juvenile record was sealed.

"Then the grand screw-up, aggravated assault for which you received a sentence of five years in the big house. Then a development I don't quite understand." Tristan slid his right hand back along his belt to the hilt of his gun, tapping it twice with his middle finger, before hooking his thumb in his front pocket. "Why a man with this history wound up in my town."

"Was that a question?" Ayden asked as though they were discussing something as mundane as the weather, not his criminal history.

Tristan scowled. "You're trouble. You don't belong with the decent folk of my county. You definitely don't want to be messing with my sister."

A flutter of movement in his periphery drew Ayden's attention. Scooter, the recluse who lived on the first floor of the house with his mother, was peeking out between the dusty blinds on the bay window. Upstairs, Rizzo and Willard, twins who occupied the attic, glared down unabashedly. *Great.* One of them was bound to rat him out to the landlord who already started every conversation he spoke to Ayden with, "I don't hold with nobody breakin' the law on my property. You cause any trouble, you're out." As if he had trouble to cause. All he wanted was peace and quiet while he tried to figure out how to live like other people did, people like Sophie and her friends, regular, upstanding citizens.

Wanting to get out of sight, Ayden dismounted, rolling his bike toward the back yard. As little as he wanted a cop in his home, he less wanted a confrontation in the front yard with Rizzo and Willard looking on. Not that it would make much difference. They'd hear everything anyway. The walls were paper thin.

Tristan grabbed his arm. "Don't you walk away from me!"

Ayden forced himself to stop, taking a moment to maintain his calm. "I'm going to put my bike away so we can talk inside."

"We'll talk right here."

Conceding in spite of his desire to deck the man, Ayden leaned his bike against the side of the house. "What's this about?" The sheriff's presence here was definitely going to cause him grief already so he decided to get on with it and bring the meeting to its conclusion.

"It's about crime. And punishment."

"Look, I haven't broken any law." He shoved his fists into his pockets when they instinctively clenched.

Tristan eyed him critically. "A leopard can't change its spots. Lately there's been an increase in drug-related crimes in the county, biker gangs moving into the area."

"That has nothing to do with me. I was never in a biker gang."

"You were a member of the Grex, don't deny it." Tristan leaned into Ayden's space and it took all of his self-control to keep from removing him physically.

"I was not. I collected for them. Different thing," Ayden replied, working hard to control the tremor in his voice caused by suppressed fury. "I haven't been back in five years. And, though I do drive a motorcycle, I am not in a biker gang. I don't peddle drugs. In fact, I haven't broken the law since moving to Ancora."

Tristan must have gauged something from Ayden's demeanor because he settled back on his heels. The change in proximity allowed Ayden to harness his aggression, to keep it from building toward violence.

Tristan's expression morphed through a range of expressions until his pale brown eyes brightened a moment. "With your contacts in Over-the-Rhine you would be uniquely placed to be a conduit for drugs into my county."

The very idea of setting foot in Over-the-Rhine made his palms sweat and his hands shake. He simply wasn't sure he could go there and not slip into his old ways. God had given him a great gift and he wasn't going to squander it.

Tristan pointed directly at Ayden's chest. "I want you away from my sister and I want the names of the people bringing in the drugs. We may be able to help each other."

Ayden snorted. "Yeah, like a cop has ever helped me." Cassie was dead because of the cops, refusing to investigate the teacher, Kevin Torrent, and taking away her protection by removing Ayden to prison. The cops had hounded her for weeks leading up to his trial, arresting her for prostitution, possession, anything they could think of. The taste of bitterness was sour in his mouth. "I'm not interested. I don't want any part of drugs or any other trouble."

"Maybe if you help me out a little, you could prove yourself worthy of—"

"I'm. Not. Interested." *Lord, help me keep my temper.* He blew out a breath, feeling a calming coolness permeate his chest. "Look, I've got a new life now. My past is behind me. The last thing I want is to go back."

"If it turns out that it's the Grex moving drugs here, you'll be implicated." Tristan pointed at Ayden's chest. "I'll see to that. You'll be out of my county and back in prison faster than you can utter a prayer."

I am not going back to prison. "I can't help you. I'm sorry."

Tristan's dark eyes glittered malevolently. "If you're not now, you will be."

Ayden followed Tristan around to his brown-and-white county car just to ensure he departed. The landlord, Hamish Oskar, was just getting out of his battered tan sedan. Ayden groaned. *Just great.*

Chapter Seven: Moving Violations

Ayden noticed the flashing lights in his mirror before he heard the blip of the siren. Shoulder-checking, he glimpsed a brown sheriff's county car trailing him. *Just great!* He was already late meeting up with Sophie at the library because of Gael Somerset. Tempted to accelerate, he instead pulled to the side of the road, hoping the car would pass by.

It stopped.

"Remove your helmet, sir. Keep your hands where I can see them."

Ayden complied, wondering, *what now* as he tracked the approach of the uniformed woman. She was tall, dressed in brown, reminding him of a tree. Not a willow. *No way.* More like a gnarled oak, strong and sturdy. As she came abreast of him, he noticed her name, Reynolds.

"Licence and registration."

"What's the problem, Officer Reynolds?" Ayden asked as he withdrew his wallet from the back pocket of his neatly pressed jeans, producing his licence and the registration for his bike. As much as he resented paying insurance on a motorcycle, he wasn't going to give anyone an excuse to give him trouble. So he followed the rules, licence, registration and insurance.

"You were travelling in excess of the speed limit. This is a county road, not the speedway."

"Speeding? I couldn't have been going more than fifty."

"The limit here is forty, sir." She walked back to her cruiser, carrying his identification.

He stretched, intending to put the bike on its kickstand and stand up.

"Remain on your motorcycle, sir."

Ayden slumped back down.

After what felt like ages, Reynolds returned, handing back his ID, taking out her ticket book and writing. She ended with a flourish and tore the sheet off. "You'll need to pay this at the county clerk's office. You have fifteen days."

"I can't believe you're giving me a ticket for ten miles an hour over."

"We've been told to keep an eye on you, Mr. Breckinridge."

What? "By who?" he asked but he already knew. "No, let me guess, Sheriff Tristan."

"Whom, sir." She actually corrected his grammar. "Drive safely. And keep to the speed limit."

Reynolds returned to her cruiser and made a U-turn, heading back toward town.

Great. That's just what he needed, more money out of his pocket. And now he was really late meeting up with Sophie. Between her family and friends, he couldn't get ahead.

⊂⊃∞⊂⊃

Sophie checked the front parking lot and then the west lot again but there was still no sign of a red Suzuki motorcycle. Ayden had arrived at two o'clock that afternoon. He'd helped Sophie get things ready for the reception and then he'd left at four-thirty saying that he was having supper with Kiran and would return by six. She wasn't sure how he expected to eat in the allotted time but, hey, she would be glad to see him again. She'd laughed more this afternoon working with him than any other time she could remember.

She checked her watch once more. It was now five minutes to eight. The ceremony was over and most of the guests were merely milling, sipping wine and making conversation. Sophie made a last circuit of the main reception room and then returned to the window.

"Hey."

She spun, astonished to see Ayden. "You're late. I was getting worried."

"Worried? Or annoyed?" he said, studying her through his peripheral vision as he rocked back on his heels. He looked…taut was the only word she could think of to describe him.

"Maybe both," she admitted. "What happened?" A tray of hors d'oeuvres clattered nearby. Sophie glanced over to see one of the wait-staff crouching down as he scooped skewered cheese balls into his hands.

"I'll tell you later," he said, tilting his head to see her better.

She chewed her lip a moment, considering, and then agreed. "Okay."

Squeezing her fingers, he muttered, his relief evident, "Thank you."

She was warmed by his gratitude. "Have you had supper?"

"No." He patted his stomach. "Anything good left?"

She smiled at him. "The good stuff's in the small reception room. Come on."

Mrs. Preston, Mr. Violet, and Mr. Porter, members of the Library's Board of Directors walked by on their way toward the audio-visual corner. Sophie gave them a smile and a wave.

Ayden snagged her sleeve. "You changed. You look nice, really nice."

"Really nice" from Ayden was the same as "lovely" from others. She blushed lightly, pleased by the praise. Knowing she would see him tonight, she'd bought a new dress for the occasion, an alizarin-crimson pleated tea-length dress with sheer sleeves and a flared skirt. "Thanks. I like your shirt." He was wearing a royal blue short-sleeved button-down with a pattern of fine orange lines. The collar had those little buttons to hold down the tabs. It was faded but clean and pressed.

His eyes dropped to her mouth and he stuffed his hands in his front pockets. He had a habit of doing that around her but she noticed it never happened when he was talking to Kiran.

"Eyes," she said softly.

Tilting his head, his blue eyes rose. His stomach rumbled.

She laughed softly, starting toward the foyer on her way to the small reception room. "Let's get some food."

"Sophie Anne."

Sophie stilled at her father's unexpected voice. What was he doing here? He had never taken an interest in her career before except to bemoan her wasted talent. After all, Cincinnati's children weren't worth the expense of a college education, were they? "Dad."

Stuart Paetan wore his trademark black pinstriped suit. And a frown. He'd always preferred his children to call him *father* or *sir*.

Stepping aside, Stuart gestured toward an arrow-straight man beside him and Sophie looked up, way up, past the man's expensive suit and silk tie to the tiny triangle of dark hair on his chin. Then she craned her neck to see into his hatchet nose. She quickly dropped her gaze back to his tie, pale blue silk with yellow rosebuds. *Gack.*

"This is Regis Maxwell, a chemist by profession, who, by grit and innovation, has worked his way up so that he is now Vice-president of Research and Development for Paetan Pharmaceuticals," Stuart said. *Ah, yes*, Sophie thought. *The business that Granddaddy built from his sweat and inspiration that you sold off for profit so that you could play mayor to the little town of Ancora.*

Regis immediately extended his hand, his fingers ruler-straight. Taking his hand, Sophie wondered whether her father would produce the man's *curriculum vitae* next.

"Hello, Mr. Maxwell." His hand was dry and cold, his fingers thin and soft. *Icky.* But when she tried to withdraw, he held on.

"Call me Regis," the man said without a smile.

She tugged again, beginning to feel uncomfortable. "You're in charge of research? What are you working on these days?"

"We have an interesting project on the go, reducing the side effects of methylphenidates and other medications used to treat hyperactivity in children," Regis replied.

Her palm was beginning to sweat in Regis' grip. "That's like Ritalin, isn't it? I heard that high school and college students are using those types of medications to improve their focus and concentration."

Regis sniffed loudly. "What people choose to do with the pharmaceuticals we supply is entirely their responsibility."

Ayden extended his arm across their clasped hands, presenting his own.

"Pleased to meet you," Ayden said.

Regis was compelled to release Sophie's hand to shake Ayden's, either that or create a fuss. Stuart would not like that. He hated anything remotely smacking of disorder. Relieved, Sophie was finally able to withdraw her own hand.

"You are?" Stuart asked. His brows were furrowed in consternation, as though he felt he should know Ayden but couldn't place him.

"Reck," Ayden replied. "You must be Sophie's father."

Stuart's eyebrows twitched in a parody of surprise. "Stuart Paetan, mayor of Ancora. You work at the library?"

"No," Ayden said.

Stuart waited for more but to no avail. He turned back to Sophie. "Regis."

"Yes, sir." Regis seemed to take the cue, whatever it was, bobbing his head three or four times before droning on in his nasal voice. "I've been working closely with accounts and it seems that a charitable offering would go a long way toward meeting our tax obligations this year. Your father suggested you could give me a tour of the library to see about a possible donation."

That was interesting. *A donation?* Public libraries could always use donations. "I'd be happy to give you a tour. Perhaps if you call the library tomorrow, we could arrange something."

"Why not now," Stuart said. Though it didn't sound like a question, Regis repeated it as such. "Why not now?" he asked, brushing his hand along her arm.

Ayden stiffened beside her. Glancing aside, she tried to judge his mood. Was he jealous? Was this another one of his "hot button issues"? She did not want to deal with that right now. She had enough on her mind with the reception and now her father's appearance.

"I'll come, too," Ayden muttered. It wasn't a question.

"Perhaps, Rex, you should join me," her father said. So he really had no idea who Ayden was. He'd accepted him as a colleague named Rex. That was probably for the best.

Uncertain what would happen next, she sighed in relief when Ayden moved away with her father.

Regis reached for her elbow but she stepped aside, half turning away to suggest he precede her toward the reference section on the second floor. He politely obeyed but she thought she detected frustration on his grim mouth.

Sophie conducted an abbreviated tour, expounding on all the ways that a donation could be used to support literacy in Cincinnati, ending in the DVD section in the rear corner of the first floor. Regis seemed attentive but...

"So what kind of donation do you think the company would make?" she asked.

"That would be handled by another department," he replied, staring at her mouth. What was it with guys and her mouth? Was it weirdly shaped? Did she have a piece of rice stuck to her lip? She ran her tongue around to check.

Cupping her forearm, Regis leaned down as if to kiss her. Shocked, Sophie pulled away, subconsciously guarding her mouth with the back of her hand. Before Regis could react, Ayden was there, yanking him back from her.

"Hands off!" Ayden was fearsome with a barely controlled rage. His left hand was clenched in Regis' expensive silk shirt, making the buttons pull and fabric crease. His right hand was fisted at his side.

"Ayden—" she began, glancing around to see if anyone was watching. Fortunately, the DVD section was just around a corner in an L-shaped alcove.

"Don't," he said. One shot of a word. He didn't even turn to look at her as he said it. His attention was all on the man he held in his power. Because as much as Regis was a good five inches taller than Ayden, he was no match for Ayden's solid power and fighting experience. Instinctively, Regis seemed to know that. He began to babble. Ayden shook him once. "Shut up." Ayden's voice was low, menacing. "Get out."

Regis nodded like a bobble-head.

Energy seemed to gather in Ayden's body and Sophie was sure he was going to throw a punch but instead he thrust Regis away from him and stood his ground.

Staggering back a few paces, Regis seemed as surprised as Sophie at his sudden freedom. He brushed his palms up and down his body as though checking to see that all parts remained intact and then pointed, taking a half-step toward Ayden and opening his mouth. Ayden merely shifted his weight toward Regis who fell back a step, turned abruptly and practically jogged away and out of the library, not even turning as Stuart hailed him on the way past.

Ayden's body was still rigid and she could see that his hands were trembling. But anyone who thought that was a sign of weakness was deluded. He was barely managing to control his fury. She paled to wonder, if this was the new and improved Ayden, what had he been like before?

Tentatively, she reached for him.

"Don't."

She pulled her hand back, murmuring, "Sorry." But remorse was not what she felt, more like uncertainty with a healthy dose of irritation. She was glad he hadn't punched Regis but she didn't appreciate being spoken to in that manner.

She watched Ayden as he stared at the print of Van Gogh's *Starry Night* on the wall over her shoulder, brushing his fingers through his hair once. Twice. The red dragon on his forearm rippled as he clenched and unclenched his fist. When he shoved his hands in his back pockets, his dress shirt rode up, revealing the bird tattoo on his biceps.

"Thank you," she said, narrowing her eyes at him, entirely uncertain what he was thinking. "For not fighting."

He dropped his gaze to meet hers, his blue eyes hard, glacial. "He was touching you."

That gave her pause. "So?" she asked slowly.

"You like that guy?"

"No." Actually, he disgusted her with his simpering deference to her father and his arrogant assumption that she was interested in him.

"Cause if you're with me, I don't want you kissing other guys."

"What?" she said indignantly. A few heads turned her way. She grabbed his arm and towed him further around the corner, away from the other guests. She no longer suffered uncertainty. She was sure that she was angry. "There is so much wrong with what you just said."

He opened his mouth but she didn't let him speak even a syllable.

"Firstly," she poked him in the chest.

He grabbed her finger, continuing to hold her hand not ungently. "Don't poke me."

She yanked her hand free. "You are not the boss of me. You do not get to order me around or control my actions."

He opened his mouth. This time she presented her palm and he snapped his mouth shut.

"Second. How dare you think that I would kiss another guy when I'm here with you?" She stomped her foot. "And C—"

"Three." Was that a grin on his face? Was he amused? She slapped him on the chest. A muscle ticked in his jaw.

"C! The same rules apply to you, you know. We're together. So you can't be kissing other women, or going out with them or sleeping with them."

That got a reaction from him. "I'm not!"

"Good." She crossed her arms over her chest and turned part-way to glare out the window overlooking City Hall next door. "I didn't kiss Regis. And if he tried to kiss me, that is *not* my fault." She glanced at Ayden's face and then away. "It's not like you've kissed me either."

He shifted his weight to meet her gaze. "Do you want me to kiss you?"

She shrugged one shoulder. "Not if you don't want to."

"I want," he said. She glanced over and then couldn't look away. His eyes were dark, intense, only a narrow rim of pale blue showing. He moved slowly, aligning their bodies then brushing the hair back from her face, his fingertips lingering on her skin. Cupping her face gently, he leaned in close. "This argument over?" he murmured, his breath tickling her lips.

"Yeah," she said huskily.

His kiss wasn't like she expected. There was no roughness or demand, merely a sweet press of his lips to hers, a gentle pressure that started a tingling in her mouth which spread to her toes and back up to warm her belly.

Standing amongst the shelves of action-adventure movies, the platinum lights from City Hall highlighting the auburn in his hair, Ayden rocked back on his heels and then settled on his feet. "You're not afraid of me. Are you?"

Astonished, she said, "No. Am I supposed to be?"

The relief she saw in his eyes was humbling. What she thought mattered a great deal to him. She was important to him. "Why didn't you let me touch you before?"

He lowered his hands beside his thighs, spreading his fingers wide, palms forward. "I just needed a minute. Sometimes I react before I can think it through. I didn't want you to get hurt."

Moving slowly, she slid her palms up his chest to rest on his shoulders, pausing to smooth a nonexistent wrinkle in his shirt. Hooking his arm around her waist, he drew her closer. She felt his kiss on her shoulder and then the side of her head. She hugged him, wrapping her arms around his neck, inhaling the scent that was uniquely Ayden, cedar and after-shave. He kissed her again, moulding his mouth to hers.

Sighing, Sophie extracted herself from Ayden's hold. "I need to speak to my father." Taking a bracing breath, she strode across the first floor, past the large-print fiction and nonfiction sections, toward her father who was currently talking on his cell phone. "How could you?" she hissed at him when she got close enough not to draw too much attention.

He continued his phone conversation for a moment more and then disconnected. "You are single. He has a promising future. Conduct yourself accordingly."

Sophie's mouth dropped open. A gasp escaped.

Dismissing her, Stuart looked beyond her. "Ah, Rex. Good to see you again. I'd appreciate it if you would see where Regis has gotten to," Stuart said. "I want to hear his impressions of my daughter."

Was he kidding? *Not a chance.* Because who was she kidding? Her father *had* no sense of humor.

"It's Reck, sir, not Rex. Breckinridge." Sophie watched the slow dawn of recognition in Stuart's expression. "Yeah. That guy. You, sir, should be ashamed of yourself. Your daughter is not a commodity. She is a beautiful, intelligent, courageous woman." Ayden drew himself up and for the first time ever, Sophie's father hesitated, looking uncertain for a fraction of a second.

"I was wrong to leave you with your mother. I see that now," Stuart said and then strode confidently away.

A wash of emotion churned in Sophie's chest. Shock. Hurt. Gratitude. Wonder…had Ayden just stood up for her, sent her father packing with his tail between his legs? She very much thought he had. Tiptoeing up, she kissed him, heedless of the few remaining library patrons milling about. Banding his arm around her waist, Ayden pulled her close, prolonging the kiss. She sighed blissfully.

When he eased back, she continued to stare at his mouth, mesmerized by the pleasure it imparted. She knew she should check in with his eyes to see what he was thinking but she couldn't seem to shift her attention from his mouth.

Chuckling lightly, Ayden tipped her chin up. "Eyes," he said.

Flicking her eyes up to his, she grinned broadly. "Oh."

They cleared up so that by ten, they were able to lock up and follow stragglers out.

Rather than get into her car, Sophie leaned on the roof, looking across at Ayden where he waited beside his motorcycle. Standing there in the dimly lit parking lot, the music from *Lonny's* and *Kip's Bar* vibrating through the night, she could still feel the glow of his kisses and she didn't want the evening to end quite yet. "Would you like a cup of coffee?"

"Like, coffee coffee?" Ayden said, looking at her strangely.

"What?" She frowned. "I'm asking if you would like to follow me to my house, come upstairs, drink a cup of coffee, and then go home. Well, I think I might have milk instead of coffee."

"Is that all?"

"Well, I think I have cream and sugar," she said, squinching her eyebrows quizzically.

"All right," he said slowly.

"I'll see you there." She figured if he was too confused to get there, she'd have her milk on her own. But he followed and knocked on her door two minutes after she arrived.

"Have a seat," she said, gesturing at her kitchen table.

He slid his palm across the top. "Not a bad finish. Pine?"

"What's fine?" she said, turning on her coffee maker and retrieving a prepackaged single-cup coffee packet from the tin on the counter.

"Your table. Is it pine?"

"Um, I don't know." She glanced over her shoulder at him. "Does it look like pine?"

He dug his thumbnail along the ridge of the table. "You've got a lot of buildup here. How often do you sand it down?"

Tossing some ice in a glass, she poured milk over it for herself then returned to making coffee for him. "Never, Ayden. It's just a table, a place where I eat."

"Don't belittle the importance of having a place to sit and eat."

She stopped before setting the cream and sugar on the table, computing what he'd just revealed. "What kind of table would you prefer to have?"

"Teak."

"Like the flower you made for me?" She glanced toward her bookshelf where the little flower sat displayed on a bookstand.

"Yeah." Moving over, he looked pleased to find it there, touching it gently with his fingertip. "I'm making a dining table. It's something I always wanted as a kid."

Of all the things a child could want, what did it reveal when the desire of his heart was a place to sit and eat? "Can I see it sometime?"

"Sure. After I find a safer place to live."

Okay. She could accept that. For now. "So, what happened today, what made you late?"

"Your friend happened."

"Why? Which one?"

"Gael. She was at Kiran's when I arrived. Claimed she'd left her purse in Kiran's office on Sunday and, since I had borrowed the keys, did I know what happened to it."

"What? She accused you of stealing her purse? Sunday to Thursday, don't tell me she didn't miss her purse for four days. She lives with that thing attached to her shoulder. And you? I was with you the entire time. Was she accusing me of stealing, too? How dare she?"

Ayden cupped her shoulders. "Shh. Calm down." He chuckled lightly. "I wish you'd been there today. You'd have taken care of her."

Sophie looked him in the eyes. "Did she really accuse you of stealing from her?"

He shrugged one shoulder. "She did, either directly or indirectly. As if I'd make a copy of the key and sell it to local hoodlums. What would they expect to steal from a minister's office? Theology books?"

"What did Kiran do?"

"Convinced her not to call your brother. Insisted we search the church for the purse. Found it, sitting on the toilet tank in the ladies' washroom."

Sophie stormed across the room and grabbed her telephone.

"What are you doing?" Ayden asked.

"I'm going to give her a piece of my mind."

Ayden reached across her and pressed the disconnect button on the phone. "Just let it be."

"No way. She has been nothing but rude to you. I don't like that, but accusing you of stealing, that crosses the line."

"I've already caused enough trouble between you and your friends. I don't want to be the cause of any more. Let it go. It's dealt with."

"I was with you the entire time."

"I know. Let it go."

"I know you would never do that."

Ayden took the receiver from her hand and gently replaced it. "I know."

Sophie's heart ached for this man. The world had dealt him some savage blows but in the end he'd let Jesus take over his life, and it was the church people giving him the hardest time. That wasn't right.

Stepping into his body, she wrapped her arms around his waist, resting her cheek against the soft cotton of his shirt. "I like your new shirt," she murmured against him.

"Thanks," he murmured back.

She moved in closer until they were pressed together from shoulder to knee and kissed his chest through the soft cotton. "You smell nice."

Stiffening, he placed his hands on her shoulders. "Soph, I need you to let go." His voice was gruff and tense.

Astonished, she released him and stepped back. He looked angry. Had she done something wrong? Was he still angry about Regis, or her father's interference? Hurt and rejected, she turned away.

He stopped her, taking her arm to halt her egress. "Sophie, I just…I need to know what you mean."

"I don't understand."

Ayden walked away a pace and then turned back. "I don't know how to do this, Sophie. I know how to be friends and I know how to—"

He used a word that Sophie didn't often hear. Shocked, she stiffened. "I don't like that choice of vocabulary. If you think it's okay to talk to me that way—"

"I don't," he said, holding out his hands in a placating gesture. "What I mean is that I don't understand relationships."

"I don't know what to say to that."

"When you…touch me like that, what do you want?"

She blushed deeply, the heat radiating out from her cheeks. But she didn't even know why. "A hug? A kiss? I don't know," she said miserably.

"This idea of saving the, uh, physical parts of a relationship until later is…confusing to me. I've never had any sort of relationship that moves toward something. I'm thinking that for you, this idea of, uh, waiting for, uh, yeah. It took me a while to realize that was the expectation. I'm not programmed to wait. It's been a real struggle for me and now to have you so close and not be able, uh…yeah." He laughed but there was no humor in it.

And finally she understood. This was about sex. And dating. And eventually marriage. "Don't forget that God created marriage and all that goes with it. He made us passionate and loving. He made the parts and how they fit."

Surprised, he chuckled. "I guess."

"Um," she began, not really sure if she wanted to ask the question but realizing that she definitely needed…and wanted to know. "That means you've, uh, done it before."

"Done it?" he said ironically, his mouth quirking. "Yeah. I've done it. In fact, the first thing I did when I got paroled was spend a week in bed with a woman."

"Oh." She was disappointed by that information. "But that's before you became a Christian."

"Soph, I got to be honest with you. That wasn't the last time. Even after I got saved, I slept with women. Old habits are hard to break and it takes time to learn new patterns."

"You know you can't anymore, right?"

"Yeah."

"While we're dating, we're not going to do that. And you can't with anyone else. In fact, if we get married one day, I'll be all you get for the rest of your life."

"I know."

"Are you…okay with that?"

"Yeah." He smiled crookedly.

"Oh. Okay."

"Soph, do we have to keep using euphemisms?"

Surprised, she laughed, one explosive "ha". "No. Sex. See I can say it. I, uh, haven't."

"I'm sorry that I have. I wish I could be…clean for you." She saw regret clearly printed in his eyes.

"It is what it is, I guess."

"As much as I regret it, I can't undo what I've done. You need to think about that."

She nodded. He was right. She couldn't just say it was okay until she was sure that it was.

"So what do we do about this?" she asked softly, gesturing between them.

He shrugged one shoulder. "I don't know."

"Um. What do you want to do?" She blushed, a brisk warming of her cheeks. "I mean, besides that."

Rather than laughing at her awkwardness, he raised his head and met her gaze. "Hold you. And protect you. Talk to you and hold your hand." He paused and then chuckled wryly. "And kiss you some more. I think about kissing you a lot." He reached out and gently brushed his knuckle beneath her eyes and across the bridge of her nose. "Especially these freckles here."

"That's all right," she said, feeling the warmth of her blush everywhere. She liked the idea that he thought about kissing her. It made her feel attractive. She also liked that he was attracted to so much more than just her looks. Appealing features changed, morphed, faded, but true beauty lasted forever and beyond it all. "There are lots of things we can do between friendship and, uh, the other thing." There she was, back to euphemisms.

Stepping over, he took her hand. "I want something real with you, Sophie, but I have no idea how to get there from here."

"Boundaries, I guess." Her blush deepened. "Tonight…the kisses…were nice. Very nice. Holding hands, hugs, kisses." She shrugged, embarrassed. "I don't know. But the real McCoy waits for marriage."

"Is that a Star Trek reference?" he asked, a smile pulling at his mouth before he sobered again. "There are a lot of barriers to cross between here and marriage."

She nodded. "I guess if we go slowly enough, we'll find out if we can surmount them."

Lowering his head, he touched his mouth to hers in a gentle kiss. Pulling back, he flicked a gaze to her eyes and then back to her mouth, stepping closer. His arms encircled her. This kiss was longer.

"That was nice," Sophie said dreamily, her hands resting lightly on his upper arms.

"It's, uh, getting late. I should head out, let you be," he said, backing toward the door, never breaking eye contact.

"Okay. Good night."

He opened the door and then came back, giving her a lingering kiss on the cheek directly on the freckles he'd touched earlier. "See you."

"Maybe Sunday at church?" she said.

"Count on it."

"Early night," Mr. Kimutai said through his open window. She couldn't tell if he sounded pleased or disappointed. "Good," he said gruffly, making his opinion plain.

Ayden chuckled. "Yes, sir. Good night."

Chapter Eight: Ecstasy

Today was a good day. Ayden tucked his hands behind his head and let the cool air in the room caress his bare chest. Light filtered in through the yellow pillowcase that he'd tacked over the one narrow window in his basement apartment giving the room, in spite of the light-sucking effect of the dark panelling, an unexpectedly golden glow. The usual sensation of subterranean dark was superseded by a sensation of warmth and promise. Okay, that was definitely sickeningly chimerical…if that was even a word. Ayden sighed. And then smiled. In a few minutes he'd get out of bed, shower and dress for church, where he would see Sophie. Any day when he saw Sophie was a good day, wildly fanciful or not.

It had been six months and one day since they'd met on the lawns of the Hope Wesleyan Church. They spent two or three evenings a week together and at least part of most Saturdays. And it was fine. Good. Amazing. His recovery was ongoing but she seemed to accept that. He was learning to guard his reactions, both ire and passion. She was learning not to push him. And she only poked him when she was really, really angry.

Today he would see, perhaps they'd drive to Dayton and walk in the park, or go into Cincinnati to see the baby gorilla at the zoo. Anything would work. Anything would be fun, as long as they were together.

His cell phone rang and he rolled out of bed to fetch it from the pocket of his jeans where they lay crumpled on the floor.

"Hey, Soph," he said, grinning foolishly at the notion that she'd made the effort to call him when she would be seeing him soon.

"Hi." Her voice croaked through the phone.

Immediately alert, he asked, "What's wrong?"

She spoke in a rush, a rapid hyponasal croak. "I'm sick. I need to ask you a favor. I feel lousy and I just can't face crawling out of bed to teach Sunday school today. I've called everyone but no one will help so I got in contact with the parents and Sandy Tripper—you know, Tommy's dad—said he'd take the class for me if I could get the materials to him. But I don't like to leave a man alone with all those little kids. It just leaves the door open for trouble and that's no way to repay someone who's doing me a favor. So would you please help him with the class?" She sneezed three times, sniffed loudly and then added, "Please?"

"You're asking me to teach Sunday school?" he asked, flabbergasted.

"I know it's last minute and you constantly tell me you don't know much about kids, but I really need your help."

"Sophie. That's not fair. You know I'd do just about anything for you, but those people do not want me with their children." Was she crazy? The problems this could cause were beyond imagining. At least *he* didn't want to think about them.

"Please, Ayden. You wouldn't be alone. And Sandy's fine with it. I guess Tommy talks about you all the time; like how you ride this really cool motorbike, and always get down low to talk to the kids." Her voice was almost gone. "You could stop by and pick up my bag of stuff. If you just read the story and let them color the pictures and then play a game…Sandy will lead it. It's just to provide a safety net for him." She coughed again.

This was nuts. Crazy. People would be up in arms. This could rain storms down upon him. "Okay. I'll be by in twenty minutes or so."

"Thank you," she whispered. "Bye."

"Bye."

Ayden's stomach clenched and went right on clenching until he felt sick. This could go so wrong, unaccountably wrong. He dropped to his knees beside his bed. *Lord, help me. I want to do this for Sophie but I don't want to deal with the consequences. People do not want me around their children. In fact, the people of that church don't want me at all. If not for Kiran and Sophie, I'd be all alone. I've been alone so long, Lord. Help me.*

Twenty-five minutes later, Sophie answered his knock and tugged him into her home. On her table was a stack of coloring pages. David and Goliath. She flipped open a Bible story book and then bookmarked the page that he or Sandy Tripper would read to the kids. On a piece of printer paper, she'd jotted down the rules to a simple game. She showed him the bean bags he'd need to play it.

Once she'd loaded it all in her "bag of stuff", she thanked him, the word coming out on a sneeze.

"Couldn't I just leave the bag for Sandy and then come back here and make you soup?" he asked, desperate to escape his doom.

"Why can't you do this for me?" she said, anger giving her voice strength.

"Don't use guilt on me, Sophie. It's not fair," he said, letting his own anger show. Snatching the bag from the table, he strode to the door, pausing a moment with his hand on the knob. "No one in that church wants me there. You think they want me looking after their children?" He was feeling almost desperately angry now. "And guess what? If Sandy Tripper screws up, no one can send him back to prison." He slammed out her door, jogged down the steps and roared away. He didn't bother to look back to see Mr. Kimutai shaking his fist out his window at the noisy intrusion.

It was still early when Ayden reached the church, a few people filtering inside. On his way up the front steps, he stopped to help Mrs. Gordon make it up the last few. Once inside, he turned toward the basement but was halted by her surprisingly tight grip on his arm.

"Thank you, son. I believe you are one of the sweetest men here." She patted his cheek with her arthritic hand. Stunned, he watched her shuffle into the sanctuary.

"Mr. Reckless." Ayden felt a tug on his pant leg and looked down into the eyes of a little flame-topped boy. He crouched down to listen. "You're helping my dad teach me t'day. I think your motorbike is so fast. My mom hates it when I'm loud but if I had a bike like yours I'd go so loud every day." Tommy grinned up at Ayden.

"Thanks," Ayden murmured in response, but it seemed to be all Tommy needed for he dashed into the sanctuary and then back outside again.

As he rose, Ayden felt a hand slap his shoulder. He tensed and turned, ready for a fight, only to be greeted by an older version of Tommy's grin, topped with cropped, blonde hair rather than red.

"Rick, right? Or was it Ayden? Sophie Paetan tells me that you're helping me out today," Sandy Tripper said.

"Yeah. Uh, Reck, actually. I've never done this before. I'm not sure I'll be of much help."

"You and me both," Sandy replied, still grinning. "My wife went into labor with Talia, my daughter, on Tommy's fourth birthday and I got left entertaining six hyperactive four-year-olds for two hours." He shook his head in wonder. "Never thought I'd do that again."

Ayden relaxed a bit. So he wasn't the only one feeling out of his element. "Are you sure you want…my…help?"

"I sure don't want to do it alone," Sandy said guilelessly. "Did Sophie send the stuff?"

"Uh, yeah." Ayden held out the bag.

Taking it, Sandy searched inside. He looked disappointed. "I was hoping she'd include candy."

Ayden laughed in surprise. "For bribery?"

"Just to keep their mouths occupied," Sandy said. "Five-year-olds have big opinions."

They started down the stairs to the basement. "Hey." Ayden had an idea. "What about cookies?"

Sandy paused on the stairs and turned to him. "Cookies are good."

"I happen to know that Mrs. Gordon delivered oatmeal raisin cookies to Kiran's door yesterday afternoon. You go ahead and set up and I'll get some."

"Excellent." Sandy slapped him companionably on the shoulder.

Ayden ascended the stairs two at a time and then jogged over to the parsonage. He knocked and then went inside, not at all concerned about entering without permission. Kiran would most likely be at the church preparing for the service.

Leaving a note explaining the soon-to-be-absent treats, he dumped the cookies into a paper bag he'd found on the counter, which, given the greasy stains, he suspected had once contained the renowned cheddar biscuits from Todd and Philippa's grandmother. No wonder Kiran was growing a paunch on this steady diet of grandmother baking. Ayden bit into one of the cookies as he made his way back to the church. He'd been so nervous this morning he hadn't eaten breakfast. The cookie was good, just a little crunchy. Perfect.

"Cookies?" Sandy said by way of greeting.

Ayden opened the bag and let Sandy take one. He finished it in two bites.

"You the man, dude."

"Good ole Kiran, always giving to the poor."

Sandy laughed. "Yeah. Poor us."

Ayden helped Sandy set up and then just tried to stay out of the way once the kids came down. Tommy introduced his father to the other kids and then turned to Ayden.

"That's Mr. Reckless," he said.

Sandy tried to correct his son but Ayden told him it was all right and handed out the cookies. The kids cheered.

"Miss Paetan always makes us wait till the end for treats," a little girl named Su Jin Li said.

Ayden wondered how Sophie was feeling right now.

"Nicky," Sandy said. "Sit down."

Ayden noticed the little dark-haired boy in the grey argyle sweater-vest for the first time. His face was flushed, his pupils were dilated and the hair around his face was damp with sweat. He reached out to touch the mint green wall of the classroom and then stared in confusion at his fingers.

"Nicky," Sandy said, reaching out to take the boy by the elbow. Nicky flinched away, looking around wildly. Then he stood on a chair, waving his hands around.

"Does he usually act like this?" Ayden asked Sandy.

"Nope. I don't understand it. He's usually well-behaved, the calm to my wild guy."

Grasping Nicky's upper arms firmly, Ayden lifted him to the floor and crouched in front of him. "Nicky? Do you have an older brother or sister?"

Nicky's head bobbed a few times. "Yes." Grinning wildly, he said the name with glee. "Tony!"

"Thanks for telling me that," Ayden said, keeping his voice friendly and cheerful so as not to scare the little guy. "You're doing great, Nicky. Did you go into your brother's room and find some candy?"

Pausing a moment while handing out the beanbags for the game, Sandy shot him an inquisitive look.

Nicky nodded. "Yes."

"What color was it?"

"Yellow." Nicky snapped the word out rapidly.

Dread filled Ayden's chest. "Did it have a picture on it?"

Nicky nodded, grinning again. "A happy face."

Ayden rose, tucking Nicky under his arm. "Sandy, do you have a cell phone?"

"Yeah. Yes." Sandy's brows furrowed, revealing his confusion.

"Call 911. Tell them a little boy has taken his brother's Ecstasy. Tell them we've induced vomiting."

"Where are you going?" Sandy asked him but Ayden was relieved that he also extracted his cell phone from his pocket.

"To make him throw up."

Once Nicky had emptied his stomach, he clung to Ayden and cried, snot and tears creating a damp spot on his shirt. Sandy met them outside the kindergarten classroom.

"Take the kids to another class," Ayden commanded. "Get Nicky's parents and meet me outside. Are the paramedic's on their way?"

"Got it. Yes. ETA five minutes," Sandy said.

Ayden could hear Sandy speaking to the woman in the next classroom as he ran up the stairs. Within two beats, Sandy followed Ayden out with Nicky's family behind him.

"What have you done?" Nicky's mother grabbed her son from Ayden's arms.

The boy's tears intensified. "Mom~my," he cried.

"Reck may have saved your son's life," Sandy said.

A siren sounded in the distance, rapidly growing closer.

Nicky's father, a swarthy, dark-haired man, grabbed Ayden by the arm. "What happened?" He looked and sounded terrified and furious.

"Nicky got into his brother's Ecstasy," Ayden said, working to remain calm in the face of the man's aggressive stance. Some habits die hard. This man was afraid for his son. He wasn't a threat to Ayden.

"My son doesn't do drugs."

"Frank," Sandy said, taking his arm and inserting his shoulder between Ayden and Frank. "I heard him admit it. Nicky found a pill in Tony's room that he thought was candy."

"Oh. No. Please." Frank turned to the teenage boy behind him. "Tony?"

Tears welled in Tony's eyes. "I'm sorry, Dad. It was Cami's. She asked me to keep it overnight. I didn't take it. I don't do drugs, Dad. I'm sorry. I didn't know Nicky would find it."

"Tony." Anguish filled Frank's eyes.

"Dad." Tony's word contained a plea. Frank wrapped an arm around his shoulders. "I'm sorry, Mr. Reck," Tony said, his father's shoulder muffling his voice. "I'm sorry, Dad."

"It's okay, son. It's okay," Frank said, setting his son back from him and placing a hand on his shoulder. As the paramedics pulled up, Frank extended his hand to Ayden. "Reck."

Ayden nodded. "Let me know what happens."

Nodding first, Frank and Tony rushed over to join Nicky and his mom.

"What have you done?" Gael said, appearing at Ayden's elbow, fisting his shirt.

"Gael," Sandy said, taking her arm. "He probably saved the boy's life."

"What happened?" Kiran said, striding up. The entire congregation spilled out of the church behind him just as the paramedics loaded Nicky and his mom into the ambulance.

"Little Nicky D'Angelo found Ecstasy in his brother's room and mistook it for candy. Reck figured it out and emptied the little guy's stomach, made me call the paramedics," Sandy said.

Suddenly, men and women were hugging Ayden and shaking his hand and slapping him on the back.

"Let's wait until we hear from the hospital," Ayden said cautiously.

"You saved him?" Gael said. Her voice was a bare whisper.

"I hope so," Ayden replied.

Kiran rounded up the congregation and sent them inside to pray for Nicky and Tony and their family. Some close friends and cousins set off for the hospital to support the D'Angelos.

"Are you okay?" Kiran asked Ayden quietly.

"Not sure yet."

"Why don't you head over to my house? I'll meet you there soon," Kiran said.

"No. Thanks."

"I don't think you should be alone, at least not until we hear from the hospital," Kiran said, concern in his eyes.

Ayden looked up and met his gaze, saying, "I want Sophie."

"Good," Kiran said, surprising him. "I'll call you there once I hear."

"Thanks," Ayden said.

"Anytime, Reck."

Ayden drove his Suzuki to Sophie's place, taking the steps up to her front door two at a time. The door opened before he placed knuckle to wood.

"Come in," she croaked at him. Her face was flushed, her eyes bloodshot and her nose raw and red. She looked wonderful.

She hugged him, squeezing him tight around the waist. Ayden rested his cheek against her hair. He knew this now. Sophie had taught him well. Hugs were about affection not sex. He was learning to give her what she needed from him. He was learning to read the signs, the way her body brushed up against his when she wanted to be held, the way her fingers brushed over his in invitation. He was learning how the good guys balanced their own physical desire with their lady's emotional needs. But this was the first time that she had given to him at a time when he needed it, and he drank it up, letting her affection, her friendship, her compassion, fill the lonely places in his heart and drive away the fear of all that would be lost if Nicky D'Angelo died.

"Kiran called and told me what happened," she said, turning her head to rest her cheek against his chest so that he could hear her speak. "I'm so sorry, Ayden."

"What?" He pulled back from her, holding her away from him so he could read her expression. "Did he hear from the hospital?"

"No." She scanned his face, her expression confused. "I just meant putting you through that. But I'm glad you were there because he probably would have died if you hadn't been." Grabbing a hold of his belt loops, she hauled him back toward her.

But what if Nicky was not okay? What if the boy still died or stroked-out? Ayden well knew how quickly people could turn on you. When you came from the poverty of inner-city Cincinnati, small town people treated you with suspicion, disdain. His needs, his desire to do good, to be something new in Christ, was inconsequential to these people. *Oh, Lord, I just want to be Yours.*

"Ayden, honey?" Sophie said, trying to pull back to see his face. He shifted closer, turning his head so that she couldn't see the fear in his eyes. "Honey, I need you to let me go."

"Just a little longer," he murmured.

"Why are you afraid?"

How does she know that? He'd spent his lifetime hiding his fear from the world around him. In his world, fear accomplished nothing but inviting violence. "What makes you think I'm afraid?"

"You won't let me see your eyes. You only do that when you're scared of what I'll see. I figure this event has upset you and, rather than feeling good that you were there to help, that the people of the congregation banded in support of you, you've assumed that they're getting ready to turn on you," she said. "Am I close?"

Close? When had he let her inside his mind? This close was dangerous. This close might see into his inner self and discover things he did not want her to know.

Ayden released her. "Let's give Kiran a call. Maybe he's heard something."

"Okay."

The call went straight to voicemail so Ayden left a message to call him at Sophie's right away.

"If he's at the hospital, his phone is probably turned off," she said, sitting down on the sofa and pulling a brightly colored afghan around her shoulders. She patted the cushion beside her. "Come and tell me what happened."

"Kiran told you. Do you want some tea or soup or something?" he said, moving into the kitchen. When she didn't respond, he turned toward her. "Sophie?"

"If I let you make tea, will you come and sit with me? I promise not to look you in the eyes," she said.

"Do you *want* tea?"

"Not really. Not right now," she said. "But I do want you."

He paused. He could do this. She needed him, for whatever reason, and all he had to do was hold her close and wait for news. He'd deal with what came next. The Lord would stand by him even if the little town of Ancora wouldn't.

His mind was resolved. He sat down next to her, wrapping an arm around her shoulders as he kicked off his boots. Leaning into him, she hugged him around the chest. He kissed the top of her head.

"You did nothing wrong, Ayden. If I had been there I would have assumed Nicky was misbehaving. Five-year-old boys can be silly. It never would have occurred to me that he'd taken a drug. The D'Angelos are good people and Tony is a good kid. I had heard that he was running with a fast crowd recently but I never would have suspected him of bringing drugs into their home," she said. "You did everything right. No one can blame you."

He snorted at that.

She was silent for a moment. "You're right. People blame others lots of times for things that aren't their fault. But I don't blame you. And Kiran is so proud of you. He said Sandy couldn't stop berating himself for not seeing the signs. He's so grateful that you were there because he knows if it had been him alone, Nicky could be dead."

"Gael—" he said but she cut him off, sitting straighter.

"I don't care what Gael or Pia or Tristan or any of the others say. You are a good man, Ayden, and I'm sick and tired of listening to you berate yourself. Why do you care what the others think?"

She really was gorgeous when she was angry. The burden weighting Ayden's chest lightened a fraction. "I have to care to a certain extent," he said. If he lost his chance here in this little town, where would he go?

"'Trust the Lord with all your heart and lean not on your own understanding. In all your ways acknowledge Him and He will direct your paths'," she quoted. "He'll take care of us."

Gripping her shoulder, he pulled her back against him and, though she resisted for an instant, she quickly acquiesced, wrapping her arms around him again. "It's easier to do that when the consequences aren't so severe," he murmured against her hair.

"I think it's the opposite. It wasn't until I stepped out from under my father's influence, trusting in the Lord to protect and provide for me, that I finally understood what it meant to trust in the Lord," she said. "He won't let us down."

Lord, help me to trust You through this no matter what happens to Nicky or how the church people react. "I'll do my best."

"No one can do more than that," she said.

Her telephone rang and Ayden jumped to answer it. "Yeah?" he said by way of greeting.

It was Kiran. "Ayden, Nicky's okay. They want to do some more neurological tests but they think he's going to be fine. The doctor told Frank and Alana that you saved their son by reacting so quickly and emptying his stomach. They've told Nicky that Mr. Reckless is a hero."

"No, I'm not," Ayden said. "Thanks for calling."

"You did good, Reck," Kiran said. "Come over later and we'll talk."

"Thanks, Kir."

"Well?" Sophie said as he hung up the phone.

"He's okay," Ayden said. Suddenly his knees felt weak. Collapsing into a kitchen chair, he dropped his head into his hands, leaning forward to rest his elbows on his knees. Ayden couldn't hear Sophie moving closer over the roaring in his head but he felt her fingers sink into his hair. The sensation was incredible. And comforting. As the noise in his head quieted with the soothing sensation of her fingers in his hair, down his neck and across his shoulders, he reached out to her. Banding his arms around her waist, he pulled her close and buried his face against her.

She stood there, sick as she was, until he was finally strong enough to release her. Leaning down, she kissed him on the forehead. He shifted her body, guiding her down to sit on his lap so he could kiss her, losing himself in the comfort of her mouth. "You taste like cough syrup."

She looked dazed as her eyes fluttered open. "Cherry," she whispered.

Her gaze followed as he licked his lips. "Mmm, cherry."

She touched his mouth, tracing his lower lip with her index finger. "You'll get sick."

"Maybe." He wasn't sure who moved first but her mouth was on his, open, tasting, exploring. The sensation shot through him, hot and cold all at once. "Worth it," he murmured when she pulled back.

"Wow," was all she said.

He needed to go. He wanted more, to lose himself in her body, but he wouldn't do that to her. She'd already given him enough. She'd stood by his side through a crisis. She'd given him affection, trust, confidence. He kissed her on the cheek just over his favorite cluster of freckles. "You probably need a nap and I should go and talk to Kiran."

She nodded, her eyes still a little unfocussed.

"Can I come back later?" he asked.

She nodded again and he grinned. He'd kissed the words right out of her. "Get some sleep, Sophie."

Mr. Kimutai stopped him on the landing. "This girl deserves respect."

"Yes, sir, she does."

"Not usual for her to miss church."

"She's sick."

"Ye'd best take care of her then."

"I intend to." Jogging down her steps, he felt lighter than he'd felt in months, almost as amazing as the day he'd given his heart to Jesus. Not quite, but a potent reminder that God intended good things for his life.

Chapter Nine: Hero to Zero

Ayden hung his coveralls in his locker and then sat on the bench to remove his work boots. Three weeks later and remembering little Nicky's triumphant return to Sunday school still brought a grin to his face and lightness to his chest. "My daddy says you're a hero, Mr. Reckless."

"Reck." Ayden looked up, tracking Barney Tomlinson's approach, clipboard in hand. "Mr. Hagerty wants to see you."

Ayden's grin disappeared. "Sure." What was this about? Hagerty rarely interacted with his staff during work hours though Ayden was highly suspicious of his activities after-hours.

"Now."

"Right." Ayden retied his boot. He had a little time. He was supposed to pick Sophie up in an hour and drive her home because her Avalon was at the mechanic's getting an oil-change and tune-up. Given the position of the bus stop where she had stubbornly insisted on waiting, and the temperature outside, he didn't want to be late.

Exiting the locker room, he crossed the factory floor and took the stairs to the second floor offices. Knocking on Hagerty's door, he entered when commanded to.

"Reckless. The Wrecker." Hagerty rolled the words on his tongue. About fifty or so, he had the thick white hair and body shape of Santa Claus, but in contrast to the jolly man himself, the smile that curved Hagerty's mouth did not twinkle in his pale yellow eyes. He was dressed in his usual attire of a snow white golf shirt, black zippered sweater, and black adidas jogging pants. Reclined behind the desk with his arms resting on his ample belly and his eyes at half-mast, he gestured toward a grey metal folding chair across the desk from him. "Sit." It wasn't an invitation.

Ayden sat in the folding chair, the deferential position making him feel five years old again.

"You've been here...what? Eight months now?"

"Yes, sir," Ayden said.

Hagerty grinned, though the expression held more malice than humor. "Sir. Hah. Respect. I like that." He belched. "I know that some men find the work here to be..." He paused to rub his hand over his five o'clock shadow which seemed to have extended its term significantly, and then dug between his teeth with his thumbnail. "Simple. Repetitive. Unskilled." Hagerty pulled his thumb back to examine what he'd retrieved. "But, in fact, I recruit men with a certain set of skills, if you know what I mean." Hagerty winked at Ayden.

"I'm not sure, sir," Ayden said, but he feared that he did, given Hagerty's use of Ayden's nickname from his enforcer days. Very quickly upon starting at the furniture factory, he had recognized a commonality amongst the employees. There were a disproportionate number of ex-cons, particularly men and women who, like Ayden, were under the heightened vigilance of recent release.

Hagerty picked up a letter opener from his desk and pointed it at Ayden. "You have a certain set of skills, appreciated by some but not by others."

"Okay."

"You're a hard worker. You're on time and you never call in sick. You had that one occasion with your landlord but I understand that. What's a man to do?" Hagerty scratched beneath his chin with the letter opener, making a scritch-scritch sound. "I have a new...opportunity," he paused, lending weight to the word, "for you, if you know what I mean."

Had Hagerty supplied an escape hatch? Was an opportunity a choice? "I'm all right with the job I have, Mr. Hagerty. I'm not looking to move up."

Shifting forwards, even the pretense of humor disappeared from Hagerty's expression. "I'm looking for someone to head my security department, Reck. Wrecker. Reckless and irresponsible." He pressed the red button on his intercom, one long buzz. "I'll be in touch."

The door behind Ayden swung open and crashed against the wall. Ayden tensed, but he didn't make the mistake of looking afraid.

"Strike. Bull. Take Reck here and introduce him to Hammer and Toss. I'm considering him for a supervisory position."

When Hagerty rose, Ayden rose, and then turned to face the two men flanking the open door. Ayden had seen the men around the factory, usually at the end of the afternoon shift, never in the mornings. They were identical goons, six-two, two hundred sixty pounds, dressed in matching navy blue security guard uniforms which did little to hide the prison tattoos adorning every visible surface of their skin. Unfortunately, Ayden could read the code within the symbols. These men were experienced, violent criminals.

Strike, so named because he'd reputedly killed a man with a ten-pin bowling ball, wore his long black hair tied back in a ponytail. His intensity never faltered. The bald-headed Bull narrowed his eyes at Ayden as he cracked his knuckles.

Yeah, he really didn't want to be their boss.

CRBO

Sophie scanned the street for a red motorcycle. Last out by a good fifteen minutes, she'd locked up the library and now stood in the far corner of the parking lot beneath a burnt-out streetlight. In fact, only the flickering argon lights of the *Pick 'N' Go* across the street brightened the deserted bus stop. Oh, why had she insisted that Ayden pick her up here? She would have been far safer taking a taxi to a more secure location and meeting him there. Just as he'd suggested. She really wasn't very good at listening to reason.

A trio of men approached from the direction of *Lonny's Snooker 'n' Pool Hall*. In certain situations, the presence of three men wouldn't have bothered her at all. Say, if she was sitting in church and they walked in wearing pinstriped suits. Or if she was at the zoo with Ayden watching the baby gorilla explore its paddock when three men pushing strollers entered the enclosure. In this situation, however, being ten o'clock at night, and standing alone at a poorly lit bus stop in a neighborhood of restaurants, bars and pool halls, with only the keys in her bag as a weapon to defend against the decidedly scary looking guys moving nearer, she was afraid. Hugging her chest, she tried to become as small as possible, hoping to go unnoticed.

Talking loudly, words and phrases full of profanity, the three men lumbered closer. One wore a black trench coat with the sleeves cut off, likely to reveal the colorful art on his arms. His thick, blonde hair fell back in waves from his face. However, the eighties fashion *faux pas* did nothing to lighten the intensity of his gaze which had zeroed in on Sophie. She shifted closer to the bus enclosure, hoping to hide in the slightly denser gloom there. She didn't want to go inside, not at the risk of being trapped.

The blonde man's two companions were shorter and stockier and wore leather pants and jean jackets. Black bandanas covered their heads. They hung back as Blondie swaggered closer.

Sophie's chest squeezed tighter at each step he took. No longer simply afraid, Sophie had progressed to truly frightened. Trying a new tactic—since looking smaller hadn't helped—she braced her shoulders, trying to appear confident. Oh, how she wished she had Ayden's dragon. Right here. Right now.

"Haven't seen you around here this time o' night," Blondie said, tossing his empty bottle over his shoulder.

Flinching as the glass clattered on the pavement, she replied, "Hmm," using Ayden's noncommittal response while subtly edging away. Her heart rate sped until she could feel it throbbing in her chest.

Blondie jerked his chin toward her while he stepped closer, close enough that she could smell him. Her stomach rolled. *Ugh!* He smelled like beer and weasel feet. "Pretty hair. Bet it feels like silk." As though he'd said something clever the other men, Stout and Stocky, called encouragement, or rather, a profane, disgusting version of encouragement.

"Back off." Ayden was suddenly there, fisting Blondie's coat and slamming him against the bus shelter. The tight squeeze of fear loosened from Sophie's chest. For a moment. Her relief left her vulnerable. When Blondie wound up to punch, his elbow connected with her cheek. The force of the impact snapped her head around and propelled her against the clear plastic wall. *Oof! Ow!* Sliding down the smooth glass, her backside hit the ground while her cheek throbbed in time to her rapidly beating heart. Vainly she tried to haul in a breath to shout a warning as the other two men rushed into the fray swearing a profane death to Ayden.

The fight progressed right there in front of her, grunts, moans and the revolting sounds of fists on flesh. Cowering on the ground, she covered her head with her arms, not certain whether she was protecting herself or vainly attempting to block out the horrible sounds of fury and suffering. Bile rose to burn her throat. She had to do something, to make it stop. Hands vibrating in time to her fear, she scrabbled through her purse, searching until she produced her cell phone, brandishing it high. Swallowing hard, she sucked in a breath to shout, "I'm calling the police," hoping to make the men hesitate. It didn't work.

Twisting, Ayden snatched the phone from her hand and shoved it into his back pocket. "No cops." Huddled pathetically on the asphalt, she studied her empty hand as though it should mean something. But she couldn't process the thought, couldn't begin to imagine why her hand was empty. Standing slowly, she thought she should ask him what he meant. She opened her mouth but no sound escaped, nothing but air sawed through her lips. Air, but no oxygen. Her lungs pumped to rectify the situation, her shoulders heaving in effort.

Ayden's arm came around, shoving her backwards. A piece of pipe whooshed past her ear. She cried out, recoiling. A scream was building. She could feel it. Pressure pushing, pulling, ripping at her insides, making her shudder as it rose up within her. Clutching at Ayden's sleeve, she tried to halt it, stop it, force it to retreat. He shook her off, turning to deflect the pipe which was aimed at his head.

Blood. Everywhere. Thuds. Cracks. Vomit. Sophie gagged. *Move. Get away. I have to get away from here!* "Stop it. Stop it! Stop it!" Sophie screamed.

Ayden glanced at her then delivered a driving punch to Blondie's head. He dropped like a stone. Horror. Panic. Revulsion coursed through her in waves.

Stout advanced. Where was the stocky guy? Ayden snatched up the pipe and swung. Stout howled as it connected. Ayden drew back his arm. But Sophie was finished. Done. Beyond control. "Stop! Ayden, no!" she shrieked.

When the pipe clattered to the pavement, Sophie realized that the other men were gone. She was alone with Ayden.

Breathing heavily, Ayden scanned the environment for any new threats. Once he was certain that they were safe, he lowered the piece of pipe and approached Sophie where she stood huddled against the bus shelter. "You okay?" The pain hadn't hit yet but it soon would. He needed to get Sophie to safety before that happened in case Blondie and his friends returned with more. "Soph?"

Eyes wide and face white with fear, Sophie hugged her elbows tightly. However, the posture couldn't hide the trembling in her frame. She looked like she was going into shock. He needed to get her inside and warm.

"Hey, it's okay." He tried to sound soothing though it was difficult with adrenaline rushing through his system. She'd obviously been frightened by those guys. He reached out to pull her into his embrace not sure if she needed comfort more or warmth, trying to provide both. She jerked out of his grip, backing away. He grunted at the pull the move put on his battered ribs. "Soph. They're gone. You're safe." What was wrong with her?

She shook her head vehemently. Her voice was high-pitched, almost hysterical. "No. Don't touch me, you brute. You lied."

Lied? Brute? What was she talking about?

"You said you were done with that life but you haven't changed. You haven't changed, you're still a thug. You're a…a…a…wild animal. Don't touch me!"

Ayden's chest caved in as he realized that the fear in her eyes was all because of him. Blanking his expression, he forced his culpability aside to deal with later. Right now, he needed to get her home.

Standing well back, he reached an open hand toward her. "Come on. I'll take you home."

"No. I'm not going with you."

If she had been holding a knife, she couldn't have cut him more deeply. He stilled his heart so his emotions were frozen. "You're in shock. I need to get you home. I'll leave you alone after that."

She shook her head. "No. Call me a taxi."

He thought about that. They were twenty minutes from Ancora. A cab would cost a fortune. "I'll call Kiran. Okay, Sophie? Kiran can take you home. Go into the bus shelter where it's out of the wind. Do you want my jacket?"

"No." Moving jerkily, she turned her back on him, entering the bus shelter and sitting on the bench, staring into nothing.

Kiran came, loading Sophie in the front passenger seat of his little Ford Focus, the car he called his Evangilator. "Ram's meeting us at my grandparents'," he told Ayden as he rounded the hood of the car. "Meet us there."

Ayden nodded. The journey passed in a fog as the pain from his injuries screamed to be heard. Soon after Kiran led Sophie inside, Ram arrived in his silver Mazda Miata, removing a red and white first aid kit from his trunk. "Hey, Reck. What's up?"

Ayden simply shook his head, following Ram to the front door where they were met by Ram and Kiran's grandfather.

"Dada." Ram launched into Hindi so Ayden couldn't follow the conversation. However, he could see that Mr. Rao, senior was not pleased to have his eldest grandson, the prodigal, at his door.

Kiran appeared at his side. "Dada, I need Ram to help me. He has become a nurse, a man who helps others. I seek only permission to bring him into the house so that he can assist me."

Mr. Rao finally nodded and stepped aside.

"We'll use the den," Kiran said, leading Ram and Ayden into a darkly-panelled space furnished with bookshelves, a desk and two easy chairs. "My grandmother is giving Sophie some tea now and a sympathetic shoulder. I called Pia and asked her to come so she can drive Sophie home when she's ready."

Ayden slumped against the door. *Just great.* Pia hated him as much as Gael and the others. Ayden's head throbbed and his entire body started screaming in indignation.

"You look rough, buddy," Kiran said, scanning his body. "Maybe we'd better get you to the hospital. We can call the police on the way, though I think it would be better to report this to the Cincinnati PD rather than Tristan."

"No police. No hospital." Ram and Ayden said it at the same time.

"Kir, this man does not need that. I can patch him up." Ram spread his supplies out on the desk. "Get your shirt off."

Drawing a deep breath, Ayden braced himself as he pulled his T-shirt up, stopping with a grunt when the movement caused him too much pain. "You'll have to cut it off," he said breathily.

Retrieving a pair of scissors from his First Aid kit, Ram cut up the middle of his shirt and then carefully peeled the fabric back to reveal his purpled ribs. Ram whistled under his breath. "That's gotta hurt." He removed the last of the tattered fabric, handing it to Kiran. "There're more bruises on your back. You're going to be a swollen, purple mess by morning."

Kiran accepted the soiled fabric, holding it between thumb and forefinger and then dropping it into the trash. "You sure you don't want to go to the hospital?"

"No. Can't afford even an aspirin," Ayden muttered. Kiran didn't offer to pay, something for which Ayden was grateful.

Ram palpated his side, checking for deeper damage. "Ribs?"

"Just bruised."

Ram eased him into the desk chair and then started to clean the wounds on his face with gauze and hydrogen peroxide. He pulled the rent flesh above Ayden's eyebrow together to apply butterfly bandages.

"All right, man," Ram said, standing back to survey his handiwork. "What happened?"

Ayden described the fight and then Sophie's reaction to it.

"I can understand why she's upset," Kiran said.

"I was defending her. What's wrong with that?" Ayden asked. He was feeling truly bewildered.

"Did you know she bumped her head when you threw her against the bus shelter?" Kiran said.

"What?" Ayden started to rise, to go and see if she was okay, but Ram shoved him back into the chair. "I didn't throw her, Kir. I needed to get her out of the way, to a safer position. She was just standing there," he said, exasperated.

"He didn't mean to hurt her, Kir," Ram said.

"Still. To see that violence up close. She's not from that world."

Ayden hung his head. "No. She's not."

"She said you grabbed her phone, wouldn't let her call for help," Kiran said.

Ayden checked his pockets, retrieving her phone from his back pocket where he barely remembered shoving it. "I didn't want the cops there." He handed the phone to Kiran. "You better give it back to her."

"Of course he didn't want her to call the cops, Kir. He's got a record," Ram said as though he couldn't believe how naïve his brother was being.

"You frightened her, Reck. She was shaking and sobbing all the way here, barely holding on," Kiran said.

Ayden heard the door slam and a female voice calling a greeting.

"Pia." Ram said the word, tracking her progress into the house as though he had X-Ray vision. Ayden knew that the Rao's had cut Ram off when he went to prison. How long had it been since he'd seen his little sister? Ram jerked his attention back to Ayden and Kiran. "What he did is not unforgiveable."

"Nah," Ayden said. "Kiran's right. I blew it. She'll never get past this. You didn't see her, Ram."

"You made a mistake, Reck. I'm not denying that. You lost control. Overreacted. But she's wrong to say you lied to her. You're not the man you were a year ago, much less five years ago."

"Not much improvement though. Anyhow, if she can't handle this, how is she going to handle the other crap I've done?"

"Give her time, Reck."

"She's better off without me." Ram cuffed him on the back of the head. "Ow. Injured man here. You're not much of a nurse you know."

"I am an excellent nurse. She's lucky to have you."

Kiran furrowed his brow. "I'm not so sure about that. I'm your friend, Reck. I know you didn't mean to upset her, but you have. It was only a little drunken flirting. He didn't even touch her." He adjusted his glasses, sighing deeply. "I'm going to check on her. I'll catch up with you guys tomorrow."

"Talk to her, Kir," Ram said. It wasn't a request.

"What am I supposed to say?" he asked, incredulous.

"What he did was a mistake, not unforgiveable."

"Leave her alone," Ayden said overwhelmed by a gnawing ache deep in his gut. His eyes burned. He hadn't felt this desolate since Cassie overdosed. What was wrong with him? Sophie was just some chick. Except that she wasn't. She was important to him, she mattered. The world, everything, was better when he was with Sophie. Now, he'd lost her. "It never stops," he murmured. "I'll never be free."

"Of what?" pausing, Kiran asked.

"My past."

Gripping his shoulder, Ram pushed him back. "That is so not true, man. Tell him, Kiran. Is every man doomed to be bound by his past mistakes?" Ram's gaze challenged Kiran.

Kiran hesitated then gained momentum as he spoke. "When Jesus sets you free, you are undeniably, absolutely free." Looking up, he met Ram's gaze even though he seemed to be speaking to Ayden. "John 8:36 says, 'Therefore if the Son makes you free, you shall be free indeed'. No qualifier. It doesn't say you'll be free if you just tithe enough money to the church, or you'll be free unless you did something really bad or made a mistake. It says that you will be free."

"Don't feel free," Ayden muttered but rather than petulant, he felt hopeful.

A smile pulled at Kiran's mouth, a look of burgeoning wonder in his eyes. "It's true that you are dealing with the consequences of your mistakes but you are not captive to them. Trust the Lord and He'll provide a way out of this situation." His gaze dropped to Ayden's. "Your way forward may not include Sophie, however."

"I guess I'll take what He'll give me," he said sadly.

"Then trust the Lord."

Chapter Ten: Barriers

"And they all lived…" Closing the library book she'd just finished reading, Sophie prompted the children seated before her, gesturing for them to finish with, "happily ever after." Their parents filtered forward to lead them out of the special reading room, the room Sophie had dubbed *The Dragon's Castle* because of the elaborate mural which dominated the rear wall.

After the last child exited, Patrick Jackson, in full-blown security guard pose with his barrel chest puffed out, legs planted equidistant, one hand on his holster and his radio in the other, took up a position blocking the doorway. A former Army sergeant, Patrick wasn't a particularly tall man but he had the natural authority to look intimidating when he chose.

"You got a problem," Patrick said gruffly. "Hoodlum hangin' round yer car."

"Really?" Sophie followed Patrick out to the main lobby where she could look out over the staff parking lot. Indeed a man was lying on the hood of her car, his booted feet resting on the bumper, his head pillowed on his arm which rested against her windshield.

"You want I should call the poh-lice?"

"Um." Sophie looked a little closer. At that moment, the man turned his head and she recognized him. "No. It's all right." It was Ayden. A host of butterflies took flight in her stomach. "I'll see to it."

"Ye' sure, missy?"

She wanted to sound confident. "Yep." It had been a month since Ayden's bus stop fight. For the first week after, there'd been nothing but silence. She'd seen him at church looking miserable as she knew she'd looked as well, but aside from that, he'd stayed away and silent. Then flowers had started arriving on her doorstep. When she asked, Mr. Kimutai informed her that the "hoodlum" had been dropping them off in the early morning. Then she'd discovered that the flowers were from Mrs. Carter's garden, meaning that he now had the seniors on his team. Next to arrive were handmade cards with verses from the *Song of Solomon*, not the really racy ones though. Then boxes of tea arrived, along with handmade chocolates, most likely made by Mrs. Gordon, and dozens of small gifts. She knew they all came from Ayden though he claimed none.

Sophie made her way down the steps to the parking level and then over to her car. Ayden must have heard her because he sat up, sliding down the slope of her hood to the ground.

"You off soon?" he asked.

"Yes. What are you doing here?"

Producing two tickets, he said, "I thought maybe we could go to the movies, to see that new thriller you were talking about a while ago." His voice sounded even, unemotional. The bruises had faded from his face but a new pink scar adorned his eyebrow. He'd cut his hair. When had he cut his hair? He wore bangs on his forehead with a tapered cut on the sides and back, a businessman's cut. It really did help him cast off that rough appearance he'd had when she'd first met him. "Soph?"

She realized that she'd stopped listening. What had he asked? Go to the movies? Her heart accelerated and her throat squeezed tight. "I don't think that's a good idea." She saw a subtle shift in his expression but she wasn't sure she could decipher it.

"All right," he said, tucking the tickets beneath her windshield wiper. "Just, uh, don't take another guy, okay?"

His face looked calm but his eyes reflected sorrow. She knew just how he felt. "Is that a not-so-subtle way to ask if I've started seeing someone else?"

"No. Uh, yeah." He shoved his hands in his front pockets, his eyes dropping to her shoes and then back up to her face. "Are you?"

"Are you?"

"Not really interested in other men," he quipped.

She almost smiled. Oh, how she wished he would give his promise to her, his pledge to cast off violence forever. "I'm not either."

He nodded as he turned away. "Take care. Okay?"

"Okay." No promise. Not even an apology.

He ambled over to his motorcycle.

"Ayden." She wasn't ready for him to go. "Thank you for all the gifts."

He stopped, turning only his head to see her from the corner of his eye, nodding a few times.

"I was surprised, actually," she said. Something was keeping her from letting him leave. "I thought you were going to leave me alone."

"I did. At first. But Ram kept at me. And I didn't really want to lose you." He strode back over to her. "Are you ever going to be able to forgive me?"

She clutched her arms across her chest. "You've never apologized."

He looked stunned, like she'd just flicked a wasp up his shorts. Shaking it off, he said, "I frightened you and for that I'm sorry."

"But not for fighting."

"Those guys were harassing you."

"They were just being jerks. You didn't have to beat them up."

"Guys like that only understand one language."

This conversation wasn't going anywhere she wanted to travel. She had waited a month for him to show up so they could discuss that terrible night. And all he had to offer her was justification for his actions. "It felt horrible, Ayden, to be caught in the middle of that. I hated it."

"I'm sorry, Sophie." He leaned his hip against the fender of her car. "I'm a work in progress. Maybe people think that once you give your life to God, He suddenly shifts all your history, all your experiences, out into the darkest regions of space—"

"He does, though. He casts your sins away as far as the east is from the west." She flung her arms wide.

"Yeah. He does." His voice was gaining energy. "But what he doesn't do—or at least he didn't do it for me, or many of the guys I know—is to suddenly free me from my reactions. I have to claw my way beyond them. He walks beside me step by step but I have to walk the path with Him, the grinding, uphill grade. Every moment of every day I have to battle the desire to settle my problems with my fists. Because you know what? Violence does solve some issues. It protected you from those guys whether you want to admit it or not." Sophie watched as his eyes filled with sorrow. "I'm a mess, Sophie, a bad man who can only say I'm not as bad as I used to be. If you want a guy who is good then I suppose it's best we finish things now." He backed away. "I wish you a happy life. You deserve it."

"Ayden!"

He didn't respond, he simply got on his bike and roared away.

Sophie locked herself in her office and cried.

Chapter Eleven: Early Grave

Jaxen set his ringing cell phone on the back counter of his classroom and pressed speakerphone. "Hey, Uncle Arlo. What's up?"

"Watchyou doin' right this instant?"

Jaxen rolled his eyes at the amusement in his uncle's voice. "I'm cleaning paste from my trousers."

Arlo snorted in laughter. "Boy, you sure you made the right choice?"

"Better paste on my pants than a refrigerator on the hood of my cruiser. You need something?"

"Did you sic a reverend on me?"

"Nope. If a reverend came to see you, Arlo, it had nothing to do with me. Who was it?"

"Some Injun fella. Friends with that neighbor gal."

Who was this pastor visiting Uncle Arlo? Was the grumpy, old man finally opening the door to God? "Paetan, isn't she? The mayor's daughter?"

"Suppose so." Arlo snorted. "You believe that load he be tellin' me about love and sal-va-tion? That reverend got no idea what I done in my life."

"I do. You know I do. 'I am persuaded that neither death nor life, nor angels nor principalities nor powers, nor things present nor things to come, nor height nor depth, nor any other created thing, shall be able to separate us from the love of God which is in Christ Jesus our Lord.' You can't do anything too bad to be forgiven. My life is proof of that."

Arlo was silent for a long time, so long that Jaxen paused in his activities to pray that maybe the man would finally reach out and grab a hold of grace. "Was me who sent yer ma away," Arlo said quietly. "Our daddy had left and twas up to me to keep the family goin'. When she wouldn't give up her fast livin' ways, I kicked her out."

Jaxen' heart ached. If not for that, maybe he would have had a chance, here in Ancora rather than the mean streets of Seattle. "Interesting that God brought me back here."

Arlo grunted and disconnected.

You do work in mysterious ways, Lord.

CR8O

"I'm sorry, sir. You can't pay a speeding ticket with cash. We have instituted a new policy."

We? As in Mayor Paetan? Ayden tapped the bills on the granite counter at the Clermont County Clerk's Office. The walls were painted beige and trimmed in blah, not unlike the pinched-face clerk behind the wicket. "Then how am I supposed to pay it?" This was the fifth ticket he'd received since arriving in Ancora nine months ago. One more and he'd lose points on his licence.

"We accept credit cards and money orders."

"I don't have a credit card."

The clerk shoved the ticket back toward him. "Money orders can be purchased at the bank or post office. Good day."

Money orders cost and he only had one more day to pay the ticket. *Why is this happening? I haven't done anything wrong.*

Pocketing the cash and ticket, Ayden shoved his hands in his pockets and stalked out, through the parking lot, around the back of the county office and across the field behind. He began to run. Soon he found himself breathing hard, knocking on Kiran's door.

"Hey, Reck…" The greeting died on Kiran's lips. "What do you need?"

"You got a job that needs doing? Smashing things?" He'd lost Sophie but her family was still harassing him. The frustration was building toward an explosion.

Kiran studied him a moment and then disappeared inside, returning in a pair of rubber boots. He gestured for Ayden to follow him around to the side of the parsonage, pointing to a spot on the grass. "I need a hole. At least four feet deep."

"Got it." Ayden found a shovel in the shed, divested himself of his jacket and rammed the point of the shovel in the earth. *Why? Why? Why?* The question hammered through his head in time to the shovel as it punctured the earth.

As the haze of anger began to dissipate, Kiran appeared with a glass of lemonade. Ayden wiped it across his forehead, the condensation cooling him before he drank down the sweet tartness. "Thanks. How's this looking?"

Kiran studied him rather than the hole. "Two feet longer, if you please."

"Sure." Ayden dug until his muscles burned and his chest heaved with the effort. Sweat poured thickly down his face.

"Hey." Ayden looked up to see Kiran standing above, his hand extended down toward him.

Ayden took hold and hoisted himself out of the hole. "What's this for?"

"Have a look."

Ayden looked down to see a hole four feet deep, two feet wide and six feet long. It looked like a shallow grave.

"This is what you're going to need if you don't find a way to channel your anger," Kiran said.

"Yeah, I know." Ayden wiped his muddy hands on his jeans. His anger had already cost him heavily. He missed Sophie, her absence in his life like a visceral ache.

"What happened?"

Ayden told him about the tickets and then went on to tell him about Tristan's second visit to his house which had been a rerun of the first. "I haven't done anything wrong."

"You were traveling over the speed limit."

"The first time it was ten miles an hour! Who gets a ticket for that?"

"It was justified."

"But now they won't even let me pay!" Ayden felt his blood pulsing behind his eyes.

"Why don't you pay me and I'll put it on my card. I can go over with you now before the office closes."

Gulping first, Ayden sucked in a deep breath. Not many people were willing to help an ex-con. Kiran never even hesitated. Ever. "Yeah. Thanks. That would work."

"No problem. Now what are you going to do about that hole? It's a hazard, don't you know."

Ayden grinned. "You want it filled in?"

"Yep. Then come back to the house. I want to show you something."

"Sure."

Ayden filled the hole. His back ached and his shoulders burned. And it felt good. The anger had burned itself out in the midst of hard work.

Returning the shovel to the shed, Ayden called through the door to Kiran who appeared a few moments later. Kiran led him around the parsonage toward the woods near the river, the same river he'd rowed with Sophie. His chest caved in as loss echoed in his heart. Kiran pointed to the cords of wood haphazardly stacked, creating what Ayden had thought was a fence of some sort.

"Pastor Baker, the man who served here before me, had two teenaged sons, two young men who were headed for trouble. He had the idea to help them start a business that would also allow them to use up some of their angst. He made a deal with a few woodsmen in the area to buy wood and then have his boys chop the lumber into firewood and sell it. There are lots of hunting cabins around here and most are heated by woodstoves. Now, I bequeath it to you."

"I can't make money off something that belongs to the church."

"It doesn't. Baker paid for the wood out of his own pocket. He could never get his sons interested, so the wood just sat."

"There's a lot of wood here."

"He didn't feel right cancelling his orders. Many of those men relied on the income to get them through. So the wood just kept coming. You chop it and sell it. Give your ten per cent to God's work and it's square. It's a good way to burn off anger and to give you a little extra income."

"I don't know what to say."

"First, you say, thanks. Then you come with me to the county clerk's office so we can pay your fine. Then you let me order pizza and wings and we watch the game together."

"Thanks. I'll order the pizza. And, yeah, I'd like to watch the game."

"Don't be a dork."

Ayden laughed. For the first time in two months.

Chapter Twelve: A Friend of a Friend

Ayden caught himself gazing out the front window of the parsonage once again, over the church lawns toward Riverside Park where he and Sophie had walked—when was it? Nine months ago? Sophie called it their second date. Ayden felt a sad smile pull at his mouth. Some date. He'd hollered at her and then vomited forth his life story.

He sighed morosely. And now, Sophie was lost to him. And he'd moved into the parsonage with Kiran because Hamish Oskar had taken one look at him after his fight and evicted him. Who could he go to? The sheriff? The town council? Yeah, right. And then, last night, on his way home from work, Deputy Reynolds had seen fit to impound his motorcycle for three days, stating that his licence plate was improperly displayed. *As if.* He'd split two cords of wood that day.

"Hey." Kiran walked into the room. Ayden hadn't heard his approach, further evidence that he was losing it. "There's a call for you." He handed Ayden the cordless phone.

"Who is it?" Ayden asked, holding his hand over the mouthpiece.

"Reggie Dundas. He wanted to know how to reach you. Don't know why, before you ask." Kiran shrugged. "I need to run over to my grandparents. You okay?"

Ayden scowled at him. If Kiran asked him that one more time, he was going to blow his stack. In spite of Ayden's stare of intimidation which he knew had made men quail, Kiran just shrugged again and departed.

Ayden looked at the phone. Reggie Dundas. Deputy to Sheriff Tristan Paetan. Skinny. Nervous. Sophie's friend.

"Yeah?" Ayden answered the phone.

"I tried to warn Sophie that you were not to be trusted. Do you have any idea how many ex-cons re-offend?"

Ayden didn't have the patience for this. "What do you want?"

Reggie cleared his throat but through the noise Ayden heard the murmur of voices in the background, followed by a muffled, "This morning. Yes." Reggie cleared his throat again. "Wait a minute." Ayden heard a door open then close and then Reggie came back on the line. "I'm calling because of Sophie. I just want to make that clear. I don't trust you. I don't know what she sees in you. But I'm her friend. So, here it goes. Local law enforcement agencies are meeting in June to discuss organizing a taskforce because of the increase of illegal drugs in southern Ohio. In preparation, Sheriff Paetan has asked me to...keep tabs on you. He seems most interested in having me find any connection that may," he paused, adding in a mutter, "or may not exist between you and illegal drugs. But Sophie cares about you, so I'm calling to give you a chance. Stop whatever you're involved in. Get out before you get caught and hurt Sophie further."

Wait. What? Sophie cares or cared, past tense?

"Are you listening to me?" Reggie sounded irritated. "You're in a mess-load of trouble, a real cluster-twist. Meet me at Dagwood's Finest in fifteen minutes."

"Reggie, is Sophie okay?" Ayden was desperate to know.

Reggie cleared his throat. "She's fine. Are you going to meet me?"

"Yeah. Yes. You're sure she's okay?"

"Yes." Reggie sounded exasperated. Well, it was his own fault for bringing up the subject. "Fifteen minutes."

Dagwood's was about fifteen blocks from the parsonage. He'd been borrowing the Evangilator for work but with Kiran at his grandparents' house, he was stranded. Without his bike, Ayden would have to practically jog to make it on time.

Grabbing his wallet and a jacket, Ayden set off, walking briskly through Riverside Park. He hopped a few fences and took a few unauthorized shortcuts, making it to the deli in seventeen minutes. Reggie was sitting at a table in the back, sipping coffee and eating pumpkin pie. He didn't offer any greeting other than, "You're late."

"My bike's been impounded," Ayden said, adding in a mutter, "as if you didn't know. I had to walk." He didn't want to offer excuses with the man so hostile but he also didn't want to burn any possible bridges that might help him connect with Sophie. And discover the tense of her caring. Even if she didn't want him, he would still do anything for her.

A startlingly buxom woman approached, platinum blonde waves around her face, black skirt far too short given her middle age. Her nametag read Essie. "What can I get you?" she asked, snapping her gum in such a characteristic manner that Ayden thought for a moment they'd landed in a sixties diner.

"Coffee, please. Black."

"Sure thing, honey." Reaching across him, giving him an eyeful, she upended his cup and filled it. Ayden averted his eyes.

"You want a refill, deputy?" Essie asked.

Reggie blushed, even his ears turning a deep crimson. Grinning at his obvious discomfiture, Essie refilled Reggie's cup and then flounced away.

That was as long as Ayden was willing to wait. "What's this about?"

"The sheriff...Tristan...he really hates you being involved with his sister."

"Yeah. No kidding. He's been harassing me for months."

"What do you mean?" Reggie asked, looking truly perplexed.

"Reynolds has been pulling me over. Tristan has been arriving at my door spewing threats."

"Really? Clarissa?"

"If Clarissa is Reynolds, then, yes. What's this about drugs?"

"I saw your rap sheet, Reck. You're a drug dealer."

"I haven't dealt drugs since I was fourteen. Whatever is going on here, it has nothing to do with me."

"But that would be your juvenile record?" Reggie paused thoughtfully. "Gang activity?"

"I'm not part of any gang, never have been." Ayden held Reggie's puzzled stare. He hadn't done anything wrong.

Clearing his throat, Reggie leaned forward, "Tristan desperately wants to connect you to this drug conduit."

"I'm not involved."

"Are you involved in any criminal activity?"

Ayden leaned forward, using his posture to emphasize the truth of his words. "No. I told you."

Reggie sat back, scratching the peach fuzz on his cheeks. He looked pensive, muttering, "I wondered how Sophie could fall for a criminal."

"Did she tell you that?"

"That you're an ex-con?" Reggie looked confused.

"No." *That Sophie has fallen for me.*

Reggie cleared his throat. Once again. Ayden wanted to present him with a cough drop but since he didn't carry any the point was moot. There was something different about Reggie today compared to the quivering mass he'd been on the night they'd bowled together. Well, Reggie had bowled. Ayden had spilled hot cheese on Sophie. And yet, somehow, she'd forgiven him.

Reggie took the last bite of his pie, rapping the clean fork on the table. "Pia and I watched a movie with Sophie last weekend and all she could talk about was how fights on television were so different from the real thing and if we cheered for the good guy on TV then why not in real life. Do you have any idea what she was on about?"

"Hmm." Maybe Sophie did still care about him. Maybe it wasn't a lost cause. *Lord, I want that so badly. Please show me what to do.* "So what happens now?" Ayden asked.

"You keep your nose clean. Then Tristan can't touch you."

Chapter Thirteen: Reconciliation

Sophie had walked every trail in Riverside Park but it hadn't eased the ache in her belly. Maybe sitting would help. The bench was partially shaded by a nearby Tatarian Maple tree, its greenish-white flower panicles catching the bright sun overhead. Sit in the shade and add to her misery or sit in the sun, feeling betrayed that the day could be bright when life seemed so dim. Finally, Sophie slumped down in the middle of the bench.

Had it really been nine months since she and Ayden had met just a few hundred feet away on the lawns of the Wesleyan Church? The time had flown by. Until two months ago when her life had ground to a halt. This had been the longest, most miserable time of her life, perhaps even worse than the time of her parents' divorce.

"Hello."

Sophie looked up to find Kiran watching her closely. She hadn't even noticed his approach.

"How are you doing?" Kiran said, sitting beside her. He chose the side of the bench in the sun. Optimistic, perhaps?

She shrugged.

"You look quite miserable."

She snorted. "Gee, thanks." She shifted away from him, deeper into the shade. Why? Misery loves shadow.

"This wouldn't have to do with Reck, would it? Because he's been as grumpy as a giraffe in a neck brace."

Drawing in a breath to deny the connection between her feelings and her desertion of Ayden, she sighed instead. Did she really feel like she'd abandoned him? Had she? "I miss him, Kiran."

"Why?"

She was startled by the question, but she shouldn't be. If she and Ayden were in a relationship…well, they had been in a relationship…then she ought to know why she liked him. So she thought about it, considering her response. "He's fun. Intelligent. He stood up to my father. Did you know that?" She turned on the bench to face Kiran. "He actually stood up to a man who uses power and manipulation as though they were carpentry tools."

"What else?" Kiran asked quietly.

"He likes me for who I am. I never have to pretend with him. He doesn't expect me to be perfect, just me." She traced an imaginary line on her leg. "He puts up with all the crap people give him just because he spent time in prison. And he has plans." She glanced up at Kiran. "He wants to make furniture. Did you know that?"

Kiran nodded.

"And he's brave."

"In what way?"

That question hit a little too close to her reasons for stepping away from him. Didn't it? Avoiding the answer, she just shrugged.

Kiran ignored her lapse. "Those are pretty powerful reasons."

"They are, aren't they?" There were lots of reasons to like Ayden Breckinridge.

Kiran was studying her face so she avoided his gaze by scanning the park for the ice cream vendor. But that only reminded her of their first day in the park, the day that Ayden had told her his story.

"I'll tell you one thing," Kiran said, tapping her shoe to get her attention. "If I had to walk down the streets of Over-the-Rhine, I would take my brother Ram and Ayden Breckinridge. How about you?"

She knew exactly what he was trying to do and she wouldn't be fooled. "He totally lost control. He would have killed that man."

"But he didn't. You know, Sophie, I see the struggle in Reck's eyes when conflict comes. In the old days, even in his early days as a Christian, he was getting into fights daily. But it's been months since he decked anyone. He *has* changed."

"Do you think…he'd ever hit…me. Or a child?"

"Never. He lives by a code. It may be different than what we grew up with but he never falters. He would never harm a woman or child. I'm not saying he's not prone to being obnoxious but you're safe physically."

"Kiran, what if I'm wrong? I feel like…I want to ignore the fight and pretend it never happened. But it did." She sighed. It still made her shaky to think about it.

"Have you talked to Reck about what happened that night?"

"Yes. Kind of. No, not really."

"Sometimes it takes a little perspective to understand a person's motivations. My family doesn't know this but I maintained contact with Ram from the moment my grandparents kicked him out."

She hadn't known that, but she'd guessed it.

"I saw my brother at his worst *and* I saw the power of God in his life. Even though he didn't have a lot of support—certainly none from his family—when he first gave over his life to God, God was so real to him. That's when I decided to become a minister, actually. If my brother, who had carried on a life of crime on two continents was brought to his knees by the Father's love, then that was something I wanted to be a part of." He adjusted his glasses, a thoughtful expression on his face. "During that time, I read a lot of books about cons turned Christian. The problem as I saw it was that most of the books were written about people who'd undergone a dramatic, immediate change. But what I saw in Ram was something much slower, more gradual, and I came to believe that that was a much more common experience. I think of my own life. I have to make choices daily, situation by situation, to act and react the way God wants me to. It's not automatic. I just have a lot less to fight through to get to the good choices." Kiran scratched his chin thoughtfully. "Reck is so different than he was a year ago, two years ago, five years ago. What will he be like a year from now? Ten years? Twenty years?"

Wasn't that basically what Ayden had told her the other day at the library? "It's risky," she muttered.

"Some of the best things are." Kiran slapped his hands on his thighs, pushed off his knees and rose. "I'm off to the Carters' to weed the garden. Reck is at the parsonage...just in case you were wondering."

Sophie smiled with a little ray of hope. "Yeah."

Knocking on the parsonage door, she called out, "Ayden? Ayden."

"Hey," he said, opening the screen door between them. Her heart sped just at the sight of him. Not only because of his rugged good looks and the way he filled out a pair of jeans, but because the sight of him reminded her of the times they'd spent together, his tenderness, humor, and fierce loyalty. "Kiran's gone over to Imogene Carter's."

"I wanted to talk to you, actually."

"Yeah?" he said, surprised. "Come in." Stepping back, he held the door for her. "Do you want some coffee? Or, I know, milk with ice."

"Sure. Either is fine."

Ayden poured milk into two glasses, adding ice to one and chocolate syrup to the other. He set them on the kitchen table and sat. "Everything okay?"

"Not really."

He immediately tensed. "What's wrong?"

"I miss you." She hadn't meant to blurt that out but it was the truth.

He didn't react at first. The room went silent; it seemed like even the birds outside were quiet in the charged atmosphere.

"I miss you, too," he said quietly, evenly, still not revealing any emotion. He was waiting for her and since he'd been the last to offer anything she guessed that was fair.

"I wondered if we could talk about what happened that night at the bus stop." She dropped her gaze to the table, tracing the whorls in the oak with the tip of her index finger.

"Sure." He turned his glass round and round with his hands.

Forcing herself to take a sip of her milk, she said, "First off, I wanted to tell you that I'm sorry I called you a brute."

His eyes shifted and he drew in a quick breath. "Thanks for that."

"It...It frightened me when you fought those guys at the bus stop. No, not really frightened, more like upset me. Made me sick, even. I just felt so overwhelmed and I didn't know what to do with the emotions." She took another sip, not really tasting the chilled beverage. "I've spent most of my life hiding how I feel. In my family, emotion was considered something to be controlled or punished. I learned quickly that I either had to hide my feelings or they would be used against me. So I'm not real good at dealing with high emotion." She traced the condensation on her glass. "I thought if I just stayed away from you then I wouldn't have to deal with it."

"Did it work?" he asked, reaching out to skim his fingertips along her knuckles.

She peeked up at him. "I guess but, wow, it wasn't worth it."

His gaze lightened a fraction. "I didn't know of any other way to get those guys away from you. It never occurred to me to try any other approach than my fists. I saw that blonde guy bothering you and the world turned red."

"He was only being obnoxious. I mean, they really scared me...and I don't know what would have happened if you hadn't come along...but I don't think you needed to fight. There may have been another approach that would have worked."

He seemed to accept that. "Yeah." He blew out a breath. "I do fight a lot less than I used to. When I first became a Christian, Ram told me that rather than trying to be perfect all of a sudden, I should simply try to do better than yesterday. If I hit ten people yesterday, then today I needed to hit only nine."

She laughed in surprise. "You know, I've watched people and said, 'How can a Christian behave that way?' I've never looked and said, 'Wow, what would that person be like if they weren't a Christian?' I think maybe I'm as judgemental as I accuse my father and brother of being."

"You're not, honey. No one could accuse you of that. You're sweet and kind."

"I am, though. I judged you. When you threw that first punch and I heard the sickening thud as your fist connected with Blondie's face, I judged you. I thought that I was open-minded, willing to see beyond your past to who you really are, to see you through Jesus' eyes. I didn't even come close. I saw only what I wanted to see." Reaching out, she rested her hand on his. He placed his other hand on top. "I'm sorry."

"You have nothing to apologize for. I put you in the middle of a dangerous situation without once considering that you could have been hurt by it. I acted without thought. If it's any consolation, I am trying to find other ways to channel my anger."

"That's good. But what if someone tried to kill me or something, then I'd need you to fight. But most of the time, I don't want you to fight."

"Okay. I can live with that."

"You're not a wild animal."

He shrugged. "No. You were right about that."

"No. A wild animal wouldn't love his little sister so much. You wouldn't try so hard to make me happy."

Her hands held warmly between his, he leaned across the table until his mouth was a breath away. "This argument over?" he asked.

"Yeah," she said. Her voice was husky with anticipation.

He kissed her. This wasn't a tender press of his lips to hers like their first kiss. This was a kiss of reunion, firm and clinging.

Opening her mouth, she invited him deeper, missing his flavor, looking for a reassurance that he still belonged to her.

Releasing her hands, he reached out to cup her face. His elbow knocked a glass and milk spilled in a chocolate river across the oak table and into Sophie's lap. Gasping at the cold, she pulled back, standing abruptly to escape the chill.

He looked shocked a moment then scrambled to grab paper towels off the counter. But Sophie laughed. Ayden paused in dabbing milk off her jeans to meet her gaze. Humor sparked in his eyes. "You're my kind of woman," he said.

She didn't say "We'll see" like last time because this time she knew that he was right. They both stood there grinning at each other until the milk dripped right into her sneakers.

Dropping her gaze to scan her apparel, she then looked up. "I guess I'd better go home."

His brow furrowed and his smile fell away. "Do you have to go? It's been…well, it's been weeks," he said as though that said it all.

"I know, and I don't really want to go but," she gestured toward her outfit, "I'm covered in milk."

"I have some sweatpants you could wear, and a T-shirt."

"Not the bloodstained one?"

"No." His cheeks took on a tinge of pink. "I use that one as a rag. I do have others though."

"You mean here?"

"Yeah." His brow furrowed.

"Why are your clothes here?" she asked.

"I, uh, am staying here at the moment."

"Why? Was your neighborhood just too dangerous?"

He laughed. "No. Not for me. But, uh, when I showed up after the fight all bruised and bloodied, my landlord kicked me out."

"In violation of your lease?" she asked indignantly.

"What lease, Soph? I got a room and threats. That was my lease."

There was no aspect of his life unaffected by his past, she thought sorrowfully. "If you have something for me to change into and a washcloth, I would like to stay a while. I don't really have anything else I need to do today." And the thought of wearing his clothes made her feel all tingly inside.

"Okay. I'll grab something—"

"Is your table here?" she asked, interrupting.

"Yeah. We put it in the parlor. We had to push all the other furniture to the side to fit it in. But it's here."

"Oh, Ayden, can I see it? Please?"

He smiled. His eyes were soft. "Yeah. Get changed before you start to sour and I'll show you."

"Awesome!"

Leaving her clothes to soak in the bathroom sink, she skipped down the stairs to find Ayden in the parlor. He was right, the room was absolutely packed-out with a pale blue settee and matching chairs, a maple coffee table and sideboard, and a beautiful teak wood dining table that she was sure would fit ten people or more. It was gorgeous, sanded and varnished smooth with elegant ornamentation on the corners and routed into the edges. The legs were elegantly scrolled.

"Ayden. This is so beautiful!" she said as she ran her hand along the smooth surface as far as she could reach.

He shrugged. "Thanks. I've been working on it a while."

"Did you do all the beautiful carvings on the corners and the legs?"

"Yeah." He shrugged again, shoving his hands in his front pockets.

Turning into him, she wrapped her arms around his neck and tiptoed up to kiss him. His hands slid out of his pockets and wrapped around her waist, pulling her close. "If you can make furniture like this, sweetheart," she said. "You could definitely do this for a living."

"I've been saving up to rent a place in Silverstone, about ten minutes from here. It used to be a shoemaker's shop so there is lots of work space and a large open area for projects like my dining table. There's an apartment upstairs and I…well, I could start making furniture to sell, go into business for myself. I've been talking to the landlord. He hasn't had any interest in the place for years. If I'll take it as is, he'll give me a break on the first few months of rent and pay for any supplies I need to fix it up. In exchange, I'll give him a cut of any profits for the first three years to cover the expenses."

She hugged him tightly again then bounced back. "I could buy the place for you. I can cash in some of my shares from Granddaddy's business and buy it outright. We could refurbish it. Or just take out a long term lease. That actually might bring better returns because of the tax deductions. My accountant would like that. He's always pestering me to invest and consider deductions." She turned to him, clapping happily at the idea only to come to a complete halt at the expression on his face. She stilled. "What's wrong?"

"I'm not going to live off my girlfriend."

"But, Ayden, I have lots of money. I could easily live off my trust fund alone not to mention the money I get from my shares in Paetan Pharmaceuticals."

He was unmoved by her words. "I'm not taking your money."

"I don't understand." She felt tears burning the backs of her eyes. Perhaps there never would be a time when they could make this relationship work.

He must have guessed her thoughts because he moved in quickly, anchoring her hips with his hands. "Soph," his voice was gentle, "with my job at Hagerty's and the little side business that Kiran found me, I will have enough saved a few months from now. I just need to build up enough capital before Hagerty decides to make me his head of security. I'm not looking forward to that conversation."

"Wait. What?" She pressed her palms against his chest to give a little distance but didn't try to break his hold. "Hagerty wants to give you a promotion? That's a good thing, isn't it?"

Did he have some kind of neurotic fear of success? *Is this what happens to people who spend time in prison? Do they all live with the feeling that they don't deserve good things?*

"It's not truly a promotion. He just wants to use my street skills to keep the employees in line."

"What street skills?"

He released her and turned away, sighing. "Nothing."

Grabbing his arm, she tugged. "Don't lie—"

He swung around. "Hey." he said loudly, defensively, and then gentled his voice. "I haven't lied to you, Sophie."

"But there are things you're keeping from me, aren't there?"

"I suppose," he replied cautiously.

"There has to be trust between us, Ayden. Trust means telling the truth—"

"I am," he insisted.

"And sharing our lives. Keeping things from me is as bad as lying. If we can't be honest and open with each other then we don't have a future." She turned to go but he grabbed her.

"I didn't know that." Still holding her as if he was afraid she'd run, he shoved his other hand through his hair in frustration. "You act like I should know these rules but I don't. It's not like I'm trying to screw things up between us. I'm actually trying. Really hard. To make things work."

Epiphany. "You mean the rules of a healthy relationship?"

"Yeah," he said belligerently.

Ayden didn't know how to have a relationship, he didn't know how to trust. Or be trusted, probably. "Oh. Okay. First, no lying. Second, be open about stuff."

A wry smile twisted his mouth. "Stuff?"

She grinned. "Uh huh. Like, for example, what street skills?"

He studied her expression warily. "I was a collector for the Grex."

"That's a gang, isn't it?"

"Yeah."

"You were in a gang?"

"No. I collected for them, occasionally delivered punishment."

She blanched at the implications. "Oh. And that's what Hagerty wants you to do for him?"

"Yeah. Not exactly. But close enough."

"I don't think you should do that."

He laughed but there was no humor in it. "No kidding. But I still need my job there. I don't have enough money yet to lease the place in Silverstone."

Lord, there has to be a way to fix this. What should we do? "What if…what if I invested in your company?"

"I will not take your money for myself. It's yours."

"No, honey, listen. I wouldn't give you money, I would invest capital. We would draw up a legal document that we both sign that tells how much I put in at what schedule and what you are required to pay me out of your proceeds."

Shoving his hands in his back pockets, he rocked back on his heels, clearly considering her proposal. "It would be like a business partnership?"

"Yes. All legal and everything. I would be basically shifting a few of my shares from Paetan Pharmaceuticals to Reck's furniture…whatever. Or maybe I should use my trust fund. It matured on my last birthday. What do you think?"

"I guess it wouldn't hurt to talk to a lawyer."

A grin split her face. "It couldn't hurt."

Brushing the hair back from her cheeks, he caressed her face with the backs of his fingers. He seemed to want to visually feed on her features. But she wanted to kiss so she moved in and pressed her mouth to his. He captured her face and breathed her in.

"Ah-hem." They broke apart guiltily at Kiran's voice, though they had nothing to be guilty about. Not only Kiran, though, Gael and Cora Johnson stood with him, looking amused, angry and amused, in that order.

"I'll be with you in a moment," Ayden said to Kiran.

Chuckling lightly, Kiran led Cora and Gael out of the parlor and into the dining room.

"We can continue this discussion later." Kissing her nose, Ayden took Sophie's hand and tugged her into the dining room with him.

"Hello, Mr. Reckless. I believe that's what the young ones call you," Cora Johnson said, patting Ayden on the cheek. She had a knowing look in her eyes. Sophie felt herself blush.

"Hello, Miss Johnson. You're looking lovely and spry today. Is that a new dress?" Ayden said. Sophie was stunned. While she'd noticed that many of the single seniors thought he was quite wonderful, she'd never heard him put on the charm.

"Why, yes, it is. Nice of you to notice." Sophie could have sworn that the woman was blushing. Imagine that. "Call me Cora. Now, I have a business proposition for you, young man." She retrieved some pages from her purse and spread them on the table. "I would like a buffet hutch just like this one for my dining room." She pointed at the specifications listed on the page. "Now I went to that place where you work, Hamburgerty's or somesuch, but that crook of a furniture salesman says that it costs three thousand, five hundred dollars to buy this one." Cora straightened. "I'm on a fixed income, don't they know?" She huffed in disgust. "I will pay you two thousand, five hundred dollars to build one for me."

Ayden betrayed no emotion except the subtle lift of his eyebrows. Spinning the page on Kiran's maple dining table, he studied it for several minutes, extracting a pencil from his back pocket and making some calculations in the margins. "I could do it for two thousand but you'd have to accept it made from cedar not cherry and maple."

"Done." Cora grinned broadly, extending her hand and shaking Ayden's firmly. "How much will you need as start-up funds?"

"Wait," he said, stopping her hand as she rummaged for her cheque book. "I don't have the facilities at the moment. I won't have a workshop for another couple of months."

"I wanted it in time for the Easter holidays," Cora said, frowning.

"Ah-hem." Sophie cleared her throat, casting Ayden a meaningful glance.

"On second thought…" He grinned slowly then made a few more calculations on the page. "I wouldn't have the finishing completed in time but I could have the piece usable."

Miss Johnson thought about that. "By 'finishing' what do you mean?"

"The carving on the doors, the jigs on the top margin, the fine details."

"Fine. We have a deal." She wrote out a cheque and handed it over. "You'll have to write in your proper name because I have no idea how to spell Breckinraider."

Ayden chuckled. "No problem, ma'am."

Kiran led Cora out.

"You put her up to that. Didn't you, Sophie?" Gael said, accusing.

Sophie blanched as Ayden's smile disappeared.

"I thought so," Gael said, viciously pleased.

"Gael," Kiran's reprimand startled Sophie, nearly as much as it surprised Gael. "It's time for you to leave."

"Oh, Kiran, you don't mean it," Gael said but her expression showed her doubt.

"Oh, but I do," he said. "I've listened to your rudeness to Reck and I've let it go. He's a big boy and perfectly capable of looking after himself. But that was an attack on Sophie. It's enough."

"Kiran," Gael said but Kiran's mind couldn't be changed and she finally left in a huff.

"Not necessary, Kir," Ayden said quietly, his emotions simmering beneath the surface.

"Yeah. It was." Kiran turned to him then nodded at Sophie. "You might want to deal with this. I thought things were looking up when we walked in."

Ayden turned to see her pale face. "I didn't get that work for you, Ayden."

Ayden's features went all soft and gooey and he reached out to gently brush his fingers along her cheek. "I know. I love you, baby."

Her breath hitched. "You do?" she asked in wonder.

"Was there ever any doubt?" he said and kissed her.

Kiran was long gone by the time they came up for air.

෬෨

Tristan sat behind the polished walnut Villa Toscana desk in his office at the Clermont County Municipal Building. Even though the old sheriff had chosen to use the large modern glass-walled space in the center of the sheriff's department, Tristan preferred this more private corner. Anya, the part-time Communications Officer and part-time dispatcher, occupied the larger office instead, giving her line-of-sight over the front entrance as well as the pod of interconnected desks where his deputies sat. The holding cells could only be reached by passing between the deputies and the dispatcher.

Closing his window blinds as well as the half-glass oak door that proclaimed "Sheriff" in gold paint, Tristan awaited an important private call. Except the voice he heard on the other end was unexpected.

"Sheriff, this is Iris Okoye. I am the attorney for Paetan Pharmaceuticals. I have been given instructions to inform the members of the Board of Directors that there is the possibility of an imminent change. One of our shareholders, your sister, Sophie, is considering cashing in a few of her shares. If you would be interested in purchasing these, you have thirty days to buy them according to your grandfather's instructions."

"Am I correct in assuming that a review of the company's finances will follow if there is a change in ownership?" Tristan said.

"That is correct. The review will occur fifteen days after Ms. Paetan signs the intention documents."

"I'd like to meet with you before the shares are offered elsewhere." Tristan barely restrained his frustration. She was doing this for Breckinridge, he was sure of it. If Sophie cashed out, it could bring attention to the little relationship Tristan had with Regis Maxwell.

"Once I receive confirmation from Ms. Paetan, I'll have my secretary get in touch to make an appointment."

"Great." Tristan rang off and then dialed again. "Regis? We have a problem."

◌৪৯

Sophie answered the knock on her door. *Oh, snap.* Glancing through the peep-hole, she saw her parents standing on her front stoop. Her father was dressed in a three-piece black pinstriped suit, matching tie, and dress shoes. Hair and beard neatly coiffed as usual. Dressed in pale blue silk and pearls, her mother cowered behind him, clutching her matching purse. Why did she allow him to dominate her life? They were divorced. And as far as Sophie could surmise, the fault had been her father's, though no one would ever tell her the real story.

"Sophie Anne." Her father used her name as he would a formal title not the name of his youngest child.

Leaning in close, he offered his cheek as he stepped inside. Hesitating a moment, particularly because she didn't believe in the bond the action suggested, she kissed his freshly shaven cheek. Why did her father find it necessary to groom before seeing her? Ayden came to her in all conditions. She especially enjoyed when he came straight from the factory with the scent of cedar dust in his hair because he "couldn't wait to see her".

"What is this I hear about you spending time with a criminal?" her father said. No pleasantries. No "how are you?" Just blat.

She thought of being evasive or simply refusing to answer but discarded both ideas. Either would only prolong her father's visit, an outcome she didn't desire. Particularly since Ayden would be arriving any minute now.

"He's not a criminal. Ayden is an ex-con, it's true, but he's also a carpenter and a Christian," she said.

"It is all very well and good for Reverend Rao to consort on a regular basis with the criminal element. I even understand why he would extend a hand of Christian charity to this man who has sought to work toward redemption through the church. But it is quite another thing for my daughter to consort with a known criminal," he said. "Particularly one who is clearly only interested in your inheritance." Stuart stepped into her space but she refused to back down. "You are not going to drag my name through the filth." He gestured toward Lucy, pinning her with a fulminating glare. "Are you just going to stand there?"

Her mother stepped forward, wringing her hands, her purse swinging like a pendulum on her arm. "Sophie, dear, be reasonable. Your father only wants what's best for you."

"My father wants what's best for *him*. And how dare you accuse Ayden of being mercenary. Do you think a decent man couldn't love me for who I am?"

"A decent man." He mocked her derisively.

"Stuart." Lucy said his name but there was no force behind it. It was more of a plea than anything else.

He frowned down at her. "Well, what do you say to your daughter?"

A knock on the door cut off her response but not her father's snort of disgust. The smile that greeted her fell away to a bland expression when Ayden noticed her parents. "Good evening, Mayor Paetan. Mrs. Paetan," he said very politely. Sophie grasped his hand in gratitude.

Lucy gave a half-hearted smile that traveled only as far as the corners of her mouth, while Stuart totally ignored him.

"You will end this affair and begin to spend time with someone more suitable," Stuart said, his tone hard and uncompromising.

Ayden stiffened beside her but his face didn't betray his angst.

"Good-bye, Dad. Mom," Sophie said, leaving no doubt that she wished them to leave.

Chapter Fourteen: Elbow Grease

Ayden lifted his hands from her eyes and Sophie gasped. "It's wonderful!" Spinning a slow circle, she inspected the large room. Workbenches lined the walls and a large worktable dominated the central space. "I mean, it's filthy, but so awesome. There's easily space to work on a dining table, a hutch and—I don't know—something else as well. Will any of these tools be useful to you?"

"Some," he replied, grinning, clearly enjoying her response. "Did I tell you it used to be a shoemaker's shop? As the town of Ancora grew, Silverstone shrunk until it couldn't support the cobbler anymore. As cars became more accessible and cheaper to own, people made the trip into Cincinnati to buy pre-fab shoes."

Sophie hugged him and then spun away to explore, enjoying his pleasure and pride. A doorway at the rear of the shop led to a small storeroom. Forcing the stubborn door open a crack, she peeked inside, sneezed, and then gave up, ascending the stairs to the upper floor.

"Wait. I'll get the lights for you," Ayden said, brushing past her.

Now illuminated, Sophie could see an open-concept apartment with angled eaves. There were two small Hopper windows along the side, a rear-facing horizontal slider that looked out over a vacant lot, and two large casement windows overlooking the front parking lot. Through these, she could see the lights of Silverstone to the west and a pale blue line she thought was the Little Miami River. The same Little Miami that ran through Greenland Forest also flowed south from Ancora into William Harsha Lake, and then south again to its source just west of Silverstone.

The apartment was a good-sized space for a bachelor. Or a young couple just starting out. She smiled, pacing toward the rear. "This could be the kitchen. That looks like a stove outlet." She spun back. "Your table would be perfect right in this spot. We could hang a light over the center, maybe a simple chandelier. Oh, and that crystal bowl my grandmother gave me on my sixteenth birthday, that would be perfect beneath it, the light, that is." She turned to the right. "If you put up a wall here, this could be your bedroom. And this little space between there and the bathroom could be for storage. And right here would be your living room. Do you think you'd want—"

Ayden cut her off by resting his fingertips gently on her lips. He replaced his hand with his mouth, murmuring, "I love you."

Wrapping her arms around his neck, Sophie kissed him, stretching up on her tiptoes to get closer. She settled back on her heels when he pulled back.

"Was I getting a tad carried away?" she asked, smiling into his eyes.

"No. I just needed to kiss you," he said but before he lowered his mouth to hers again, a noise downstairs warned them they had company. "Must be Kiran to help clean up."

"Maybe," Sophie said enigmatically.

Ayden tilted his face to see her expression more clearly. Whatever he detected made his brows furrow. Sophie gave him a quick kiss on the lips and then skipped away and down the stairs.

"Hey, Reck," Kiran said. Ayden stepped into the workroom and froze, surveying the group before him. Kiran stood with arms outstretched, indicating those around him including Ram and Pia, Sandy Tripper, Frank and Tony D'Angelo, Reggie Dundas, and last but not least, Miss Cora Johnson and her grand-niece Mary.

"Well?" Cora said. "What are we waiting for? Get to praying, pastor, so we can clean up this mess."

Kiran laughed and called everyone to prayer. Ayden still looked dazed at the "amen" so Cora took over as administrator and handed out the tasks.

The group washed and lugged, toted and swept. Sandy, Frank, Ram and Ayden maneuvered Ayden's dining table in and up the stairs. Kiran and Reggie assembled an old bedframe that Kiran had salvaged from the parsonage attic.

After four hours of labor, Sophie went out for pizza and salad. Once a buffet was assembled on the teak dining table, Kiran told Ayden to say the blessing.

"You'd better, Kir. I'm not much for that kind of thing," Ayden said, fighting a blush which Sophie could see rising up his neck.

"No, thanks," Kiran said, bowing his head. When the others followed suit, Ayden shot Sophie a look of silent desperation. She took his hand, holding it tightly in hers and then bowed her head.

"Uh, right," Ayden began, rocking back on his heels. "God, I don't know much about praying out loud, but I guess you know that." He cleared his throat and then swallowed hard. "I want to thank you for this food." He sighed deeply. "But most of all, uh, I want to thank you for a new life. Um, for Kiran and Ram and Sophie. For Sandy, Frank, Tony, Reggie, Pia, Mary, and Cora. I've never had this many friends who weren't trying to score drugs off me. I guess I shouldn't have said that, God. But you already knew." He cleared his throat again. "Thanks for second chances. Amen."

"Let's eat," Sandy said, clapping his hands together with enthusiasm. "I'm starving."

While everyone else followed suit, Sophie leaned up, resting her head on Ayden's shoulder a moment, whispering, "Nice job".

Ayden grumbled something in reply, making her laugh.

Once the pizza was consumed, the others got back to work downstairs, leaving Sophie and Ayden to finish upstairs.

"Sophie?"

"Yes," she said dreamily, carrying a stack of empty pizza boxes across his soon-to-be living room.

"Where did this refrigerator come from?" he asked sternly. "This top-of-the-line stainless steel refrigerator?"

"Cora had the stove in her basement," she said, slowing, the dreamy smile dropping from her expression.

"Fridge, Sophie," he insisted on knowing.

She chewed her lip anxiously. "Sandy's wife was elated to get rid of the apartment-style washer and dryer and get a new set."

Crossing his arms, he drew himself higher.

"I couldn't find a fridge anywhere, no one had a spare. I had to give you a housewarming present, didn't I? It wasn't the most expensive or anything. And I got the one with the ice machine because I like ice cubes in my milk. I assume I'll be spending time here, so I need it." She finally lapsed into silence and then grumbled, "I'm not going to apologize."

Something in her expression spoke to him and he relaxed visibly. "I'll pay you back." So he was willing to accept her gift. Kind of.

"No, you will not," she said sternly. "I understand that you want to do this on your own but you will not rob me of the opportunity to do this one thing."

Tilting his head, he studied her in silence for a long moment. She maintained his gaze, barely restraining the urge to pout. She was not going to back down.

"Okay," he said. "Thanks."

She relaxed visibly. "You're welcome."

Extending his hand to her, he drew her close. "You do realize that ice cubes in milk is gross."

She laughed.

Kissing her, one smack on the lips, he took her hand and towed her along. "Come on. Let's finish up downstairs. Then I'll drive you home in your car and take a bus back."

"You don't have to do that. I can drive myself home." She pulled back, halting his progress. "Stay here. Sleep in your new home."

He kissed her. "I need to know you're safe." Guiding her through the door, he shut the apartment door behind them. "Someday soon maybe you won't need to go home."

She stopped and turned on the stairs. "Like if we were married?" Sophie's heart rate quickened. Was he really talking about marriage?

Cupping her shoulders, he turned her around and nudged her down the stairs. "Hmm."

"Yes, Ayden," she said, turning back to him. She was ready to marry him.

"Really?" He'd brought up the topic yet he seemed completely taken aback by her positive response.

"You've got company," Cora called up to them with a twinkle in her eyes. She was standing at the bottom of the stairs and had clearly heard their discussion.

"Who is it? Everyone I know from Ancora is here," Ayden said.

"The one man looks like a scruffier, angrier Santa Claus but the other two are definitely not elves."

Chapter Fifteen: Who is Guarding your Six

"Wait inside," Ayden said to Sophie. He didn't want her or any of his friends to witness what was to come. "In fact, keep everyone in here."

"No," she replied, trailing him out the large sliding metal door of the workshop. Ayden immediately stepped in front of her.

"Mr. Hagerty."

"Bit of a dump," Hagerty said.

Ayden felt Sophie bristle. Reaching back, he squeezed her fingers, hoping she would understand his meaning. *Be quiet. Don't attract attention.*

"But I see some po-ten-tial, if you know what I mean," Hagerty added. "Be a shame if something happened."

Bull cracked his knuckles loudly. "Ye might need some insurance, jes' to keep the little lady safe."

"Well said, Bull," Hagerty said, nodding his approval at the man's words.

"Why, you—" Sophie began, starting forward. Ayden jerked her back before she could get in front of him, squeezing her fingers. He didn't want to hurt her but he needed her to obey. Better sore fingers than to let Bull get his hands on her.

"That's a good thought, Mr. Hagerty," Ayden said, unflappable.

"You'll be at work Monday," Hagerty said and it was definitely not a question.

"I handed in my notice," Ayden said.

"I assumed that was…a misunderstanding." At Hagerty's words, Strike and Bull moved in closer.

Ayden released Sophie's hand, retrieving and handing her his keys. "Go in and lock the doors. Keep everyone inside," he said quietly.

"No," she whispered.

"Do it now." Even in his quiet tone he knew she could hear the command in his voice. Clearly torn by indecision, she reached for his hand but he batted her away, hissing, "Now." After a word that sounded surprisingly like "harrumph", Sophie backed away. Soon he heard the door open and shut. He didn't hear the lock engage. She really was frustrating in a crisis.

Ayden returned his attention to the three men in front of him. Bull was cracking his knuckles again. "Let's cut to the bottom line," Ayden said.

Hagerty frowned as the conciliatory tone left Ayden's voice. "The bottom line, if you know what I mean, is that you are not free to leave my employ. I did not take you in, give you a job when no one else would, so that you could be bull-headed and strike off on your own," Hagerty said. Slowly, his unintentional use of his henchman's names filtered through and he laughed loudly.

"It'd be a shame if somet'in' happened to the pretty lady," Strike said.

The security light on the front of the building suddenly turned off, plunging the parking lot into darkness.

"Turn it on," Hagerty demanded.

"I didn't turn it off," Ayden replied, bewildered.

Objects clanged and feet shuffled and without warning, the area was flooded with light, revealing Hagerty's naked astonishment. Ayden cast a wary glance to either side, not wanting to let his attention drift too long from the dangerous men in front of him. *What is going on?*

Reggie stepped forward to stand beside Ayden. "What seems to be the problem here?"

"Everything's okay, Reggie. I'll handle this," Ayden said.

"You'd best listen, tiny," Hagerty said, disdain in his voice.

Ayden heard Reggie gulp but he didn't back down even as Bull and Strike snorted their derision at the badge he produced from his back pocket. "I can't do that. Mr. Hagerty, is it? You're trespassing on Mr. Breckinridge's property. I'll have to ask you to leave."

Strike stepped forward, menace in his very posture. "Go 'way, squirt, 'fore you get hurt."

Arms out in a gesture of peace, Ayden stepped ahead of Reggie. "There's no need for this to escalate."

"You are very wrong about that, Reck." Hagerty pointed at Ayden's chest. "Now I'm going to have to hurt you."

Strike and Bull started forward and Ayden took a step away from Reggie to give himself space to move, room to protect himself and Reggie and Sophie and the others. Ram took up a position on his other side, sinking into a defensive posture.

"No one's going to be hurt today." That was Kiran's voice.

"Kir," Ayden began but he was cut off by the sound of the metal double-door opening behind him. He glanced over his shoulder to see everyone, Frank, Sandy, Sophie, Pia, and even Cora and her grand-niece fanning out behind him. They each held something in their hands, a baseball bat, a lug wrench, a hammer. Cora raised her arm, brandishing a cell phone.

"You'd best get out of here, you nasty man. I've called the local sheriff," Cora began. Hagerty snorted. "And the FBI. You're in a lot of trouble. So I suggest you get out of here before they arrive in," she checked her watch, "Exactly seven minutes."

That gave Hagerty pause. "We're not finished, Reck. You won't always have your friends at your back."

"Oh, yes, he will." Sophie stepped forward, raising a rolling pin threateningly. *Where did she get that?* "Don't come back."

The sound of a siren filtered through the air.

"We gotta go, Mr. Hagerty," Bull said, already backing away.

"This isn't over," Hagerty threatened though with less conviction this time.

"Yes. It is," Ram replied.

Hagerty, Bull and Strike piled into a black SUV and drove off in a cloud of dust.

Cora led a cheer. "Hurrah!"

There followed much back slapping until Ayden called a halt to it. "Wait. Just wait." He turned to Reggie. "You called Tristan? So now he'll have more reasons to harass me? Or even arrest me?"

"What do you mean?" Sophie said.

Reggie blushed, ducking his head. "Well, not exactly."

"The sirens?" Ayden asked.

Reggie shrugged. "The, uh, siren is from Sandy's phone."

Sandy held it up and demonstrated. "Tommy keeps reprogramming my ringtones."

"But I really did call the FBI. And asked them the address of the local farm-something-or-other," Cora said.

"Gran," Mary said, appalled.

"Local field office," Reggie said, grinning brightly.

"Ayden?" Sophie said.

"Thank you. All." Ayden hugged Cora and shook Reggie's hand firmly. He then pulled Sophie into his arms. "You scared the life out of me. Why can't you ever do what you're told?"

She stiffened in his arms but he wouldn't let go. He needed reassurance that she was safe.

"Well done, Reggie." Kiran shook his hand.

Ram hugged his brother. "Very brave, lil bro."

Sandy slapped Reggie on the back. "Impressive, deputy."

But all Ayden cared about was Sophie.

"When were you going to tell me that my brother has been harassing you?" Sophie said, trying to wriggle her elbows between them. "You—" Sophie's voice rose in consternation, speech tumbling out until Ayden finally just stopped her words with his mouth. Not a good idea. It might work in the movies, where the female protagonist melted against her man in the moment of crisis. Sophie, however, bit him, not hard enough to draw blood, but hard enough to make him pull away.

"Ow. Hey. What was that for?" Ayden protested.

She simply shoved out of his embrace and walked away, back into the workshop. That couldn't be good.

"You never told her what was going on, did you?" Reggie asked, his intonation carrying an accusation.

"You really do have a rare talent for upsetting her, Reck," Pia said, surprising him. Though there had been no more hostility between them, she didn't usually speak directly to him. "After all the gifts I delivered for you are you going to mess it up now?"

Ayden sighed, brushing his fingers through his hair. "I was just trying to protect her. Why does she think I need to tell her everything?"

Ram, Reggie and Kiran shrugged while Sandy and Frank made comments about incomprehensible things in marriage. Finally, Cora stepped into the circle of men. "A woman wants to know that she owns her man's heart," Cora said as though they were simpletons.

"What does love have to do with information?" Ayden asked.

"Sophie needs to know you trust her, Reck. She needs to know that she is every part of you." Cora jerked her chin toward the upstairs windows of his apartment. He followed her gaze to see Sophie watching him.

Frank placed his hand on Ayden's shoulder. "I don't understand much about my wife except that she's worth a little humility. Is Sophie?"

"Yeah," Ayden responded thoughtfully.

When he entered the apartment, she was standing in the center of the space, her arms crossed over her chest. Her expression was difficult to read because of the shifting emotions in her eyes.

"You're right," Ayden admitted. "I should have told you about Tristan." Her eyes widened in surprise. "I thought I was protecting you." Sophie's arms dropped to her sides and she tilted her head quizzically. She stood there watching him and he absolutely didn't know how to react. "Are you mad at me?" he finally asked. Might as well know.

She hugged herself again. "I can't believe you think you have the right to boss me around."

"What?"

"You said I should do what I'm told."

"I didn't…that's not what I meant. I just meant that you don't listen."

"You are not the boss of me." She stamped her foot like a toddler.

But he knew he daren't laugh. This was serious. "I don't want to boss you around, I want to protect you. But you won't ever do what I ask you to do. I'm learning to share my life with you and to let you do things for me, like buy a refrigerator and invest in my company, but you still question everything I ask you to do," he said. "Sort of like you don't trust me."

Sophie's mouth gaped open and her arms dropped to her sides again. Then her shoulders slumped. "You're right," she whispered. "I didn't realize it. My father controlled every aspect of my childhood even after my mother left him. I guess I'm a little oversensitive to feeling under the dominion of someone else."

"I don't need to dominate you, Sophie. But I would like to be trusted."

"I'm sorry."

"Then come here," he said forcefully.

He watched her struggling with herself; her eyebrows furrowed and her lips thinned. "You come here," she finally said.

He grinned broadly and complied, walking over and pulling her close. "With pleasure."

"Guess I still need to work on that following instructions thing."

"Mmm," he said. "Let's start right now, honey. I want you to kiss me. Immediately."

Chuckling breathily, she wrapped her arms around his neck and he pulled her closer, kissing her.

"I love you," she murmured against his mouth. "I'm so proud of you."

"Marry me, Sophie."

From the doorway came a resounding cheer.

⊂୧୨⊃

Sophie answered the knock on her door. "I'm really busy right now…" She stopped trying to latch her necklace and stared in surprise. "Mom. What are you doing here?"

"I was at the market today and heard Pia Rao talking," she said, fidgeting with the strap on her matching purse.

"That's nice." Sophie walked away to fetch her flowers from the refrigerator. Even with only three months to plan her wedding, things had come together surprisingly well.

"You look lovely, Sophie."

"Thanks." Sophie glanced down at the white dress she was wearing. A simple white chiffon tea-length with a wide silk belt and lacy sleeves, it was pretty. Elegant. She and Pia had picked it out together.

Lucy turned to study the Paetan family photo that hung over Sophie's television. She reached out as if to trace the frame then retracted her hand. "I know your father is a hard man, but he loves you, Sophie."

Her mom was topic-leaping or maybe Sophie's mind was wandering, missing segues. "Mom, it's not about whether he loves me or not. It's the fact that he doesn't behave in love toward me. Look, I don't have time for this conversation today."

"Pia says you're getting married. Today. To Ayden Breckinridge."

Aha. Now it made sense. Her mother was here at her father's behest to talk her out of it. That wasn't happening. "Yes, I am."

"I'd like to come," Lucy said. Then she finally met Sophie's gaze. "I'm asking your permission to attend your wedding."

What? "Why?"

Lucy walked across the room, fingering the afghan, picking up the teak daisy and studying it. "You're my daughter. I love you and I want to know that you'll be happy."

Sophie's heart softened. "I will be happy, Mom. I love Ayden and he loves me."

Lucy stilled, fidgeting with her purse. She sat elegantly in the overstuffed chair and then stood again. "I know that he does. He stood up to your father."

"Yeah." Sophie smiled softly at the memory. "He did."

Lucy's bleak gaze met Sophie's. "There are a lot of mistakes I've made." She sighed heavily. "So many. With you. Viv. Tristan. Your father. I understand why he can't forgive me. But I promise you that I will be a good mother-in-law to Ayden."

"Forgive you? Why would Dad need to forgive you? He's the one who had an affair."

"No, Sophie. It was me. He was such a cold and distant man and I was lonely. He refused to change, refused to forgive me for wanting him to. Still. I couldn't stay in a marriage that I had betrayed. So I divorced him. But he has such traditional values that he never really took it to heart."

Epiphany. "Is that why you feel so obligated to him?"

"Well, of course. I deserve his condemnation. I don't deserve to be forgiven. I am willing to pay for my mistake for the rest of my life."

"Oh, Mom. God forgives us by grace. You can't earn it. It's a gift from God. You are forgivable. You don't deserve to be punished forever for your mistake. It's true that your mistake broke your marriage vows but it doesn't have to haunt the rest of your life, not if you are truly sorry. Let God forgive you, Mom, whether Dad will or not."

Dampness sparkled in Lucy's eyes. "You are the sweetest, wisest daughter a mother could have." Lucy kissed Sophie on the cheek then cleared her throat. "However, this is your day. This is not about me."

A faint flutter of hope tickled Sophie's heart. "Okay, Mom. If you have your car, you can follow me to the church."

Lucy's face broke into a happy smile that lifted the corners of her eyes. "Thank you."

Chapter Sixteen: Matrimonium Interruptus

Ayden applied the last swipe of varnish to the walnut bookcase ordered by Mr. and Mrs. Peach of Silverstone, the first commission he'd received from a complete stranger. Once he delivered the bookcase and the final load of firewood to the local hunters, he would have enough money to buy a sapphire and diamond engagement ring for Sophie. Which kind of ridiculous because they'd been married for three months. But she had admired the white gold ring on the day they'd purchased their wedding bands. Turning away from it, she'd said, "Let's get these," indicating a matching set of blended white and yellow gold bands. "The two metals meld together, becoming one substance. Just like us." Now he was going to complete her set with the sapphire ring. And then he was going to thank her for marrying him, melding her life with his, and making him happier than he had a right to be.

His cell phone rang from his back pocket, pulling his mind out of his memories. Wiping the varnish from his hands on a rag, he answered, taking the now familiar trek up the stairs to their apartment. "Yeah?"

"Mr. Breck-in-ridge?"

"Yeah." Ayden paused on the top step.

"My name is Erich Fravenfeld. I'm a case worker with the State of Ohio. Did you know a Faehr Koenig of Whetsel Alley in Cincinnati?"

"Yes." That short roadway that marked the beginning of his world; burnt-out buildings, shotgun high-rises and the City Gospel Mission guarded the entrance and exit to the tiny neighborhood. Drunks, druggies and gangbangers used it as a shortcut to evade the police.

Silence a moment as if Fravenfeld expected more. When Ayden remained silent, waiting, Fravenfeld coughed and continued. "When was the last time you had contact with Ms. Koenig?"

The last he'd seen Faehr she was lying in bed with a hangover, telling him he'd have to find a new place to stay because she was moving to Cleveland to make a fresh start. Ayden's brows furrowed. "What is this about?"

There was a pause on the other end of the line. "There's been an incident. I'm sorry to inform you that Ms. Koenig has passed."

Passed? "She died?" The air hissed out of Ayden's lungs. *Faehr. Dead?* "What happened? How?"

"She was shot and killed in her apartment. It's seems to have been a drug deal gone awry."

Poor Faehr. He should have been shocked by the news but he wasn't. She just could never extract herself from addiction. Stabbing his fingers into his hair, Ayden sat heavily on the top step. "Is there anyone to take care of funeral arrangements?" Faehr had been estranged from her family since adolescence. Had things changed for her?

"Her body was interred three weeks ago."

"Three weeks?" Faehr was gone. *Lord, did she ever find peace?* "Why are you contacting me now, after the fact?"

"There's a…complication. I understand that you live in the area. Could you come into Cincinnati and meet with me?"

Ayden opened the door to the apartment then paused. "Why? What's going on?"

"I think it would be better if we spoke in person. Can you come to the Community Learning Center on Montgomery Road? As soon as possible would be best."

"I don't understand. If Faehr is dead and buried, what do you want from me?"

"Faehr left a letter with me, sort of a last will and testament. It instructs me to contact you." Fravenfeld's voice changed. "Which was difficult, I must say. Will you come?"

Faehr had been his friend when he'd had no other. They'd scraped and clawed their way through the streets of Over-the-Rhine, determined to survive, escape. He had. But what had happened to Faehr? "Yes. Yes, I'll come. Can you tell me more?"

"I'll share what I know when you arrive. I'll need you to bring some identification."

Ayden checked his watch. It was only just past noon. "I can be there in forty minutes." He shut the apartment door again.

"That would be best."

Ayden sent a text message to Sophie to let her know that he was going into Cincinnati because she tended to get annoyed when he disappeared for hours at a time without telling her where he'd gone. *Go figure.* Then he rolled his bike out into the rain. It seemed fitting, cloudy to commemorate his return to the dark days of his past.

He made it as far as Bach-Buxton Road before the flashing lights of a brown and white Clermont County Sheriff's car intruded on his journey. He dutifully pulled to the shoulder beneath a stand of trees and removed his helmet. Watching in his side-view mirror, Ayden could see Tristan finishing his coffee before stepping out into the rain, pulling on a brown rain slicker and sauntering over.

"Goin' mighty fast, weren't you, lad?"

"I was beginning to think you'd lost interest in me, sheriff. I haven't been pulled over in three weeks," Ayden said, shaking water off his sunglasses.

Tristan's eyes lasered in. "Watch your tone." He pulled out his ticket book. "Licence and registration."

Retrieving his wallet from his back pocket, Ayden handed over the well-thumbed documents.

"Nasty day to be headin' into the city," Tristan said.

"I have some business to attend to."

"Nothin' to do with drugs, I hope."

The funny thing was, from the tone in his voice, it sounded like it was Tristan's dearest wish that Ayden would return to a life of crime. *I suppose it is.*

"Sophie has been missing family dinners."

"Is that right? We haven't really talked about it."

"Maybe you should." Tristan handed back the documents and tore the ticket out of the book. "Our granddaddy built this town."

"He was a pharmacist, wasn't he?"

"Created a new drug then built the factory to supply it. Gave this town a stable source of jobs."

"That's great. Am I free to go?"

Tristan leaned menacingly into Ayden's face. "You'd best show a little more respect."

"Oh," Ayden replied. "I have a great deal of respect for my wife."

"Your what?"

Ayden started the engine and roared away. He could see Tristan's mouth gaping wide in the reflection from his mirror. So Sophie hadn't told her family about their marriage. And neither had Lucy. Now that was interesting.

Through Newton, Madison, and Norwood, Ayden took the old highways. With less traffic, he was able to let his mind wander over the past. Faehr. His best friend. They had dumpster-dived for food as preschoolers, dodged the gangbangers and cops to survive. Together, they'd perfected the art of shoplifting, busking, bullying and avoiding school. Together, they'd sold drugs but only Faehr had succumbed to their lure.

Arriving at the Cincinnati CLC, Ayden parked his bike. Though he was not at all certain that he was ready to revisit his past, he entered the building. With its grey walls and linear architecture, it was more reminiscent of a prison than a place of learning and care.

Ayden introduced himself to the receptionist who called Fravenfeld down to meet him. Clad in black jeans and a navy sport coat, the man was short, stocky and wholly blonde.

He extended his hand. "Mr. Breckinridge. Thank you for coming."

"Call me Reck."

"Let's speak in my office. Follow me."

They took the elevator up to the third floor and then walked down a long hallway past a series of offices occupied by individuals who all seemed to be in the midst of an irritating phone call.

"Right in here." Fravenfeld motioned into an office with beige walls, brown carpet and a taupe metal desk.

"Tell me what's going on," Ayden said, impatient to discover the purpose of this mysterious meeting.

Fravenfeld sat behind the desk. "Before we begin, I need to collect some information from you."

"Such as?" Ayden sat in one of the two green Hospitality chairs across from Fravenfeld.

"Where did you meet Faehr Koenig?"

Ayden sighed. *What the hay.* "We grew up in the same neighborhood."

"What kind of a relationship did you have?"

What was their relationship, friends, occasional lovers, partners in crime? "Look, I'm not sure why that's any of your business."

Fravenfeld studied him a moment and then flipped the file closed. "You have a criminal record."

"Yeah. That's no secret." Ayden's ire was rising.

"My understanding from your former parole officer and a local minister is that you had a…" he paused a moment, "life-changing experience shortly after prison."

"Yeah." Being inside a state building was making Ayden feel petulant. Nope, downright surly. What right did this man have to question him?

"You're a carpenter?"

"Yeah."

"Are you able to support yourself at that?"

"I do okay."

"It can take quite a while to build up a private business to the point of profit."

"What's your point?"

"Can you support yourself financially?"

"Yeah. I work part-time cleaning up around a lumber yard to make up the difference for now. Just started a couple weeks ago."

"Are you involved romantically?"

"I'm having a hard time understanding why this is your business." Ayden was really annoyed now. Sophie had nothing to do with Over-the-Rhine or anything in his past.

"Bear with me, please," Fravenfeld said.

Gritting his teeth over his instinctive negative response to being questioned, he replied, "I got married three months ago."

"Married?" Fravenfeld frowned.

"Yes." Holding up his left hand, he thumbed his shiny, new ring.

"To Sophie Paetan?"

Ayden's brow furrowed. "How did you know that?"

"The minister." Fravenfeld checked the file again. "Kiran Rao." He struggled over the pronunciation of the Indian name. "He spoke very highly of you."

"That's good," he said noncommittally. Kiran? What did Kiran have to do with Faehr? What was he doing discussing Sophie with strangers?

"We just want to be sure." Fravenfeld ripped a sheet of paper from a notepad and wrote something down on it. "This is where Ms. Koenig's possessions are being held." He fished another sheet of paper from his desk. "You may want this as well." Fravenfeld stood and held out his hand. "Call if you have any further questions. I'll need to meet with you before you return home."

Studying the pages, a photocopy of Faehr's letter and a requisition for medical tests, Ayden's last hope evaporated. What would this mean to Sophie?

Fravenfeld paused a moment, fidgeting with the pages on his desk. "We have resources to help you cope."

Ayden's stomach caved. "Am I the only one?" he asked.

"I'm sorry. My understanding is that there is no one else. Only you."

Ayden nodded slowly. Of course. *Lord, why does it have to be so hard?*

CRSO

"Ayden, have you seen my keys?" Sophie asked as she slipped her feet into her black pumps.

"Huh?"

"My keys?" She stood, pacing to the sofa to check beneath the cushions.

"Yeah."

"Ayden. What's wrong?" She looked beneath the laptop on the dining table, rifled through the pile of bills she'd been perusing earlier, and then turned over the crystal bowl in the center, spilling out the potpourri inside. Nothing. "You've been walking around like a zombie all evening."

"There's, uh, something I need to talk to you about."

She waited but he continued to stare at her shoes. "Well? What?"

He glanced at her face then turned to open the refrigerator, the door creating a barrier between them. He ducked inside. "I, uh, drove into Cincinnati today."

"I know. Thanks for letting me know." She scooped the dried rose petals back into the bowl and then followed him into the kitchen. "Did you have a delivery or something?"

"No."

She waited but he just stood there studying the interior of the fridge. Skirting the door, she ducked down beside him.

"What do you want in here? Milk? I bought chocolate syrup yesterday. It's in the cupboard."

He grabbed the milk jug and then froze in surprise to find her standing beside him. Rolling her eyes, she backed away, taking a glass and the syrup from the cupboard and setting them on the counter side by side. Setting the milk on the counter, he bracketed it with his hands, leaning down as if he was studying the interior of the glass.

"Would you just tell me what's going on," she said, exasperated.

"Are you sure I have to?" Raising his eyes, he met her gaze bleakly. He obviously saw her blood pressure rising because he quickly said, "Never mind. You told me before. Rule number two." He sighed deeply. "I met with a social worker."

"A social worker? Why?" she said.

He sighed.

"And?"

He brushed his hands roughly over his face. "Faehr was his…" He stopped. "Is it called a patient or a client or what?"

Her eyebrows winged. He was officially driving her crazy today. "Who is Faehr?"

"Oh. Uh. Faehr Koenig. We grew up together and, you know, hooked up from time to time."

"Hooked up," she repeated. That better not mean what she thought it did. "So something happened to Faehr?"

"Yeah. She was shot."

Immediately contrite, Sophie said, "Oh, Ayden. I'm sorry. Was she…was she someone special?"

"I don't know. Yes?" He raised his brows in question.

"She was or she wasn't, Ayden." Counting to ten in her head, trying to find the patience Ayden obviously needed from her, she endeavored to move the conversation forward. "What did this social worker have to do with Faehr?"

"I guess, she, uh…Faehr, that is…the social worker was a man…Fravenfeld…odd name."

"Ayden." She reprimanded him then softened her tone. "What did the man want?"

Ayden paced away then turned back. "Faehr left a letter with this guy, Fravenfeld. There's, uh, something she left me…that affects you and me."

Sophie blanched. "Like a disease?"

"No." He brushed his hands over his face. "Like a son."

"What?" Her eyes widened in astonishment.

"I have a son." He leaned back on his elbows on the counter.

"How? When?" She gulped. Had he cheated on her?

"No." Every now and then it was like he could read her thoughts. "I didn't cheat on you. It happened years ago. The kid is four or five."

"You have a child you just forgot to tell me about?"

He straightened. "I didn't know. She never told me."

"Why would she keep it a secret?"

"To protect him? I don't know." He hung his head.

And then a terrible thought occurred to her. "Are you in love with this Faehr?"

"She's dead."

"Oh." Sophie felt a confusing blend of remorse and relief at that.

"And no, I don't love her. I never loved her, not like that. We did, uh, spend time together."

"You slept with her." *Please deny it.*

He nodded miserably. "It must have happened just after I got parole because that's the last time I, uh, saw her. But she's dead now, killed in some drug-related incident they think. The kid's in a foster home."

"Are you…are you sure he's yours?"

Defeat moulded his posture. "Yes. No. I don't know. She said he was…in the letter. I, uh, took a paternity test but the results won't be in for several days. Fravenfeld said he'd try to hurry it up."

She glanced at her watch. "I have to go."

The color drained from his face. "Of course."

"My mother—"

"Don't." He held up his hand. "Don't bother to explain." He walked across the room, slumping down on the sofa.

"Are you okay?" she asked.

He nodded, not meeting her gaze. The door clicked shut. Ayden's chest was tight, squeezing his heart. His lungs wouldn't expand to draw in air. Panic fluttered through his limbs. A loud sound escaped, rasping past his vocal chords. When the second spasm squeezed his chest, he realized that he was crying, and not just a gentle weeping, but gut-wrenching sobs. He fell to his knees beside the coffee table, burying his head in his arms.

"Oh, God. Why? Why now? Why give me the hope of a normal life if you were just going to snatch it away? Oh, God." *Oh, God. Oh, God. Oh, God.*

"Ayden?" He heard her voice but he wasn't sure if he only imagined it. She'd left, hadn't she? His wife had walked away once she'd heard the depths of his youthful depravity. "Ayden." Her arms wrapped around him warm and solid. Was he hallucinating, creating a world where he could find comfort? She kissed him on the head. This was too real, too sensual to be a hallucination. His woman, the love of his life, his wife, was here. Now. "Oh, Ayden. Don't cry, baby. It'll be okay. We'll figure it out. I'll call my mother and tell her we'll have to postpone supper. I'll stay here with you. Don't cry."

He couldn't catch his breath so he couldn't reply. Turning, he clutched at her, absorbing her warmth, her presence. She held onto him just as tightly.

"I, uh, thought you'd left me." His voice was hoarse from all the crying.

"Ayden, it's the second Thursday of the month. I was going to my mother's for supper."

He nodded because a fresh flood of tears had started. He hadn't cried since he was a child, not even when the landlord had beaten him and locked him in a closet all night, not even when he got word that Cassie had overdosed. But now, the thought of losing Sophie because of a mistake from his past had overwhelmed him and here he was squeezing her close, crying like a baby.

He wondered for a moment if his kid had cried when they told him Faehr was dead.

"Ayden?"

"I'm okay."

"Let me call my mother and then we can talk about this some more."

"Yeah. Good." While she used the phone, he washed his face, sticking his head under the cold water tap, hoping the temperature would clear his mind. When he exited the washroom, she was in the kitchen stirring chocolate syrup into a glass of milk which she offered him. He accepted it, asking, "How do you, uh, feel about this?"

"I don't know, to be honest. How do you feel?"

"Depressed. I've been…Soph, the past three months have been the happiest of my life. I'm sorry I screwed it up."

"This doesn't have to mean that we'll never be happy again."

"Doesn't it? I grew up without a father, Soph. I swore I would never do that to another boy. But I did. I," he gulped, "used her when I needed comfort…without even considering the consequences."

She brushed his wet hair back from his face, petting his head sweetly. "You were young. You didn't know."

He gazed over her head at their wedding picture which hung in place of pride above the television. Sophie, in her lacy white dress, stood beside him, clutching his hand, looking at him like he was the best thing in the world. He would have wall-papered the place in it if he could have. "Don't kid yourself, I knew. I did wrong so often that my conscience stopped working but that's no excuse. I knew what we were doing was wrong. I'm sorry."

"Have you met him, your son?"

"Yeah. He's little."

She chortled, wiping a tear from her eye. "I guess he would be. Can I meet him?"

"Yeah. I'll, uh, arrange it."

"Okay." Wrapping her arms around him, she kissed him on the cheek and then nestled her head against his shoulder. "It'll be okay."

"How is this okay?"

She didn't respond but what really was there to say?

Chapter Seventeen: Impetuosity

Ascending the front steps of Mr. and Mrs. Black's tan Craftsman's bungalow in Pleasant Ridge, Cincinnati, Sophie slipped her hand into Ayden's to find it sweaty and trembling. She wanted to offer him reassurance but was too nervous to try. He clenched his other fist, lifting it to knock on the mauve door, turning to her before he connected. "I love you."

"I love you, too. It'll be okay."

He nodded, rapping briskly on the door. Shoving his hands in his back pockets, he rocked back on his heels. Sophie pulled his right hand out and wrapped her fingers back around it.

A silver-haired man who was leaning on a cane opened the door. Dodging between the cane and the man's left leg, a little boy emerged. "There's nuffin' good on TV. I'm goin' outside," he said. He was small for a five-year-old, wiry and underfed with a muffin-top of curly auburn hair. His deep blue eyes shone from his dirty face. Darting beyond Mr. Black's reach, the boy skidded to a halt in front of Sophie. "Who are you?"

"I'm Sophie. What's your name?" she said.

"Owen Koenig." He gestured to Ayden. "That guy's my dad, I guess. I never knowed it but my mama told him so he comed t' see me here where I gotta stay wif this guy." He gestured vaguely at Mr. Black.

"Oh," she said stupidly, slanting a look at Ayden. He looked vaguely green, that sickly shade of chartreuse that usually meant someone was about to heave.

"Yeah. My mama got deaded and my nana don't wanna keep me so that guy," he gestured vaguely at Mr. Black, "taked me here." Owen tilted his head and put his hands on his hips. "You live here?"

"No. I, uh, don't."

"Oh." He looked disappointed. "You know that guy?" He gestured vaguely at Ayden.

Sophie nodded.

"Like he's your boyfriend guy? My mama gots guys like what come and get on her bed and then I gotta go watch TV cause they…" Moving more quickly than his appearance suggested possible, Mr. Black covered Owen's mouth with his hand, the last few words coming out muffled.

"Owen, you can't say things like that to a lady," Mr. Black admonished him.

Sophie glanced aside at Ayden. Oh, yeah, he definitely looked ready to vomit.

Peeling Mr. Black's hand from his face, Owen looked up at Sophie. "*You* take me outside?"

"Why don't you go have a snack?" Mr. Black said but it sounded like more of a plea than a suggestion.

"I don't need another apple. Don't you gots any good snacks?" Owen's mouth twisted in disgust.

"Owen," Mr. Black reprimanded him. "Use your manners."

Owen simply crossed his arms over his chest and stuck out his chin, saying, "I'm only sayin' the truf. You gotta tell the truf y'know," before storming back into the house.

As though nothing unusual had happened, Mr. Black extended his hand to Ayden. "Good to see you again, Mr. Breckinridge."

"Thanks." Ayden shook his hand. "This is my wife, Sophie."

"Pleased to meet you. Come in. Mrs. Black made tea."

Sophie could hear thumps and exclamations coming from other parts of the house as Mr. Black led them down the hallway past a living room decorated in mid-seventies greens to the bright eighties kitchen at the back of the bungalow.

A woman in her fifties with hair dyed a hickory brown, welcomed them. "Hello. Hello. Come in. Come in. Owen!" she hollered. "Stop thumping around. And wash your face."

"I jus' playin' the checkers like you said," he hollered back.

"Silas, go and check on him," she said in that same enthusiastic manner. Mr. Black lumbered off, the tap of his cane helping Sophie track his progress. It sounded to her like Owen was long gone by the time he reached the checkers.

"I take it you received the results of your test?" Mrs. Black asked, moving objects around the kitchen in a pattern that seemed pointless to Sophie.

"Yes," Ayden said. His skin still held a greenish cast. "99.67 % certainty."

"Have you made a decision as to what you want to do with him?" Mrs. Black said.

A clatter sounded followed by a gruff exclamation. "I dunno," Owen hollered.

"Mrs. Black?" Sophie said. "Could I go and see him?"

"Who, dear?" she said, pouring out four cups of tea.

Sophie glanced at Ayden who looked faintly ill and completely distracted. "Owen," she said. Wasn't it obvious?

"No need to bother. Silas will bring him in." Mrs. Black moved to the doorway. "Silas! Make sure he washes his face, it's time for tea!"

Ayden flinched and Sophie had an almost irresistible urge to giggle. She slipped her hand onto his leg, squeezing once. Flinching again, he glanced at her and some of the green faded from his pallor.

Owen appeared at the door to the kitchen, skidding to a halt. His wet bangs were testimony to Mr. Black's attempts to wash the dirt off his face. "You gonna make me eat a apple again?"

"You may have one cookie," Mrs. Black said. "Sit down at the table."

Mr. Black stumped into the room, sweating profusely and breathing laboriously. He dropped heavily into a chair.

Owen rifled through the cookies, spilling them onto the table until he found some with chocolate. He snatched two and ran.

"Owen!" Mrs. Black yelled after him, bustling out of the kitchen in his wake. After much fuss, most of which Sophie heard in muffled shouts, Mrs. Black returned, limping slightly with two half-eaten cookies in her hand, one with the chocolate licked off. "I sent him to his room. I understand you have some difficult decisions to make, Mr. Breckinridge. Consider carefully." Setting the half-eaten cookies beside the sink, Mrs. Black took a jelly cookie, consuming it in two bites then taking another. "Owen is a child who needs an experienced caregiver, someone to provide structure and clear expectations. He has many needs with his delays in enunciation and grammar. We've committed to taking him to speech therapy twice a week and to see the child psychiatrist at the hospital. I used to be a volunteer reader at the local school when our children were small so I know all about supporting literacy. We can provide what's best for Owen. He'll settle in here."

Now Sophie felt ill. This couldn't possibly be the best place for that little boy.

Ayden stood abruptly. "We gotta go." He reached down and grabbed Sophie's hand. "Let's go."

"Call if you would like to visit again," Mrs. Black said. "Owen! Say good-bye."

"Why I gotta say that?"

"To be polite!" Mrs. Black shouted back.

"Bye!" he yelled.

CRSO

Ayden and Sophie lay side by side on top of the antique Log Cabin quilt on their bed, not touching, not speaking. In fact, they hadn't spoken a word since leaving the Blacks'. Ayden finally broke the silence. "Are you angry with me?"

"Of course not." Sophie curled onto her side away from him.

"You know if I tell the tiniest fib or leave out the smallest detail, no matter how insignificant, you rip me to shreds yet you're allowed to lie your face off." The bed moved as he rolled to sit on the edge, positioning his back to her.

"Fine," she snapped, leaping out of bed and whipping around to face his back. "I cannot believe you were so stupid. How could you have unprotected sex? How could you have sex with a drug addict? Huh? It was such high risk behavior."

"High risk behavior." Spinning to face her, he replied, mocking her voice and manner. "Fancy words for..." Then he used a foul word to describe the act of making love.

Rigid with indignation, she said, "If you say that word to me ever again, I will slap your face off."

Clenching his fists, he automatically crouched defensively and then shook it off. Turning to the wall nearest him, he slapped his palms against it, the sharp smack loud in the room. Facing her, the bed still between them, he said, "No hitting. You know that." The intensity in his voice eased, though not in gentleness, more like earnest desperation. "I need you not to hit."

The raw pain in his eyes touched her more than his words, more than the events of the day. "It's okay, Ayden. I'm sorry for threatening you. I won't hit." She knew that he still feared reacting without thought and hurting her.

"Thank you." His voice rasped with the tight control he was keeping on his emotions. He made no move to approach her and she realized that he was still so upset that he didn't trust himself to be gentle, which meant that he was more upset by the encounter at the foster home than she'd realized. The realization made it easier to express her feelings.

Sighing sadly, she said, "I guess it doesn't help for me to pretend I feel the way I *think* I should rather than the way I actually *do*."

"Uh uh. It's not like I can't tell when you're mad at me. I wish you'd just tell me and put me out of my misery. It's not like it's a secret."

Emotion hit her in a wave, tears welling in her eyes. Yet the sound she made was more of a laugh, a soggy, drizzling laugh. "Yeah. I'm not so good at hiding my feelings, not from you." Her smile dropped away. Tears coursed down her cheeks as her lips trembled in her struggle for control.

Ayden rounded the bed, reaching for her then drawing back, shoving his hands into his hair since he wasn't wearing any pockets. "You never have to hide from me, baby."

"I wish you hadn't had sex...before me," she said wretchedly.

"I'm really sorry." There was agony and regret in his voice.

Releasing her breath on a sob, she flung herself against him. His arms came around her to draw her closer than a whisper, gripping her tightly to his body as he let her sob out her grief, perhaps hoping it would clean out some of his as well. After her crying faded into occasional shuddering breaths, she remained leaning against him, her cheek resting against his bare chest, against the smooth skin over solid muscle there; the muscles that had been toned by years of violence and, more recently, by good hard physical labor. His body was powerful; she knew this even as he held her tenderly, his lips occasionally brushing her neck, her shoulder, her temple.

She trailed her fingers along his shoulder and down his arm, pausing to caress his forearm over his tattoo. "Why a dragon?"

His head dipped toward her ear. "One day when I was a kid, I found this stack of comic books in the trash behind our apartment building. One was about this dragon that attacked a village, carrying off the wealth of the people. The whole countryside feared that dragon. That's what I wanted, to be feared. One of my mom's regulars around that time had a dojo where he taught martial arts. I begged him to teach me and he did. Even after he stopped using my mom, he still let me hang out and take classes. When I got my brown belt, he paid for me to get the tattoo."

"How old were you?"

"Fifteen."

"You know, in Chinese culture, dragons symbolize power, strength, even good luck." She stroked his arm, tracing the dragon's body with her fingertips.

"I love you," he murmured, his breath fanning her hair. "You mean everything to me. You're my good luck. God is my strength and power."

"I love you." She kissed his chest.

Tears welled in his eyes and fell down his cheeks. "Sorry," he muttered.

She chortled in an expression of relief, their argument fading like mist. "At least I'm not the only one blubbering."

"I don't blubber," he said indignantly but she felt him smile.

They were going to be okay. *Thank you, Lord.*

Chapter Eighteen: Best Interests

Sophie lay in bed staring at the ceiling while Ayden showered. He was due to meet Mr. Fravenfeld at 7:30 am so that they could go over to the Black's and pick up Owen. This would be Ayden's third visit with the social worker as he tried to decide what was in Owen's best interests.

The Blacks seemed to feel that Owen should remain with them, that they had the experience to deal with the issues arising from Owen's early childhood. Mrs. Black was able to rhyme off the long list of diseases and disorders that resulted from poverty, abuse and neglect. She knew all the isms and disorders.

Ayden wavered because, while he didn't feel he had any skills to be a parent, particularly not to such a troubled child, he resisted the idea of passing on his responsibilities to others. The thought of leaving the little boy with the Blacks made Sophie's stomach hurt. But Owen wasn't her son.

Ayden's cell phone rang and Sophie picked it up from the bedside table. "Hello?"

"Mrs. Breckinridge? It's Erich Fravenfeld."

Sophie's tummy fluttered. Her married name was still so new. "Yes?"

"Something's come up and I'm not going to be able to meet Reck at the Black's."

"Okay. I can let him know. Is it okay if he still goes?"

"Of course. He is the boy's biological father. He has open access unless he chooses to abdicate his parental rights."

"Why would he do that?"

"If he chooses to leave Owen in the foster care system."

"So he would have to permanently make Owen not his son or else he needs to take him home?"

"Exactly. I understand he's struggling with the decision."

"Yes. You could say that. Owen is just so needy with his speech delays, his attachment issues, behavioral issues and academic delay..." Her voice trailed off. Owen would need therapies of all kinds for years to come.

"What is your opinion?"

"I don't really think I can have one."

"Is that how your husband feels?"

Was that how he felt? "I don't know. We haven't discussed it."

Fravenfeld made an impatient sound. "You are Reck's wife and Owen's stepmother. That gives you the right to an opinion."

"How difficult would it be if I decided to adopt Owen?"

"You are married to his father." Fravenfeld's voice quickened. "It would be quite simple with Reck's agreement. But, Sophie, it would be best if you decided quickly. Owen needs certainty. He's been cast adrift all his life, moving from place to place with his mother, different men in and out of his home. Now, he's at the Blacks but he doesn't know where he's going to be tomorrow. He knows that Reck is his father but really has no idea what that means."

"I understand. I'll speak with Ayden today."

"That would be best. I must go."

"Thank you, Erich."

"You're welcome."

Ayden emerged from the washroom in a cloud of steam. "Hey, sleeping beauty. Who was on the phone?"

"Erich Fravenfeld."

His outlook fell. "More pressure to decide?"

"Yes. You could say that. Ayden? Do you think I should have an opinion about what to do with Owen?"

"Of course. Why wouldn't you?" He looked plainly confused by the question. "I've been kind of surprised that you haven't wanted to talk about it."

"I thought...well, I thought I shouldn't because he's not mine."

"But I'm yours, right?"

Her face softened and her insides went all gooey. "Yes."

"Well, then, so is he."

She felt better. "Let's talk tonight. The longer we wait, the harder this is for Owen."

"Agreed." He eased her back into bed, pulling the blankets up to her chin. "Go back to sleep. I'll take him to a park and then out to breakfast. The Blacks have some medical appointment this morning but they expect to be back by noon or so."

"Love you."

He kissed her again. "I love you, too."

ⱭⱭ

Sometime later, the telephone woke Sophie from a sound sleep. "Hello?" she said blearily.

"Soph. Sorry."

She brushed the sleep from her eyes, sitting up. "Ayden?"

"I have a problem. They told me I could have the time off but now they've called me in to work and I have Owen with me. The Blacks won't be home for another few hours." Ayden spoke quickly, the words coming out in a jumble.

"I never said I wouldn't help. Is that what you think?" she said, sitting up in bed. "That you have to do this alone?"

"Yeah. No. I know it's not what you were planning for the day but can you take him?"

"Yes. Of course." She checked the clock. "Can you bring him home?"

Silence for a moment. "I've only got the Suzuki and, frankly, I don't trust him on it. We walked to a park," he said grimly. "But I can have him back to the Black's and meet you there."

"I'll come get him. I can be there in an hour."

"Half an hour?" Ayden sighed. "Or I'll be late."

"No problem. I think I'll bring him back here, though, if that's okay. I think it'll be easier."

"Sure. Yes. Let the Blacks know. Thanks, sweetheart, you're a life saver."

She smiled at his enthusiasm. "Just like the candy. See you soon."

Sophie broke speed records showering, dressing and driving to the Black's. Ayden essentially tossed Owen, his booster seat, and a backpack into the rear of the car and then roared off on his bike.

Sophie walked around to buckle Owen in properly. "Good morning. How are you?"

"Hungry. That guy said he got no time and you can give me breakfast. You give me breakfast?" Owen asked. He seemed subdued, the usual rapid-fire delivery he'd used when she'd first met him had slowed and he looked worried.

"Why don't we go out to a restaurant? Do you like pancakes?"

His eyes brightened a little. "Yeah. I like blueberry jam." Then his eyes fell. "That guy done wif me?"

"Pardon?" Sophie said. She had noticed the immaturity in Owen's speech and grammar that Mrs. Black attributed to the "environmental neglect inherent in his impoverished and underprivileged situation". Sophie found it rather charming even though she couldn't always understand him.

Owen looked into her face, searching for something. "He gonna come back?"

"Oh, yes, Owen. Ayden's coming back. He was called into work so he asked me to spend the day with you."

"You tell the truf?" he asked, his brow furrowed.

"Yes. He is definitely coming back."

Owen's expression brightened though she thought his eyes still carried the darkness of doubt. Reaching in, she pulled the seatbelt out to draw it around him. Owen halted her hand. "I no need that."

"Pardon?"

"I no need that belt. This seat is dumb." His lower lip looked as droopy as a deflated balloon.

"It's the law, Owen. Boys as old as eight years old have to sit in a booster seat and even grown-ups have to wear a seatbelt."

"Why?"

"It will keep you safe."

He huffed but didn't interfere again when she pulled the belt across his chest and fastened it.

Pulling into the parking lot of Dagwood's Finest in Ancora, Sophie walked around to get Owen. But by the time she reached his door, he'd already unbuckled himself and was halfway across the sidewalk.

"Owen, wait, please. Hold my hand." Sophie jogged the few steps to catch up with him, her arm extended.

He stopped, looking at her hand in disgust. "Why you wanna hold hands?"

"To keep us together," she replied, sensing that any reference to him as young or a need for compliance would not be welcome.

Finally, he shrugged and grabbed her sleeve, towing her toward the door of the restaurant. As she opened it, he darted through and ran down the main aisle, surveying each booth until he found one to his satisfaction. He plopped himself down in it. Sophie sat beside him, not at all willing to be all the way across a table from him if he decided it was time to depart.

"Hey, Sophie." Essie Taylor greeted her as she placed two menus on the table. "Who's this little guy?"

"This is my friend, Owen. Owen, this is Miss Taylor," Sophie said.

"Call me Essie," she said, winking at Owen. He watched her from saucer-shaped eyes. "What'll ye have?"

"Pancakes, I think. And do you have blueberry syrup?" Sophie said.

"Why, yes, we do. Along with Canadian maple," Essie said. "Coffee?"

"Yes, please," Sophie said. "And two milks. I'll have ice in mine."

"Milk?" Owen finally spoke up, his intonation making his meaning clear. "I don't do milk."

"We've got chocolate milk," Essie said persuasively, speaking directly to him.

"Yeah. Okay," Owen said, shifting closer to Sophie.

"Thanks." As Essie walked toward the kitchen to place their order with the cook, Sophie turned her attention to Owen. "So do you want to know what we're going to do today?"

"Yeah. Okay," Owen said, shifting onto his knees facing her.

He had beautiful eyes, a bright blue. In contrast to his olive complexion and auburn curls, they seemed to shine from his face. "After breakfast, we can go to my house and color some pictures or play a game and then we'll go to my work in the city." It didn't make a lot of sense to drive home then back to Cincinnati but Sophie was completely uncertain what to do with Owen. At least at home she knew she had toys to amuse him. And it was only a twenty minute drive back to the library.

"What you do there, in a city?"

"I work in a library."

"Whatsa libaree?"

Surprised, Sophie said, "It's a place with lots of books and people come and borrow the books so they can read them."

Essie arrived with the pancakes. Owen grabbed for the mini syrup pitcher and upended it over his plate. Sophie tipped it back before the entire contents had puddled over the edges of the plate.

"Why you gotta do that?" Owen slapped the table with his hand.

"Watch," Sophie said, pointing to the puddle of syrup on his plate. "If we add any more blueberry syrup, it will overflow and make a mess."

"I like blueberries," he insisted, pursing his lips in determination.

"Good. But if you eat all this syrup, you will feel sick to your stomach." She indicated the remaining syrup in the pitcher. "Eat what you have and if you need more syrup later, you can have some."

"O~kay," he said, the word drawn out on a sigh. He grabbed his fork and then paused. "You gonna do the prayin' fing like my guy?"

She smiled gently. Ayden was teaching Owen to ask the blessing before meals. *Awesome.* "Yes, please. Do you know any words?"

"Nah. Just thankya, thankya, thankya," he said, shaking his head in bewilderment, his curls flapping around his face.

"How about this one, God is great..." She repeated the grace she'd learned from her mother as a small child. "Amen. You can learn those words, can't you?"

"Yeah. I'm not dumb." He repeated it rapidly. And flawlessly.

"That's really good, Owen. You have a good memory."

He shrugged one shoulder and ducked his head.

Sophie brushed her fingers through his unkempt curls. "I mean it, Owen. That's smart to be able to learn something so fast."

Looking up at her, his eyes wide in wonder, he said, "You think I'm a smart guy?"

"Yes, I do."

"Hmm," he said in that same noncommittal way that Ayden had.

Sophie hugged Owen around the shoulders and then started to eat.

"These is good," he murmured, his mouth stuffed full.

Sophie ignored the breech in etiquette for the moment, instead, agreeing. The second Owen finished eating he slithered to the floor and took off toward the door. She dropped a twenty on the table and chased him out, arriving at the car in tandem with him, much to her relief.

Back at the apartment, Sophie retrieved a couple of kids' board games from the closet, games she used with her Sunday school class. When she returned to the living room, Owen had emptied his backpack on the floor and was playing with four wooden cars on the coffee table.

She picked one up and examined it, noticing that each one had been carved in the shape of a well-known sports car, a Ferrari, a Lamborghini, and a couple others she didn't know.

"Where did you get these, Owen? They are really cool."

"My guy, he maked 'em for me in a workshop. He telled me he like cars too." Owen met her gaze. "He grumpy all a time but he make good cars."

"Wow," she said. Ayden had taken the time to build these for his son. A lump formed in Sophie's throat. *His son.* There would be no fresh start for Ayden. His past would always be there with him. Could he deal with that? Could she?

"You wanna play?" Owen asked shyly.

"Absolutely," she said, sitting cross-legged across the coffee table from him. "Can I have the yellow one?"

"Uh huh. That one a Porshy."

"Hey, wait. I have some blocks we could use to build bridges and towers and stuff," she said enthusiastically, rising to retrieve them.

They'd played for an hour when Sophie realized that she needed to get ready or she'd be late for story hour. Packing up the backpack, she washed Owen's hands and face, much to his chagrin, and then they drove back into Cincinnati to the Cin-Ham.

Head down, Owen followed the footprint tiles on the floor which led to the children's section. Then he raised his eyes. "Wow!" His face shone with wonder, his arms stretched out as if he was trying to embrace the shelves and shelves of books.

"You know all these stories?" he said, clearly awed.

"Not all of them," she admitted. "Do you like books?"

"I like stories," he said.

"Maybe before we leave, we can borrow some for you to take home."

"Forever?"

"No, not forever, for three weeks," she said, smiling.

"Okay."

Reaching down, she took his hand and led him to her office. When he spotted the dragon's castle, he halted, wonder printed anew on his face.

"You live here?" he asked breathlessly.

"No. You've been to my home, Owen. Remember?"

"There's a dragon. My guy gots a dragon," he said, ignoring her words.

Ayden's dragon of power, the marauder.

"An' there's a horse guy."

"A knight."

Furrowing his brow, Owen turned to her. "Not nighttime."

"A knight." She grabbed a piece of paper and a pencil from her desk and wrote the word for him.

He glanced at it and then said, "I wanna live here."

Chuckling, Sophie gathered what she needed for story hour. She gave Owen little jobs to do and he seemed happy to help. During the first story, he couldn't seem to sit still, roaming throughout the room, touching and picking up everything his hands alighted on.

On the spur of the moment, Sophie grabbed a book about knights and dragons and started to read. Transfixed, Owen paced over, stepping between children, even pushing one boy's head out of his way, until he was sitting right in front of the open pages of the book. The children grumbled but eventually settled to the story.

"…the end," Sophie said, shutting the knight book.

"No," Owen said. "Read more."

"I will," Sophie said. "This book is by a Canadian author and is about an aardvark and all his friends…"

"No." Owen reached up and shoved the book aside. "Read another knight book with a K." Standing, he fisted his hands on his hips. "Right now."

What was she going to do? Owen was ready to fight. She couldn't let him get away with this behavior but she also wasn't sure what he would do if she thwarted him. And she didn't really want to find out.

"I yike dat one," said a little girl, about three years of age. She stood as she spoke, her voice gentle and sweet as she twirled her ponytail around her fingers.

"Knights is better," Owen said, pointing to the picture on the wall behind Sophie.

"Horsey good," the little girl agreed. "I yike dat one." She pointed to the book in Sophie's hands.

Owen dropped his head, shaking it as he tapped his foot on the floor. "Okay." He pointed to the little girl and then to the carpet at his feet. "You sit here. I don't care 'bout this one."

She obeyed, gracing Owen with a toothy grin. Sophie breathed a sigh of relief. Owen sulked, lying on his back with his feet against Sophie's metal desk, his shoes beating a rhythm to match his impatience. But he didn't disrupt that story or the next.

Finally, the parents arrived and Sophie could relax, knowing that he wasn't going to explode. But she still kept an eye on him as she chatted with the parents.

Near the door, Mrs. Porter and Ms. Dunphrey were deep in conversation. The littlest Porter was in the stroller fussing, reaching toward the floor, trying to escape. Mrs. Porter reprimanded him sharply, shaking the stroller to quiet him. It only seemed to aggravate him.

In an instant, Owen was beside Mrs. Porter. "Hey." He tapped her hand where it lay on the stroller handle. She gave him a dirty look and went back to her conversation. Scowling, Owen dropped to his knees and crawled under the stroller. It rocked and Sophie rushed over to prevent the baby from toppling out.

"What are you doing?" The woman frowned at Owen. "Get out of there."

Owen stood, presenting a pacifier. He popped it into the littlest Porter's mouth. The baby's eyes rolled back in his head in an expression of absolute bliss. "You gotta watch a baby," Owen said, reprimanding the mother.

Mrs. Porter's look of horror started when the dirty pacifier entered her son's mouth and morphed into anger as she turned her gaze on Owen once again. "You're a very rude boy," she said, waggling her finger at him. "Miss Paetan, who does this ruffian belong to."

Mrs. Breckinridge, Sophie wanted to say. Instead, she swallowed her irritation at Mrs. Porter's condescending tone in order to help her husband's son. "Me," she said. She was responsible for Owen. "He's with me."

Mrs. Porter looked shocked. *It would have to be the wife of the chairman of the library board that Owen insulted.* Mercifully, the other parents quickly exited with their children. "He is rude and disrespectful not to mention a hazard…"

"He was only trying to help your son," Sophie said, her ire warming on Owen's behalf. Okay, maybe he was rude but he'd only been telling the truth. Sophie had entertained both of the Porters' older children in her reading group and they clearly lacked for adult attention. This little guy had simply dropped his pacifier and couldn't sleep without it. As a matter of fact, due to Owen's intervention, he was now contentedly suckling and dozing.

"I will definitely be speaking to my husband about this," Mrs. Porter said.

"I'll see you next week," Sophie said, putting her arm around Owen's shoulders. The Porters would be back, Sophie knew. Normally the children attended with a nanny, providing Mrs. Porter with a morning free of her offspring, an event she seemed to covet.

"Hmph," Mrs. Porter said, gathering her middle child and pushing the stroller out.

Once they'd gone, Sophie slumped into a kiddie chair, suddenly exhausted.

"You gotta watch a baby," Owen said, clearly disgusted with Mrs. Porter. Then his expression shifted to uncertainty. "Right?"

Taking his hand, Sophie drew him close. "That was nice of you to get the pacifier for the baby. And it was nice of you to let the little girl...her name is Wanda-Joe...hear the story she likes."

"I b'long a you?" Owen asked.

The question was so out of left field that Sophie was confused, both by his grammar and his intent. So she simply pulled him into a hug and then kissed him on the cheek. He resisted at first and then sighed in resignation, begrudgingly submitting to her affection.

"We go now, my Sophie?" he asked, pulling out of the hug.

She smiled at his use of possession. "We need to clean up and then we can go back to my house."

"Okay."

Before leaving, Sophie tried once again to contact the Blacks. Unsuccessful, she led Owen out of the library and back to her Avalon. Once she managed to get him belted in so they could head back to Silverstone, Owen decided that he was suddenly critically hungry. So, instead of hopping on the 471 as she would normally do, Sophie turned onto E 7th. She knew there was a Dunkin' Donuts a few blocks away on Walnut.

But really, the boy needed something more substantial than a donut, particularly in view of what Erich Fravenfeld had said about the effects of poor and unbalanced nutrition on early growth and development. In other words, Owen had grown up eating an abundance of cheap, over-processed, carbohydrate-rich foods and what he needed was fresh fruits, vegetables and meats.

As she drove the streets neighboring the public library, avoiding the plethora of crater-sized potholes, she noted the appalling lack of supermarkets. There was an abundance of fast-food joints and corner stores but nothing that would serve a salad, not one with green things in it anyway. She headed back to the highway.

Exiting the 471 at Highland Heights, another unfamiliar neighborhood, Sophie realized that she'd never really explored Cincinnati before. She used the highway to commute to her job, the zoo, and a few other museums and galleries, but she'd never taken the time to notice the reality of the city. If you looked up Cincinnati on the internet, you were met with beautiful nightscapes of fine architecture, paddleboats and lighted bridges. The reality was something very different indeed. A desert of culture, of opportunity. A food desert. And this was where Owen had spent his young life. As had Ayden.

Driving past yet another under-repaired street punctuated by walkways that led to either boarded-up houses or empty lots, she finally spotted a deli situated between a Laundromat and an empty parking lot where someone was selling used clothing off a coat rack. Since there were no chairs in the little deli, Owen and Sophie ate in the car. By the time they made it to the apartment, she was feeling slightly ill.

"I watch TV?" Owen asked.

Sophie agreed because she suddenly felt very ill. Racing to the bathroom, she vomited, retching out her entire lunch and half of Hong Kong, it seemed.

As the retching subsided, she felt a small hand on her back. "You okay, my Sophie?"

"I think I have food poisoning." That would teach her to order extra mayonnaise at an unknown deli. "Are you feeling sick?"

"No. Me good." He put his little arm around her shoulders and eased her to sit against the wall. "You want me get you the smelly drink?"

"Pardon?"

"When Mama got sick, she maked me get her the smelly-whiskey drink. Then she always go to sleep, even in a middle of cartoons." He shook his head in disgust at the memory. Then his face brightened. "You want some?"

"No, thank you. But I think I'd better lie on the sofa while you watch cartoons." She pushed up to flush the toilet and then rinse out her mouth. Owen put his arm around her waist and helped her to the sofa.

"I make you tea. Mama get the tea and put the fiery stuff in there," he said. "You got a pot to boil a water?"

Did his mother let him mess with boiling water? "I can have some tea later, sweetheart."

"Why you no let me make it?" he asked, annoyed.

"I don't want you to get hurt. Boiling water can burn you."

The transformation of Owen's features was astonishing. Sophie couldn't hope to track the emotions he experienced in those few moments.

"Okay," he whispered, staring at her with wonder-filled eyes.

Holding out her hand, she gestured him over. "Come sit with me. I'll rest and you can watch TV. Okay?"

He nodded enthusiastically, jumping on the sofa, making her stomach heave again. Then he settled. She was afraid to go to sleep, not sure what Owen would get into unsupervised. But she must have drifted off because when she woke, he was setting a mug on the coffee table beside her.

"Oh, Owen, I didn't want you to use the stove," she said, taking him gently by the arm.

"I no did it. I promise." He crossed his fingers over his chest.

The sound of a key in the door sent Owen running to fling it open in spite of Sophie's protest. Ayden entered.

"Hi, guy," Owen greeted him. Ayden reached down to ruffle his hair, stilling when he saw Sophie lying there.

"What happened? What did he do?" Ayden asked, shoving his fists in his pockets dejectedly, clearly expecting the worst.

"Nothing. In fact, he made me tea because I was feeling sick," Sophie said.

Ayden's brow furrowed and he glanced down at Owen who suddenly looked uncertain. "I turn a hot water on and put a bag in a cup and so I don't boil a water cause my Sophie say she want to keep me safe."

Ayden lifted an eyebrow and glanced over at Sophie. "Did you understand any of that?"

She smiled softly. "I did. Ayden, I like your boy a lot. He deserves a hug for the way he helped me today."

Looking surprised, Ayden shut the door behind him and lifted Owen into his arms. "Thanks for looking after Sophie," he said.

"Welcome," Owen replied easily. "I watch TV?"

"Sure," Ayden replied, putting Owen down. Then, kneeling beside the sofa, he brushed Sophie's hair back from her forehead, kissing her there. "You want to tell me about your day?" His touch was tender, his voice gentle.

So she did. "He really has a good heart, Ayden. He showed me the cars you made him. When did you do that?" she asked but didn't bother to wait for an answer. "You're a good dad."

Ayden shrugged one shoulder. "I don't have a clue how to do this, honey. It's easy to do it badly, really hard to do well. I just don't think I'm cut out to be a father." His voice dropped to a whisper. "He's probably better off without me."

"I don't think so. I think you have the skills to be a good father."

"I wish…" He sighed morosely. "He's a handful. Maybe he's better off with the Blacks. They have years of experience…"

"We can't leave him there," she said. She sat up. Ayden sat beside her, gathering her close. "I think we should keep him."

"You do?"

"I would even like to adopt him, if that's okay with you."

"Okay? You really want that?"

"I want us to be a real family. He's never had that I don't think. Every child deserves to feel permanent."

His outlook fell. "I just don't know."

She touched his face, caressing the darkening whiskers on his cheeks. "Look, I'm feeling much better now. Why don't we take him to the park? It will give us more time together and we can talk."

"Sure. I heard from the Blacks. They asked if we could keep him until supper time."

"That would work. Owen? Come over here, please," Sophie said. He glanced over his shoulder at her and then leapt onto the end of the sofa. Perching on the arm, he rested his chin in his hands. "I know about a really cool park that has a river beside it and a man who sells ice cream, and there's a slide and swings."

"Oh, boy!" Owen said, clapping exuberantly. Suddenly, his face fell. "My dad guy go away again?"

"Nope," Ayden replied. "I'm coming, too."

Sophie exchanged a meaningful look with Ayden as Owen perked up again. There was definitely a bond forming between them, or at least the potential for one.

"We goin' on a motorbike?" Owen asked with his voice full of hope.

"Why don't we go in the car?" Sophie suggested with an amused grin. After spending the morning with Owen, she understood Ayden's reluctance to put him on a motorcycle.

Holding a fistful of his pant leg, Owen stuck close to Ayden as they walked to the car. But as soon as they parked, his anxiety fled and Owen was out of the car, running across the road into Riverside Park and directly toward the small cluster of vendors at the park.

"We're going to have to teach him a few lessons, I think," Sophie said as she hurried after him. "He did the same thing earlier."

Ayden reached him first, grabbing him by the shoulder and spinning him around. Crouching down, he held him firmly by the upper arms. "You can't just run off like that, Owen."

"Why not? My Sophie say I can have ice cream." Owen pouted, his lip extended dramatically.

"Little boys who run away don't get ice cream," Ayden said firmly.

"Ayden." Sophie tried to stop him but it was too late.

Owen's deep blue eyes shimmered with tears. "You lied," he said fiercely. "You say I can get ice cream. You don't tell the truf. I don't wanna be wif you. I hate you." Jerking out of Ayden's grasp, Owen flung himself at Sophie's legs, holding on tightly.

She stroked his hair and patted his back. "Ayden," she said in reprimand. "That wasn't necessary. You can't expect him to suddenly know how to behave. He's clearly never had any boundaries."

"I don't need you to tell me that I don't know what I'm doing," he said and stormed off toward the benches beside the river.

"It's okay, Owen." Sophie continued to soothe the boy until his tears subsided. Holding him back from her, she crouched to get face to face, taking his little hands in hers.

Owen looked around bewildered. "The dad guy gone?" he asked mournfully. "Jus' like my mama don't come back."

"Your, uh," Sophie's heart beat with pity for the motherless boy, "daddy isn't gone, Owen. He's a little upset so he went for a walk, but he knew that I would take care of you." She pulled out the tail of her shirt and wiped Owen's face. Then she offered him her hand. "Come on. Let's go see your daddy."

Sophie walked with Owen to the bench by the empty wading pool where Ayden sat with his head in his hands. Approaching, she called out to him. He looked up to meet her gaze. A host of expressions flashed across his face: anger; despair; fear. Sophie's heart clenched anew in pity, now for the fatherless man she'd married.

"Can we go to the slide? Owen could play and you and I could talk," she said.

Owen peeked up at Ayden through his curly bangs, hope in his eyes.

"Yeah." Ayden's voice was gruff. He rose and Sophie took his hand, entwining their fingers.

Trying something new, Sophie first delineated Owen's boundaries before stepping back to talk to Ayden. Scanning his face, her heart ached in her chest at his apparent misery. So she hugged him. Owen groaned and muttered something about grown-ups before he jumped up on a swing.

"Come push me," he hollered at them.

Releasing her, Ayden said, "I'll go."

Sophie walked with him, standing back while Ayden pushed Owen a couple of times before the little boy jumped off and raced back over to the slide, trying to climb up on his knees.

"If Faehr chose not to tell you about Owen when he was born, why did she leave him to you?"

He shoved his hands in his pockets. "I guess...somehow she'd heard that I had...turned my life around. The letter says she wanted to give," he gulped, "our son a better chance."

He looked so culpable. "That's a good thing, honey. Nothing to feel guilty about."

Propping his shoulder against the swing set, he continued, "Faehr spent her childhood passed around among family members who didn't want her, foster parents who didn't take care of her. She was unloved. Abused. Neglected. I think she wanted to spare her kid the same experience." He glanced over at Owen who was now trying to find a way to slide down backwards. "I guess she hoped I'd be an improvement over state-approved strangers," he said. "I'm sorry, Soph. It wasn't enough that I brought my messed-up history to your door, now I've brought a permanent burden."

"Ayden sweetheart, he's not a burden. He's a little boy, a gift from God, a compliment."

He quirked a brow. "What compliment?"

"God thinks we can do this. We can be the parents that Owen needs. But if we're going to do this properly, we've got some hard work ahead of us. I'll get some parenting books from the library and we probably need some child psychology books as well, maybe even a counsellor. I can check out the phone book for speech therapists and maybe even a tutor. But to begin with, you can stop acting like a dork." Ayden inhaled sharply, clearly shocked by her accusation. "Owen won't know the rules until we teach him. You can't punish him for doing something he doesn't know he's not supposed to do."

Ayden gazed over her shoulder at the little boy who'd changed the shape of his future and then back at this woman who meant everything to him. "You want to do this? With me?" he said. "Because I don't think I can do it alone."

Sophie's decision was made. "Yes." Sliding her arms up his chest to link behind his neck, she tiptoed up to kiss him. "I love you. I think you'll make a great father. I married you, hoping that one day we'd have children together. Why wouldn't I raise a baby you helped create?"

"Soph." His eyes glittered with emotion, with passion and love and something deeper. Brighter. "I love you."

Owen groaned. "Why you gotta kiss all a time? I over here playin' and you kissin'. Bleah!" He leapt off the slide and started swinging with his belly propped over the swing.

Sophie chuckled, pulling back. "Let's get him some ice cream."

Nodding, Ayden called Owen over. Owen ignored him.

"Go to him, touch his shoulder and then talk to him," she instructed Ayden. "Oh, yeah, you need to apologize for walking away. That really scared him."

Ayden winced at her words. "Owen." He touched him on the shoulder. "If you can listen to me now and come, I think we should get an ice cream cone."

"Wow, wow, wow." Owen jumped up and down and then ran over to Sophie. He hugged her and then took off toward the vendors.

"Owen. Stop!" Ayden's voice boomed across the space. "Come here."

Owen hesitated, looking back at Ayden and then longingly toward the ice cream wagon. He shifted from foot to foot and then abruptly ran back to Ayden.

"Make sure he knows you noticed he did what you asked him," Sophie said in a stage whisper. Ayden looked at her. "Tell him you're proud of him."

Ayden dropped to his knees in front of Owen, taking his little hands in his larger calloused hands. "That was awesome, Owen. I'm proud of you." He stood, keeping one of Owen's hands firmly in his. "Hold my hand or Sophie's hand and then we'll walk together to get ice cream."

Owen looked back and forth between them, chewing his lower lip as he debated. Sophie finally just took his hand and started walking.

Once Owen had consumed, for the most part, his chocolate ice cream cone, he ran off to the rubbish bin in the park and then started toward a leashed German shepherd on the path.

"Owen, stop." In two strides, Ayden was beside the boy, stopping him with a firm hand on his shoulder.

Sophie jogged over to join them. "You can't just run up to a strange dog."

"Why?" Owen demanded to know. "I wanna pat a doggie."

Sophie knelt down in front of him. "There are rules about dogs."

Owen frowned at her and tried to pull away from Ayden's solid grip. "You gots too many rules, lady. I don't gotta listen to your stupid rules."

Ayden crouched down and turned Owen's body so they were face to face. It was clear that, while Ayden was able to set aside his frustration for moments of time, it didn't take much for the emotion to come roaring back. So this was what Owen meant when he said that Ayden was always grumpy. "You are not going to speak to her that way. If you keep being rude I'm going to take my hand and smack your...behind."

D. C. Shaftoe

Owen dropped to his haunches and curled into a ball with his arms over his head in protection. His voice emerged muffled. "I no do it. Okay. Okay?"

Ayden clenched his fists in frustration as he scanned the environment to see who was observing. "This kid is a minefield," he said through gritted teeth.

Sophie sat down on the grass, tugging Ayden down beside her. "This kid," she imitated his intonation, "has obviously been hit before and not with a simple tap on the bottom like you intended." She turned to Ayden, frowning. "That *is* what you intended?"

"Yes, of course," he growled at her.

Owen squeezed his body tighter in response.

"Stop it, you're scaring him," Sophie hissed at Ayden. "Just talk to him."

While Sophie watched Ayden swallow down his frustration, she rested a gentle hand on Owen's back. Owen flinched.

When Ayden didn't speak, Sophie finally asked, "Who smacked you, Owen?"

His muffled voice emerged. "Lotsa guys. They gots big hands like that dad guy and big hands hurt."

"Did your mommy smack you?" Sophie asked.

"Mama, you mean? Yeah. But she don't hit hard," Owen said, peeking up at her. "The guy who comed and deaded mama hit me till I fell asleep."

Sophie gulped and noticed that Ayden was clearly touched by the boy's words. "Owen. Your daddy was going to open his hand and give you a little smack." She brought her hand gently to the fleshy part of the boy's exposed hip.

Owen lifted his head. "That don't hurt," he said with disdain.

"He doesn't want to hurt you. He wants you to remember," Sophie said and Ayden nodded.

"Remember what?" Owen asked, now curious.

"The rules," Sophie said.

"Hmph." Owen flopped onto his back in the grass. "I telled ya you gots too many rules."

"Owen," Ayden began, his voice shooting a warning, but Sophie stopped him with a touch on the arm.

"The man who smacked you until you passed out broke the rules, Owen. The man who hurt your mommy—your mama— broke the rules," Sophie said.

"Oh," he replied, rising to his elbows to look at Ayden. "You wanna smack *him*?"

"Yeah," Ayden muttered gruffly.

"He needs to go to *jail*, wouldn't you say?" Sophie asked Ayden, reinforcing her statement with her narrowed eyebrows.

"Yeah," Ayden said grumpily. Then he held his hand out toward Owen. "I'm not going to hurt you, Owen."

"You promise?" Owen watched him through gimlet-eyes.

"Yeah. But you do need to follow my rules."

"Why?" Owen tilted his head quizzically.

Ayden scanned Sophie's face, clearly looking for inspiration. "So I can keep you safe." He said it almost like a question.

"If I don't go wif you, I don't gotta listen to your rules," Owen said, thrusting his chin out stubbornly.

"I guess that's true," Ayden said, keeping his voice carefully neutral.

"Cause I lived in lotsa places that don't got so many rules." Owen sighed dramatically. "But I'm tired of new beds and new dad guys. You gonna keep me?"

Ayden met Sophie's gaze and she could see the vulnerability in his gaze. She leaned in to kiss him on the mouth and then pulled back a fraction, ignoring Owen's groan. "Say, yes," she whispered.

Ayden kissed her quickly and then turned to Owen. "Yes, we're going to keep you."

Owen jumped into Ayden's lap. "Okay." The word he chose was so blasé, but the brilliant grin on his face eclipsed the sun.

Chapter Nineteen: Social Rules

Sophie had insisted or they wouldn't be here. Ayden had carefully avoided potentially embarrassing situations since Owen had come to live with them three weeks ago. But Sophie had insisted that the boy needed to attend Sunday school. So here they were, the three of them, together at church.

As soon as Owen started to wiggle in his seat, which was about five minutes into the service, Sophie produced two stubby pencils and a notebook with mazes and dot-to-dots. She leaned down to whisper in his ear and then Ayden watched the little boy sink to his knees in front of the pew to use the seat as a table.

Ayden stretched his arm along the back of the pew behind Sophie, giving a lock of her tawny hair a light tug. She glanced over at him and he smiled at her, gesturing with his eyebrows to indicate her brilliant idea. She smiled back, clearly pleased at his praise.

"See that?" Owen said.

A few people turned at the intrusion but soon settled back with their eyes to the front. Sophie leaned down to whisper to him. When the music began, she encouraged Owen to stand on the pew between them for the songs. Then he returned to the floor. During the announcements, Owen seemed to feel he needed to compete with Kiran's voice but Sophie leaned down again, placing her fingers over his mouth and whispering to him.

Ayden relaxed. His son wouldn't win any prizes for silence or attention but things were progressing. No dirty looks had been thrown his way though it was true that he and Sophie couldn't hope to get anything from the service.

"See that?" Owen said.

He didn't seem to get the concept of whispering. Sophie leaned down, placing her fingers over his mouth again.

"Don't stop my lips!" he hollered at her. "Why you gotta do that? I gotta tell you somefin' and you keep stoppin' my lips so they can't talk..."

The words went on and Sophie's attempts to quiet Owen went on and head after head turned to watch them. Feeling the flush of public humiliation suffuse his skin, Ayden stood and, leaning over Sophie, he grasped Owen's upper arms and lifted him up and over. Hugging his body close, Ayden walked them straight down the aisle toward the back of the church, seeking a quick exit. But, of course, Sam Jeong was serving as an usher today, using the opportunity to chat quietly with a man Ayden didn't know.

Both men stopped speaking as soon as Ayden started down the aisle. "You need to teach that kid some manners," Sam said.

"Can't teach what he doesn't know," the other man responded.

Ayden ignored them both, quelling the desire to take his frustrations out on their hides in Kiran's church. Jogging down the steps, Ayden crossed the lawn and the road to Riverside Park. He set Owen beside him on a bench.

"Don't you even think about getting off this bench," he said firmly, warning his son.

Owen looked left and right and then dropped to his feet. Ayden scooped him up and set him on the bench a little more firmly.

"How long I gotta stay here?" Owen asked annoyed.

"Until you and I have a chat," Ayden said.

Owen narrowed his eyes, studying Ayden through the slits. "What we gonna chat 'bout?"

"Being quiet. And Sophie."

"Yup. I know. You gotta tell her, no more stoppin' my lips. What she thinkin' she doin'?"

Ayden clenched his fists in a spurt of frustration. Sophie was a natural mother, instinctively understanding little boys and their unique take on life. Ayden, however, had to fight all his natural instincts to try not to react as he wanted to, to endeavor *not* to behave in the manner that the men in his life had. What had the men in his life taught him? When the going gets tough, depart? How to beat the crap out of someone smaller than you? How to intimidate and crush vulnerability? *Lord, please, give me just an ounce of Sophie's calm. Please.*

"What. Do you think. Sophie meant when she put her fingers on your lips?" Ayden asked deliberately.

"Don't talk. But I gotta tell her somefin'."

The boy had no sense of self-preservation. "She meant, be quiet, or, if you have something very important to say, whisper."

Owen tilted his head quizzically. "Whatsa whisper?" He was intrigued now.

Ayden demonstrated. "It's when you need to talk softly because it would *be rude* to speak loudly."

"Why it be rude to talk?"

"In church, you're supposed to be quiet while the people up front speak."

"Why?"

Why? I don't know. "Because…well, because other people want to hear what they say."

"I want my Sophie t' hear me."

"Sometimes you have to wait."

Owen pouted, his entire body slumping. "I forget."

Suspicious that Owen's humble reaction was not contrition, Ayden asked, "Forget what?"

"I forget t' tell my Sophie and then she don't know what I say."

"If you really, really need to tell her, you have to whisper very, very quietly."

"Why?" Owen asked again but Ayden could see no impertinence in his manner, only sincere curiosity. Sophie kept telling him to look beyond Owen's words to the intentions of his heart. Okay. What was Owen really asking and why?

"Respect." Ayden couldn't believe that word had come out of his mouth. His entire life, he'd been reprimanded for not showing respect. How often had he been told that he would amount to nothing because he lacked respect for authority? "To some people, we show respect because they are good people, like Pastor Kiran. He is a good man, a godly man, so we treat him with respect."

"How?"

Ayden chewed the inside of his lip. He didn't have the skills to answer questions like this. But he had to try because there was no one else for this boy. "When he talks, we're quiet and we listen. And we think about what he says and try to do it."

Ayden held his breath, hoping…Owen nodded…and Ayden released his breath. The boy got it. Maybe.

"My Sophie a good man?" Owen frowned. "Not a man, a lady."

"Yes, Sophie is a good lady, a godly woman. But we also listen to Sophie because we love her. So even if we don't understand what she's doing, like stopping our mouths, we listen to her and try to be nice."

"Okay, guy."

Relieved, Ayden checked his watch. "It's time for Sunday school. Do you think you can behave if I take you to class?"

"Wif my Sophie? Yup." His countenance fell. "My Sophie be mad?"

Ayden knew she wouldn't be mad at Owen. She seemed to have an uncanny ability to cope with things that Ayden found humiliating. "Do you want to fix it?"

"Yep. Uh huh."

"Then you need to apologize to her. You were very rude, yelling at her in church. I'm sure she was embarrassed." *I know I was.*

"How does me 'pologize?"

"You say, 'I'm sorry for yelling at you' to Sophie. Okay?"

"Okay."

Ayden took Owen's hand and led him back across the road to the church and then quietly through the side entrance, directly to the kindergarten classroom. As usual, a din echoed from the room, making Ayden smile. Sophie had such fun with the kids.

Knocking lightly, Ayden opened the door, letting Owen lead the way in. Tommy and Nicky were sitting on the floor constructing boats out of newspapers while Sadie-Jean Billings, Kandace Walters, Su Jin Li, and Rafe Washington colored a four-foot-square picture of a whale.

"Hey, Mr. Reckless," Tommy called from his spot on the floor and Nicky looked up and smiled shyly. The other children called similar greetings.

"Come on in, Owen," Sophie said, looking relieved.

Owen shuffled over, very serious, to stand in front of Sophie, his eyes on the toes of his shoes. "I'm sorry," he said, glancing back at Ayden. "For yellin' for you t' stop stoppin' my lips." He looked over at Ayden again. "That good?"

Sophie met Ayden's gaze over the children's heads, smiling at him. He nodded for Owen's benefit and then rolled his eyes for Sophie's.

Sophie crouched down to hug Owen. "It's okay. I forgive you."

His entire body lit up with renewed energy but Ayden wanted to collapse in exhaustion. This being a dad thing was a lot harder than he'd ever imagined. It also reminded him how deeply he'd missed having a father figure in his own life. It was no wonder he was parentally clueless.

"Would you like to help color the whale or make a boat with Nicky and Tommy?" she asked Owen.

Owen stilled, tilting his head and chewing his lip as he considered his options. "Boat." He glanced up at Sophie. "Please."

She smiled down at him because he looked so proud that he'd remembered a polite word. She gave him a sheet of newspaper and asked Tommy to demonstrate how to fold it into a boat. Owen sat right between the other two boys.

Ayden shoved his hands in his pockets because he was itching to touch her and this wasn't really the right time.

"Are you going back up?" she asked him.

"I don't really want to face them upstairs."

She walked into him and gave him a quick hug. "You could stay and help me."

"Any time," he said, wry relief in his voice.

The rest of the class went peacefully. Well, except for the fact that Owen got frustrated and crumpled his hat because he "couldn't make it right" and Sophie only just managed to stop him from leaping on Nicky when he snickered. Then, somehow, she managed to get the two boys laughing together.

Ayden remained in the classroom until all the children were retrieved, hoping to avoid the censure he was sure awaited him from the members of the congregation. It didn't work.

When Sandy arrived to collect Tommy, he was already chuckling. Or still chuckling. Ayden wasn't sure. "Welcome to the Daddy Club, man." Sandy slapped Ayden on the shoulder as Frank guffawed, joining in on the ribbing.

"Oh, there you are, young man." Cora Johnson shuffled into the classroom, coming right over to Ayden and resting her thin hand on his arm. "I wanted to make sure you know that I am so glad you have brought that young man to join our congregation. My youngest brother, Theodore—we called him Dorie—was just like your young man. My father could never accept him. He always made him feel bad and wrong. Eventually Dorie gave up and became the man my father believed him to be. That made me sad. But your patience with your little man pleases me. I sneaked out the door behind you and watched from the church steps. You didn't harm that poor child. You talked to him. And I could see the smile in his eyes as you returned. Well done, Reck." She placed a cold hand on his shoulder and tugged until he leaned far enough that she could kiss his cheek.

"Owen, come here," Ayden said, waving the boy over. "I'd like you to meet Miss Johnson."

"Hey, Johnson," Owen said, waving distractedly.

Cora laughed.

"You could say, 'Hello, Miss Johnson'," Sophie prompted him.

"Really?" Owen looked up at her with an expression of mild distaste. "If you say so." He turned back to Miss Johnson and said very solemnly, "Hello, Miss Johnson."

Cora rested her hand for a moment on Owen's head. "Hello, Owen." Leaning on her cane, she managed to lower herself to say confidentially, "It takes a while to get used to being quiet in church, doesn't it?"

"Yup. Always rules, rules, rules wif this guy," Owen said, jerking his thumb over his shoulder in Ayden's direction. Ayden blushed.

Cora laughed again. "I'll tell you what, I'll bring a candy every week and, if you can mind your father and your..." She stopped, looking at Sophie.

"My Sophie?" Owen said.

Cora met Owen's gaze with a firm nod. "Yes. Then I will give you the candy. How does that sound?"

"I like it a lot. You got ice cream?"

"Owen," Ayden said and then covered his eyes in embarrassment.

"Sorry. It's a candy or nothing." Cora stood straight.

"I take a candy," Owen said.

Ayden poked him in the shoulder.

"Oh. Uh, thank you?" Owen said as though he wasn't quite sure that's what Ayden was prompting for.

"You're welcome. See you next week."

"Thank you, Cora," Sophie said, giving the woman a kiss on the cheek, bringing a pleased smile to her face.

Then Sophie had her arms around Ayden's waist and was resting her cheek on his chest. He released his tension on a sigh, murmuring, "Prison was less stressful than this."

Gathering up their things, they followed Owen upstairs. "Gotta pee," Owen shouted and then took off back downstairs.

"Do you need help?" Sophie called after him.

"Nope. Nah ah."

Ayden grinned because Sophie chuckled so happily.

"Sophie Anne."

Ayden's grin turned to a silent groan. Not him again. Mayor Paetan blocked their exit from the church, wearing a navy pinstriped suit, floral tie, and shiny black shoes. His white hair and beard were perfectly coiffed. Lucy stood meekly at his side. Neither made eye contact with Ayden.

"I have heard a disturbing rumor about you," Stuart said.

Ayden heard Sophie sigh. "Hi, Dad. Hi, Mom."

Stuart frowned in disapproval. When did that man approve of anything?

"Ayden, could you please check on Owen?" Sophie said.

"He'll be fine."

"Please."

His lips thinning in disapproval, he agreed reluctantly. "I'll be right back," he said in warning to Stuart then started down the stairs.

"Who is Owen?" Lucy said, only to be ignored by all.

"Your brother tells me you are planning to cash in some shares. I warned you that this criminal was only after your money. Stop the process at once." Stuart crossed his arms over his chest.

"He's not after my money. He is incredibly stubborn about it in fact."

"I don't understand how you became involved in this sordid affair. And now I hear there is a child involved," Stuart said.

"Is that Owen?" Lucy asked.

"There's nothing sordid about it. We're married." Sophie could feel a blush warm her cheeks.

"The child?" Stuart said the word as if it contained profanity.

"Ayden has a child from a former relationship."

"Disgraceful," her father said.

"Yes. It was disgraceful, the conditions that led them to make that decision, the loneliness and pain in their lives that made them believe that physical pleasure could substitute for love," Sophie said. "But Owen is *not* disgraceful. I wouldn't exactly call him delightful because he's a real firecracker, but he is hilarious and wonderful, and buried beneath that mouth of his is a sweet boy who just wants someone in his life he can rely on."

Stuart stepped into her space but she refused to back down. "Separate yourself from this man at once."

Anger built up inside Sophie but Owen blasted up the stairs at that moment so she swallowed it down. He ran into the sanctuary, changed his mind and ran back to Sophie, skidding to a halt in front of Stuart. "Who are you?" he demanded to know.

Sophie crouched down beside Owen, taking his hand. "He's my dad guy."

"What?" Stuart said, vibrating with displeasure.

"He a good dad guy or bad?" Owen asked, looking her straight in the eye.

Leaning close, she whispered confidentially in his ear, "Not very good."

"Sophie Anne, stand up and speak to me properly," Stuart said.

"Owen?" Lucy whispered, reaching out a hand and then immediately withdrawing it.

A bland expression on his face, Ayden emerged from the stairwell silently and came to stand behind Owen, resting one hand on the little boy's shoulder and one hand possessively at the small of Sophie's back.

Stuart brushed his palm along his beard, but as was his way, he didn't let his body betray his anger in any other manner. "Your behavior is disgraceful—"

Ayden started to reply but Owen interrupted him. "You don't talk rude to my Sophie!"

"How dare you?" Stuart frowned indignantly down at the little boy. He grabbed the shoulder of Owen's shirt with the clear intention of shaking the child. Owen went ballistic, jerking out of her father's grip and flying at him, pounding Stuart's legs with his little fists.

"You don't touch me! You don't smack me. It's against the rules. My daddy says you can't smack me."

Ayden crouched beside his son, trapping his flailing hands. "It's okay, son. I won't let him hurt you. Or Sophie." Ayden's voice was calm and firm but loud enough to be heard over his son's shouts.

"He breaked the rules. He breaked the rules, Daddy." Owen flung himself into Ayden's embrace, his arms and legs clamped around Ayden's body. Ayden held him tightly, murmuring reassurances as he stood, facing Stuart.

"We're leaving," Ayden said. Taking Sophie's elbow, he pulled her closer. "And until you repair your behavior toward your daughter and our son, you'd better stay out of my way." Ayden looked like a man that no man would choose to disobey.

"Your son, Sophie?" Lucy asked.

"Yes, Mom," Sophie replied.

"Your son! I should have guessed," Stuart said with spite and disgust. "Outrageous. You have betrayed your heritage," her father said. "I no longer consider that we share a name."

"That's fine by me," Sophie replied. "But you better learn how to spell Breckinridge."

Sophie came when Ayden tugged her forward, down the steps and to the car. He settled Owen in his booster seat with remarkably little fuss and then rounded the trunk to open her door.

"Thank you," she whispered, leaning up to kiss Ayden. He returned her kiss, hard, possessive.

"He breaked the rules. Right?" Owen said from the back seat as though trying to reassure himself that he'd done right.

"Yes, he did," Ayden said, settling in the driver's seat. His voice was hard and uncompromising.

"You know what, Owen Koenig Breckinridge?" Sophie asked, reaching back to pat his knee.

"What?" He looked afraid of what she would say.

"You two guys are my heroes."

"Heroes is the good guys right?" he said, his eyes wide in wonder.

"Yes, darling. You and your daddy are the good guys," she said.

Owen shifted his gaze toward Ayden. "You mad, Daddy?"

Ayden's features softened. This was the first occasion where Owen had called him Daddy. "I'm a little mad at Mr. Paetan but I'm not mad at you."

"We have ice cream?" Owen asked with a calculating expression on his face.

Ayden laughed. "Ask your Sophie, champ. Maybe she has some cookies 'n' cream in the freezer."

Owen scowled, muttering, "Don't want cookies, jus' ice cream."

Chapter Twenty: Kindergarten

Sophie held Owen's hand tightly as they entered Ancora Elementary School. His auburn curls flapped around his face as he swivelled his head to and fro, trying to absorb everything within his line of vision and beyond.

"I hafta go to school, my Sophie?"

"Yes, sweetheart. School is fun. You'll learn lots of new things and you'll have lots of kids to play with. It will be great."

His upraised eyes betrayed his skepticism but he didn't pursue the matter as Sophie led him to the office. There were three adults behind the desk, a tall man drinking coffee while gazing studiously out a window, a young woman rifling through a filing cabinet, and an older, rapier-thin woman tapping a pencil on a desk blotter. She wore a telephone headset.

"Hello, I'd like to register a child for kindergarten," Sophie said. Owen started trying to climb up Sophie's leg to see so she picked him up. No one spared her more than a glance. "Excuse me."

Owen slapped his hand on the counter. "My Sophie talkin' to you."

Sophie blushed hotly as every eye turned to her. "It's okay, Owen," she murmured.

A sour look on her face, the thin woman, clearly the school secretary, finally met her gaze. "Can I help you?"

"Yes, thank you. I need to register this little guy for kindergarten." She indicated Owen.

"The school year started two months ago."

"Yes, I'm aware of that. It would probably be helpful if I could speak with the principal."

The secretary ignored the suggestion, asking, "Do you have his records, immunizations, birth certificate?"

"Yes." Sophie put Owen on the floor beside her and pulled the documents out of her bag. Since Owen had come into her life, she'd taken to carrying a large purse filled with anything she could think of to keep him out of trouble. "Stay right here beside me, okay?" she said to him.

"Yeah," he said, clearly distracted by the pictures of dinosaur skeletons tacked to the bulletin board across the hall.

Spreading the documents across the counter, Sophie waited patiently as the secretary made her way over, checked each document and then mumbled something about making copies.

When Sophie glanced down to check on Owen, she realized that he wasn't there to check on. He'd disappeared without a trace. She experienced a presage of disaster. "Owen?" she called quietly. "Owen." *Oh, no.* "Excuse me," she said, trying to gain the attention of the coffee drinker. The filer was nowhere to be seen.

"You need something?" he finally replied, draining his cup. He looked familiar.

"Yes. The little boy I came in with? He seems to have stepped away…" Her voice drifted off as the sounds of shouting filtered through the morning sounds of school. "Oh, no."

Amused, the coffee drinker moved to her side. "Follow me," he said.

The familiar sounds of an indignant Owen grew louder as they moved down the hall, joined by the shouts of a very displeased adult.

"…that down, right this instant!"

"I on'y lookin' at it."

Coffee Man pushed the door to a classroom fully open revealing what looked like a group of ten-year-olds gathered around a middle-aged woman in a pink pantsuit who was wagging her finger down at a five-year-old boy. Owen. There was a display of internal combustion engines supplemented by a variety of dinky cars and a model of an Edsel in the center of the room.

"Owen," Sophie said, rushing to his side. In each hand, he fisted a dinky car. "Put them back."

"Mrs. Warner. How are you today? Isn't it always amusing when the Kindies escape?" Coffee Man said, relieving Owen of the cars in a deft move and then handing them to Mrs. Warner. He muttered, "Move him out."

Sophie scooped a protesting Owen into her arms and scooted back to the front office. The secretary was back, waiting impatiently to return Sophie's documents. She didn't want to let go of Owen to stuff them in her purse so she kept them gripped in her fist. "Thank you. Good-bye," she said. She wanted to get out of here fast before anything else happened. The secretary waved her off.

Coffee Man was chuckling as he rounded the corner. When he saw her, he approached. "Warner's a grumpy one. Not the greatest first impression for the little guy. I'm Jaxen Foxx." He extended his hand and then, when he realized that hers were full, he reached out and squeezed her fingertips.

"You're Mr. Kimutai's nephew," Sophie said, finally realizing where she'd seen him.

"Yep. I've seen you coming and going next door. But not in a while." He ruffled Owen's hair lightly. "You starting kindergarten, buddy?"

Owen frowned at him. "They say I gotta," he said grumpily.

"You'll like it, I promise. I like kindergarten the best," Jaxen said, shifting his attention to Sophie. "Uncle Arlo would love to see you again. I think he misses you." He ruffled Owen's hair again and then wandered off with a smile.

"Oh." Sophie turned back to the secretary. "Who is the kindergarten teacher?"

"Mr. Foxx."

Thank you, Lord.

಴ಇ

"Daddy?"

D. C. Shaftoe

Owen walked out of his bedroom wearing his pale green dinosaur pyjamas, his hair still damp from his bath. He held Rover the platypus in his arms, the stuffed animal that Sophie had insisted he needed from the Greater Cleveland Aquarium gift shop. She must have been right because he slept with it every night.

"What's up, champ?" Ayden held his hand out toward Owen who climbed into his lap, hugging the platypus between them. Ayden wasn't surprised that the boy was still awake. Tomorrow was his first day of school and, based on Sophie's description of registration day, Owen was already infamous; an inauspicious start to the year.

"My Sophie gone?" Owen's deep blue eyes searched the room.

"She went to visit her mommy for the evening." Ayden had encouraged Sophie to maintain a relationship with her mom. He could see no harm in the woman and it wasn't like they had much family between them. So Sophie had agreed to resume their suppers which she'd curtailed after her father's obnoxious encounter at the church. "I hear you two went to see Mr. Kimutai today."

"He the guy what yelleded at me?"

"Which time?" Ayden said. His son seemed to be in trouble most of the time.

"My *Sophie* drawed the chalk," he said as though it was definitely her fault, whatever happened. "But he yelleded..." Owen stopped and looked into Ayden's face.

"Yelled," Ayden said, guessing what he wanted. Lately, Owen had started recognizing some of his unusual grammar and looked for guidance. He was sure that Sophie had something to do with it.

"He yelled for me to stop. Was only pictures," Owen said in disgust. "No bad ones."

"Then what you did was okay."

"Yeah. Sophie told him I'm a good draw-er. She maked him take a picture on his camera and he smiled."

"You made Mr. Kimutai smile?' Ayden said, astounded.

"Yup."

Ayden kissed his forehead. "You're an amazing dude." Owen grinned. "Now why are you not asleep, dude?"

"I go to school tomorrow. You go to work. Sophie?"

"Sophie will go to work at the library in the morning, pick you up from school and then you can spend the afternoon together." *Because she is the most incredible woman on the face of the planet.*

"Her dad guy, he hurt my Sophie?"

Surprised at the question, Ayden replied, "No. He won't hurt her."

"He yelleded…yelled. Loud."

"He did. But I won't let him ever hurt her."

"You be at work," Owen said. "Me at school with Foxx."

The door opened and Sophie walked in. Owen leaned in close and whispered in Ayden's ear. "I don't want her deaded, Daddy."

Ayden winced. No little boy should have to fear such things.

"What are you two whispering about? And shouldn't you be asleep, young man?" She looked so beautiful, so full of life and joy.

"We were just having a man-chat," Ayden said. "Sophie, would your father ever hurt you?"

"Pardon?" In spite of her astonishment, she gleaned the message that Ayden sent her. Owen had been far more affected by the confrontation with her father than they'd suspected. "No, Owen. My father is not a nice man and he can yell pretty loud, but he would never…"

"Make you deaded?" Owen asked.

Sophie gulped. Ayden felt bad for upsetting her, but Owen needed reassurance. "My father would not kill me." Then she surprised him, asking, "Who killed your mama Owen?" as she sat beside them.

Owen crawled across Ayden's lap and into Sophie's arms. "A guy. A guy like your dad guy. Black and white."

"Like a zebra?" Ayden said.

"No." Owen shook his head emphatically. "Like my Sophie's dad guy. He weared clothes all black, an' white hair all over."

"Hair on his head and a beard on his face." Sophie rubbed her hands on her head and then her chin and cheeks to demonstrate.

"Yup."

"Do you know his name?" Ayden asked.

"Mama said to him, 'no, guy, you not his dad'." Owen flung his arms out. "That all I know."

Leaving the topic for the time being, Sophie tucked Owen back into bed with Rover the platypus, and then wandered back out to find Ayden in the kitchen, washing the dishes. She wasn't sure what she needed after Owen's revelation until Ayden drew her into his arms. This was what she wanted, needed, his hands on her hips, his fingertips lightly tracing patterns on the narrow strip of skin between the hem of her T-shirt and the waistband of her capris. He dropped a kiss on her lips and then sank into it. She wrapped her arms around his neck, burying her fingers in his hair, reveling in the rich thickness of it. He hadn't had time to get it cut so it was longer, as it had been when she'd met him a year and a half ago. His mouth wandered across her cheek and down her neck. She strained upward to get closer to those lips and teeth and tongue.

"This is what I miss," he murmured against her skin. "Since Owen came."

"Mmm," she replied which really didn't mean anything except that she wanted him to keep kissing her. As he kissed the line of freckles from one cheek, across the bridge of her nose, and beneath the other eye, she popped the top few buttons of his shirt to press a kiss to his chest. He shuddered and sighed, weaving his fingers into her hair and pressing her cheek to his chest. She inhaled. He smelled so good, of freshly cut cedar and aftershave. "We have kind of stopped touching each other since he came," she murmured. "But he probably needs to see proper affection. Things not like 'the guy what climbed on her bed'." She quoted Owen, making Ayden chortle in surprise.

"Okay," he replied, settling in to kiss her ear, tracing the whorls.

"Uh…" She shuddered at the delicious tickle. "Cal Zimm…uh…Zimmerman…my…uh…our lawyer called today." She was having trouble keeping a coherent thought.

"Uh huh." He moved beneath her chin and to her other ear.

"Uh. He started the…uh…process…for the shares…money will be ready…in a couple weeks…can buy a house."

Abruptly Ayden pulled away. "I'm not comfortable using your inheritance to buy a house."

Blast. She hadn't expected him to stop kissing her. "We can talk about it later."

He stepped back, sitting against the edge of the teak table. "It's not right."

"Oh, come on, Ayden. Owen is sleeping in a ten-by-eight-foot windowless room that used to be a storage closet. We need a house where he can have a yard and a room of his own. We discussed this."

"I'm…failing."

"How?" she said, her arms slapping against her legs. "You've been out of prison for what? Six and a half years? And you've started your own business, married…a truly wonderful woman…" She grinned and he returned her smile. "And had a child. You haven't beaten anyone up in months. You've only sworn twice—at least that I've heard—and you haven't had a speeding ticket in six months."

"Uh. Yeah. No. I got a ticket a couple months ago."

"If you would just go the speed limit, they couldn't stop you."

"Not true. If I stick to the limit, they only pull me over for something else. Last time I went the speed limit, Reynolds impounded my bike for an improperly displayed licence plate. It was three days before I got it back. Cost more than a ticket, too."

"Really?" She paced away and then back. Her hands clenched into fists.

"Feel like hitting someone?" he asked wryly.

"Of course not," she replied hastily.

"Oh, yeah?"

She huffed out a laugh that held no humor. "You're right. I do lie my face off. I want to plow my fist into Tristan's face."

"Yeah. Well. Welcome to my world." She expected him to look smug but all she saw was regret in his eyes.

"So how do I keep from hitting?" she asked.

His brows rose in astonishment. "You're asking me?"

"Yes." Walking over, she stepped between his feet, moving forward until she was stopped by the edge of the table. Placing her palms on his chest, she kissed him, a quick peck on the lips. "You are amazing, sweetheart. You've overcome so much to become who God wants you to be. You're my best friend, my wonderful husband and a great dad. So, tell me, how do I keep from smacking my brother?"

He paused a moment, clearly considering his response. "Well. First thing I do is shut up and try to talk myself down, pray a bit, maybe recite Psalm 51. Then when I can't stand the pressure building up anymore, I open my mouth and hope what comes out doesn't get me arrested."

Sophie chortled.

"Next, I remind myself of all the bad things that will happen if I lose control."

"Like going to prison?" she asked, suddenly sad.

"Like almost losing you." Brushing the hair back from her face, he cupped her cheeks tenderly.

"I'm still here."

"Yeah. Go figure." He kissed her, tenderly loving her with his mouth and then, in the privacy of their bedroom, with his body.

Chapter Twenty-One: The Honeymoon is Over

Sophie was almost as excited as she'd been on her wedding day. Today, in front of her mother and her best friends, she was going to adopt Owen. She would become his mommy for real.

When she arrived, Owen leapt off the front steps of Cincinnati's City Hall and raced across the lawn, vaulting into Sophie's arms. Pia rushed down the steps after him, looking harassed and out of breath. She'd clearly drawn babysitting duties.

"You taked a long time to come. You still wanna be my mommy?" he asked, his wide smile fading minutely.

"Of course I do. You're my bestest son," she said, hugging him hard.

"Mine too," he said, wiggling down. "I sure do need a mommy. Nicky at Sunday school says he gots a mommy and his mommy kisses him on a cheek every night afore bed and reads him stories and every morning makes him Loopy Fruits." He started away at a run with no more than a glance over his shoulder and a wave, halting abruptly when he noticed Lucy. His gaze darted back to Sophie. "Your dad guy comin'?"

"No, honey," Sophie replied. "Just my mom. Come here." Owen cast Lucy a wary glance but obeyed Sophie. "After the judge says I can be your mommy for always, she will be your grandma. She wants to get to know you."

Owen stood toe-to-toe with Lucy giving her a fierce glare. "I don't like the dad guy."

Heedless of the fine peach-colored silk of her dress and the price of her Manolo Blahniks, Lucy crouched down in the grass, meeting Owen face to face. "Sometimes I don't like him either.

But I do love Sophie. And you're her son so that makes you my grandson. I would like us to be friends. Would you like that?"

Owen chewed his lower lip a moment, his brow furrowed and his foot tapping the ground. "Okay. You like ice cream?"

"Yes. Vanilla is my favorite," Lucy said.

"Nilla?" Owen frowned, shaking his head, refusing to accept such a ludicrous statement. Then, grabbing her hand, he towed her toward the front doors. "Come on."

"Well, would you look at that?" Pia's eyes were round with astonishment. "Your reckless man is changing our community."

"You never really believed in the potential for redemption, did you?" Sophie said.

"I believe in salvation. But you're right. I've seen so many people continue on in the church, Christian men and women, who never really change. Sorry, but your father just keeps right on bullying the world in spite of his self-righteousness. When my brother was sent to prison, my so-called Christian grandparents turned their backs on him. I figured, if that's the way it works, then all I really needed was enough faith to get me into heaven, and then I could carry on and live the way I wanted. But God really does have the power to make us new."

"More than you can guess," Sophie said. "Like Kiran says, step by step, we become more like Jesus."

Pia hugged her. "Thank you for bringing Reck into our circle of friends. Now come on. Let's get your boy adopted."

CR&O

Sophie whistled as she set up her laptop on the beautiful teak dining table so that she could order books online for the children's department at the Ancora Library. She'd quit her job at the Cin-Ham and had taken a part-time position at the Ancora Library so she could devote more energy to her family. Sophie smiled. When she'd returned to Ancora after college to "reconnect" with her family, she hadn't imagined the family that God would provide.

Owen had been with them for six months and things were going well. In spite of the complications, she and Ayden seemed to fall more deeply in love each day. Sophie sighed blithely. She was the luckiest of wives because she had it all, passion, respect and adoration from the man she loved, her husband. She had a son who was full of energy and boundless curiosity. Life was not perfect; in fact, as Ayden said, it was a work in progress.

Today, she'd picked Owen up from school at eleven-thirty, taken him to lunch at Dagwood's Finest and then played with him for a couple of hours until she had to take time to work. Owen had just popped downstairs to watch Ayden work. And he'd even remembered to ask permission first. Things were going well.

"Owen Koenig Breckinridge, get your butt upstairs. Now!" Ayden roared.

Oh. Leaping up, Sophie jogged down to the workshop from the apartment, passing Owen running, hands and feet on the stairs to propel him faster. "Ayden, what on earth happened?"

"Look. Look what he did." Ayden gestured at the end table he was currently building for a Mr. Arbegast of Dayton, Ohio. "Weren't you supposed to be watching him?"

Tracing the deep gouges in the top surface with her forefinger, Sophie asked, "Owen did this?"

"Yes, he did. I caught him at it. The little...toad. I've had enough." Ayden strode up the stairs to the apartment.

This was bad. When Ayden started hesitating over words, replacing the profanity he wanted to say with milder vocabulary, it was a sign of the depth of his anger. "Ayden." Sophie caught up to him at the door. "What are you going to do?"

"What I should have done long before now. I'm going to spank his...backside."

"You can't." Sophie grabbed the back of his shirt.

"Don't tell me that he didn't mean it, that he has a good heart. He looked me straight in the eye and carved his initials in that piece."

Her brows furrowed in skepticism. That couldn't be accurate. Because if Owen had been looking directly at Ayden when he carved in the wood then surely Ayden would have stopped him.

"It was virtually finished. I was ready to deliver and receive payment. Now I'll have to redo the top and eat the extra costs." Ayden paced to the center of the room and planted his feet, his fists on his hips, bellowing, "Owen!"

"Ayden. Stop." Sophie stepped in front of him. "You cannot spank him."

Ayden's blazing glare dropped to her face. "Why not? You think a little chat will do it? Huh?" Sarcasm dripped from his words.

Sophie stiffened at his tone, saying earnestly, "You cannot spank that boy because he trusts us, he trusts us not to hurt him. You cannot break that trust." When he shifted his weight to turn away, she grabbed his arm. "You cannot smack a child who has been abused. It just isn't right."

"Ah!" Gripping his hair in frustration, Ayden huffed out a breath. "Soph, I can't do this. It's so hard for me. I'm frustrated all the time. The urge to hit, to smack, to pummel, it's always there. I've been solving my problems with my fists since before I could walk."

"Well, you can't do that anymore." She snapped the words out.

Ayden paced away from her. "I can't do any of it anymore." He dropped his head. "I think about leaving all the time, just walking away."

Stunned, Sophie gaped at him. "I'd be a single parent."

Ayden spun to face her, his expression enigmatic. "You would do this alone, raise my son without me?"

"Yes," she said breathily. What would that be like? What would it do to Owen? To Ayden? "But I'd rather do it together."

"What kind of man do you think I am?" he said fiercely. Then, all at once, the anger leaked out of him and, passing without touching her, Ayden flopped onto the sofa. "Where am

I supposed to learn these skills that I need to be a father when I never had one? Are they hiding somewhere inside me?" He passed his hands along his body as if searching. "Dormant?"

"'Trust in the Lord with all your heart and lean not on your own understanding. In all your ways acknowledge Him and He will direct your paths.' God is father of the fatherless."

"He better be," Ayden said harshly and then added softly, "It's my only hope." He reached a hand out toward her. "I'm not going anywhere, Soph. I'm simply telling you how I feel."

Relieved, she took his hand, allowing him to pull her down beside him. "Owen had a rough start in life. He's under a lot of strain at school. We've only been together as a family for a short time. He's not used to rules and consistency, expectations and responsibilities. His mother, Faehr, gave him no skills to cope with these things."

Ayden bristled. "Faehr did her best."

"You're kidding, right? She beat the kid. She made him lace her tea, which he prepared, with whiskey. She let her male friends pound on him. What about that is 'best'?"

Tensely, Ayden leaned forward, releasing her hand. "Her mother was a heroin addict who ran off when she was six, two years after her dad took off. She went to live with her aunt and uncle who beat the...snot out of her frequently, when they weren't drinking themselves into oblivion. They certainly never bothered to feed her on a regular basis."

Moving to the coffee table across from him, Sophie touched his knee lightly. "Not unlike your life, sweetheart. Yet you are a good father."

Ayden sighed morosely. "You know how they say that alcoholics always feel the pull toward drink? I feel the same sometimes, the constant temptation to solve problems with my fists. Or to run away."

"But you'll stay?"

He smiled sadly. "You're the best thing that's ever happened to me. Why would I give that up?" Ayden brushed his hands down his face and then back around his neck. "And you're right. Faehr should have done better for Owen. I need to do better for him." Extending his arm, he gestured her closer, invitation in his eyes. "I won't smack him."

Snuggling into his embrace, she asked, "Do you love Owen?"

Ayden blew out a breath, lifting his head to meet her gaze. "Yeah. I do. But you do have to admit that he's hard work."

She grinned. "Oh, yeah. He's a little toad."

"So what do I do?"

"What do *we* do?"

Ayden's face relaxed into a contented smile. "Yes, love of my life. So, how are we going to discipline *our* son?"

"We need to find out why he did it. Did something happen at school today? Is he getting sick? Jealous? Scared? I can go in and talk to him."

"Yeah, that would be good."

"But what then?"

"I honestly don't know, sweetheart," Ayden said. "It's going to take me a couple of hours to fix that…" His voice drifted off as inspiration hit. "I've got it!"

"Well? What?"

He sobered. "Do you trust me?"

"Yes," she replied slowly.

"Then trust me. Get Owen, please."

She studied him skeptically a moment before rising. At Owen's door, she knocked lightly. "Owen, honey. It's Mommy." There was no response from inside so she opened the door and went in. Scanning the space, she spotted Owen curled in a ball with his arms over his head in the farthest corner of the room, in the narrow space between the bed and the wall. She hadn't seen him in that posture in weeks.

Leaving the door ajar so that Ayden could listen in, she sat on the edge of the bed, right near the yellow stegosaurus on the bedspread. "Owen," she whispered softly.

"My daddy so mad." Owen's voice was muffled.

"It's understandable, don't you think?" Sophie said.

Owen dropped his arms. "He gonna hit me wif his big hands?"

Tears stinging the backs of her eyes, Sophie's breath caught in her chest. "No, honey."

"He gonna lock me in a closet?"

"No. Come here." Reaching down, she lifted him onto her lap. "What you did was very naughty, Owen."

"Me, I can 'pologize," he suggested.

"'I'm sorry' would be a good start."

"Sorry, then all done. Right?" He looked up, hope in his eyes.

"No, honey. You are still going to have to be punished."

Owen's affect fell and his lip quivered. "I'm scared."

Sophie hugged him tight. "Don't be scared. Go and talk to your daddy."

Shaking his head, he buried his face in her shoulder. "No, no, no."

She held him a while, murmuring reassurances. Then, carrying him to the door, she put him down and gave him a little shove toward Ayden.

"Owen. Come here." Ayden's voice brooked no argument.

When Owen looked back at her, Sophie nodded, smiling reassuringly and gesturing him forward. His body stiff, his lip quivering, he took a few steps and then jerked to a halt.

"Come here." Ayden dug deep for calm.

Reaching the penultimate point of the journey, Owen stood just out of reach. Ayden extended his arm in an inviting manner. Softening his voice, he said, "Come here, son."

Leaping into his arms, Owen buried his face against Ayden's neck. "I'm sorry. Please don't smack me on a bum!" Breaking down, he sobbed.

The boy's anguish touched Ayden's heart and he hugged him hard until Owen's sobs quieted into little hiccups of sound.

"Soph, can we have some tissues, please?" Ayden said gently. When Sophie brought the box over, he took two and held them to Owen's nose. "Blow." Owen honked to clear his nose. "Again." Ayden wiped the tears from his flushed cheeks.

"I'm sorry, Daddy. You smack me now?" His piteous voice visibly moved Ayden.

"I'm not going to smack you, Owen."

Owen breathed a dramatic sigh of relief.

Ayden set him on his knees so they could speak face to face. "You damaged the table, though, didn't you?"

Owen nodded pathetically.

"Does it belong to you?"

Owen shook his head.

"Do the tools belong to you?"

Eyes widened, Owen shook his head again.

"Mr. Arbegast hired me to build that table. Now it's damaged and I have to buy a new piece of wood and spend the time sanding a new surface. A new piece of wood costs money, money that could be spent on…" Inspiration hit. "Ice cream."

Ayden had made his point. Owen's lips trembled. "I like ice cream. How me fix it, Daddy?" he asked quietly, his bright blue eyes wide and wet.

"I want you to understand how much work it takes to repair something that's broken. So you're going to watch."

Owen perked up a bit. "After me play?"

"No."

"After…" He didn't seem to know what else could delay his doom.

"Now. We'll start now but will likely have to finish tomorrow."

"Okay, Daddy."

Ayden hugged him then set him on his feet.

"I'll see you both a little later." Sophie gave Owen a reassuring squeeze.

"I go to a workshop?" Owen asked querulously.

"Yep. Later. First we need to go to the lumber store and buy a piece of maple for Mr. Arbegast's end table."

"In a car? We get ice cream?" Owen began dancing in excitement.

Ayden's expression was quelling.

Owen stilled. "No. No ice cream. I like ice cream," he added in a mutter.

Tough. Ayden was tempted to say it aloud but he refrained.

CЯᏰᎧ

"Daddy? Do you gots green paint for dinosaurs?" Owen asked the next afternoon as he sat on a stool at the counter in the workshop.

"Um." Passing over a small pot of water-soluble Cyan green, Ayden took a moment to admire Owen's handiwork. "Hey, champ. That's a good picture." He had a good eye for someone so young, and consistency of form; all the dinosaurs always looked like dinosaurs.

Owen frowned, his voice subdued when he responded. "Tammy drawed a picture. Wif dinosaurs. Not as good as me." His lower lip shot out in a pout.

"Well, maybe she's not as good at drawing as you are."

"I told her that...told her that."

Uh oh. Ayden had an idea of where this was going.

"I telled...told her it was no good and all wrong and Foxx said, 'no' I should not say that. He told me I'm not nice. I on'y sayin' the truf. I got so mad I drawed all over her paper and Tammy, she cried so loud and Foxx got mad at me and I had to go 'way from a table." Owen looked up with misery stamped on his face. "Foxx say he dis'pointed wif me."

"It sounds like you hurt Tammy's feelings," Ayden said.

"What you mean?"

Ayden dug deep for calm and inspiration. In fact, he asked the Lord. And received an answer. "Was Tammy being naughty when she drew her picture?"

"No. Just a bad draw-er."

Ayden ruminated on that a moment. "I like to build furniture, right?"

"Uh huh." Owen's face twisted in confusion, clearly wondering why his father was talking about chairs instead of dinosaurs.

"I work hard to make good, solid furniture."

"Yeah, you make it nice."

"But there are lots of people in the world who make better furniture than me."

"Nuh uh." Owen shook his head vehemently. "You gotta be the best."

"No, champ. I don't. I've gotta *do* my best. That's all anyone can ever ask of me. If Tammy's picture was her best then that's great for Tammy."

Crossing his arms, Owen insisted stubbornly, "You gotta tell the truf."

"The truth is one thing but your opinion is another," Ayden muttered darkly. Opinions so often sprouted from selfishness and cruel ignorance and frequently led to labels that followed you, dogging your life-steps. By the age of ten, he'd been labeled a loser, a reprobate, a no-good son-of-a-whore. There had never been an adult in his life to offer him a word of kindness or, more importantly, hope.

"What's a 'pinion?" Owen asked transparently.

Shaking himself out of his musings, Ayden thought about how to answer Owen's question. "It's the idea we have that might be true and it might not be."

"Like lying?" Owen tilted his head quizzically.

"Not lying, not usually. More like something you think..." He paused, groping for a way to explain. "But maybe other people have other ideas. Mr. Foxx thought Tammy's picture was good. I'll bet he thought your picture was good."

"He said I need more blue sky. But Tammy had no blue sky." Owen emphasized the point with his hands, painting the imaginary expanse.

"In Mr. Foxx's opinion, your picture needed more sky but Tammy's didn't," Ayden said. "But opinions are something we don't have to tell other people because sometimes our opinions might hurt their feelings."

"Like make them cry?" Owen's brows furrowed.

"Yes, exactly like that."

"I didn't wanna make her cry. I on'y want Foxx to like my picture."

"I think I understand. You were feeling jealous so you made a mistake, got angry and reacted badly." That was definitely something that Ayden well understood.

"Yeah." Owen groaned loudly, pathetically.

And here was an opportunity to offer his son hope for a better tomorrow. "Do you want to fix it?"

Hope lit Owen's features. "Yeah."

"Tomorrow at school, you need to apologize to Tammy for saying rude things and for damaging her picture."

Chewing his lower lip, Owen thought about that for a while, long enough for Ayden to think the boy had no intention of following through. And long enough for Ayden to think that they were going to have to do something dramatic to help Owen understand.

"Okay." Owen finally conceded.

"Good." Relieved, Ayden brushed the sawdust off his hands onto his jeans and then pulled Owen into a hug. If he could accomplish nothing else as a father, Ayden was going to let his son know that yesterday's mistake did not need to determine the course of his life. He was going to give Owen something positive. Hope. But how? Sophie was constantly telling him that Owen needed verbal reassurance of their love. So Ayden gave it. "I love you."

"I love you, Daddy." Okay, now Ayden understood why those three words were so important. His chest was flooded with warmth at the little boy's sincere words.

Music was blasting through the apartment as Ayden led Owen upstairs, bringing lightness to Ayden's spirit. When Owen went off to play with his cars, Ayden found Sophie dancing and singing softly as she washed the dishes. When she noticed him, she smiled buoyantly. No one else had ever smiled at Ayden in such a manner, like their life was made better by his proximity.

"How are things going?" she asked, sashaying over to him.

Taking her sudsy hand, he spun her into his body, her back to his front, swaying to the music together. "Teachers have too much influence," he muttered.

Leaning her head back against his shoulder, she looked up at him, frowning, clearly puzzled. "What do you mean?"

Ayden kissed up the side of her neck to the silky soft skin below her ear, then stayed to nuzzle as his hands pressed her closer. She relaxed against him, her question forgotten. Pushing her collar aside, he laved the cluster of freckles he'd discovered on her shoulder. "You're amazing," he murmured against her skin. "So good."

"Because of my superior grace and dance-ability?"

"Hmm." Turning her body, he kissed her, taking his time, lavishing attention on every surface of her mouth until she was breathless and weak in the knees.

"Mommy?" Owen appeared beside them. "I have ice cream?"

They kept their arms around each other. "We don't have ice cream, sweetie."

His face fell. "The table done. Right, Daddy?"

"Yes, champ. It's finished."

"No more ice cream?" His lip shot out, quivering.

"I can deliver the table tomorrow and, once Mr. Arbegast pays me, maybe we can buy some ice cream."

"Yes, yes, yes." Joyfully, Owen jumped up and down then stilled. "You not mad anymore? You forgive me like they say in a Sunday school?"

Ayden scooped him up. "Yes. Just like they say in Sunday school."

"Ice cream today?" he asked.

"Tomorrow," Ayden repeated firmly. "I'll deliver the table in the morning."

"Then when I pick you up from school, we can buy some ice cream and a few other groceries," Sophie said.

"Oh. School." Owen wriggled free of Ayden's grip and ran to his cubby by the coat closet where they kept his backpack. Unzipping each and every pocket, he rifled through until he produced a pale blue sheet of paper. Jogging over, he offered it to Sophie. "Foxx says he needsa talk t' you."

Sophie accepted the page, reading it through and then handing it to Ayden. "This is dated from two days ago." Crouching, she got face to face with Owen.

He avoided direct eye contact, fidgeting with the sleeves of his shirt. "You mad at me. Foxx mad at me. I'm ascared. Then, today, Foxx say to give you the note." Owen's gaze shifted to Ayden. "I say sorry to Tammy t'morrow. I promise." He made a cross with his fingers over his chest.

"Who's Tammy?" Sophie asked.

"I'll explain later," Ayden said. And he knew that this was the moment, this was the time when he could give his son a better chance than he'd had. "It's going to be okay, Owen. Tomorrow you can apologize to Tammy and then Mommy will talk to Mr. Foxx. Everything's going to be okay."

"I don't like when you mad at me," Owen whispered.

Sophie pulled him into a hug. "Even when we're mad at you, we still love you. We will always love you." Owen gripped her tightly. "You don't need to be afraid to bring us notes from school. Whatever happens, we'll always be there for you."

"Forever?"

Exchanging a meaningful look with Sophie, Ayden crouched beside them, wrapping them in an embrace. "Forever."

Chapter Twenty-Two: Eddy's

The next afternoon found Sophie pushing a grocery cart laden with ice cream and sundae toppings from the doors of the Red Barn Market across the parking lot to her Toyota Avalon while corralling Owen between her body and the cart. She listened with half her attention as he chattered away, the sound rising from between her arms. With the other half, she monitored his position relative to the moving vehicles around them, trying to predict the moment when he would dart this way or that. He was developing into a helpful little guy, carrying and fetching for her, but still tended to act without thought of the consequences.

"I help you," he said, darting beneath her arm as they reached the proximity of the trunk. "I have the keys to open a trunk?" he asked looking up at her hopefully.

"I'll do it, sweetie. Remember the rule? Only Mommy is allowed to use the car keys."

Owen frowned, pouting for a moment before nodding once. He remembered. He had a good memory, but his thoughts didn't always process before he acted.

Sophie did her best to refrain from correcting him as he swung the grocery bags into the trunk regardless of their weight or contents. She'd learned early on to keep the eggs separated and under her constant vigil. For the bread? Well, she and Ayden had simply become accustomed to eating deformed toast and sandwiches.

"It's all in. Thank you, Owen. You are a great help," she said, holding him by the shoulder as she closed the trunk to prevent any last minute idea that might cause him to reach back into the space.

"You think I did good?" he asked, wonder in his eyes. He was still unaccustomed to compliments.

"I think you are great," she replied, hugging him tightly.

Beaming, he hugged her back as earnestly.

"Now, once you're buckled in, we can go home and meet Daddy. Then, can you guess where we're going for supper?"

"Grandma Lucy's?" he asked.

"Nope." She kept a tight grip on his hand. "Think pizza."

"Hmm. Good pizza or the yucky stuff wif mushyrooms and blechy peppergreens?"

Sophie drew out the words. "The bestest pizza of all."

"Wow, wow, wow!" Owen jumped up and down. "Eddy's! Let's go! Let's go!"

For once, getting Owen into his booster seat was going to be easy. She gave herself a pat on the back for forward thinking, tucking the strategy away. Give Owen a reason to get in the car and thus prevent the argument.

"I sit in the front," he said definitely. "Then I can tell you where t' go t' get home faster and then we go to Eddy's." The last word he said as a substitute for "hurray".

Well, so much for that theory. "You have to sit in the booster seat in the back, sweetie. It's the law. You know that."

Scowling, Owen insisted, "I don't wanna go in a back. I can't see nuffin' back there."

Sophie glanced around to see a few shoppers openly watching them. *Thanks a lot. Oh, Lord, please don't let him embarrass me.* Sophie felt instant contrition. *Sorry, Lord. This isn't about me. Help me to help Owen.*

Bottom line? Owen simply had to obey this rule. There was no way around it, no negotiating. Without intending to, she fisted her hands, resting them on her hips and glaring down at him. "We are not leaving this parking lot until you are safely belted into your seat. I will stand here all day if necessary."

"I get ice cream?" he asked slowly.

Oh, the temptation to make his ice cream dependent on compliance. But she couldn't. They had promised Owen ice cream. She couldn't renege on the deal. But she needed to come up with a reasonable consequence if he didn't comply. "Ice cream is not for grocery store parking lots. It is for home after supper at Eddy's. In order to get home and then to Eddy's and then home again, you will need to sit in your seat with your seatbelt on. If it takes too long, the ice cream will melt."

Even at the threat of melted ice cream, he took the time to consider his options. Heaving a sigh of disgust, he demanded to know, "Why they gotta make rules all a time?"

"Well," Sophie returned the question to him, feeling very Socratic. "Why do we have rules about seatbelts?"

"Hey, lady. You need some help?" Sophie glanced around, startled to find a hulking middle-aged man watching them from a few feet away. How had he gotten so close without her noticing? She felt a moment of trepidation as she surveyed his tattoos and skull bandana.

"We're fine. Thank you," she said, trying to infuse confidence and warning into her tone and then added quietly to Owen. "Get in the car now."

Owen squinted at her, determination written in bold caps on his expression. "No."

The watcher chuckled. "They do grow up, ma'am. It may not seem so now, but one day you'll laugh. Good luck."

Astonished, Sophie watched him walk away toward a woman of commensurate age. The woman kissed him before they mounted their luxury motorcycle and drove away. A smile pulled at Sophie's mouth. Love was everywhere.

"I sittin' in a front, Mommy." Owen grabbed for the doorframe, scrambling to get into the driver's seat.

No way. Not happening. Determined, Sophie took hold of him around the waist. "You will sit in your seat in the back."

"Leggo! Leggo!" Releasing the doorframe, Owen slithered through her grip. Shoving at her, he spun and ran right into the edge of the door. "Aaah! Mom~my!"

A goose-egg-sized bump appeared almost immediately. Feeling sick to her stomach, Sophie scooped him up. "Oh, sweetheart. Are you okay? Oh, my baby boy, that must hurt so much." Owen clung to her, sobbing against her shoulder.

Fishing her keys out of her pocket, she opened the trunk, getting the ice cream and positioning it against his forehead. His cries quickly settled into hiccups "Wh-what you doin', my Soph—" Hiccup. "Mommy?"

"The cold ice cream will help your poor head feel better."

He hiccupped. "Mommy?"

"Yes, sweetheart."

"I belong to you? I—Am I your baby?"

Sophie pulled back to see his expression. "You're my baby. I love you, Owen."

"I don' wanna sit in a back," he said, but he seemed to be testing rather than demanding because he tilted his head to study her response.

"I still love you, even when you don't want to sit in the back."

He pushed the ice cream away and then settled in her arms. "I don't need a ice cream."

Sophie wasn't positive what he meant by that so she just hugged him, kissing his forehead carefully so as not to hurt his poor bump. Returning the ice cream to the trunk, she shut it and placed Owen in his seat. He let her fasten the seatbelt without comment.

She still felt shaky as she sat behind the steering wheel. "Let's go home and pick up Daddy. Do you still want to go to Eddy's?"

"Yep," he said calmly.

Chapter Twenty-Three: Consequences

The telephone woke Sophie at five o'clock the next morning. The three of them had had a wonderful time at Eddy's—if you didn't count the cardboard-flavored pizza—and then they'd returned home, deciding to make one giant sundae in a mixing bowl, loading it with every topping they could find in the house including Owen's favorite breakfast cereal. Half of it had ended up melting in the sink but Owen had giggled all the way through.

"Yeah?" Ayden answered the phone. He immediately sat up against the headboard. "Yes. Absolutely. She'll come. Fifteen minutes. Got it. And, sir? I hope she's okay."

Sophie came alert in an instant. "What's going on?"

Ayden rang off. He took her hand, kissing it. "That was your father. Your mom's had an episode, at least that's how he referred to it. He called an ambulance. I guess she asked for you so he's coming to pick you up to take you with him to the hospital."

"Of course. Yes. I can drive and meet him there." She was out of bed and dressing before he'd finished.

"There's no need to drive, he's on his way here. And I'll need the car to take Owen to school."

"But aren't you helping Kiran and the others paint the sanctuary today?" she asked, sitting on the edge of the bed to pull on her socks.

"I'll just be a little late. No problem."

"Owen needs to be at school by eight-fifty and—"

Ayden brushed his fingers lightly over her lips. "I can handle it. Go and see your mom."

"Okay. I love you."

"Love you, too."

Sophie jogged down the stairs after peeking in on Owen to make sure he was still sleeping.

"Bye."

"Bye, honey." Ayden followed her down, kissing her again. "Don't worry. We'll be fine."

Ayden watched until she slipped into the Beamer beside her father.

"What happened, Dad?" she asked.

"They're not sure but she kept saying she couldn't breathe," he replied. He was immaculately dressed as usual, wearing an earth-brown three-piece-suit. His hair and beard were neatly coiffed. And he frowned when she called him "Dad". Some things never changed.

Sophie reached across to squeeze his hand. "She'll be okay."

He glanced at her, releasing her hand. "Of course."

⊂⊃⊂⊃

Jaxen was just finishing the attendance when Owen Breckinridge barreled into the classroom, completely ignoring the school secretary who bustled along several paces behind him, reciting a litany of reasons why he shouldn't run in the school.

"Good morning, Owen," Jaxen said, suppressing a smile at the comical sight.

"Hey, Foxx," Owen said over his shoulder as he jogged across the classroom, coming to stop beside Tammy Watkins who greeted him with a toothy grin.

"Good morning, Mrs. Crowder," Jaxen said as the secretary came to a halt, wiping the perspiration from her brow with a tissue she'd produced from the pocket of her pale green dress.

"It's no wonder that boy doesn't follow the rules," she said huffily. "That father of his is so rude."

Jaxen's smile dropped away. In his opinion, Owen was doing extremely well given the life from which he'd emerged, a life not so distant from Jaxen's own miserable childhood. As a matter of fact, Jaxen's hope for the little boy was enhanced because of the dedication and love that Sophie Breckinridge openly displayed toward her adopted son. That love would make the difference in this boy's life, far more than condemnation from misunderstanding adults.

Mrs. Crowder had more to say. "That Breckinridge man walked right in the front door ten minutes after the bell. When I asked him to go back and come in the proper door, he refused. He said, wasn't it better that Owen was at school rather than coming in through a specific door. Can you believe that kind of attitude? We have rules here for a reason. For the safety of the children." She sniffed haughtily. "And, look," said Mrs. Crowder pointing at a nasty looking contusion on Owen's forehead. "Who do you suppose did that?"

"Did you ask his father?" Jaxen asked.

Mrs. Crowder looked appalled. "He's a criminal. I didn't dare."

"How do you—" *know that?* Jaxen wondered. Though it was rumored and hinted at, it wasn't common knowledge that Ayden Breckinridge had spent time in federal prison.

"What seems to be going on here?" Ms. Byers, the principal, asked, making her rounds as she typically did after the morning bell.

"It's that Breckinridge boy again," Mrs. Crowder said as if that explained it all.

Jaxen scanned the children to see that several of them were listening to the conversation. He needed to distract them. "Ms. Smith?" He called the educational assistant over. "Could you please start circle time?"

"Sure, Mr. Foxx." As curious as she obviously was, Zoe Smith took control, leading the children across the room and settling them with their backs to the adults.

"What about the Breckinridge boy?" Ms. Byers said, glancing back and forth between Jaxen and Mrs. Crowder.

"His father brought him today," Mrs. Crowder said. "Very late. And he was so rude. *And* the boy has a huge lump on his head."

"A lump?" Ms. Byers asked. "Owen Breckinridge. Come here."

Owen glanced over his shoulder, pursed his lips in annoyance and then turned back to the circle.

"You see?" Mrs. Crowder said. But Jaxen wasn't exactly sure what they were supposed to see.

"I'll get him," he said. With no more than a word and insistence, Jaxen returned with the boy in tow. In order to head off the interrogation that he was sure was building he crouched down in front of Owen. "What happened to your head, buddy?" He touched Owen's forehead lightly beside the bump.

Owen glanced over at the circle and then back at Jaxen, down to his shoes and then to his hands. "I hit my head on a door."

Mrs. Crowder gasped. "You see? What did I tell you? Every abuser tells the same story."

"Just a minute," Jaxen protested. "We don't know what happened."

Ms. Byers held up her hand for silence. Mrs. Crowder snapped her mouth shut on whatever else she'd been planning to say. "Owen," Ms. Byers asked. "Did your daddy hit you?"

"My mommy don't let my daddy hit me," Owen said. "I, uh...can I go back to circle?"

"Yes," Ms. Byers said. Owen trotted off. "It certainly does seem that his father has violent tendencies. I, er..." Ms. Byers led Mrs. Crowder and Jaxen into the hall. "Shortly after Owen was registered here, the sheriff came to me...for a confidential conversation...something he felt, as principal, that I should know." She cleared her throat and then lowered her voice. "Mr. Breckinridge has spent time in jail." Mrs. Crowder nodded knowingly.

Not so confidential if the school secretary already knows. Who else was made privy to this information? Jaxen sighed, rubbing his forehead with his fingertips. Jaxen knew of Ayden Breckinridge, AKA The Wrecker, from his days on the Cincinnati PD though Ms. Byers didn't know of that connection. For the same reason, the staff here knew very little of Jaxen's past. Because he'd found that even the merest hint of his previous gang activity had been met with shock and horror. The full disclosure of Breckinridge's rap sheet would be met with the same horror. The past was the past. The real question in Jaxen's mind was whether The Wrecker had managed to change his life as Jaxen had.

"I'm calling the sheriff," Mrs. Crowder said.

"I don't think we have any other choice," Ms. Byers said.

Jaxen didn't want to land a man working toward recovery in the hot seat but he didn't see any other option. He nodded sadly in resignation. "I'll talk to Owen later and see if I can get the whole story from him. You should also get in touch with his mom, Sophie. She's been my main contact with the family."

"A very good idea," Ms. Byers said.

Lord, please help Ayden Breckinridge today.

⋘⋙

Kiran had finally convinced Mr. Gordon to come down off the step-ladder and let Ayden take his place with the paint roller. At seventy-eight the man had no business climbing ladders for any purpose. His wife was no help. She stood at the bottom haranguing the man with instructions. Ayden felt an inexplicable desire to chuckle, wondering if some day he and Sophie would be the ones driving their friends crazy.

"Hey, Reck. Missed a spot."

"Ha ha, Sandy. You're a riot," Ayden retorted. Working with Sandy was a lot like working with a five-year-old. They'd do just as well enlisting Sophie's Sunday school class to help.

"Breckinridge, get down. Immediately!"

Ayden glanced down to see Tristan Paetan at the bottom of the ladder with Reggie and Reynolds flanking him. They were all dressed in their dirt-brown uniforms, clearly not here to help.

Blast it. "I'm not even on my bike. How could I be speeding?" Ayden quipped, returning to his painting. It wasn't bad enough that the sheriff was harassing him every time he drove out of town, now he'd started following him around.

"Reck," Kiran said in warning.

When Ayden heard the click, he knew exactly what it was. Glancing down, he confirmed that Tristan had pulled his Smith & Wesson out of his holster and cocked it, aiming it directly at Ayden's spine. Energy gathered in Ayden's muscles as his brain engaged to try and harness his instinctive reaction: fight. "What's going on?" he asked through gritted teeth.

"Get down here." Tristan snapped out the words.

"What's this about, Tristan?" Kiran asked.

"This has nothing to do with you, Kiran," Tristan said harshly. "Stay back. I don't want to be forced to arrest you as well."

Ayden didn't want to bring trouble to Kiran so he backed slowly down the ladder, keeping his hands visible. As soon as his foot hit the floor, Tristan fisted the back of his shirt and shoved him face first against the ladder, jabbing him between the shoulder blades with his handgun. Humiliation and pain rose up within him, morphing into indignation which felt a lot like fury. Twisting abruptly, Ayden grabbed Tristan's wrist in one hand, shifting the barrel of the handgun toward the ceiling, and then fisted Tristan's shirt with the other hand, keeping him at a distance. "Back off," Ayden said through gritted teeth.

Reynolds gun came out.

"Wait! Whoa!" Kiran tried to get between them but Reggie held him back. Vaguely, Ayden heard Mrs. Gordon weeping as Sandy, Frank and the others stared on in bewilderment.

Reynolds pressed the barrel of her pistol against Ayden's temple, the cold metal digging into his flesh, the nip of pain like a bucket of cold sense on his ire. "Release the sheriff!" She was getting panicky and Ayden realized that he was much more likely to be shot because of her agitation than any supposed crime he'd committed. At that range, she'd splatter his brains all over the freshly painted walls.

Slowly Ayden released Tristan. Tristan slammed his pistol into the side of Ayden's face. Taken unawares, he wasn't prepared for the vicious attack. Blood dripped into his eye as the impact opened a wound over his eyebrow. He swiped it away. This was the part where he would normally use his fists to take his opponents down. But the last time he'd fought, he'd almost lost Sophie. He wouldn't risk it again. Praying for patience, he struggled against his desire for combat and tried to wait and see what would happen next.

"You're under arrest for assault on a minor," Tristan said, spinning Ayden and pressing him against the pale yellow wall. All Ayden could think was that his blood was going to ruin the excellent paintjob.

"What assault?" Kiran said.

Tristan shoved the back of Ayden's head, smashing his cheek into the freshly painted wall. "His kid showed up for school with a bump the size of a baseball."

"That's what this is about?" Ayden said, resisting Tristan's grip. Tristan got one wrist confined by the cold metal of a handcuff but it wasn't until Reynolds joined the fray that they managed to get the second secured. "I didn't hit him," Ayden said, struggling. "Did you ask him what happened? He was out with Sophie and he bumped his head on the car door." Ayden's blood pressure was rising fast.

"Yeah, right. I walked into a door," Tristan mocked him. "Why can't abusers come up with anything better to say? So predictable." He jerked Ayden away from the wall. The paint came off as well, sticking to Ayden's clothes and the left side of his face.

"I didn't hit Owen. I wouldn't." Except that he had wanted to smack Owen after he'd damaged the table. Did that make him an abuser in training? No. Not as long as Sophie was there to talk sense to him. But what if there were no Sophie? "I did not hit Owen. Ask Sophie."

Tristan clenched his fist in Ayden's paint-covered shirt, jerking him close. "You leave my sister out of this, you filthy piece of..." He uttered such foul descriptors that even Reynolds looked shocked.

"Sophie would never let you get away with saying that," Ayden said for no reason he could deduce. "Reggie, call Sophie. Ask her what happened."

"We tried," Reggie replied. "She's not answering."

"Shut up!" Tristan spat as he reprimanded his deputy. Shoving Ayden ahead of him, he said, "I blame you, Kiran, for bringing this criminal into our peaceful community."

"Kiran," Ayden called. "Sophie's at the hospital."

"Shut it!" Tristan said, shoving Ayden hard enough that he stumbled over the doorframe.

"She's at the hospital with her father. Lucy's ill!" It was the last chance he had before Tristan shoved him into the back of his Clermont County sheriff's car and drove him to jail.

Chapter Twenty-Four: Not Guilty

"Mrs. Breckinridge?" A nurse in baby blue scrubs entered Lucy Paetan's hospital room. "There's a telephone call for you at the nurse's station."

"Oh. Okay." Sophie patted her mother's hand. "I'll be right back."

"Sophie Anne." Her father frowned at her and she found it vaguely annoying. He'd had no issue taking dozen of phone calls today. What was wrong with her taking one?

Ignoring him, she walked to the nurse's station, taking the proffered phone. "Hello? This is Sophie Breckinridge." It still gave her a little thrill to use her married name.

"It's Ms. Byers calling from Ancora Elementary. We've had some difficulty reaching you. In the end we contacted the mayor's office, knowing that Mayor Paetan was your father. They forwarded us to him and he let us know you were there at the hospital and not to be disturbed, however—"

"What do you mean? If there's a problem at school, you can always contact me." Had her father really told the school not to get in touch with her? "Is something wrong with Owen? Is he sick? Has he been hurt?"

"Owen has not been picked up yet."

"What?" She checked watch. It was after one. "My husband was supposed to drop Owen off and pick him up today. Hasn't he come?"

"He did drop him off." Ms. Byers cleared her throat. "We noticed that Owen had a bump on his head."

What does that have to do with this? "Yes. Did Ayden explain what happened? Our arrangements were kind of rushed this morning so I forgot to remind him to."

"Is that how the bump happened? His father?"

What? "No. Oh, no, not at all. It happened yesterday at the shopping mall. Owen was being a little pickle about getting in his booster seat and when I insisted, he pulled away and fell into the car door. Why would you think it was Ayden?"

Ms. Byers spoke very slowly as though she was considering each word. "There has been a misunderstanding. We thought that Owen had been...injured by his father. We called the sheriff."

"Oh, no! The sheriff? Ms. Byers, my husband is a good man. How could you think he would do such a thing?" Tears sprang to Sophie's eyes.

"He does have a record of violent crimes," she said but it sounded like a lame excuse to Sophie.

"People are not bound by their pasts. They can change." Tristan thought Ayden had smacked Owen. "Oh, I can't believe this." What would her brother do now?

"I am sorry if this causes difficulties for you. However, Owen still needs to be picked up."

"I can be there in twenty minutes. Tell Owen I'm coming. And please tell Mr. Foxx I'm sorry to inconvenience him," Sophie said, hanging up. *How can this be?* Returning to her mother's room, she started to explain that she'd have to leave when the doctor entered the room.

"Mrs. Paetan, you're looking much better now. I'm going to give you some medication that you can take when you feel these episodes coming on. You've taken this before, I believe."

"Yes, Doctor Jones," Lucy said meekly.

"Before?" Sophie said. "What happened, doctor? What caused her episode? Was it her heart?"

"No, not at all. It was a panic attack. I'm sure it was very frightening. My wife suffers attacks and she says it can feel like you're dying. But, fortunately, you are very healthy, Mrs. Paetan." After handing her the prescription, he turned to Stuart. "The next time you wish to have a discussion with your ex-wife, I suggest you wait until daylight rather than waking her in the wee hours of the morning." He pinned Stuart with a glare and then smiled gently at Lucy and departed.

"What is going on?" Sophie asked.

Stuart scowled. "She was talking about turning her shares in Paetan over to your husband's child. I needed to speak some sense into her."

"What?" Sophie was flabbergasted. "You're kidding me. You have to be. I cannot believe that you induced a panic attack by bullying my mother in the middle of the night. Over something that is none of your business."

"I'm still planning to set up a trust fund for Owen," Lucy said with just a hint of adamantium in her voice. "You have not changed my mind, Stuart."

Sophie leaned down to kiss her mother. "Thanks, Mom. I love you. I need to go pick Owen up from school." She pointed at her father. "You! Don't have a clue."

"Sophie Anne Paetan."

"Breckinridge, Dad. Forever."

Sophie had a nurse call a taxi to Ancora Elementary. Ms. Byers met her at the front door. "Thank you for coming, Mrs. Breckinridge. Mr. Foxx kept Owen in the classroom. He's an unofficial member of the afternoon kindergarten class at the moment."

"Thank you," Sophie said, her mind still spinning with images of Tristan and Ayden and allegations of child abuse. She turned toward the primary hallway.

"I have a feeling that we…" Ms. Byers stopped her with a hand on her arm. "*I*…may have caused a problem. We had difficulty reaching you."

"My cell phone was off at the hospital." Sophie took it out and turned it on, finding five voicemail messages, three from Kiran, one from Reggie and one from the Clermont County Sheriff's Department. She listened to the first. "Sophie, it's Kiran. Tristan arrested Reck. He said Reck hit Owen. Call me." Sophie's heart thudded in her chest. *Oh, no!* "I think you did cause a lot of trouble, Ms. Byers." Sophie strode away down the hall, knocking on the door frame as she scanned the kindergarten room for Owen.

"Mommy!" He sailed across the room and into her arms.

"Did you have a good day?" she asked, trying to sound normal when what she felt was dreadfully anxious.

"You okay, Mommy? You comed so late." Owen's brow furrowed darkly.

"I'm very sorry, sweetheart. Something unexpected happened. But I hope you knew that I would always come."

Jaxen had made his way over with Owen's jacket and backpack. "Sophie. It's good to see you. I think you might want to check in with your husband—"

"It's a little late for that," she snapped at him. "Why would you think that..." She gulped, glancing down to see Owen listening with interest. "Owen hit his head on the car door when he and I were at the grocery store. Nothing to do with...his father."

"I suspected as much. Sometimes a rap sheet works against you in unexpected ways. I'm sorry."

"I have to go. And now I have to take this little boy to the..." She stopped. The last thing she wanted was for Owen to think he was being taken to the police station because *he'd* done something wrong.

"Why don't I keep him here until you get things straightened out? And Sophie, I'd be willing to make a statement that, once Owen told me the whole story, it was clear that his father didn't injure him. Unfortunately, when Ms. Byers questioned him, he gave an enigmatic response. But once I investigated a little bit, I got the rest of the story."

Owen was swiveling in her grip, watching his peers playing around the room. "Owen, honey, would you like to stay in afternoon kindergarten a little longer? I can come and pick you up a little later?"

"Hmm," he replied. "Foxx, you stay here too?"

Jaxen smiled. "Yes. I'll be here."

"Okay," Owen replied happily. He started off and then turned back. "You come back. Right, Mommy?"

"I will always come back, Owen. I promise."

"Okay." He skipped off and immediately joined in on a game on the carpet that involved small cars and large blocks.

"Thank you," Sophie said. "I'll be back as quickly as possible."

"Owen is doing really well, Sophie. You and your husband are doing a good job."

"Thanks. Now I just have to convince my brother, the sheriff."

Sophie called Kiran on the way over, asking him to meet her at the sheriff's office. Then she called Cal Zimmerman, her lawyer, and told him everything she knew. Cal agreed to represent Ayden.

One of the hardest things she'd ever done was to wait in the parking lot for Kiran and Cal to arrive, given that her husband was unjustly imprisoned inside the building. Kiran arrived first, telling her about the incident at church.

"Oh, Kiran. He must have been so humiliated. Just because he has a record, law enforcement thinks they can treat him as badly as they choose, that he deserves it. It's not right. He would never harm Owen. Even if he did give him a little smack on the behind—which he hasn't—he would never knock him about."

"I know, Sophie. I'm sorry this happened. Your brother certainly seems to have a problem with Reck."

Cal arrived and the three entered the sheriff's office together, going directly to the large glass-walled office and knocking. Reggie walked over from a series of desks nearby.

"Sophie." Reggie greeted her, looking paler than usual.

"Where's my brother the sheriff?" she asked angrily.

Tristan strode out of his office. "What are you doing here?"

Sophie flushed red with wrath. "You have to ask? I'm here to sue you for wrongful arrest. And assault. And slander. And anything else I can think of. Get my husband out here now!"

The entire office went quiet. "You!" Tristan stepped into her, his fists clenched. Sophie stood her ground. "He's filth! A scumbag who only married you for your money." Tristan poked her in the shoulder in time with his words. "Get out of here and let me do my job."

A strange calm settled on her. "You know?" She turned to Kiran. "I understand why Ayden finds it so irritating to be poked." Turning her back on Tristan disdainfully, Sophie walked toward the door to the holding cells. Cal took over, preventing Tristan from following her.

"With what has my client been charged?" Cal asked.

"Your client?" Tristan looked astonished a moment then just plain mean. "Assault and child abuse."

"Based on what evidence?"

"The school principal."

"Did the principal witness the abuse?" Cal asked. Sophie stopped to listen.

"No. Not exactly," Tristan said, his voice losing some of its energy. "She said she asked the boy and he said…"

"His exact words," Reggie spoke up, "were 'my mommy don't let my daddy hit me'."

"Well, yeah, that's true," Sophie said, turning back. Taken out of context, she could see how the words could be misconstrued. But surely an experienced peace officer wouldn't take a child's poor syntax as his only evidence. "Owen's teacher, Mr. Jaxen Foxx, is willing to make a statement that Owen told him that his father did not hit him. The principal heard only one poorly organized sentence."

"Mrs. Breckinridge," Reynolds said, stepping forward. Tristan scowled at her but remained silent when Cal started taking notes. "What *did* happen?"

"I took Owen to the Red Barn Market yesterday. When it was time to get in the car, he refused to put his seatbelt on in his booster seat. When I insisted, he tried to climb in the front seat. I picked him up but he wiggled out of my arms and, when he tried to dash away, he ran into the edge of the car door."

"He really did run into a door," Reynolds said thoughtfully.

"Yes," Sophie insisted.

"Are you releasing my client, Sheriff Paetan, or am I starting proceedings against you?" Cal asked.

"Get him." Tristan snapped out the words. Reggie moved away toward the cells in the back. "Regardless, Sophie, that guy is only after your money. He's got you liquidating shares in Granddaddy's company."

"What I do with my shares is my business, Tristan. It has nothing to do with you or Dad. In fact, I no longer want anything to do with you or the name Paetan. I will be liquidating *all* my shares. I want nothing more to do with any of you."

Tristan blanched. He looked suddenly afraid, rushing into his office and closing the door. What was that all about?

"Soph."

Sophie spun to see her husband. His clothing was covered in stiff, dry yellow paint as was the left side of his face. A trickle of blood oozed down, making an obscene crimson path through the mellow paint.

"Oh, Ayden." Sophie ran to him, wrapping her arms around him. He didn't return the hug. "It's all explained, honey," she said. "We're going to sue for wrongful arrest." She pulled back. "Are you okay?"

"Is Owen all right?" he asked, his voice subdued.

"Yes. Mr. Foxx has him at school. We can pick him up and go home."

"Where's Tristan?" Ayden asked.

"Hiding in his office," Sophie replied.

"This lawyer of yours?" Ayden said.

"I'm here, Mr. Breckinridge." Cal shook Ayden's hand. "I'll handle things from here on out. Why don't you take your wife home and get cleaned up?"

"I didn't do anything wrong," Ayden muttered.

"That is more than evident, sir. Be sure that this won't happen again," Cal said.

"And no more speeding tickets," Ayden said petulantly, pinning Reynolds with a glare.

"It seems to me that the sheriff was concerned about the wrong individual," Reynolds said. "If you stay to the speed limit, sir, there will be no more trouble."

Ayden nodded stiffly, either because the dried paint hampered his movements or to hide his convoluted emotions.

"Reck." Reggie offered his hand. Ayden narrowed his gaze then shook it. Reggie's cheeks darkened in a blush. "I'm sorry. There is clearly no reason to monitor your behavior."

"Come on, sweetheart," Sophie said, tugging on Ayden's arm. "Let's get our son and go home."

"Fine." Noticing him for the first time, Ayden nodded at Kiran.

"I'm sorry this happened, buddy," Kiran said, hugging Ayden companionably.

"Yeah, thanks," Ayden muttered.

"I'll make sure everyone knows," Kiran said, his eyes bright with compassion.

"Thanks." Ayden pulled back and they shared the silent communication thing that Sophie never could decipher. It seemed to bring Ayden some comfort.

"Ayden, are you okay?" she asked softly.

"I'm yellow," he said.

A smile pulled at her mouth. "Yes, you are." She flung her arms around him and this time he returned her embrace.

"Let's get Owen and go home, baby." He guided Sophie out the door with his arm around her waist.

Epilogue

Sophie ran the red rubber spatula around the mixing bowl one last time, removing the remnants of the cake batter into the pan. The pan she then slid into the oven.

"We havin' a party for a choc'lit cake?" Owen asked watching her every move, his little pink tongue popping out to lick his lips in anticipation.

"Actually, Uncle Kiran is having a party for us."

"How come?"

Sophie picked Owen up and placed him on the counter so they could speak eye to eye. "For Daddy's birthday."

"Am me...am I comin'?"

"Of course."

"Who else is comin'?"

"Tommy Tripper and his family..."

"Talia's comin'?" Owen said outraged. "We don' need girls at a party. You can come, Mommy, but no lil' sister girls."

Sophie chuckled. "She is Tommy's sister and part of his family."

He harrumphed. "She be's a pest."

"She *is* a pest. Most little sisters are."

"Who else?"

"Nicky D'Angelo and his family. Uncle Kiran's sister and brother. Miss Johnson..."

"She bringin' candy?"

"I don't know. Maybe. Probably since she knows you'll be there," Sophie said. Owen looked very pleased. "Mr. and Mrs. Gordon..."

"She bringin' cookies?" he said hopefully.

"I think she's bringing Daddy's favorite oatmeal cookies."

"Uh huh. They's good."

"Deputy Reggie. Mr. Foxx…"

"Foxx is comin'?" Owen said surprised.

"Yes. He and your dad are becoming good friends."

"Foxx is my friend?" Owen asked, doubt shading his eyes.

"Yes, of course." Sophie helped Owen down off the counter. "Can you please get the card you made for Daddy this morning?"

"Yep. Yeah. Sure." He ran off toward his bedroom, the teeny room which had, several months ago, been a storeroom. It would soon be a storeroom again once she and Ayden gained possession of the home they'd purchased in Ancora.

"Tristan's being investigated for embezzlement." Ayden's abrupt arrival pulled Sophie out of the kitchen and into his arms. He dropped a newspaper onto the teak dining table right on top of the photographs of the house that Sophie had been studying with Owen earlier, trying to decide which bedroom in the new house would be his own. At the moment, he seemed to feel that the garage would suit him best. She'd keep working on it.

"What do you mean?" she asked, opening the paper to see a picture of her brother being led away from the Clermont County Sheriff's Office in handcuffs.

"Who's that?" Owen asked, skidding to a halt at her side with a colored piece of construction paper clutched in his right hand.

"My brother," Sophie said, suppressing an urge to chortle. "It looks like he's got some questions to answer."

"Yeah. He was embezzling from Paetan Pharmaceuticals and then, to compound matters, he and that chemist, Regis Maxwell, were in league to start producing an addictive form of that Rita-whatsit Maxwell was working on. They were planning to turn it into a street drug, hoping to take advantage of the increased drug traffic in the area recently."

"I can't believe it," she said, plopping into a kitchen chair. "I knew he was a jerk. But I didn't realize just how big a dodo-brain resided beneath the sheriff's hat."

"That's why he didn't want you to mess with your shares," Ayden said.

"Oh, my goodness, you're right! That's probably why he was so obnoxious to you. Selling shares requires a review of the company's finances. That was a safeguard my grandfather put in place."

"Yeah. It was that investigation that exposed his crime." Ayden pulled her up and into his arms. Kissing her palm, he turned her hand over to admire the beautiful sapphire ring adjacent to her wedding band. He kissed it once. "You know, you should be a little more prudent about who you associate with."

Startled, she met his gaze. And then she laughed.

"What we laughin' 'bout?" Owen asked, coming to push between them.

Ayden scooped him up and held the three of them together. "We are laughing about life, champ. And God."

"God is funny?" Owen asked, perplexed.

"God is great," Ayden said. "Don't ever forget that, son. God loves us and wants good for us. He can even take guys like you and me, from Over-the-Rhine, and make us new and good."

"God likes us," Owen said smiling.

"More than you can imagine."

Psalm 51

1 Have mercy upon me, O God, according to Your lovingkindness; According to the multitude of Your tender mercies, blot out my transgressions. 2 Wash me thoroughly from my iniquity, and cleanse me from my sin. 3 For I acknowledge my transgressions, and my sin is always before me. 4 Against You, You only, have I sinned, and done this evil in Your sight— That You may be found just when You speak, and blameless when You judge. 5 Behold, I was brought forth in iniquity, and in sin my mother conceived me. 6 Behold, You desire truth in the inward parts, and in the hidden part You will make me to know wisdom. 7 Purge me with hyssop, and I shall be clean; wash me, and I shall be whiter than snow. 8 Make me hear joy and gladness, that the bones You have broken may rejoice. 9 Hide Your face from my sins, and blot out all my iniquities. 10 Create in me a clean heart, O God, and renew a steadfast spirit within me. 11 Do not cast me away from Your presence, and do not take Your Holy Spirit from me. 12 Restore to me the joy of Your salvation, and uphold me by Your generous Spirit. 13 Then I will teach transgressors Your ways, and sinners shall be converted to You. 14 Deliver me from the guilt of bloodshed, O God, the God of my salvation, And my tongue shall sing aloud of Your righteousness. 15 O Lord, open my lips, And my mouth shall show forth Your praise. 16 For You do not desire sacrifice, or else I would give it; You do not delight in burnt offering. 17 The sacrifices of God are a broken spirit, A broken and a contrite heart—These, O God, You will not despise. 18 Do good in Your good pleasure to Zion; build the walls of Jerusalem. 19 Then You shall be pleased with the sacrifices of righteousness, with burnt offering and whole burnt offering; then they shall offer bulls on Your altar.

References Consulted

1. http://ohioline.osu.edu/hyg-fact/1000/1082.html
   (December 9, 2013)
2. http://www.socialareasofcincinnati.org/report/Chapter2
   .html (July 1, 2013)
3. http://cincinnati.com/blogs/opinionati/2010/10/04/over
   -the-rhine-ranks-among-uss-top-25-most-dangerous-
   neighborhoods/ (July 1, 2013)
4. http://news.travel.aol.com/2010/08/31/cincinnati-slang/
   (July 5, 2013)
5. http://thetyee.ca/gallery/2004/11/24/Prison/ (July 8,
   2013)
6. http://allthingswildlyconsidered.blogspot.ca/2009/08/g
   angs-in-ohio-you-better-believe-it.html (Oct 5, 2013)
7. http://legal-
   dictionary.thefreedictionary.com/Police+Corruption+a
   nd+Misconduct (Oct 25, 2013)
8. http://news.travel.aol.com/2010/08/26/safe-and-
   dangerous-areas-in-seattle/ (Oct 26, 2013)
9. http://oncampus.macleans.ca/education/2009/03/09/bra
   in-candy-can-ritalin-turn-you-into-an-a-student/
   (November 23, 2013)
10. http://www.studylight.org/com/acc/view.cgi?bk=18&c
    h=37 September 28, 2013)
11. http://www15.uta.fi/FAST/GC/mobspeak.html
    (September 30, 2013)
12. http://www.cmausa.org/ministry/ (October 6, 2013)
13. http://cincinnati.com/blogs/opinionati/2010/10/04/over
    -the-rhine-ranks-among-uss-top-25-most-dangerous-
    neighborhoods/ (October 19, 2013)
14. http://www.dmv.org/oh-ohio/safety-laws.php#Child-
    Car-Seat-Laws (November 23, 2013)
15. http://www.satp.org/satporgtp/publication/faultlines/vo
    lume12/Article5.htm (November 27, 2013)

16. White, E.B. (1952). Charlotte's Web. N.Y., N.Y.: Harper & Row Publishers
17. http://www.topix.com/forum/city/chillicothe-oh/T8RPTDCC0OG7CGC7O (Oct 5, 2013)
18. http://thetyee.ca/gallery/2004/11/24/Prison/ (September 30, 2013)
19. http://www.youtube.com/watch?v=7MFItVyCprA (November 27, 2013)
20. www.waitingtobeglong.ca
21. www.focushelps.ca
22. Focus on the Family (2012). *Attachment in Adoption.*
23. http://enquirer.com/editions/2001/07/16/loc_over-the-rhine_under.html (December 30, 2013)
24. http://nwgangs.com/king-county-gangs.html (December 29, 2013)
25. http://www.nytimes.com/1983/02/15/science/self-sabatoge-in-careers-a-common-trap.html (January 13, 2014)
26. http://www.mediad.publicbroadcasting.net/p/wvxu/files/201210/Cin_reportFINAL.pdf (February 8, 2014)
27. Cruz, Nicky & Martin, Frank, *Soul Obsession: When God's Primary Pursuit Becomes Your Life's Driving Passion*, Waterbrook Press, Colorado Springs, 2005.

D. C. Shaftoe

Excerpt: Award-winning novel, Assassin's Trap

Shards of glass scattered across John Brock's chest. Pain seared through his shoulder. *Blast!* He couldn't tell if his shoulder was broken or not. And he didn't take the time to check, because through the shattered window, someone was groping for his keys ... first a pry bar, now the hand that wielded it.

While wrestling with the disembodied hand, John swung his aluminum travel mug up and over his throbbing shoulder, ecstatic that he'd taken his coffee to go. The mug hit with a solid smack, and John grinned in satisfaction at the grunt of pain that followed.

Not pausing to weigh the options, John accelerated directly toward the gunman positioned in the building ahead, spoiling the shooter's aim, and then slammed on the brakes. A body hurtled past and onto the asphalt. *Gotcha, you git!* Reversing, John spun the car 180 degrees, grinding the protesting gearshift straight to second as the staccato of automatic gunfire obliterated the rear window.

John wrenched the steering wheel sharply right, bouncing off the curb but continuing forward. He glanced in the rearview mirror. A blue sedan pursued him. *Crap!* With the sedan behind and a fire engine blocking the street ahead, he was trapped. So when he noticed the narrow alley on his left, he turned into it.

Shifting his Volvo C30 to the left of the alley, John accelerated straight at a blue rubbish tip. At the last second, he cranked hard on the wheel, spinning and bouncing the car off the far wall of the alley. The airbag punched him in the face. Through the ringing in his ears, he could still hear the blue sedan crash headlong into the tip.

After clearing his vision with a shake of the head, John tore his Glock from the glove box, disengaged the safety and chambered the first bullet. Holding his gun at the ready, he moved in slowly, scanning the seats in the vehicle. He saw only the driver slumped groaning over the steering wheel, loosely holding a submachine gun. John disarmed the man easily, tossing the SMG beneath his own car.

"Raise your hands. Step out of the car," John said, adopting his best military voice, the voice that clearly conveyed that refusal was not an option.

"Hah!" A chuckle bubbled from the driver's frothy lips. "Y'all are dead, Brock," he said in a lazy Texas drawl. Then he raised his left hand slowly like a 6-year-old playing cowboys. "Bang bang." The chuckle morphed into a bloody cough, and John stepped back to avoid the crimson spray. *Yick!*

Wheezing in a breath, the Texan continued. "There's more a-comin'."

More? John's anger ratcheted up a notch. "Who are you working for?" The Texan sneered derisively, and John repeated the question, the heat in his voice freezing to a deathly chill. "Who are you working for?"

But it was too late to find out. The blaggard was dead. *Blast!*

John checked through the car and searched the man's pockets to find ... nothing. No identification. No clues. Nought of any use.

And then it started to rain. *Of course it's raining! It's London in winter.* John slapped his hands down on the roof of the blue sedan in an uncharacteristic release of temper. "Aargh!" Flipping open his mobile phone, he called his second-in-command.

"Horace Hibbert." The man's deep bass tones filtered through the phone, and John could picture the affable giant running his fingers through his neatly trimmed afro.

"Hibb, I need your help. I'm in an alley just west of Aldersgate somewhere near St. Bart's Hospital. Are you still at Carter's campaign office?" John said.

"Things're fine down our end. It was a small bomb, not much damage," said Hibb.

"It's not that. I've been involved in an ..." John paused, looking for a benign word to describe the situation. "Incident."

"Do you want me to send the plods over?" John could hear the concern in Hibb's voice.

"No, only you." John rang off. *There's more coming.* The threat replayed in John's mind as the rain poured down his already soaked body, the chill on his skin matching the chill in his heart.

When his mobile rang, he checked the caller ID. It was his wife. If he let the call go to voicemail, she might worry—and frankly, he could use a little Caroline about now.

Pausing to wipe the water from his phone, he answered, trying to keep his voice easy and light. "What's up?"

"Hi, sweetheart," Caroline said. "The Home Secretary called. He wants to meet with you when you're finished at the campaign office."

"Cheers," he replied.

"John. What's wrong?" Of course his wife would hear right through the attempted calm.

"Nought. The car's broken down, but don't worry, Hibb is on his way to me."

"Darling, what happened?" He heard the edge that accompanied the concern in her voice. This past year, since John had begun going on operations again, they'd argued endlessly, it seemed, about disclosure; she wanted to know where he went and what he did on his operations, and he refused to tell her, hiding behind the Official Secrets Act. John simply couldn't put Caroline at risk by revealing classified information that would likely only put her in danger or terrify her and send her running from him—information such as the fact that assassins had just attempted to terminate his existence using a pry bar, a blue sedan, and an SMG.

"John. What happened?" She sounded annoyed by his hesitation in responding.

"A spot of car trouble, but I'm all right, I assure you. Do you think you could get a clean suit ready for me? I'll meet you on the third floor in the medical suites," he said.

"John." He could hear the frustration in her voice, and then the moment when she gave in. "Okay," she said. Her voice quavered, but he couldn't tell which emotion set it to quake—anger or anxiety. "How long?" she asked.

"Not long. I'll need to drop the car over to the panel beater, I'm afraid," he said.

"The what?" she said. Normally, he would have chuckled at what his wife termed the English-Canadian Vocabulary Gap, but there was no humour in him.

"Body shop," he clarified.

"Oh. That's fine. Are you sure you're all right?" she asked again.

Oh, just tickety-boo. "I'm fine. I'll see you shortly," he replied.

Within minutes, Hibb arrived, carrying an umbrella to cover them both. At his approach, John straightened, framing his emotions into a look of confidence and control.

"I take it this was no simple crash," Hibb said, gesturing at the Glock in John's hand.

Outstanding deduction! John swallowed his sarcasm, replying instead with a decisive, "Correct." Providing Hibb with a rundown of the events, he quickly moved on to a plan of action. "I need to get an ID on this fellow." *And then I need my wife.*

"How did he know where you'd be?" Hibb asked, clearly puzzled.

"Bomb in London. Political target. Not difficult to guess that I'd make my way here eventually." *If he somehow knew that I was the Head of Counter-Terrorism for MI-5.* "The plods and fire services have all other accesses blocked, making this the most likely route," John said. It all sounded so reasonable until you realized that only a handful of people actually knew what John did for a living.

"John, do you think he …" Hibb nodded at the dead Texan "… had summat to do with the bombing of Carter's campaign office? Could he have planted the bomb to draw you out?"

"Let's find out," John responded fiercely.

"You're looking ragged," Hibb observed, eyeing him up and down. "Need a lift to Casualty?" John shook his head and then froze at Hibb's next question. "What are you going to tell Caroline?"

Holding his section chief's gaze, John replied tonelessly, "That's not your concern." And then, for some reason he couldn't fathom, he continued, "I told her I had a spot of car trouble."

"You really think she's going to be satisfied with that?" Hibb asked.

Why did I even answer? On most days, John was glad that Caroline had agreed to be his administrative assistant. She was a brilliant analyst, well-respected and liked by her colleagues, unfortunately to the point now where they had become quite protective of her. On other days, like today, John wished he could return to the time before Burma when he'd been the undisputed autocrat of his section: *Ironheart*, the ultimate spy, his emotionless life neatly compartmentalized.

"You're my officer, not my counsellor," John grumbled.

Hibb muttered something unintelligible in response— unintelligible, but clearly spoken with intent.

John rose threateningly. "What did you say?" Heat flushed his cheeks.

Unperturbed, Hibb replied, "I said, that would be an underpaid job." And then he opened his mobile to ring for a clean-up crew to collect evidence and sanitize the environment, returning it to backstreet London normal.

The "sanitation unit" arrived, and John briefed them on the evidence he wanted collected. Then he hitched a ride with Hibb back to Thames House, headquarters of MI-5. Caroline met him on the third floor, wearing black slacks and a cream-coloured blouse. John thought she looked both angry and concerned ... and beautiful.

Her chestnut hair was swept into the new hairstyle she was trying out, a "fred" or a "wedge" or some such. Her round face held a softness. In fact, her entire body and her spirit held a softness he loved, and his hands itched to touch her familiar curves. But the expression on her face held him in check. Even though she stood several inches below his six feet, she was nonetheless very intimidating with her hands on her hips. Her deep brown eyes looked annoyed—but always, always, he could see her love for him written clearly within them.

"Car trouble?" Caroline asked, and her scepticism was blatantly evident in her voice and manner. "John, what happened? You've got a cut over your eye. Your shirt's been shredded by ..." She scanned his clothing, looking up to meet his gaze. "Broken glass?"

"An accident. The airbag deployed." He supplied the minimum required information, always hoping that she wouldn't ask for more.

He didn't miss her sigh as she stepped closer and slipped off his ruined blue silk tie and his suit jacket. Her warm fingers brushed his skin as she undid the buttons on his powder-blue shirt, revealing the long welt across his chest and shoulder.

"That ... was not caused by the airbag." Her fingertips gently traced the bruise, and he was tempted to hum happily at the tender contact. "It looks like someone hit you with a baseball bat or an iron bar," she said. Really, she was much too clever to dupe, so rather than argue or lie, he remained silent. She might suspect that he was attacked, but if he didn't confirm it, she didn't need to feel the fear of danger. "John!" She clearly wanted to question him, interrogate him really. "Wha—"

And then he just didn't want to argue, so he began to sing. "'Safe in your arms. Far from alarms...'" He moved minutely closer to her. "'Kiss me again...'"

"I don't know that one," she said, and the grim line of her mouth relaxed just a little. "Didn't Boyzone sing that?"

"No, my love. It was written by Victor Herbert and Henry Blossom for the Broadway show 'Mlle Modiste'." And he held his hands out palms-up in a gesture of surrender, begging her for comfort. "Please?"

He watched her struggle for a moment more, and then her arms were around him, her love erasing the fear and frustration from his chest.

"Never mind. I'm glad you're okay." She pulled his head to her shoulder. He slid his arms around her waist, sighing against her and kissing her neck. For a moment, he was fascinated by the trail of goosebumps his cold lips left behind.

"I love you, Caer," he murmured against her skin.

Shivering lightly, she stroked her fingers through his wet and sweaty hair. "I love you too, my bear."

Pulling back, he let her remove his shirt. He waited patiently as she washed his cuts, applied a butterfly bandage above his eyebrow, and kissed his bruises better. Everything felt better when Caroline took care of it.

"Why won't you tell me what happened?" Caroline asked. Her voice was soft and sad.

"It's nothing you need to worry about," John assured her. "I'm fine."

"You know," she said, "just because you say that, doesn't mean I actually stop worrying."

Sighing morosely, he pleaded with her, "I don't want to argue. I hurt. I have a headache ..." He knew she saw the sorrow in his eyes, because he didn't bother to hide it. And because she really was incredible, she let him off the hook. He pulled her close, so relieved to have her in his arms, loving him. Loving him in spite of all it took to be married to Ironheart, the ultimate spy.

Soon after, bandaged and dry, John rode in the back of the service-pool car on the way to Whitehall, the centre of Her Majesty's Government. As they wove their way along the Embankment, the grey clouds even parted for a moment, revealing a rare glimpse of the sun's rays shining through the London Eye.

"Shall I wait for you, sir?" the driver said.

"Yes. I shan't be long," John replied, stepping out of the car. With a nod to Big Ben, England's famous clock tower, John walked past the wrought-iron fence and on into the Cabinet Office to meet with the Home Secretary, Sir Desmond Stanway.

"Good afternoon, Mr. Brock," said Sir Desmond, simultaneously offering his hand in greeting and undoing the straining button on his suit jacket to make room for his hefty belly before he sat.

"Good afternoon, Home Secretary," John replied. He remained standing out of deference. "I have a preliminary report on the Carter bomb. The explosion occurred today at 5:45 a.m. in the campaign office of Nigel Carter of Her Majesty's Loyal Opposition. Three casualties. No fatalities. Four groups have stepped forward claiming responsibility, but none is credible."

"I want you to make this a priority. I've arranged with Commander Winters of the Met to coordinate your efforts with Counter-Terrorism Command. I'll expect you to offer your gratitude for his cooperation in person," Sir Desmond said.

Excuse me? "Of course, sir," John said. *How much manpower is necessary to investigate one simple bomb? And why am I expected to glad-hand the Met?*

"Very good," Sir Desmond said, gesturing for John to sit before he continued. "Before you leave, I have an urgent matter to discuss with you. The Chairman of the Joint Intelligence Committee passed this information on to me. Apparently, MI-6 intercepted a communiqué that originated in Mumbai, India, and terminated in Drammen, Norway. They believe the receiver to be one Tor Grendahl, a known—"

"Mercenary," John said. "What is the message, and how does it concern MI-5?"

Silently, John took the sheet of paper the HS offered. It read: "Locate: Pet Badger. Very Precious. Reward If Found Dead." And beneath the heading was John's own picture, taken in Moor Mead Garden from the looks of it, likely when he was walking their dog, Rufus.

Steeling his expression and releasing no emotion, John replied, "Thank you, sir. I'll look into it."

"I have spoken to Special Branch and been assured that they will organize protection for you and your wife," Sir Desmond said. "You live in Twickenham, do you not? They can have a security team in place within the hour. You are a fine officer, Mr. Brock. The Crown has no desire to lose your services."

"Thank you, sir, but I'll organize my own protection." *That way, Caroline will never have to know.*

The HS watched John silently for a moment, and John could read his concern plainly in his eyes. "Very well, Mr. Brock. It is your prerogative."

John rose, shook the man's hand, and departed, returning to the pool car. *This is why, against the culture of English security and law enforcement, I always have a handgun at the ready.* John sank into thought, not even noticing when the car stopped.

"We're here, sir," the driver said as they arrived at the Millbank entrance to Thames House.

John pulled himself mentally back to the present and exited the vehicle. He walked through the door with the tourists, making a left and then a right to the door marked "Staff Only," swiping his security pass and entering the restricted zone. He mounted the few steps, paced along a corridor and then passed through the bulletproof security pods and onto the Grid, the office space for Section G, Counter-Terrorism.

Aubrey Davies met him with a statement that was likely meant to be a question.

"There's been some chatter from our assets in the Indian arms trade during the last forty-eight hours," said Aubrey, a long-time veteran of the Security Services. His domain was the technology of espionage and counter-espionage. His brilliant intellect stood side-by-side with his social ineptitude within a 55-year-old body complete with hunched shoulders and squinty grey eyes permanently lined from spending too much time chasing down ones and zeroes.

"And we're only hearing about this now?" John asked.

"Shall I pass the information on to MI-6?" Aubrey said, reaching up to scratch along the edge of his receding hairline as though to stop the glacial decline of his youth.

Something about Aubrey's manner warned John that his question had a deeper meaning. "Should I assume that you're not content with that course of action?" John asked.

"It seems to me that, given the dodgy source of the rumours and the information Caroline uncovered about the Jammu Kashmir Liberation Front, there may be a connection here that MI-6 might overlook," Aubrey said.

John released an internal *ah*. "Very well. Keep a copy of the information and pass along the Indian rumours. Agreed?" John said, gauging Aubrey's reaction, knowing he'd guessed right when the man released a satisfied smile. It was important to let his officers feel appreciated, something Caroline was seeking to teach him.

But rather than return to work, Aubrey remained, alternately tapping a pencil against his trouser leg and his lower lip.

Eyeing the graphite stains, John furrowed his brow to express his impatience with the man's stalling. "Out with it, Aubrey."

"Well," Aubrey began slowly. "I understand that Caroline's had her issues with the telephone system, but ..."

Issues? John mused. That was an understatement. Caroline consistently disconnected the Home Secretary and, on more than one occasion, had set off the emergency shutdown protocol when she was meant to transfer calls.

Aubrey cleared his throat and continued. "Er, Caroline ... well, stone the crows! She has an uncanny ability to see to the heart of people and the issues surrounding them. We could make much better use of her talents as an intelligence analyst rather than an administrative assistant." John felt his gaze tighten, and he noticed Aubrey hesitate before continuing. "Er, remember the Smythe case? None of us understood the significance of what she detected in his banking patterns. What about the ex-minister Sheldon? She sussed him out the first time she met him ... and informed us all that the man was having an affair ... which turned out to be the truth. And with the mistress of the ranking Russian officer in London, who was a KGB agent."

"They're called the FSB now," John reminded Aubrey tersely for the umpteenth time.

"Nevertheless. She's very bright," Aubrey said. His voice was suddenly sure and definite.

John frowned, belying his next words. "I'm grateful, Aubrey. It's not really possible for me to promote my own wife." *And don't think for a moment that I would ever allow her to be involved operationally. She is much safer as she is, answering phones and typing reports.*

John's gaze drifted across the room to the desk where Caroline sat, mercifully oblivious to the danger of a hit man. John had made a long list of enemies in his time, first with Special Forces' Maritime Terrorism Command and then with MI-5. His enemies were not the sort to cringe at the thought of using his wife as leverage against him. The very idea chilled his heart.

"I don't mean to waffle on about it ... but, there! I may have a word with the DG," Aubrey said.

Sir William Jacen has always had a soft spot for Caroline. Will he listen to Aubrey? "Anything else?" John asked, eager to end this conversation before his wife overheard them talking about her. The last thing he needed was for Caroline to decide that she wanted a more active role in the defence of the realm. When Aubrey shook his head, John asked, "Have you seen Hibb?"

"Nipped down to Human Resources to get Ryan's new badge sorted," Aubrey said.

"He's lost it again?" John inquired, feeling the familiar thrust of annoyance that Ryan Carstairs' ineptitude always seemed to elicit. He would never understand how the young man came to be recruited. If John hadn't been in Burma at the time, Ryan never would have been assigned as a field agent on his team. The young ginger-headed blighter was a liability.

"Indeed," Aubrey replied. "Hibb should return shortly." Aubrey retreated to his lair, the computer and technology laboratory of the Grid.

Crossing the Grid to Caroline's desk, John paused to watch her studying the computer screen before her, every measure of her body immersed in her task. Fear rolled through his belly. A contract on his life was nothing new, but he'd never before had something to lose—never before that one remarkable day in a dingy, terrifying prison in Burma when he'd met Caroline ... and loved her. Defying all the odds of his hard and lonely life, she'd loved him in return. She'd married him, taking his name, taking his life as her own.

For a moment, he gave in to the need to have her attention focused on him. "Could you please ..." he began, leaning forward on his arms. Watching her eyes shift from the computer, he saw the furrow of concentration ease from her brow. And she smiled at him. She could smile with the greatest joy. As her gaze settled on him, though, her smile reversed into a frown.

"What's wrong now?" she asked.

Her question took him by surprise. "Nought, sweetheart," he replied, but he knew that she didn't believe him because she narrowed her deep brown eyes in scepticism. How she could see through him was a mystery. He had earned the nickname Ironheart in part because he maintained complete control of his emotions and was adept at hiding them from others. But somehow, she always knew.

"John." She interrupted his thoughts, warning in her voice. "I can tell there's something wrong. And don't give me that 'nought' crap, because it won't fool me." And he thought he loved her more in that moment than ever before, because she could always somehow find the "real John Brock." However, he did *not* want her to worry about him. After escaping with him through the jungles of Burma, she deserved a little tranquility. So he fobbed her off.

"Operational issues. Nothing for you to worry about," he replied. But she frowned at him and his heart sank within him. *Is it lying if I'm only keeping the information hidden for her own good?* Hoping to deflect her mood, he changed the subject and made his escape. "Could you please send Hibb in when he arrives?"

She nodded, but the frown didn't shift. Covering a heavy sigh, he tucked his anxiety away. The truth was, he never wanted to go back to life before Burma, before Caroline. He would never survive it.

Ten minutes later, Hibb knocked on his office door.

"Come," John said, inviting Hibb into the glass-walled heart of the Grid.

Sitting behind his modern oak desk, John motioned for Hibb to shut the office door and take a seat, which he did, settling his gigantic frame into the straight-backed wooden chair across from John. Horace Reginald Hibbert—the name was as large as the man. An enigma to the majority of his colleagues, Hibb somehow managed to maintain a transparent Christian world view amidst the shadowy translucency of espionage. John had quickly detected within Hibb the character of a good man, and promoted him. Hibb fulfilled his role as Section Chief perfectly, because everyone trusted Hibb.

"Bad news from the Home Sec?" Hibb asked. His voice was easy and light.

Without a word, John retrieved the folded sheet from his pocket and handed it over. Hibb seemed unfazed by the message, refolding it and raising his eyes to meet John's.

"Badger-Brock. That's twee," Hibb said. "This the third contract you've had on your life?"

"Fourth, actually, but that's not my concern," John replied.

"Is Special Branch providing security? I don't suppose you'll be moving into a safe house or anything convenient like that?" Hibb asked.

And here was where things got tricky. John carefully kept his face void of emotion as he said, "I don't want Caroline to know."

"Aye?" Hibb's eyes widened in astonishment. "Why?"

"That's not your concern," John said. "I want this to stay between you and me, and I want you to liaise with Special Branch to organize discreet security. You can put a couple of blokes on me if you like, but I want Caroline and the house covered. Understood?"

"Aye, sir. Wouldn't it be safer to simply tell her?" Hibb said.

"No. She's either with me at home or safe on the Grid," John said. *If I'm careful, she'll never know.*

"And when you're on assignment?" Hibb asked.

"I'll deal with that when it becomes necessary."

Sneak Peek: Book 2 of the *Second Chance* Series

"You okay, Grace?"

Grace glanced over at her husband, Barnard "Bud" Marek. Broad-chested and broad-shouldered, just a hair under six feet, Bud sported a Grizzly Adams beard and a full head of wiry auburn hair. Beneath his grizzled brows, the most piercing blue eyes peered at her now and her heart fluttered. He was so strong and masculine and yet beneath his tough exterior beat the heart of a sweet and sensitive man.

"We've been foster parents for five years. I like to think of our ranch as a haven for troubled adolescents. But we've never taken a small child," she said, turning in her seat to face him across the console in the Jeep Cherokee. "Why do they think we can help?"

"We're the last resort, at least that's the impression I got. It's us or an institution." Shoulder-checking, he took the dogleg at Greybull on US-14.

"He's only three years old, not even four yet. How can things be so dire?" she asked, tucking her blonde hair behind her ear.

His eyes tracked the movement and she smiled. They'd been married six years now but he still looked at her like she was a feast and he was a starving man. "He's been in six foster homes in the past six months, including three placements on the Crow Reservation."

"Why?"

"The little fella put two foster moms in the hospital and took a chunk out of a Rottweiler."

Grace chuckled. "Sorry. I know that should horrify me but, really, at least he can defend himself."

"*He* attacked the *dog*, Grace," Bud said wryly.

"Poor little boy," Grace said, sighing sadly. "And they don't even know his name?"

"No. I guess the mother, Carla Rydel, was a prostitute and she never registered their births."

Grace frowned, asking, "What do you mean *their* births? I thought we were driving from Wyoming to Montana to meet one little boy."

"Didn't I tell you? There were two children in the home. Apparently, the mother's pimp killed her and dumped the body in an alley a couple of blocks away. It was three days before someone came forward to say that the children were missing. By the time the police found the home, the baby girl had died. The boy was underneath the crib, dehydrated, half-dead. He looked Crow so they took him to the Reservation but no one had any idea who he belonged to. They were happy to foster him but..."

"He bit a dog," Grace said drily.

"They've brought in a couple of different psychiatrists and given him about five labels, Oppositional Defiant Disorder, Childhood Schizophrenia, Severe Autism," he said, shaking his head and frowning.

Nudging the turn signal, he turned into the parking lot of the Big Horn Department of Public Health and Human Services. "Here we are."

She huffed, disgusted. "Hasn't it occurred to anyone that you don't need a diagnosis to explain why a child who witnessed the murder of his mother and then watched his baby sister die bit by bit while locked in a room, that those events alone would explain violent behaviour?"

Bud brought her hand to his lips, a look of sweet love in his eyes. "Come on."

Watching him as he rounded the hood, she let him help her out of the truck. Not that she needed the assistance, but she recognized that he took pride in being a gentleman. At five-foot-two, a hundred-and-ten pounds, she was small enough that Bud could have slung her over his shoulder and carried her inside. But he would never raise a hand of harm to her. Always his gentle soul won out.

D. C. Shaftoe

Slipping her hand in his, she walked beside him into the building to meet what seemed to be a committee of professionals.

"I'm Elizabeth Hardin, Child Psychiatrist." The imposing woman shook both their hands and then turned to introduce the others. "This is Aislynn Warner who was assigned as a Child Protection Worker to this, uh, child. Bertram Yellowtail representing the Crow Tribal Council, and Harvard Lee, Paediatrician. We have all heard wonderful things about you both." She paused a moment and then frowned severely. "We are very concerned about this little boy. We believe that you should—"

Grace cut her off. "Before you tell me anything else, I want to see him. What do you call him?"

"He only responds to Kid," Aislynn said.

"Kid? We'll call him Seth, the child who carried on the legacy of Adam." Grace turned aside to Bud. "Shall we?"

Bud nodded, camouflaging a grin. "I think we're ready to see him," he said to the others.

Dr. Hardin looked ready to burst with suggestions and strategies but she finally conceded and led them to the large two-way window in the playroom. Through it, Grace could see a moderately-sized space with little chairs and tables, toys, storybooks, crayons, and colouring books. There were six or seven children in the room playing. A pair of boys was taking turns racing dinky cars down a ramp they'd fashioned from bricks and blocks. A trio of girls were engaged in play with a kitchen set, clearly arguing about who got to be the baby. Another girl and boy were colouring at one of the tables.

But there, well away from the others, sitting and rocking in the corner with his back to the wall, was a young boy. Seth. With two objects clutched in his little hands. He was very thin but tall for his age with raven black hair which was dull and tangled and hanging to his shoulders. He had a dusky complexion with obsidian eyes under hooded lids. His face should have been ruddy and round with plump cheeks but instead he looked gaunt and pallid. Grace's heart broke for the poor traumatized lad.

"There's a real geography of space going on in there," Bud observed. And he was right. There was a clear zone around Seth into which the other children never ventured.

"Look," Bud said and Grace followed his point. One of the dinky cars had gotten away from the racing boys, rolling within reach of Seth. Protecting his space, Seth sprang to attention, growling and leaping like a wild beast at the little boy who ventured too close in his quest to retrieve it. Shrieking, the boy abandoned his car, running to the other side of the room. Once the boy had scampered away, Seth settled back to rocking.

"Interesting," Grace murmured. "What's in his hands?"

"He found those on his first day here," Aislynn said. "One of them is a comic book hero, I think, and the other is a mermaid doll."

"Mhmm." Grace watched the repetitive actions Seth performed with the dolls.

"Repetitive and perseverative behaviour. A clinical sign of Autism," Dr. Lee said.

"Hmm," Grace replied. Was he speaking as he bumped those dolls together? If he was, what was he saying? "Does he speak?" Grace looked at the professionals around her.

"No," Dr. Hardin replied.

"Language delays. Another sign," Dr. Lee said.

"I want to get closer," Grace said. Ignoring the explanations as to why she shouldn't enter the room, she gripped Bud's hand, striding inside. Finding two child-sized chairs, they sat. Grace shifted her chair right to the edge of Seth's zone of protection. Bud followed suit.

"He repeats the same actions," Grace muttered. Bud grunted in agreement. "One comic book figure. One mermaid. I wish I could hear what he's saying."

When she shifted in her chair, Bud grasped her arm. She turned to look at him, narrowing her gaze. "I am going over there. That poor child has been left alone for far too long. For goodness' sakes, his mother left him locked in a room..." Her speech slowed as realization struck. "That's it. That's what it's all about."

Jumping up, she crossed the room, past the racers to pull out the bin of action figures from the cubbies along the one wall, rooting around until she found a mailman in a traditional dark blue uniform which she hoped would do the job. And then she moved slowly toward Seth who had alerted and was tracking her every movement. He growled low in his chest, a noise that sounded frighteningly like an irritated Rottweiler. That was far enough, she decided, and sat cross-legged on the floor.

After a few minutes, Seth resumed his pattern of movement. Soon Grace could detect words and then whole phrases. Shifting closer, she listened again from start to finish.

"Grace," Bud said with a note of warning in his voice. She motioned for him to stay back.

Once more through the sequence and she knew she was right. Grace scooted closer, keeping her movements smooth and slow so as not to startle the boy.

"Boss," she said. Other than the narrowing of his eyes, Seth didn't react. "You must not hurt Carla. It is bad to hit mommies."

Grace shifted even closer and then moved her blue-uniformed mailman right up to the male action figure, the one Seth referred to in his mumble as Boss. "You will stop right now." Graced pushed the mailman-cum-policeman against Boss, meeting Seth's resistance with her own. "I am a policeman. I say that you cannot hurt Mommy." Then she turned her attention directly to Seth. "Boss hurt Mommy. Boss is bad. Give him to me. He has to go away." Grace held out her hand.

For the first time, Seth met her gaze directly. "Bad," he said.

Grace heard the gasps of adult voices behind her but she ignored them. Seth's startled gaze flicked up, beyond Grace. She sat up taller to capture his attention again. "It is bad to hurt mommies. I'm sorry you had to see that, Seth," she said while motioning for him to hand over the Boss.

He tilted his head. "Seth."

"Seth," she repeated, keeping her hand out, palm up. "Give me the bad man. He has to go away. He can never hurt you again. He can never scare you again."

Seth looked at the Boss figure in his hands and then held it out to Grace. She took it, placed it behind her out of view. "I'm sorry, Seth," she said, holding out her arms to him.

Seth leaned forward, placing his palm on her cheek. His cavernous eyes bored into her and Grace read despair in his expression. A child should never experience despair.

Slowly drawing him onto her lap, she wrapped Seth in a hug. "Would you like to come home with me?"

"Babygirl?" he whispered, his dark eyes dull with grief and exhaustion.

"I'm sorry, honey. She died," Grace said.

"Mommy dead. Babygirl dead." He looked up at her. "Home?"

"You can come to my home and live with me." Grace gestured for Bud to come closer. "Come live with us." Sitting on the floor beside Grace, Bud reached around, embracing them both. Seth narrowed his eyes at Bud and a low growl erupted in his chest. Grace leaned over slowly and kissed Bud on the cheek, over the fuzziness of his beard. The wariness subsided and Seth leaned into Grace.

"Are you hungry, Seth?" she asked.

"Baloney sandwich," he said. "An' a apple."

"Bologna sounds fine," Bud said. "And maybe a milkshake."

Seth furrowed his brow at the big man by her side. "Don't know milkshake."

"You'll like it," Bud said.

"Ready to come to our home?" Grace asked.

"Home," Seth repeated.

D. C. Shaftoe

Reckless Association

ISBN: 978-0-9937176-0-4 (sc)
ISBN: 978-0-9937176-1-1 (e)

www.ingramcontent.com/pod-product-compliance
Lightning Source LLC
Chambersburg PA
CBHW030027180626
46810CB00001B/242